AF574501

$14.95

BIRTHRIGHT

BIRTHRIGHT

A Novel

CLAY BLOUNT

NewSouth Books
Montgomery

NewSouth Books
P.O. Box 1588
Montgomery, AL 36102

 Published in the United States by NewSouth Books, a division of NewSouth, Inc., Montgomery, Alabama.

Library of Congress Cataloging-in-Publication Data

ISBN 1-58838-145-5

Design by Randall Williams
Printed in the United States of America

For Amie and Alex.

You are the greatest.

Prologue, 1863

Winston Carthage tried to stand, but his knees refused to support him. His burdensome right leg throbbed and his arms felt like dead weight. He slipped back into the leather chair with a grunt. He was too tired to move, too exhausted for clear thought. Thankfully, the worst day of his life was over.

He watched through bleary eyes as dusk discreetly melded with night. The window above his desk was streaked with water. Sheets of rain pelted the ground as if God had opened a tap and, distracted by something or other, forgotten to see it closed. How could men be motivated to fight in such weather? How much was enough? Then he remembered his own day and an admission of hypocrisy swept over him. He was no better than any of them. Not today. Never again. A moment's outrage, a single bullet, and he had ceded the moral high ground forever. That place now belonged to other self-important souls.

Flustered, he tried again to rise. He felt impossibly old, too old even for modest pleasures, yet age wasn't his immediate problem. Nearing his expected years, his health had always been good. But a simple head cold had marched inevitably down to his chest. He'd helped it, working like a pack mule in the rain. What had seemed so important this morning now seemed foolish. Pneumonia, the indiscriminate killer, stalked him. How long did he have? A month? A week? Less? War had smothered his hope. His family was only a memory and his will to live was weak. He would be the killer's easy target.

He stretched for his walking cane and shuffled across the hardwood floor, slumping heavily onto the daybed. Even this minor exertion prompted a wet coughing fit.

"Massa Winston?" A hesitant feminine voice called from the hallway.

"Leave me be, Lou," he puffed.

"I heard you movin' 'round and thought you might need somethin'." She was just outside the door.

"No, nothing." The pain of speaking caused him to reconsider. Something for his throat. "Bring me tea and honey."

"You oughts to eat, Massa Winston."

"A bowl of stew then," he croaked.

"Yassa." She hurried away.

His lungs rattled like percolating coffee. He was just able to raise a handkerchief and catch the heavy phlegm. He stared dully across the room. Why had he come to the daybed? He should be writing, not napping.

His huge oak desk was ten feet away, but seemed much further. With considerable effort, he raised himself again and struggled to his desk. Lou would return soon. He would rest a bit and eat. Then he would write.

A knock startled him from a semiconscious slumber. He twisted nervously and was struck by a hard coughing spasm.

"Massa Winston?"

"Yes?" he managed.

"Your tea, sir."

"Come in."

Lou, the house slave, entered, balancing a serving tray. She stole a glance at him slumped behind the desk. He didn't look up, so she stared longer than was normally appropriate. His cough had worsened and his color was ghastly. The heavy bags beneath his eyes had swollen to thumb-size. Death would see his face in the mirror.

"You want it at the desk?"

"Yes."

She carefully placed the tray in front of him.

He watched indifferently as she poured a cup of tea, laid a linen napkin across his lap, and turned to leave. "Bring me some whiskey."

"Massa Winston, you too sick for whiskey."

"I wasn't asking permission."

"Yassa, right away." But she stood fast. "You want me to see if I can fetch Doctor Purvis?"

He ignored her question. A flicker of interest stirred in his eyes. "How long have you been in this house, Lou?"

"Sir?"

"You were born here, correct?"

"Yassa. Down at the fields. My momma died when I was born." She frowned. "I never knew my daddy."

"When were you born?"

Confusion clouded her pretty brown face. Being illiterate, dates and numbers were unsolvable mysteries. "I's born in . . . thirty-seven, in the winter." She expectantly looked at him.

"I remember. Just after the new year. That would make you twenty-six years old." Winston cocked his head aside. "Do you like it here?"

"Yassa, I do."

"Is that why you didn't escape with the others?"

Her mouth opened slightly and closed again. Finally she said, "Them that left was goin' to N'awlins, but I hear the Yankees stopped 'em at Natchez." She hesitated, visibly conflicted. "I hear they have to work for the Yankees just like the Rebels. Weren't really no freedom uh-tall."

Winston regarded her. "So what will you do?"

"Sir?"

"You have options now."

"I don't understand."

"You are free, Lou."

"Free? Massa Winston, I wouldn't know—"

"Go where you like. I recommend you leave the Confederacy, but that is your choice." He searched her face, wanting to tell her she had many alternatives, but that was a lie.

Lou self-consciously smoothed her apron. "Thank you."

Winston shrugged, which was more effort than it was worth. "By this time tomorrow, it won't matter."

They both knew he was right.

"Massa Winston, would it be all right if I was to . . ." She studied her hands.

"Stay here for a while?"

"Yassa. Just for a spell."

"Why?"

"You's so sick and all."

Winston smiled, but in fact, was closer to tears. "Stay as long as you please, but as of now, you are earning a wage."

"Thank you," she said again.

"Don't thank me. It doesn't feel right."

She looked hurt. "I was just tryin'—"

"I'm sorry. I didn't mean to sound harsh."

She fidgeted with her cotton blouse. "Y'all been real good to me."

"That is a matter of opinion."

An awkward silence separated them.

Lou pushed the bowl of stew closer. "You oughts to eat."

"Yes."

"I'll be in the kitchen."

"Don't work too hard."

She smiled. "Gots to work hard. I'm earnin' a wage."

"My whiskey?"

"Yassa." She went to the liquor cabinet and returned with a decanter of sour mash and a shot glass, then quietly retreated from the study.

Winston poured a shot down his raw throat. Then another, and another. After a few lost minutes, he felt warmer. The liquor strengthened him with false resolve. He pushed away the stew and reached for a blank piece of paper. So much to say, but no direct way to say it. Nothing was easy any more, not even a letter to his son. He began:

May 17, 1863

Dear Andrew,

Please let this note find you well. You've been away so long, at times I struggle to recall your face. How are you in Tennessee? The local newspaper, a bastion of objectivity, reports General Bragg's campaign there is being expertly prosecuted. That is bracing news if one is to believe it.

I've not received a letter from you in some months. Perhaps that is to be expected. Word of your valor has reached me through many sources. My heart bounds at your accomplishment.

All is not well. My health is poor and the Yankees are coming. They will arrive soon, and I really don't care. The war in Mississippi is but lost, and Vicksburg is threatened by that persistent bastard Grant. He is tenacious and thick, a bulldog.

Vicksburg will soon fall, its former prominence a vanishing memory. I remain in our home, but the Yankees will pass this way, probably tomorrow. I shall be forced to move. Or perhaps I'll not move at all.

War—and especially a lost war—drastically alters what is considered proper conduct. The social elite and common citizen are now generally indistinguishable. We all act in ways that would have once been unthinkable. History might forgive us, but regrettably, war's epitaph is penned by the victors. This gloomy assessment doesn't excuse what I must tell you, rather it provides a better context. I wantonly killed a man. That is in itself a wretched admission, but at this moment, with liquor in my veins, my shame is tempered by details I can't provide in a letter subject to prying eyes. Suffice it to say, my motivations would not be obvious at first glance. To unearth the truth, one must know where to dig.

Come home, Andrew, and allow me a chance to explain. Beg for furlough, bribe your commanding officer, desert if you must, but please come home. And be careful. You will have enemies when you return here, enemies who will hate you only for your name.

My time is short and my only selfish wish is to see you again.

With love,

Father

BIRTHRIGHT

I

May 17, 1858

The train prepared to leave. A host of passengers sat comfortably in two coach cars, some dozed, others spoke in hushed, early-morning tones. The last person on the depot platform was a portly conductor who checked doors and inspected the giant wheels. His attention was drawn to a silhouette walking west, away from the depot, inside the fence. A vagrant.

The conductor climbed on board and waved to the engineer who tugged three times on an air whistle. The giant steam engine engaged, urging the locomotive away from the depot at a walking pace. As the cars lumbered through the first bend in the tracks, a man stepped from a copse of trees and pulled himself onto the trailing cargo car. He tried the sliding door handle, but it was locked, so he inched his way along the side rail to the access ladder, unaware he was watched by the conductor two cars ahead.

The man climbed atop the cargo car. He was remarkably nimble for his size—six foot six, hard and lean, 220 sinewy pounds, with broad shoulders that tapered to a narrow waist. His close-cut hair was the same brown color as his chin stubble. His hooded eyes were shark's gray, coldly intelligent, but small and ill-fitting his wide, ordinary face. His mouth was an abrupt, thin line, not given to normal expressions of pleasantry. At first glance, he might seem imposing, handsome in a sense. But he had long ago learned that on inspection, he frightened rather than attracted. And that suited him.

His movements were economical and calculated. Wastefulness, even in motion, bothered him. He rarely acted out of sentiment or emotion.

He saw things as he expected them to be, always on his terms, always in his time. He relied only on himself, a pure loner. He had no use for friends or casual acquaintances.Even fools gave him broad passage.

He spied a cargo hatch door and grasped its handle. The hatch creaked open. He peered into the darkness and saw a metal ladder. His enormous shoulders just fit through the hatchway. He shimmied down the ladder silently wishing for a candle. At the bottom rung, he jumped and landed heavily on the wooden floor.

"Hey," called a sleepy voice from the dark.

"Hello." The large man wasn't startled. He waited for his eyes to adjust.

"Where ya headed?" The voice was thick and raspy.

"I dunno." The large man stepped closer. "Where does this train go?"

"Vicksburg, back and forth, twice a day. My name's Clem." Clem slowly came into view, a scruffy vagrant who sat cross-legged on the floor, a bottle gripped firmly in his lap. His unkempt hair was shock-white, his eyes bloodshot.

The newcomer's birth name was Gaylord Pritchard, but he didn't offer it. He sat down a few feet from Clem. "Vicksburg?"

"Yep." Clem pulled the cork from his bottle and took a furtive swallow. A drip of the cheap fill landed on his chin. He wiped with the back of his hand and reclaimed the drip with his tongue. He offered no liquor to his visitor.

"How many stops before Vicksburg?"

"Bolton Station and Edwards Station, sometimes Clinton, too. Whole trip takes about three hours unless—"

Clem was interrupted by a pounding sound on the car's roof. The large newcomer tensed.

Clem shook his head. "Relax. Prob'ly just a railroad detective."

"A what?" His eyes were queer and unsettled.

"You ain't done this before have you?" Clem smiled. "He'll just toss us off at Edwards or something."

"Who we got down there?" A voice called from the access hatch.

Clem whispered. "Sounds like McCallister. He's a mean one."

Two weighty boots found the ladder rungs. A heavyset man climbed deliberately to the floor and stood in the hatch light. An undersized shirt stretched across his ample midsection. His legs were short and thick. His face was bearded and his left cheek bulged with tobacco. He loosely wielded a two-foot piece of oak with a carved handgrip, a polished skull-basher.

The detective spread his feet wide and squinted at the stowaways. "That you, Clem?"

Clem rose haltingly to his feet. "Yes, sir."

"Who's your friend?" McCallister grinned in the dim light.

"Can't say." Clem's voice faltered. "He climbed in when we pulled away from Jackson."

McCallister slapped the club shaft in his left palm. "You got a name, boy?" He punctuated the question with a stream of tobacco juice that splattered the newcomer's britches. The newcomer remained silent. "Ain't a talker, huh? We'll see about that." McCallister produced a key chain and unlocked the sliding cargo door.

Clem stepped forward. "Mr. McCallister—"

"Shut up, Clem!" McCallister slid the door open a few feet and the car filled with light. "The Southern Railroad of Mississippi authorizes me to throw your sorry asses off this train."

Clem tried to speak. "We was just—"

"Yeah, I know, Clem. You didn't think nobody would mind since the car's empty."

"We'll get off at Clinton. Right?" Clem turned and saw his stowaway companion clearly for the first time. He was struck by the man's eyes, recessed and gray-looking. His voice trailed off and a chill formed at his neck.

"I told you to shut up once, Clem!" McCallister bristled. "You boys got two choices. You can ride to Vicksburg like ya planned. With me." McCallister smiled through off-color teeth. "Or go that way." He jerked his head at the open door and the countryside rushing past. "We'll be at the river trestle before long."

Clem inched closer to the door.

"Stop your shuffling, Clem!" McCallister's eyes blazed.

"Mr. McCallister, my ol' body can't take jumpin' in the river. If you could spare me this one kindness, I'd be—"

"Stop movin' around, Clem! If I was the suspicious type, I'd figure you and this other boy aimed to jump me. Hold still!"

The newcomer came suddenly to his feet and grasped Clem's greasy head with both hands, one on top, the other at his chin, and twisted savagely. *Crack!* Clem's head turned almost completely around; perversely, his torso faced forward. His last vision was the newcomer's complacent face and strange eyes. Clem fell like a piece of timber on his back. His nose struck the floor first.

"Clem will not be moving." The newcomer spoke with a deep, frostbitten voice.

McCallister's mouth opened wide. Slowly, the skull-basher sank to his side.

"The jump would have killed him anyway." The newcomer spoke matter-of-factly.

"Who are you?" McCallister inched backward toward the ladder to increase the gap between them.

"You wouldn't know my name. We've surely never met." The gap narrowed.

McCallister looked down at the club in his hand. The newcomer followed his eyes. McCallister tossed it to the floor.

"Listen, fella, I got no problem with you. I'll scoot outta here and you can ride to Vicksburg, no charge." McCallister's smile eroded to a tight grimace.

The newcomer advanced.

Without noticing, McCallister backed past the access ladder and thumped into the wall.

"Mister, I wasn't really gonna make him jump." McCallister could back no further. "Let's forget this, huh?" The fear in his voice was conspicuous. "He's an old bum, ain't nobody gonna care he's dead."

The man was within six feet and still coming. "Can I count on your discretion?" With stunning quickness, he closed the interval between them and slammed a fist into McCallister's stomach. Air exploded from the detective's lungs and his chewing tobacco hurtled across the car. He doubled in agony, then felt his right arm being lifted beyond its normal circle of radius by absurdly strong hands.

McCallister's wretched scream was absorbed by the roar of the train. A ripping sound, much as a drumstick being torn from a chicken, signaled the utter destruction of his right shoulder. He might have sunk to the floor, but his other arm was seized and subjected to the same procedure, this time more slowly.

McCallister's inhuman shrieks lasted but a few moments before he slipped from consciousness. Disappointed, the newcomer regarded his misshapen hulk on the floor.

"A fly without wings . . ." He twisted McCallister's neck until it snapped. Then he twisted some more.

The conductor patiently watched the countryside in reverse through a tiny mirror thrust from his window. His train sped along at the remarkable speed of eighteen miles per hour. Passing through a right bend, he saw what he'd expected—the cargo door had been opened. McCallister had found the stowaway. The tracks straightened and the conductor held his mirror out farther. They approached the Big Black River trestle. Someone would go for a swim.

The locomotive clanged over the bridge, followed by the coach cars. The conductor watched closely and sure enough, a figure vaulted through the air and floated lazily over the railing down to the muddy Big Black, strangely, without the usual flailing arms and legs.

The conductor strained to see the water's surface, but the railing blocked his view. Had McCallister killed him? He shrugged. Wouldn't be the first time.

He focused on the tracks ahead just as a second body flew from the cargo door, balanced precariously on the bridge railing, and tumbled into the river.

❧

Winston Carthage was not a talkative man. He spoke directly and with purpose, without pretense or presumption. He might have been a politician or a leader of men, had he the instinct or desire, but such leadership held no interest for him. His life, his family, his business—these were his passions. He hid no agenda or conspiratorial thought, yet he always knew more than he said. His actions were well-considered and logical. He gave what he received and was respected for it.

He stood in the blistering mid-day heat, sweat pouring from his face, and had a contrary thought—what if he acted a madman? Who would notice? What if he danced on a tabletop or swung from a balcony. What if he crawled in the street like a beggar and spoke only in French vulgarities? What if he waded nude through a city fountain? Other than his immediate arrest, what would happen? Proper Vicksburg would, of course, notice. He would make fine conversation for the society hens. The newspapers would conclude that the stress of the lawsuit had hastened his dementia. People would stare and wonder how his next episode would take shape. After a moment's deliberation, he decided on conformity.

At just under six feet tall, Winston's broad shoulders were complemented by a strong face. He had sharp blue eyes and a dominant lower jaw. His mouth was subtly expressive, framed by thin lips and whiskers stretching from his earlobes to his chin. Tiny crinkles tugged at his eyes. His looks were pleasing, he knew. He appeared a man of means—which he was—intelligent and quick-witted, but not overcome with himself.

He glanced at his pocket watch. The train from Jackson was predictably late. The lawyer, *his* lawyer, *his* albatross, was traveling to Vicksburg for the seventh time in eight months, always by train, and since Winston paid his expenses, always first class. Winston had resigned himself to the inevitable bore of legal discussions and trial dates and depositions. He detested lawyers, just as his father had.

His attention was diverted across the street to Shelly's, a riverfront saloon. He might have a beer or two while he waited. Others who waited for the train had long since sought sanctuary there from the sun. His attorney would smell the beer on him. He needed to abstain, to keep his wits. A few beers might send him wading nude through the nearest fountain.

The lawsuit. Damn the lawsuit. How much longer could it last? How much paper could be moved from one file to another before obvious justice was reached? His attorney wouldn't answer that or any other pertinent question. Bills. His attorney was only reliable for bills.

He reached inside his jacket for a cigar and brushed his sweat-dampened shirt. May was far too hot. Unreasonably hot, he concluded. How was a man to think clearly when May felt like July? How was a man to grapple with a lawsuit brought by his own brother?

"Winston Carthage!" A voice hailed him from across the street.

Winston turned to see Samuel Morris—newspaper owner, writer, editorialist—standing before Shelly's.

Morris crossed the street and joined Winston under the depot awning. "Good afternoon."

"Hello, Sam."

"Lovely day, wouldn't you say?"

"Not really."

"And why is that?"

"Too hot for May." Winston winked. "I have a meeting with my attorney."

"My sympathies. The lawsuit?"

"Yes."

Morris noted Winston's displeased expression. "When did you last speak with Jeremy?"

"Not since January." Winston waved a hand at nothing, irritated his thoughts had been read so easily. Morris was an Alabamian, bright and handsome, equally fond of ladies and alcohol. His clothes were somewhat threadbare, but he cut a sharp figure. He had a roundish face with smiling eyes as if he knew something that only you and he shared. Winston had long ago decided Morris was smart as a whip, wasting his life, and having a fine time so doing.

"Jeremy was your father's flesh and blood. Has he no claim to *Magnolia*?"

"Morris, I shall not discuss this. My venom is better spent on lawyers."

Morris held his tongue, obviously disappointed in failing to bait his friend. They stood quietly and watched as a wagon load of slaves passed by. A dozen men in ragged cotton britches and thin work shirts were crowded together in back. The sweltering day showed on their faces.

Morris spoke. "The Jews had Moses. Who will free these people?"

Winston sighed. Abolition was Morris's favorite subject, and Winston, one of the few people with whom he could rationally discuss it. Winston, who owned more than one hundred slaves. "I shall not talk about *that* either, Sam."

Morris raised an eyebrow. "Any thought on my suggestion?"

"Really, Sam, I can't pay my slaves wages and remain in business for long."

"Of course you could." Morris searched Winston's eyes.

"Concede the advantage of free labor to my competitors?"

"You *buy* your slaves, don't you?"

"Yes, but—"

"Will you fight a war over slavery?"

Winston shook his head. "What war?"

"It's been brewing for a decade and you know it. Dred Scott, the Kansas-Nebraska Act, Congressional tariffs, I can think of many plausible avenues to war."

"The Dred Scott decision will not start a war."

"So you say. Many in the North tend to think slaves are actually people. The Supreme Court saying otherwise won't change their minds."

"Secession perhaps, not a war." Winston was less sure than he sounded.

"There's a fancy concept. A new nation founded on the backs of the disenfranchised."

"Do you know the money invested in slavery? The southern economy would collapse without it."

"No, the southern economy would collapse if cotton prices fell."

Winston hated to argue against many points with which he agreed, particularly the concept of slavery, which he privately deplored. He sidestepped. "I might run an advertisement for an overseer in the *Reader*."

Morris wagged his head as the wagon disappeared. "You've over a hundred people working for you. Promote from within."

Winston chuckled. "You are very persistent."

"A curse of mine." Morris said. "Shall we have a beer at Shelly's? This train is never coming, you know."

"Are you buying?"

Morris frowned. His newspaper, the *Vicksburg Reader,* was notoriously unprofitable. "A man of your means can ask that question? Honestly, Winston, you disappoint."

"You well know I am on an allowance."

"Ah yes, the meager stipend you draw from that escrow account. I am sure you barely manage to eat." Morris appraised Winston through thinned eyes. "Come by my office to place your advertisement. You *know* where my office is?"

"Grove Street."

"Correct. Two years I've owned that paper, and you've never darkened the door."

"And how many times have you been to *Magnolia*?"

"That is different."

"Of course." Winston smiled. "I would enjoy a beer, but I should remain sober for my meeting."

"Good luck then. Shelly's beckons."

Winston watched him leave, wondering how the two of them had ever become friends. Polar opposite attractions or something.

The train was nearly an hour late. Winston exhaled. He tried—and failed—to find reason for optimism about the meeting. His lawyer, perfunctory and dry, would offer twisted questions and convoluted answers. Eight months of litigation had pushed Winston near his snapping point. He had responsibilities, a plantation to manage. Instead, he fought his brother Jeremy for control of that same plantation. All because his father had not left a proper will, had died legally *intestate,* a despicable word if there ever was one. The primogeniture laws clearly favored Winston, but that hadn't mattered to Jeremy who had little to lose and everything to gain.

Winston's increasingly dark mood made him uncomfortable. He was a strong man, and until recently, was seldom overwrought or unduly troubled by the world around him. He was a good-natured person. That had all changed since his father's death, since Jeremy's lawsuit. For the first time in his forty-six years, he was tortured by self-doubt. Mood swings were frequent. He felt alone and weak. His father, Charles Carthage, the man he'd most admired, was no longer there to guide him. And instead of finding comfort and mutual support from his only brother, he had found betrayal.

A long, piercing train whistle jolted Winston from his thoughts. His pocket watch read twenty after three. His outward calm obscured an expanding knot in his stomach. Curtis, his carriage driver, approached.

"Train comin', Massa Carthage."

Winston raised himself on his walking cane. He had broken his leg just below the knee three months earlier while horseback riding. The break's awkward location had caused the bone to heal crookedly. His limp was permanent.

He watched for the locomotive and hoped his attorney was ready to talk business. He had arranged the use of an office in town rather than waste forty-five minutes making the three-mile trip south to *Magnolia.* Winston tapped his cane nervously on the depot planks.

The locomotive appeared, billowing smoke behind it. With a steamy sigh, it creaked to a halt. Two coach cars slowly emptied their passengers. Winston scanned the platform; finally, his lawyer appeared.

"Dobbins! Here!"

Richard Dobbins was a partner in the state's largest law firm. He was a tall austere man, hook-nosed and full-bearded, dressed in a waistcoat and tweed trousers that concealed his gaunt frame. He extended a bony hand.

"Mr. Carthage, forgive my lateness. A large tree fell across the tracks near Edward's Depot and it took some time to remove. The conductor actually requested assistance from the passengers. Imagine!" Dobbins accented his outrage with a huff.

"No inconvenience. I'm pleased you arrived safely. My carriage is just over here. Shall we?"

"Will we be traveling to *Magnolia*?" Dobbins asked.

"Actually, no. I'm sure you weren't planning to stay the night and the late train to Jackson leaves at 5 P.M. I thought we might expedite matters by meeting at the jail. I've arranged for an office there."

A visit to *Magnolia* was a special occasion, even for a well-to-do lawyer. Winston, normally a gracious host, was in no mood for guests, particularly a man as spiritless as Dobbins. Besides, if the meeting lasted too long, he would be obliged to invite Dobbins to dinner and stay the night, something he had not discussed with Elizabeth.

"Our business should be concluded promptly and I hoped to pay my respects to your charming wife—"

"On your next visit. The office was a favor from the sheriff. I don't want to abuse his hospitality. You understand, I'm sure."

Winston turned for the carriage, ending the discussion.

Dobbins shrugged and talked anyway. "The courthouse fire has been quite a burden. I'm glad we were able to change the venue to Hinds County for your lawsuit. This case might have been interminably delayed here." He spoke of a recent fire that had razed the county courthouse. All court records had been relocated to another building just before the blaze. Thus, disgruntled county employees had been suspected of arson, but the end result had been authorization for a grand new courthouse, so nobody much cared. Winston had almost naturally concluded his brother was somehow responsible for the fire as a means of changing the lawsuit venue to *anywhere* but Vicksburg, where local justice would favor the more respected, older Carthage brother. The case was now being heard in Raymond, the Hinds County seat.

Winston's one-horse carriage pulled away from the depot. Winston ignored Dobbins who chattered about the intricacies of probate law. Winston had the distinct feeling he was being watched. He looked around, but saw no one paying him particular mind. Still, the uncomfortable feeling persisted.

Several travelers milled about the depot, but none dared look too long at the immense man who wore plain clothes and carried no baggage. This was Gaylord Pritchard, and he *had* been studying Winston Carthage. As Pritchard crossed the street and slipped insided Shelly's saloon, he glanced back at the depot where the conductor trundled from car to car, searching for the absent railroad detective.

2

Vicksburg was nestled comfortably within an area of steep hills and deep hollows. The hills were a geologic anomaly, the product of millennia of wind-blown dust collecting on the east banks of the Mississippi River. Vicksburg's location gave it a commanding, if tenuous, position overlooking the grand and capricious river, so prone to change course, seemingly if only to assert its dominance. Conversely, just a few miles in any direction were vast, flat expanses of delta land, the world's richest soil, ruled by the velvet fist of cotton.

Vicksburg's population was a mixture of cultures and classes. Its roots were traced to the city's pious founder, Reverend Newit Vick, who'd had the vision to recognize the value and potential of the bluffs overlooking the river. The small town he founded had grown commensurately with the worldwide demand for cotton. As the city's agricultural and manufacturing outputs increased, the river became a natural outlet to other markets. Vicksburg developed into a thriving port as well as a production center. And like all cities of commerce linked to the water, it attracted colorful and lawless people.

This caused the city's interesting dichotomy. On one hand, the riverfront was a rough and dirty place populated by river people, roustabouts and boatmen, gamblers from New Orleans and St. Louis. Vicksburg's riverfront activity centered around the aptly named Levee Street, running parallel to the river and its long levee, the train depot, and piers, amidst the importers, retailers, and hotels. Nearby was the District, the disreputable area of prostitution clustered around Mississippi's most famous and opulent whorehouse, 15 China Street, ably operated by

Madame Mollie Bunch. The District's populace lived on the edge; nothing was sacred or permanent, and violence was more common than peace.

In stark contrast was Vicksburg's other half, the counterweight in the city's moral balance. Traditional society was dominated by the plantation culture, patriarchal families held together by the glue of religion and commerce. Manufacturing barons and big farmers, the ruling capitalist class, imprinted their moral code on society's fabric. Profit was a righteous thing, and so too should be the lives of those who pursued it in Vicksburg.

These were Vicksburg's two societies, lifestyles and philosophies at odds with the notion of co-existence, but able to do so for the sake of business. Shelly's Saloon straddled both sides of that cultural divide. Shelly's was on Levee Street at the busy Monroe Street intersection, adjacent to the seedy District but not really in it. It was a saloon, perhaps a little nicer than its counterparts, slightly more discriminating in the clientele it attracted, able to maintain a veneer of respectability. The owner, a man named Blevins, had tried to further this illusion of respect by establishing the River Club, a members-only association located on the second floor where Warren County's wealthiest men talked business and drank expensive liquor without the distraction of wives and family. They liked to be near the bustle of the docks, but marginally separated from mixing with the unsavory river people.

Acceptance to the River Club required money and clout, the pillars of elitism. But the Club wasn't purely a social outlet for wealthy men. Unlike other local business organizations, it occasionally hosted high-stakes card games. And for the members who came to drink, and did so in excess, it maintained a handful of small furnished bedrooms. Blevins neither foresaw, nor would he have cared, that some of the family men on the members' rolls would use the rooms for occasional assignations. Blevins never made it his business to pry; the club was private, he merely the landlord. For his discretion, the members were appreciative and generous.

Gaylord Pritchard took note of the River Club as he entered Shelly's.

He ordered a beer and sat down. Most of the patrons glanced in his direction, appraised his remarkable size, and returned to their drinks. All but the smallish man near the door, who watched him rather directly.

Pritchard finished his beer quickly and dropped a coin on the bar. As he rose to leave, the smallish man was standing just beside him.

"Afternoon, sir."

"Hello." Pritchard's monotone had a hard core, like a plum seed. He stepped for the door.

"My name is Sam Morris." Morris offered his right hand. "You new in town?"

"Pritchard. Just passing through." He recognized the combined look of awe and curiosity on Morris's face, a common reaction when people met him up close. He wondered why Morris was so interested in him, but without caring enough to ask, walked out the door.

❧

"Mr. Carthage, as I mentioned earlier, Judge Permutter has instructed you to provide documentation of all business transactions over the last three years in which you acted as the principal agent for the *Magnolia* plantation. He has also requested any dealings in which you and Jeremy acted jointly also be documented." Attorney Dobbins watched Winston through square, wire-framed spectacles.

"Did we not already provide him with similar documentation covering the last *five* years?" Winston planted his hands firmly on the oak table at which they were seated. He was losing patience with Dobbins and this meeting. The judge had seemed ready to decide the lawsuit weeks ago, but had recently begun to request additional information, some of which had already been given him. Winston routinely suspected that Jeremy was somehow behind the new delays.

"Yes, sir, we did, but he is looking at the case now, I believe, in the framework of real versus implied responsibilities of the two parties. A fine legal distinction no doubt, but one which is proper to consider."

"That's a very simple matter. Jeremy's responsibilities were non-existent. He never lifted a hand in the management of *Magnolia*. He was a parasite." Winston tugged irritably at his long sideburns. Elizabeth had cautioned him not to expect much from this meeting. She was right as usual.

"Mr. Carthage, I appreciate your position, but your father's will was never notarized, and it was written such that many interpretations of its full meaning are feasible."

Winston slammed a fist on the table. "What about *primogeniture*?"

"Yes, sir, that is the law. You are the oldest surviving son, so the property is rightfully yours. Unfortunately, certain judges like to . . . make new law."

"How's that?"

Dobbins coughed. "Perhaps I should rephrase myself. Judges can't really *make* law. They *can* rule that a law is unconstitutional, or that exigent circumstances allow a different interpretation. The effect is the same as making new law."

"Who is this judge to make such a determination?"

"Judge Permutter is a unique man, rather eccentric."

"Has he done this before?"

"Done what exactly?"

Winston frowned in response.

Dobbins shifted in his chair. "My review of his past probate decisions shows that he has never challenged primogeniture."

"Then he has accepted a bribe from my brother."

Dobbins coughed again. "Mr. Carthage, Permutter would jail you without a second thought for such a statement."

"Jesus, Mary, and Joseph. That land belongs to *me*. And some judge is trying to take it away."

"He hasn't taken it yet, sir." Dobbins paused and, almost inaudibly, continued. "This would not have happened if your father had contracted my services prior to his death."

"Dammit! There's little I can do to remedy that now!" Winston felt himself losing control. He knew Dobbins was right. Charles Carthage, ever mistrustful of attorneys, had penned his own will only days before his death. Unfortunately, the document was unwitnessed and thus subject to legal challenge, at least in the mind of Judge Harold Permutter.

Dobbins looked down at the table. "Perhaps we should recess for a few moments."

"Yes. I apologize for my outburst." Winston rose and left the stifling office.

❧

Winston looked out the second floor window of the jailhouse annex down on the port of Vicksburg. This could have all been so simple if only Charles Carthage had hired a competent attorney. Instead, his three-page will was a confusing mess, though its intent was generally clear, at least to Winston.

Charles Carthage had naturally wanted *Magnolia* to remain in the family. The problem with which he'd grappled was how to take care of both his sons while leaving primary control of the estate to the older Winston. Charles had loved his sons equally, but it had been apparent to him for years that Jeremy was a malingerer with no interest in *Magnolia*'s operations. Charles had assumed this was a combination of Jeremy's laziness and latent jealousy of his older brother. Jeremy's passion for deviance had been a great sorrow to Charles, who'd spent a lifetime waiting for him to grow up. But after an unremarkable childhood, then seven wasted years at three different east coast universities, Jeremy had learned little more than how to avail himself of liquor and prostitutes.

By comparison, Winston had been the perfect son. Graduating with honors from Transylvania University in Kentucky, Winston had returned home and mastered the skills necessary to run a plantation: crop management and planting strategies, animal husbandry and marketing. He had thrived in the church environment and married a Vicksburg woman, Elizabeth Dearman—she, too, the product of a wealthy plantation family.

Winston had been everything Jeremy was not. So it was with misgivings, but cause, that Charles had torn up his original will splitting his assets between them. His new will had left control of everything to the eldest surviving male Carthage, essentially re-stating the primogeniture law, but he'd added clauses and timetables whereby, under certain conditions, Jeremy might gain some ownership. And the conditions had stipulated drastic changes in Jeremy's lifestyle—marriage, sobriety, piety—meaning Winston had ostensibly inherited full ownership of *Magnolia* since there was little chance that Jeremy would ever change. Charles, rather than completely disinheriting his younger son, had left Jeremy a $10,000 bank account with no strings attached. Charles could not have known that Jeremy would spend that money paying off gambling debts and hiring an attorney to contest his will.

Winston didn't want to see his brother pushed away from *Magnolia* forever, but if Jeremy persisted with his groundless lawsuit, that was the way it would be.

Attorney Dobbins joined him at the window. "Mr. Carthage, I would like to apologize for my comment about your father."

"Apology accepted." Winston heaved a sigh and gazed at the river. The *Delta Queen* made her way around DeSoto's Point. Smoke billowed from her twin steam stacks and spray from the paddle wheels was whisked away by a hot westerly breeze. Passengers formed a human chain along the upper deck railing.

"If you'd like, we could continue our meeting."

Winston heard the words but didn't reply. His body trembled slightly and he couldn't bring himself to turn around. He'd loved his father, loved him more than anything in the world, but had never truly mourned his loss. The suddenness of it so soon after his mother's death and the legal quagmire that followed had never allowed him to mourn. He would have moments of despair, like now, when he missed and needed his father's strength and wisdom. But Winston always pushed those moments away, vowing to properly respect his father's memory when everything was settled. Only this time he couldn't fight his emotions. He couldn't box them up for later inspection.

He took a deep, halting breath and turned to Dobbins, expecting no sympathy, seeing none. He tried to speak, but a lump in his throat choked off the words. Tears slowly cascaded down his cheeks.

Dobbins, the bloodless attorney, silently retreated.

3

Winston had called an end to the meeting. Dobbins had begun repeating questions, or so it had seemed. Winston had answered with diminishing patience, then had taken a second recess during which he'd experienced another crying spell. Confused and disgusted with himself, he had sent Dobbins back to Jackson. Winston was played out. He needed to be home. He needed to see Elizabeth.

Winston now bounced uncomfortably in the passenger seat of his carriage, consumed by his thoughts. He couldn't shake his earlier feeling—someone was watching him. He was sure of it. Almost by default, Jeremy came to mind. Not that Jeremy himself would be following Winston, but someone at his bidding. Who? And why? He couldn't think. Unanswered questions seemed to define his day.

In the driver's seat, Curtis, ever silent, maneuvered the spoked carriage wheels through the ruts of Halls Ferry Road. Dusk had begun to consume the late spring day, and mosquitoes danced hungrily about in search of an evening meal.

They ascended the narrow carriage path to *Magnolia*. Huge oak and cypress trees to either side formed a canopy of green that blocked the retreating daylight. Ahead, a large deer stood in the path, alerted to the oncoming carriage.

A six-point buck, Winston noticed. Pity he didn't have a shotgun handy. The buck tensed and his nostrils flared, but he didn't bolt. Curtis brought the carriage to a slow halt as the four creatures, two men, a horse, and a deer, stared mutely across the hundred feet separating them. Winston sensed a slight breeze in his face and understood why the deer was still there—it couldn't smell them.

In a whisper, "Curtis, do you have a shotgun under the buckboard?"

"No, sir."

The buck's large head tilted at the voices, not sure if it should trust its eyes or its ears. Then it was off. With two leaping strides it crashed through the underbrush into the hollow straddling the left side of the road. Winston shrugged as Curtis slapped the horse lightly with a riding whip and the carriage continued upward. They emerged from the quarter-mile-long tunnel of green to see, three hundred feet ahead in the center of an oddly shaped plateau, *Magnolia*.

Winston's family had lived here for most of their lives, so the view did not affect him as it did others. *Magnolia* was breathtaking, designed by Charles Carthage to reflect the English castles at which he'd marveled as a child. The exterior was constructed almost entirely from brick to minimize the risk of fire. A large portico supported by four white wooden columns stretched across the front of the house connecting two massive stone turrets at either end. Brick steps approached the deep porch, and two enormous bay windows framed a wide front door. The second story was dotted with a half dozen windows and a long railed balcony. A stone driveway lined by a colorful assortment of camellias and gardenias interrupted the front lawn's gentle incline. A visiting magazine editor had once called *Magnolia* "the quirkiest residence imaginable. One expects to see a medieval knight on white steed approaching the moat as a hoop-skirted debutante sips juleps on the porch."

Curtis pulled the carriage over a small bridge that had once spanned the erstwhile castle moat. After Charles passed away, Winston had filled the moat with earth since he'd always considered it a breeding area for mosquitoes and had long tired of seeing loose hogs slop through it on hot days. Charles had never seemed to notice . . .

Curtis helped Winston from the carriage, then disappeared to the stables. Winston climbed the porch steps and paused. He should improve his demeanor. It wouldn't do for Elizabeth to see him so emotionally spent.

He struggled in his mind for words that might cast the meeting with

Dobbins in a positive light. Finding none, he opened the door and found himself eye-to-eye with Lou, a young house servant.

"Evenin', Massa Winston."

"Lou."

"Can I take your hat, sir?"

"Yes." Winston handed it to her. "Where is Mrs. Carthage?"

"She's in the sewin' room fittin' a new dress she got today." Lou backpedaled as she spoke, allowing Winston to enter.

"Is dinner prepared?"

"Almost. Be ready in a few minutes."

"Fine. Tell Mrs. Carthage I will be in my study."

"Yassa." Lou scurried away leaving Winston in the foyer. He strode through the house as gracefully as a man with a cane is able. He was met in the west hallway by his fourteen-year-old son, Andrew.

"Hello, Father."

"Good evening, Andrew. What have you there?"

"My mathematics lessons. I was working in your study. Was that acceptable?" Andrew stood a little straighter. He was short like his grandfather, but his looks were his mother's—green eyes, reddish-brown hair, fair skin, a smattering of freckles across his nose.

"You can use my study whenever you please. Just remember not to disturb anything on my desk."

"I won't." Andrew stared at his father. "Do you feel well?"

"I am fine. Why do you ask?"

"You look upset."

"I was upset earlier. I am better now."

"Did Uncle Jeremy do something else?"

"No."

"Then what?"

Winston chuckled at Andrew's directness. "I had a difficult time with my lawyer today. You will understand about lawyers when you are older."

"Catherine's father is a lawyer."

Winston nodded and frowned at the same time. "Who is Catherine?"

"Catherine Parker." Andrew blushed.

"Randall Parker's daughter. I've seen her before. She's very pretty."

"I hadn't noticed."

"Really? What color are her eyes?"

"Blue." Andrew bit his tongue too late.

Winston's laugh echoed in the hallway. "If you find her attractive, why haven't you called on her?"

For the first time, Andrew failed to meet his father's eye. "We've spoken many times at church, but . . ."

Winston remembered being fourteen and his terror of the fairer sex. "What you need is a more relaxed social setting. We are having a picnic next month. I will invite the Parkers."

"Father!"

"You will thank me afterward."

"I suppose." Andrew abruptly changed the subject. "Curtis says that white trash is still loitering on the south property."

"I will be seeing the sheriff tomorrow about that. Stay away from there in the meantime."

"Yes, sir. What do they want?"

"Handouts, I suppose."

"From us?"

"Anyone, really. They are transients; they move from place to place preying on honest citizens," Winston said.

"Oh." Andrew fidgeted. "Lou says we will be eating soon."

"Yes. Tell your mother I will join her shortly."

"Yes, sir."

Winston stepped into the study amazed at how easily Andrew could make him smile. He was so much like his grandfather, the same expressions and mannerisms. Winston seldom had to wonder what his father had been like as a child. He could easily guess by watching Andrew.

Winston's study was simply furnished, a large desk and chair before the bay window, a daybed against one wall, a two-seat sofa set against another. An unassuming liquor cabinet tucked away next to the sofa was stocked with his favorites, Kentucky sour mash and French brandy. He reached for the whiskey and poured himself a shot, then took a seat at his desk.

Elizabeth would note his dour mood as easily as Andrew. Winston despised his own weakness. He thought again of his father, the man who had never shown weakness. How had he done it? What in Charles Carthage had been the key to such enduring inner strength? Winston had seen it in so many ways. His surety in business, his unerring sense of dignity, his piety. Winston allowed himself to dwell on his father's life, this time more dispassionately, for a purpose, to combat his emotions rather than wallow in them.

Charles Carthage was a Protestant laborer from London when he arrived fifty years earlier on a merchant ship in New Orleans. Twenty-two and alone, he was a young man of undying ambition. But the truth of being a poor immigrant was harsh. Work was scarce, especially for one mistakenly perceived as an Irish "potato eater." He accepted a menial janitor's job in a seedy French Quarter cabaret where hopes were supplanted by reality. Still, he worked hard and there met Marie, a dancer, also an immigrant, from Marseilles. They married the same year and moved to a row house off Canal Street.

When Marie Carthage became pregnant with their first child, Charles took a second job as a bookkeeper-cum-janitor for a Catholic church. Fourteen-hour workdays were common, yet money remained elusive.

As Marie's pregnancy progressed, Charles's wearisome existence took a turn for the better. He met a group of Corsican businessmen in the French Quarter who made him a partner in their trading company in exchange for his bookkeeping skills. Money became more plentiful, though the long hours didn't lessen. Marie worried for her husband's health, and her concerns were justified, but for reasons she wouldn't have guessed. On a cold December night a week before Christmas, Charles stumbled home from a late night's work, bloodied and beaten. Without explanation, he collapsed in Marie's arms. Fearing for his life, she dragged him to the kitchen to tend his wounds and in so doing, discovered a leather pouch stuffed with $5 gold coins—some were bloodstained. He fell unconscious without explanation.

The next morning, Charles woke and insisted they leave New Orleans immediately despite his fragile condition. They packed their belongings and bought passage on a north-bound coach. Three days later, they spent the night in LeFleur's Bluff, Mississippi, the small trading post that would grow into the state capital, Jackson.

On Christmas Eve, Charles bought a horse and a second-hand wagon from a local livery. Having no real destination, they abandoned the coach and headed west. Late in the afternoon, they arrived at the monstrous and impassable Mississippi River. There, they took a room at a boarding house and spent their first Christmas in the community that was to become Vicksburg.

The rest was local legend. Charles used his gold to buy land. It was the last time Marie would see or know of the gold. For forty-five years, Charles never uttered another word of its origin.

Charles quickly expanded his land holdings. By the time their second son Jeremy arrived, he had amassed three thousand acres through speculation and creative purchase options. He farmed cotton and corn, using Negro slaves bought at the Natchez auctions.

Along with Charles's remarkable success came the urge to flaunt it. This he did in spectacular fashion, building his dream home, *Magnolia,* on a hilltop for all to see. It was, much to Charles's delight, the most unusual mansion in the area, christened by the local press with an obvious nickname: the Castle. Charles became an icon in the Vicksburg business community. By his death, few men in west Mississippi were more respected.

Winston took enormous pride in his father's legacy. It had been his lifelong intention to maintain that legacy, build upon it, make the Carthage name famous for generations to come. And now it seemed to all be slipping away, at the hand of another Carthage, no less.

❧

Winston heard footsteps approaching and righted himself in his chair.

"Winston, dear, I'm so pleased you're home."

Elizabeth Dearman Carthage breezed into the study and Winston immediately felt himself brighten. She was thirty-six years old, fair-skinned, slender, and attractive. She was slightly shorter than average, about five feet, with full lips and a narrow face. Her auburn hair was complemented by twinkling green eyes. Her disposition cheerfully spoke of privilege, but didn't obscure her beguiling Southern charm.

"Hello, my love. How was your day?" Winston drank her in like an addictive nectar, certain he could not specify a single thing about her he would prefer different.

"Rather uneventful." She looked at him first with affection, then concern. "You were the one with important business. Did you have a productive meeting with your attorney?"

"About as well as can be expected when lawyers are involved."

Elizabeth studied him, looking for a fissure. "Did you lose your temper?"

"Not exactly."

Winston's emotions lingered just below the surface and he risked another scene like at the jail. He also knew his wife was quite astute at assessing him.

"You didn't notice my new dress." Her eyes twinkled with concern.

"It's magnificent."

"Thank you. I felt guilty spending money like that."

"Don't."

"I put it on Daddy's credit account."

"Elizabeth!"

"It's all right, dear. Remember, Daddy forgot to buy me a birthday gift last year. He was just making up for it."

Winston grumbled.

Elizabeth continued. "And besides, I spoke with Milton Green this morning. He advised me our accounts are balanced nicely."

"Milton is a banker. He can't anticipate the needs of this plantation and the fact that all of our supplier accounts are past due. You don't plant an entire spring crop for free. The cattle and chickens must be fed. I had to buy six new slaves this year. I owe money from Memphis to New Orleans and back." He stopped, realizing the obvious. "Owing a little more to your father won't kill me, I suppose."

"You don't owe Daddy anything. It was a gift." She smiled firmly.

Winston chuckled. "Am I that predictable?"

"I don't know what you mean," Elizabeth said with a hint of tease in her eyes. She shrugged. "Pride is only a sin if you act on it." Her face became more serious. "What happened at the meeting today?"

"Nothing really. Dobbins said the judge asked for additional information. I got frustrated and snapped at him." Winston intently studied the floor. "Then I . . . completely lost my composure." He looked up at her, but self-consciously averted his gaze. Tears welled in his eyes again. He wanted her to know, but he hadn't the courage to tell her. He didn't have to.

"Oh God." She took his head in her hands and felt him shudder. His arms wrapped around her waist and squeezed tightly. She stroked his hair and made soft noises in his ear. They remained that way for a full minute. Embarrassed, Winston finally stood.

"I let a grown man see me in a moment of complete weakness. That won't do at all." His voice was resolute, but disconnected from his eyes.

"It will get better, my love. This lawsuit will end, and our lives will be normal again." She lightly caressed his cheek.

He rose and clutched her hands in a trembling grip. "Can you promise me that?"

She looked at him and said, "I surely can."

Elizabeth watched Winston walk slump-shouldered from the study. She had felt his pain, seen the desperation in his eyes. He needed her more than he could express. He was the strongest man she'd ever known, but he'd aged five years in eight months. It was terrible to see. She encouraged him, consoled him, held him, loved him—but he grew more disconsolate by the day. Because of his own brother . . .

Damn Jeremy! If only he would behave as a man. He was so different from Winston, cowardly and worthless. Twenty years ago they had competed for her affections. The contest had been brief. Winston had treated her like the gentleman he was. Jeremy had been clumsy and overly eager, too familiar with her person, distasteful. She had declined his romantic advances with polite certainty, yet he'd persisted in calling on her. She'd been forced to speak plainly, to hurt his feelings . . . to tell him she loved Winston. And he'd never forgiven her. He was still bitter, still intimidated. And he could never have her, so he still desired her. Such a tiny man.

Elizabeth had frequently considered using her influence over Jeremy, to expedite this sordid process so Winston could maintain his sanity. The time had come to try.

Sam Morris had arrived in Vicksburg a young man from Montgomery, Alabama. He felt destined to write great literature inspired by the beauty of the Mississippi River. But after a very short while, his inspiration, along with his money, had run out. So he'd taken a job at a local newspaper—the *Vicksburg Reader*—writing columns and news summaries, selling advertising, making deliveries, effectively running the newspaper for its aging owner. When the owner retired, Morris purchased the *Reader*.

He was a reluctant journalist, less interested in prose than poetry. But sometimes, the job offered more than the tedium of news stories. As owner and editor, he wrote opinion columns once or twice a week. It was his only current creative outlet and one that he savored.

Tonight he sat on the front porch of Sarah Bowie's boarding house enjoying a cigar and brandy. His companion, Terrance Holloway, was the desk clerk from the Warren County jail and a long-time tenant at Sarah's. Coming to see Holloway gave Morris the perfect excuse to stay for Sarah's dinner. She was the best cook in town by Morris's reckoning, and usually allowed him a free after-dinner drink. She had romantic intentions toward him, but he was an avowed bachelor and she a rather dowdy widow. He accepted her hospitality anyway. Free was free, after all, and her flirtations were an innocent diversion of no consequence.

Morris enjoyed May's cool evenings. He liked stargazing and good conversation, even though Holloway was not terribly bright. He was also Morris's best source of inside information at the jail.

"Winston Carthage was cryin' like a newborn." Holloway pulled on his cigar.

"Bad news?" Morris was skeptical.

"Don't know. Might've lost that lawsuit."

"Oh, certainly not!" Morris knew there was no way in hell Jeremy Carthage deserved to win the lawsuit.

The two slipped into silence. After a time, Morris rose to fetch himself another brandy. When he returned, Holloway was snoring loudly. The previous night, Morris had spent an hour trying to convince him that slaves weren't stupid but merely uneducated. That was an opinion Morris normally reserved for himself, and not, of course, a topic he broached in his newspaper. The popular and comforting public belief was that slaves were intellectually inferior; to suggest differently was dangerous, and Morris did not intend to live dangerously. Over the last thirty years, no fewer than three Vicksburg newspaper editors had been killed for printing controversial editorials.

Morris bumbled around just enough to wake Holloway. He tried to revive the debate of a night ago.

"Did I ever tell you about a Negro I knew in Decatur who could read? He worked for the man who owned the local printing press."

Holloway shook his head no, his boredom with the topic obvious.

Morris ignored him. "I went there one day to inquire about employment. The owner was gone, but this Negro was sitting in his office scanning the latest issue of the paper and didn't hear me enter. He looked up, saw me watching him, and nearly had a conniption, stammering and explaining that he was only checking the margins. I might have been amused, but this poor fellow thought I intended to reveal his secret. Imagine! A man frightened to have it known he's literate."

"Niggers ain't supposed to read. Puts dangerous idears in their head." Holloway took a swallow of beer, confident he'd added to the conversation.

"Do you feel threatened by educated people?"

"Nope."

"If Negroes were educated, would you feel threatened by them?"

Terrance looked dully at Morris. "I knew a nigger got caught reading a Bible at the Colburn plantation. They whipped him near dead."

"Precisely! But why?"

"Cuz he was reading, you simp!"

Of course, Morris, you simp. He let it drop, wondering if he were too smart or too stupid to convey his point.

The absent conversation was replaced by regular noises of dusk. Crickets furiously rubbed their legs together. A dog wailed at the moon, then a second joined in, and soon the air thickened with hoarse canine voices. The object of their attention was unfazed and the choir drew to a listless conclusion.

Morris started to speak when footsteps echoed off the dirt road. A solitary figure approached in the fading light. It was Pritchard, the gigantic man he'd met in Shelly's. Pritchard stopped in the street and seemed to consider his direction. Then he faced the front porch where Morris and Holloway sat.

Morris felt himself cringe and fought the urge to sink lower in his chair.

Pritchard approached the front gate, but didn't pass through. He stood silently, looking at the house, the yard, the two men in chairs.

Morris stole a glance at Holloway who also watched the man in the street. Holloway was uncharacteristically mute.

Pritchard reached into his pocket and extracted a cigar butt. He struck a match, momentarily illuminating his face. He flicked the match away and was again absorbed by darkness. He didn't sway or shuffle his feet. He was completely still except when the cigar came to his lips. The orange glow exaggerated his facial features. His forehead seemed unusually hooded, and his cheeks were high and pronounced. Morris hadn't noticed these physical traits when they'd spoken at Shelly's. Only the bizarre eyes . . .

Pritchard dropped his cigar to the street and methodically ground it with his foot. His movements were precise and calculated. He turned and continued walking in his original direction.

When Pritchard was beyond earshot, Morris let out his breath. He leaned to Holloway. "Do you know that man?"

"Couldn't tell." Holloway's voice was whispery. "Big sumbitch. Looked like a damn bear."

"And about as friendly, I'd say."

They sat quietly until Holloway found the courage to resume his earlier diatribe.

"I'll tell ya about slaves who can read. They'd start plottin'. We'd have alchemy."

"You mean anarchy."

"Yep. We'd have to kill 'em off or send 'em back to Africa. Hell, we could just herd 'em down to the river. Ain't none of 'em can swim." He then postulated about the white man's worst fear, the coming alliance between slave and Indian, a black and red war machine bent on revenge.

Morris paid scant attention. He'd heard it before and it struck him as patently ridiculous. His mind was elsewhere. As a journalist, it was his job to be curious, especially about new arrivals in town. And with that justification, he couldn't quit thinking about the mysterious Pritchard.

4

Jeremy Carthage raised himself from the bed. His face was boyishly handsome, full lips, a typically prominent Carthage jaw, and a light beard. His hair was brown like Winston's, but he had his mother's green eyes. He and Winston were only five years apart, but Jeremy looked much younger.

He casually observed the naked prostitute as she struggled into her corset. She had been good, as usual. Her name was Mary Tisbett, his regular sex partner of three years. She was young and talented, but the experience of her profession showed in her tired blue eyes and fleetingly seductive mouth. Enormous breasts were her job security.

Jeremy had never been married and poorly hid his disdain for women. His long relationship with Mary, though professional, had allowed her insights. She knew virtually all his sexual experience came from prostitutes, he drank to excess, he secretly loved his sister-in-law, and he deeply resented his older brother.

"Have a seat when you are dressed. We must talk."

Mary slipped on her dress. "Is this about your brother again?"

"I told you about the judge handling my lawsuit?" She nodded. "I believe he might support my claim to half the family assets."

"I thought you said it wasn't going well for you."

"Not presently."

"How do you hope to change that?"

"Winston, through his lawyer, has cast doubt on my character. I believe that may be unduly influencing the judge."

"Your character?" She fidgeted. "You *are* talking to a prostitute."

"I don't pay for your opinions!" Jeremy's nostrils flared. *"Sit* down."

"I'm very sorry." She slid to the chair. "Please continue."

Jeremy pointed a finger into his palm. "I don't have time to repair my reputation. So I must cast doubt on Winston's character, too. That's the only way to eliminate it as a factor in the judge's decision."

"Sullying your brother's reputation?" Mary frowned. "That's your plan?"

Jeremy fought the instinct to slap her. Her intelligence could be a problem. "The judge is a devout Methodist. If Winston's moral advantage is eliminated, my chances improve."

"The judge isn't assessing character. He's deciding if the will was legal."

"The will was *not* legal!" Jeremy's cheeks reddened. "My father was a senile bastard who died absent his faculties!" His fists balled and relaxed. "And you are my employee in this matter."

"Yes." Mary looked down. "What must I do?"

Jeremy's breathing steadied. "Go to Vicksburg. You'll meet a man named Pritchard . . ."

❧

Winston's nose crinkled and he brushed a hand at the tickling sensation on his face. Somewhere in his sleep, he wondered why the mosquito net had been pulled away. Slowly, he came awake, his eyes adjusting to the early morning light. Elizabeth stood next to the bed, stroking his temple.

"Good morning." Her voice was husky and full.

Winston began to sit up, but she put two hands on his chest and pushed him back down.

"Did you sleep well?"

Winston wasn't completely sure if he was dreaming. "I did."

"And you?"

"Very restful." She raised herself on the bed and sat next to him. "What are your plans today?"

"I . . . I can't recall just now."

Her hands were on his chest again, exploring.

Winston's breath caught in his throat. "I have . . . work to do this morning." A feeble protest.

"I should say you do." Her face was close to his. "You'd better begin."

With a gruff sound, Winston seized her shoulders and brought her to him. "If you molest a man in his own bed, you should expect a full range of consequences."

"I'd be disappointed otherwise."

Emmit Burnside, attorney-at-law, turned in his comfortable office chair to face his client. "Mr. Carthage, the ruling will likely go against you. We should perhaps try again to reach a settlement with your brother." Burnside's legal advice was delivered to the accompaniment of his tapping foot. He was a small, hyperactive man with a balding head and a tight pair of glasses that pinched his nose. The glasses were an affectation, meant to hide a chronic twitch in his left eye.

"Winston would never settle this case. He's a man of principle." Jeremy intended sarcasm, but it was lost on Burnside, who assumed Winston *was* a man of principle.

"Mr. Carthage, your case has always been tenuous. As I've told you previously, judges are hesitant to tamper with a man's final decree, especially in light of the primogeniture laws. Your father was smart enough to pen a passable will. Had the document been notarized and witnessed, we wouldn't be having this discussion. As it is, you should attempt a settlement or abandon the suit altogether."

Jeremy took a deep breath and tried to clear his mind. Winston would never settle. That was why Jeremy had hired Pritchard, but he had to put on a good show for Burnside.

"Fine. You have my permission to approach the other side with our latest proposal." It would be a token attempt. Winston was too goddamn proud. He considered the lawsuit a personal affront. Why couldn't he see it was just about money? He could easily pay $20,000 and still be exceptionally wealthy. Jeremy paused before his next question. "When will Judge Permutter reach a decision?"

The mercurial Burnside could remain idle no longer. He shot from his chair and paced the length of his stylish office.

"I spoke with the judge on Monday. He expects to receive a final bit of evidence from the other side tomorrow and will render a decision within a week." Burnside was briefly motionless except for his rhythmic left eye.

"Then we have a few more days?"

"I should think so."

Jeremy strode to the window behind Burnside's desk. A knock on the door interrupted his thoughts.

"Mr. Burnside, I have your breakfast." Burnside's legal secretary, a small, bookish-looking man, stepped through the door. He carried a wicker basket and two coffee cups, which he placed on the desk. Inside the basket, Jeremy could see a biscuit and an egg, probably hard-boiled. "Coffee, Mr. Carthage?" He extended a steaming mug.

"Splendid."

The secretary retreated while Burnside settled down for breakfast at his desk. Jeremy scooted out of the way and found a spot to lean against the wall.

"So, Mr. Carthage, we're in agreement on the next course of action?" It was a statement rather than a question. Burnside eyed his food.

"What you said a moment ago struck me. You know, that the judge would decide in Winston's favor. How could two enterprising men like us change that?"

Burnside's stare was blank. "What are you suggesting?"

"I'm not suggesting anything. Maybe you could suggest something."

"There's really nothing to be done."

"Judge Permutter. He's a very scrupulous man . . ."

Burnside's jaw went slack. He spoke barely above a whisper. "You can't be thinking of corrupting the judge."

"Don't be so naive." Jeremy's face was dispassionate. "You know the judge. You know how to approach him."

"Oh no." Burnside emphatically shook his head. "You're insane if you think I'll try to induce Judge Permutter."

"I'll triple your fee."

"Carthage, what you've just suggested would not only cost me my license to practice law, it would send us both to jail."

"Only if he doesn't accept."

"We'll never know. I won't do it. And if you ask me again, you can find a new attorney."

Jeremy flustered. "All the money I've paid you means you'll do what I ask!"

Burnside's eye took on a life of its own, twitching so rapidly his whole left cheek contracted. "The money you've paid me bought you the best legal representation this city has to offer. Nothing more."

"But you've always known the case couldn't be won."

"I knew nothing of the sort."

Jeremy bristled. "Nearly five thousand dollars, for what? A man who gives up?"

"A man who follows the law!" Burnside rose from his chair. "It's time we adjourned this meeting, sir. I'll contact you if your brother's attorney chooses to accept our latest settlement offer."

Jeremy stomped from the office.

❧

Winston Carthage stuffed a piece of bacon into his mouth and wiped his lips with a linen napkin. He was having breakfast on *Magnolia*'s rear veranda. The late morning was hotter than he expected. He was usually up at dawn to meet with the plantation's two overseers, but this morning, Elizabeth had convinced him that staying in bed could pay enormous dividends.

Elizabeth's smile glowed morning fresh. They did not often share breakfast. "Your appetite is good."

"Yes." He winked. "Thank you for that."

Lou appeared at the back door.

"Massa Winston, Miss Elizabeth, y'all need anything?"

Winston nodded. "I'd like half a honeydew melon."

"You can bring me the other half, Lou."

"Yessum."

Winston looked skyward. "I thought I might ride over to Brown's Lake."

"That's a grand idea! It is Wednesday after all. You haven't followed your routine in so long." She spoke of his long-time habit of fishing on Wednesday mornings. "Maybe you could take your easel with you."

Winston grunted through a mouthful of eggs. "Can't paint and fish at the same time." He pointed over his left shoulder with his fork. "New gardenias are in bloom."

"Aren't they magnificent?"

Another grunt in response.

Lou reappeared with two honeydew halves and fresh napkins. Winston pushed his plate away to make room.

Elizabeth studied him in the clear morning sun. He was only forty-six, but gray tufts dominated his hairline. His sideburns were no longer deep brown, and his skin crinkled at the corners of his eyes and mouth. The lawsuit was taxing him. Eight months of bitterness and acrimony, his brother's betrayal, the hard work of a lifetime in the balance. Jeremy's lawsuit, if he won, would force the sale of *Magnolia* with the proceeds divided between the brothers. Jeremy didn't want any part of running *Magnolia*, just the cash equivalent of half its value.

"Winston, what will Jeremy do if he loses the lawsuit?"

"I can't imagine."

"If you win, will you offer him anything? A conciliatory gesture?" She hoped not.

"Are you serious?" He saw that she was. "Not likely, though Father certainly left me that option."

"Why couldn't you establish him in a business so he could make his own way? A trading company or a retail concern?" She already knew the answer.

Winston scooped a rogue seed from the honeydew half and flicked it into the grass with a spoon. "Jeremy isn't a businessman. He's a hedonist. The laziest man who ever lived. Work involves responsibilities and he wishes no part of them." Winston brought the spoon to his mouth.

"Many people are lazy. Why is he so wicked?"

"Jealousy, I think."

"Of you?"

Winston focused on his breakfast. "Jeremy is an intelligent man, you know that. But he never found the will to apply himself. The shortest path was always the one he chose."

"Why didn't your parents demand more of him?"

"Father tried. But when Jeremy was very young, my mother doted on him. She never placed expectations on him like Father did. Her protection made it easier for Jeremy to fail."

"She was too forgiving?"

Winston shook his head. "Father once told me that when Mother was carrying Jeremy, she was desperately hoping to have a girl. And when Jeremy was born, her disappointment was compounded by a very difficult childbirth. She was told that she would never bear children again. For whatever reason, it caused her to treat Jeremy differently, almost like the girl she couldn't have."

"How awful for your mother."

Winston nodded. "Jeremy, too. She was overprotective of him. It bothered him greatly, especially when he couldn't master some of the things expected of a young man—hunting, athletics, academics."

"And you did those things well."

"Yes. Eventually, Jeremy gave up on most of it. He grew to rely on others to do unpleasant tasks and burdensome work. But I think the worst part was, it made him resentful of his own family, particularly my mother."

"And women in general."

"Pardon me?"

Elizabeth frowned. "Jeremy has very little respect for women."

"That's true." Winston looked frankly at Elizabeth. "The sad part is, my intellectual *talents*—for lack of a better word—do not greatly exceed his. I simply applied myself. He never bothered."

Elizabeth shook her head. "Jeremy was never your equal."

"I disagree, but thank you." Winston looked away, apparently struggling with his next words. "I never told you, but I offered Jeremy an additional sum of money after the reading of the will."

"Really?"

Winston nodded. "I offered to supplement his ten thousand dollar bequeathment with an additional five thousand and an ownership share on the condition he take a role in managing *Magnolia*. He said he would think it over. Four days later, he filed the lawsuit."

Elizabeth let the thought linger for a moment. She looked south across the flattened hilltop which dropped off sharply into a hollow about a hundred feet away. The back lawn of *Magnolia* was small, but perfectly landscaped. An array of rose bushes and gardenias enhanced the red brick footpath leading to a stone fountain in the center of the yard. Elizabeth took special pride in the gardens since the house grounds were her province.

"If Jeremy applied himself, he could be an asset to *Magnolia*."

Winston chuckled. "He avoids work as if it were a disease." He paused and his voice softened. "Yet when we were growing up and well into manhood, I suffered the misapprehension that he was an honorable, well-meaning person."

"When did you know the truth?" A truth, Elizabeth thought, she apparently saw much sooner than her husband.

The faintest of smiles crossed Winston's lips. "If I tell you, you must never repeat it. Not to your father, not to your brothers, not to those birds in the Cotillion Club."

"When have you known me to be indiscreet?" She affected a hurt look and he laughed. Her heart warmed a little.

"Never of course." He took a sip of coffee. "In the fall, about three years ago, Jeremy, Father, and I had a serious problem."

Elizabeth nodded, vaguely remembering an unexplained tension among the three men.

"That entire ordeal was Jeremy's doing."

"Ordeal?"

Winston tapped his spoon absentmindedly. "Among Jeremy's other faults, he is an inveterate gambler."

Elizabeth nodded again, aware that Jeremy wasn't just a gambler, but a *poor* gambler.

"It is very common for him to place wagers beyond his means to honor. He developed the habit at boarding school in South Carolina as a teenager. He would lose large amounts of money in poker games, money extended to him on credit by the other players. When he was unable to repay, he was often threatened with beatings or worse. At which point, he would write home to Father asking for money to pay unexpected school expenses." Winston's features clouded. "My father sent the money at first. Eventually, however, he penned a very explicit letter to the headmaster regarding the additional expenses. The headmaster wrote back saying there had been no additional expenses. That was when Jeremy's gambling problem was first discovered."

Winston paused while Lou cleared away the dishes, then continued. "Jeremy was disciplined by my father, but the punishment must have been inadequate, because he got into the same predicament time and again, even as an adult. Finally, the true breaking point was reached three years ago. Jeremy entered a poker tournament hosted by one of the gambling boats, a winner-take-all affair which required each of the ten participants to post a six thousand dollar entry fee. The total purse for the winner was fifty thousand dollars excluding a commission to the boat for hosting the tournament."

"Good heavens! A single poker game worth fifty thousand?" Elizabeth was truly astonished. "Such games take place on the river boats?"

"Not on the passenger steamboats, on the *gambling* boats. They never stay in any port for very long. As you can imagine, Jeremy was desperate because he didn't have the entry fee. He asked me to sign a credit letter in Father's name at the bank. I refused."

"Did he get the money?"

Winston shifted uncomfortably in his chair. "Yes. He borrowed it from a man in Jackson who . . . capitalizes risky business ventures."

Elizabeth observed her husband's discomfort and smiled. "Honestly, Winston, I know about loan sharks."

Winston raised his eyebrows but didn't comment on her use of the term. "Needless to say, Jeremy lost the poker tournament. In fact, he was the first player eliminated." Winston couldn't hide his disgust.

"Then what happened?" Elizabeth prodded.

"He was in quite a fix. This loan shark was no schoolboy chum who might blacken his eye, but a man who would do him serious physical harm."

Elizabeth was plainly baffled. "How would Jeremy ever know such a person?"

"The same way he knows thieves and corrupt businessmen and ladies of ill fame. Jeremy is most comfortable around those people. He is depraved."

Elizabeth pondered whether she should change the subject. Talking out one's anxieties was healthy, but perhaps only in small doses. Winston resumed before she could decide.

"After a time, the loan shark came for his money. He cornered Jeremy one day near the outskirts of town and demanded repayment. Jeremy probably would have been hurt, but Curtis happened by in the wagon and was quick enough to see what was happening."

"Curtis prevented Jeremy from coming to harm?"

Winston smiled. "Curtis asked directions to the sheriff's office. The loan shark caught his hint."

"How did you find this out?"

Winston's eyes twinkled, but he didn't answer.

"Oh." At that moment, Elizabeth realized Winston was closer to one of his slaves than to his own brother.

"The loan shark was a very persuasive man, and knowing Jeremy's reputation, he established a short deadline that Jeremy was strongly encouraged to meet."

Elizabeth shivered. "I've heard loan sharks will do unspeakable things to delinquent borrowers."

"If they are unspeakable, how did you learn of them?"

Elizabeth laughed despite herself. "Be serious."

Winston swatted at a fly on his coat lapel. "Jeremy's solution, as always, was to turn to the family. Only this time, he knew Father would never pay his debt. So he decided to steal the money."

"From his own family?" Elizabeth had always assumed her opinion of Jeremy was as low as Christian beliefs permitted.

"He tried. And I almost allowed it to happen." Winston pursed his lips tightly and looked away. "Father caught him,though."

"Charles? How?"

Winston fidgeted.

Elizabeth gently prompted. "Please finish. I'll never breathe a word."

Winston smiled. "As you know, most of our business is handled in large transactions. We sell our cotton to trading companies, our cattle to large abattoirs, our produce to grocers and wholesalers. Much of our business is done on credit. That is, if we sell our cattle to a slaughterhouse, the cattle are delivered, then the slaughterhouse sends us a bank note for the purchase amount. It's standard business practice. Jeremy's idea was to consign our cotton crop to a company that did not really exist. When the cotton was delivered and no payment was received in exchange, he could claim the family was defrauded by an unscrupulous company. He would then sell the cotton himself and use the proceeds to pay his gambling debt." Winston shook his head at the stupidity of the plan. "He did not have the foresight to understand the family could be bankrupted by his malfeasance."

"Losing six thousand dollars could bankrupt the family?"

"Not literally, but he attempted to swindle a good bit more, about thirty thousand."

"How was he exposed?"

"As you can imagine, the whole thing was poorly conceived, at least in retrospect. I sometimes wonder if that loan shark put him up to it. First, Jeremy formed an imaginary corporation in a vacant warehouse in New Orleans. That took about a week to accomplish and I unwittingly helped by taking him there on a business trip."

Winston couldn't quite meet Elizabeth's eye for a moment. He continued too quickly.

"The day he and I were to come home, he dragged me to the warehouse district and showed me a thriving little cotton distributorship. I was feeling . . . tired that morning and didn't pay attention as closely as I should've. The building was unmarked, but there was much activity about. Men and bales of cotton and delivery wagons, all a farce. He had arranged the warehouse one day while I was at the slave auctions. He'd hired a dozen roustabouts for an hour and rented fifty bales of cotton to have on hand when I arrived. Therefore, I saw what looked to be a viable business with a warehouse and at least a dozen employees. He told me he'd met the owners a couple of days earlier and they wanted to buy our summer crop at very attractive prices. He invited me inside to meet them knowing full well we didn't have the time, nor I the inclination. We had stayed up rather late the previous night . . ." Winston looked away again. "It was risky to assume I wouldn't *take* the time to meet new customers, but it worked."

Elizabeth quietly noted his evasiveness. "What would he have done if you'd agreed to meet the owners?"

"Bluffed, I suppose. But the whole scheme showed more initiative than Jeremy had ever exhibited in his life. Pity his goal was to embezzle from his own family."

Winston was interrupted by the appearance of Andrew at the back door. He was dressed in worn trousers and a thin cotton work vest with big open pockets at the sides. His reddish-brown hair reached almost to his collar, far too long for the summer months.

"Father, may I go with Curtis to the sugar shack?"

"What about your math lessons?"

"Mrs. Cantrell sent word that she's ill today."

"All right, you may go with Curtis, but have him hitch a horse to the other wagon before you leave. And stay away from the south property until I'm sure those vagrants are gone."

"Yes, sir."

"And Andrew, since you're excused from your lessons today, tell me: if I sell four bales of cotton for forty dollars apiece, spend seventy-five dollars in production costs and forty-five dollars in transportation costs, what is my profit margin?"

Andrew knitted his brow. "Twenty-five percent."

"Right. And if I invested my profit in a corporate bond yielding four and a half percent compounded annually, what would be my cumulative balance after ten years?"

"Winston!"

"Let him answer, Elizabeth."

Andrew feigned deep contemplation. "You'd have enough to buy me a new horse and saddle."

Winston chuckled. "A creative response, but a correct one nevertheless. Off you go."

"Thank you, sir. Goodbye, Mother!" He was gone.

"He has an excellent mind for figures. Just like his grandfather," Winston mused.

"And his father."

"No, he exceeds my abilities at the same age."

"You couldn't possibly remember your specific abilities at his age."

"I can remember I was an average student who worked very hard for decent marks. Andrew retains knowledge effortlessly." Winston rose to leave as he spoke.

"Wait! You never told me what happened with Jeremy."

"Ah." Winston fell back into the wicker chair. "Where was I? Oh yes. When we returned from New Orleans, Jeremy immediately lobbied Father to do business with his phantom company. This despite the fact that *I* was effectively in charge of the business operations of the plantation. Father told Jeremy it was my decision to make, and I was so impressed with Jeremy's enthusiasm, I authorized the cotton shipment with only a letter of credit from a New Orleans bank as collateral. The letter was a forgery, but an excellent one, I must admit."

"Did Charles stop the sale?"

"Not immediately. But by this point in his life, Father was suspicious of everything Jeremy did. He was over sixty years old, but took it upon himself—without telling anyone—to investigate this new customer. He didn't openly question my decision to proceed with the shipment. Instead, he went to New Orleans himself and discovered Jeremy's empty warehouse. The whole transaction was a sham, Jeremy was the culprit, and I was the clod who failed to protect our family's interests."

"Charles blamed you?"

"Father would suffer no incompetence, especially from his elder son."

"Yes, but surely Jeremy's betrayal was worse than your negligence."

"That was true in Father's heart, but in his head as a businessman, our misconduct was equally deplorable. We both placed the family's well-being in peril. Acts of omission versus commission, that sort of thing."

They fell into silence. Winston waited for the next question to come as Elizabeth's mind whirred to form it.

"He forgave you, though?"

Winston spoke softly. "He did leave me the plantation."

"Given what you've just told me, how could that judge in Raymond even contemplate a ruling in Jeremy's favor?"

"Because the judge has never heard what I just told you."

"*What?*"

"Mr. Dobbins informed me it would be disallowed as testimony since I have no evidence to support my assertion."

"How could the judge think you would lie about such a thing?"

"His ruling is based on law, not personal opinion. He would be obliged to ignore my testimony unless it was corroborated by Jeremy—obviously an unrealistic expectation. So it has no probative value."

"And Charles didn't keep any records, a diary, something?"

"My father was very meticulous about records and documentation, yet there's no mention of it in his personal writings. I think in the end it caused him too much shame to record for posterity. He kept it very quiet. It would've been bad for business to have such a thing aired publicly."

Elizabeth looked at her husband curiously. How could he have kept that story inside for so long? And how could Jeremy lay claim to half of *Magnolia*? Such temerity!

"I think you should go to Brown's Lake, before it's too hot."

"It's already too hot, but I'll go anyway." Winston rose again and kissed his wife on the forehead.

"Winston." She had a final question. "How did Jeremy repay the loan shark?"

"Who says he did?" He smiled and left.

5

The wagon bounced along a winding trail through the magnificent hills that formed *Magnolia*'s western boundary. Andrew Carthage basked in the late spring day, grateful to avoid his tedious math lessons. He was an average fourteen-year-old in most respects. He hunted and fished, was fully infatuated with girls, and his changing voice took strange turns at unfortunate moments. He enjoyed the new or the unusual, and had boundless curiosity. His character was reflected in his face, at once open and kind, his eyes warm, physical traits inherited from his mother. Yet he didn't lack the Carthage legacy—shrewdness and pragmatism. Winston secretly hoped that the *clever* Andrew, the one so reminiscent of his grandfather, would win the battle for his dominant personality. Andrew wasn't as exceptionally bright as Winston might think, but he was smart enough, good with numbers, already decisive and direct.

Andrew closed his eyes and raised his face to the warm sun. "Father asked me to be sure those vagrants are gone."

Curtis rubbed his white-whiskered chin. "You joshin' me?"

"No, really! He asked me at breakfast this morning."

"You didn't eat breakfast with your paw this mornin'."

"I know that. He was eating before we left. He told me then." A corner of Andrew's upturned mouth betrayed him.

"Uh huh." Curtis, who'd taught Andrew how to split rails and shoe horses, to set beaver traps and field-dress deer, knew Andrew's games better than most. The wagon clattered ahead over the grassy trail until it reached the turn to the south property. Curtis passed it without a second glance.

"Hey, where are you going?"

"Sugar shack."

"What about the south property?"

"Don't hand me nothin' 'bout the south property."

"Dammit, Curtis!"

"Hush up with that kinda talk. Just because your paw lets you swear, don't mean I gotta listen to it." Curtis glared, his face a mosaic of brown skin, a salt-and-pepper beard, and a smattering of dark freckles, outlined by bushy white hair.

"Sorry." Andrew leaned back in the seat, unchastened by his oldest friend, slave or no.

"And don' be poutin'. Your paw would skin me good if we was to get in a fix with them vagrants."

"I just want to *see* them, Curtis, we don't have to approach them."

"Nope. No sir, not today."

Andrew sighed in mock exasperation. "So we're just going to the shack?"

"That's how it sizes up." Curtis waited patiently. Experience said Andrew would never be satisfied with one rejection, that in fact, he would probably offer several outrageous proposals just to make his desired intentions sound reasonable.

"Let's go into town and buy some tobacco."

"Forget it."

"I know how to smoke."

"Knowin' *how* to do something and havin' permission is different things."

Andrew frowned impatiently. "But we can't just go home. It's not even lunchtime yet."

"Well . . ."

Andrew's face livened. "Do you remember that cave over by the bean fields?"

Curtis' yellowy eyes were opaque in the morning sun. "I ain't climbin' into any cave."

"You used to be more fun, Curtis."

"Used to be a damn sight younger, too," he muttered.

"What did you say?" Andrew beamed.

"You heard me fine. I'm old enough to talk how I wants." His broad, flat nose flared. "Young man like you don't need to be gettin' into bad habits like cussing and smoking. People think your parents is neglectful."

"Neglectful?"

"Yep."

They rode in silence until Curtis said, "I hear you got a new friend."

"I have many friends."

"Yep, but this one's pretty."

"And what would you know about that?" Andrew demanded.

"Catherine Parker is what I know." Curtis said easily. "Ain't no shame in eyeballin' a young lady. I been wonderin' what took you so long."

"I'm not ashamed and I've been *eyeballing* her for some time. It's just that, she's so beautiful, she's bound to have many suitors."

"Can't let that stop you. Better find out for sure."

"I will soon enough." Andrew reached beneath the wagon seat and extracted a bound book. "Look what I brought."

Curtis surveyed the book, then Andrew's face. "What's that?"

"It's been a long time. Don't you miss it?"

"I do." Curtis nodded at the book. "Is that a new one?"

"This, Curtis, is a very famous book. It's called *A Christmas Carol* by Charles Dickens. I think you'll like it."

"It's mighty thick. How's I gonna read all that?"

"The same way you read the Bible. I'll help."

"I dunno . . ."

"I think we should start right away. Pull the wagon beneath those trees."

On this occasion, Curtis did as he was told. The wagon rolled to a halt under a willow tree. Andrew opened the book.

"This story takes place in Europe, so some words will be unusual."

Curtis frowned. "They talk different in You-rup?"

"Completely different languages. French, German, even the British.

Of course the British speak our language, but it sounds different."

"Uh huh."

"Grandpa Carthage was British."

"I thought he was from England."

"He was but . . ." Andrew shrugged. "See, English and British are like the same thing. Never mind. Here." He opened the book, but was interrupted before he could read a word.

"Ain't that a sight! A white boy readin' with a nigger." A lean, scruffy man stepped from behind a nearby oak tree. He was joined by a second man who seized the horse's bridle, then a third and a fourth. All were emaciated and dirty, their faces sallow, their clothes ragged and thin. They were the vagrants from the south property, emboldened by hunger to drift farther north on *Magnolia* property.

"Who are you?" Andrew's voice fluttered.

"Traveling salesmen," said the first man, producing chuckles from his companions. "And who might you be?"

"Andrew Carthage," he proclaimed proudly. A hard glance from Curtis changed his answer to, "None of your business."

The leader smiled wickedly through a wiry black beard. He came closer to the wagon's buckboard and squinted up at Andrew.

"We're moving north to find work. Sadly, we have no money, so we're collecting donations from passers-by. Ten dollars would help." The leader and Curtis locked eyes for an instant. Curtis recognized the man's dangerous look. Andrew, apparently, did not.

"I'm not paying for passage on my own property."

"*Your* property. You're the man of this plantation?"

"I live here."

"So who's the owner?"

"My father."

"I see." He turned to his companions. "What's the name of this fine place?" The other vagrants shrugged. "Son?"

"You better be moving on, mister." Andrew spoke with more conviction than he felt.

The leader frowned, his thick eyebrows forming a shadowy V above his nose. "My friends and I must insist on the money. You see, we've had a bad turn of late and food has been scarce. Understand?"

The leader was close enough to reach out and tap Andrew's foot. Andrew caught a whiff of the man's powerful body odor and instinctively drew his foot back. "I don't have ten dollars."

The leader nodded and walked around the wagon to Curtis's side. "I expect this wagon won't do us much good. Lessen we take the horse too."

Andrew followed the vagrant's progress with his eyes. He imagined how his father might react to this threat. Would he slap the reins and run for it? Give them the wagon? His father always said be careful when the situation demanded it, know what the other man was willing to do. Then act boldly. Andrew drew a deep breath. "You're making a mistake, sir."

"Is that so?" The vagrant's hand slid around Curtis's ankle and with a yank, sent the old slave flying from the buckboard. He landed on his rear in the tall weeds.

"Ray!" The leader called to a companion who produced a bullwhip. He expertly uncoiled the leather rope. It sliced through the air and landed on Curtis's right thigh with a *snap!* Curtis didn't yell or flinch. He'd felt the whip often in his life, but never during his long stay at *Magnolia*; the Carthages weren't like that. But it felt the same as he remembered. He slowly rose to his feet, wishing he were thirty years younger and alone in a very small place with the leader.

Andrew watched, almost certain he could hear Curtis's ancient bones creaking as he rose.

The leader sneered at Andrew. "I wonder if your smart nigger can tell me what's about to happen to him."

"I'm warning you, mister." Andrew stared hard into his eyes.

The leader cackled. "Shut up, little man." He made a motion and the other three drew closer around Curtis. "You're pretty attached to this nigger. You can have him back for ten dollars."

"He's not yours to give."

"He ain't yours, neither."

The leader snapped his fingers and Curtis was driven to the ground by a barrage of punches. He was simply too old to fight back. He curled and tried to protect his head as the motley vagrants pounded him with their boots.

The leader chuckled. "Now listen, boy . . ." He turned and found himself staring into the double barrel of a shotgun. Beyond the barrel was a wide-eyed, young face.

"Tell them to stop." Andrew's voice was steady. The vagrants didn't have to be told. All eyes were on him. The leader haltingly stepped backward.

"Easy, son. Don't do nothin' stupid."

"I can't miss from this close, mister."

The leader turned and ran. His companions were close behind.

❧

Curtis poked tenderly at his ribs. The half-starved vagrants hadn't hurt him as badly as healthy men would have. Andrew hoisted him onto the buckboard.

"How did you know 'bout the gun? I just put it there this mornin'."

"I saw it when I put the book there." Andrew was lightheaded, unsure why he felt the need to urinate and lie down. His hands were shaking so hard he had to make fists to stop them.

"Damn good thing." Curtis wheezed and fell against the backrest. His cheeks were beginning to swell.

"Lucky." Andrew climbed on the buckboard, the color drained from his face.

Curtis gently prodded various spots on his body. Finding nothing broken, he turned to Andrew. "Were you really gonna do it?"

Unable to answer, Andrew slumped forward and shuddered.

"Hey, now! What's wrong?" Curtis straightened him. "You done mighty good, Massa Andrew, mighty good! I didn't see no fear in your eyes."

"Sweet Jesus." The words rushed from Andrew's mouth in a whisper. "I almost killed a man."

Curtis smiled and patted him gently on the back. "Not really. That gun ain't loaded."

6

Brown's Lake was not really a lake, but a pond. Its surface area measured four acres roughly in the shape of an hourglass. A twenty-foot-high bluff towered above the eastern shore. The west bank was graced with a spectacular and solitary magnolia tree. Winston had come here since he was a child. The fishing and the beauty of the spot were incomparable. In better days, he had come to the lake once a week, even in the winter. In the months since his father's death, he'd only been twice. He steered the wagon to a flat area near the northern shore where he kept a row boat, a cane pole, and a pair of paddles tucked in the tall weeds near the water. The boat was a wooden skiff he could slide into the water, bad leg and all.

At Elizabeth's insistence, Lou had prepared him an afternoon snack of fruit and a canteen, all of which she'd put in a straw basket. She'd also tossed in a jar of worms and bacon fat for the catfish. He grabbed the basket with one hand and his cane with the other. On second thought, he tossed the cane back into the wagon, preferring a limp to the infernal nuisance. And limp he did, to the weed patch where the boat rested. He pushed it into the shallows, slipped off his boots, and rolled up his pants. He carefully waded until he was knee-deep and swung his bad leg into the boat. Pushing off the bottom, he landed true. He seized the oars and stroked toward the lake's west side. Within seconds, perspiration washed his face. He grunted and removed his shirt, exposing his white chest and back to the sun.

The skiff knifed easily through the placid water. Winston had always favored rowing as a pastime and it suited him well. It was a single-minded pursuit requiring stamina and power, qualities he owned in abundance.

Winston pulled hard and the muscles in his shoulders and arms screamed for mercy. He pulled harder knowing he would regret the extra effort in the morning. He covered the distance from his launch point to the west bank in less than two minutes. He slowed to a stop beneath the outstretched branches of the giant magnolia tree. The tree and the place were special. Charles Carthage had gazed on this tree nearly thirty years earlier when he'd named the plantation.

Winston withdrew the jar of worms and methodically baited his hook. He dropped the line in the water and watched the squiggling worm sink to a few feet. He settled back in the little boat's bow, stretching his legs. Five minutes later, he received a bite. Then a second. Finally, the hungry bream took a swipe and managed to slip the worm from the hook without impaling itself. Winston never stirred from his sleep.

❧

Winston shook away cobwebs from his hour-long nap. Sticky and hot, he reached for a long swallow from the canteen. Amazingly, he'd slept for almost nine hours last night, yet here he was dropping off again only a short while later. A lazy man could grow accustomed to this schedule.

The skiff had drifted to the tall reeds near the bank. He brought in the fishing line and shoved an oar into the thick mud, pushing the boat away from shore. He tugged on the oars and in three long pulls, the skiff moved at full speed. The rowing felt good, cleansing. He decided on a quick turn around the lake and then a swim. He looked over his shoulder for a sense of direction and was surprised to see a man leaning against a tree near his wagon. He slacked on the oars and adjusted his course toward the north shore.

The man was motionless as Winston neared the landing. The skiff scraped to a stop in a few inches of water, and Winston threw his good leg over the side. The stranger still didn't move. Winston dragged the skiff to shore. Shirt in hand, he limped the few feet to his waistcoat and, most importantly, his pistol.

The man finally spoke. "Good afternoon, Mr. Carthage."

At first glance, he was huge, but otherwise unremarkable. Winston had learned never to trust first glances. He always held a man's eye long enough to see what was inside.

"Who are you?" Winston's voice was calm.

"My name is Pritchard, sir."

Winston donned his shirt, never looking away.

"I'm here at your brother's behest."

Winston stopped buttoning his shirt. He reached down and retrieved his waistcoat. He slipped it on and felt the heavy gun bounce against his rib cage. "You are the one."

"Pardon?"

"Someone has been following me. You."

"You are very observant."

"Why?"

"No reason. I wasn't sure how to approach you."

"I have nothing to say to you or, by proxy, my brother."

"I can appreciate that."

"I'll not be coerced by some hired goon."

Pritchard faintly smiled. "I'm not here to threaten you. I'm a private detective."

"Good for you."

"I normally work for insurance companies or bill collectors as an investigator, occasionally for clients who choose not to seek assistance from law enforcement officials."

"A mercenary."

Pritchard chuckled. "In some ways."

The laugh sounded genuine, but Winston saw no humor in Pritchard's face. "What has any of that to do with me?"

Pritchard ran a hand through his hair. "I was hired to locate a prostitute in New Orleans."

For the first time, Winston broke eye contact. "And?"

"She told me quite a lot." Pritchard paused. "I know this is a delicate subject for you. I came to offer a proposition, if you'll hear it."

Winston studied Pritchard. "What?"

"Simple. Twenty thousand and your brother will drop his lawsuit."

A darkness marred Winston's face. He remembered eight months earlier, immediately after the reading of his father's will. Jeremy had used the same approach. Winston had refused him then.

Pritchard spoke. "You don't seem surprised by this."

Winston was thinking and talking at the same time. "My brother is on the verge of losing his lawsuit."

"A matter of opinion, but I assumed as much. When a client uses a tactic such as this, one can infer he has reached a desperate condition."

"You speak very well for a personal detective."

"*Private* detective. Thank you."

"What if I refuse to pay?"

Pritchard tapped his chest. "I have in my pocket a signed, notarized affidavit from Michelle Tussaunt of 1125 Decatur Street, New Orleans, Louisiana, which is not only her residence, but also the location of The Carousel, a well-known house of ill fame. This document recounts in explicit detail numerous sexual liaisons between you and her, in New Orleans and Vicksburg. She gives a very complete description of you including, as I've just seen, an accurate representation of a scar on your torso. She also details some of your . . . sexual appetites."

Winston blushed. If this was a bluff, Pritchard had more information than Winston would've figured. And someone *had* spoken to Miss Tussaunt to know about Winston's "sexual appetites." The affidavit was new. Before, Jeremy had only threatened to tell Elizabeth. Now he was using legal documentation and this monster Pritchard.

"Get to the point, Mr. Pritchard."

"Judge Permutter will receive the affidavit."

Winston considered this. He folded his arms across his chest. "Do your worst."

"There are other implications."

Winston raised an eyebrow but said nothing.

"You'll read this affidavit in the local newspaper."

Winston laughed. "This is Vicksburg, Mississippi, not Gomorrah. Sam Morris and J. W. Swords would never allow such offal to be printed in their papers."

"Yes, Mr. Morris is a friend of yours, I believe. You can probably count on his discretion, but could you say the same about the other local papers? The Jackson papers, or Memphis, or Baton Rouge? I believe you have business interests in each of those places, do you not?"

"I have no interests in those places that outweigh my sense of propriety. What people will or will not print is of no concern to me."

Pritchard nodded at Winston's predictable reaction. "You are a religious man."

"I'm active in the Presbyterian church."

"What does your Bible say about adultery, Mr. Carthage?"

Winston's face flushed red.

Pritchard's expression signaled retreat. "Mr. Carthage, I've been instructed to present you with this proposal and receive an answer. But you don't have to decide right away. I won't return to Jackson until Saturday. If you care to take a day and think it over, I'll gladly meet you again tomorrow."

Winston suddenly realized that Pritchard was merely planting seeds. "I don't need a day or a minute. There will be no settlement."

Pritchard looked mildly disappointed. "Mr. Carthage, I understand your hostility toward me, but I would encourage you to think of your wife and son, your father's memory, this incredible plantation. This unseemly business could be resolved for an amount of money that would seem trivial in time."

"I think you should leave my property, Mr. Pritchard."

"I'll do as you ask, but it's not really your property, is it? Not yet." Pritchard smiled. His teeth were even and white.

Winston drew the pistol from his jacket and pointed it squarely at Pritchard's face.

"That is completely unnecessary." Pritchard shrugged his massive shoulders. "I will be at the River Club tomorrow evening at eight o'clock. Your brother gave me his key. If you change your mind, meet me there, and we'll discuss this further. If not, I'll assume your position is final. Now if you'll excuse me, I have a long walk back." With a nod of his head, Pritchard was gone.

7

Elizabeth Carthage sipped a glass of water and listened to her father berate a domestic slave. "Dammit, Harriet, I've told you a hundred times not to throw out leftover vegetables. *We have hogs to feed!*"

Harriet meekly nodded and slunk away.

"Daddy, why must you treat her that way?"

Harvey Dearman glared down his bulbous nose at Elizabeth. He had bulging eyes and a wide mouth in a permanent frown. He was as ugly as his daughter was beautiful. He nodded when he spoke, and a strand of white hair drooped across his forehead. "How else do you expect her to remember? She's a slave, dear. They don't retain like we do."

"Daddy, that's just not true. They are quite capable if given a chance." She smiled, not afraid to challenge her bellicose father.

"Are you here to pester me, dear?"

"No, Daddy." She paused and took a deep breath. "It is about Winston. Is there anything you can do to help resolve this silly lawsuit?"

A faint smile stole onto Harvey's face. He and Charles Carthage had been long-time rivals despite the marriage of their children. "What would you have me do? Your brother-in-law seems intent on destroying his own family."

"Lend me some money, Daddy," Elizabeth declared.

"Have you discussed this with Winston?"

"No, sir."

Harvey nodded. "He's as stubborn as his father."

Elizabeth didn't dispute this. "But you would lend us money, if we really needed it?"

"Elizabeth, I would never let you or your family go hungry, you know that."

"I'm not talking about going hungry, Daddy. Winston has business expenses. He's worried about maintaining the plantation."

"For heaven's sake, I'll loan him operating capital, if he needs it."

"Thank you, Daddy." She fiddled with the curls of her shoulder length hair. "You and Mr. Carthage never got on very well, but you did discuss business from time to time, right?"

Harvey nodded. "Charles and I were friendly competitors." Harvey would never admit that he *owed* the Carthage family. Charles had once privately helped Harvey keep his plantation solvent during a severe drought.

"Did Mr. Carthage ever discuss with you . . . " Elizabeth paused. If her father knew of Jeremy's cotton scheme, he could testify on Winston's behalf. But she remembered her promise to Winston. "Did he ever tell you of an instance when someone tried to embezzle money from the family? Three years ago?"

Harvey raised his eyebrows. "Embezzlement." He tried to stare his daughter down. "Who are you talking about, dear?"

Elizabeth immediately withdrew. "A man who worked for the family, an overseer."

He held her gaze a bit longer. "No, Charles never mentioned that."

Elizabeth exhaled. This had been a bad idea. She would have to think of another way to help Winston.

❧

Winston poured a brandy from the liquor cabinet in his study and tiredly hobbled to his leather chair. The house had been empty on his return from the lake and the man named Pritchard. Where was Elizabeth? The servants? He felt lonely and pitiful. He hated such feelings, they were foreign and burdensome.

He sipped at his brandy and considered the offer at the lake—twenty thousand dollars for a settlement. Jeremy's first blackmail attempt had only been ten thousand. Winston had called his bluff, knowing Jeremy wouldn't deliberately hurt Elizabeth. But things had changed. Jeremy had lived a meager existence for the last eight months and hadn't liked it. And now he had Pritchard working for him—Pritchard, who would have no compunction about any of it.

What of the affidavit? Would it matter if the whole world knew of the prostitute? It had been three years ago, for God's sake. That damned trip to New Orleans. Hiring the prostitute in a drunken state had been wrong. Hiring her in front of Jeremy had been utterly foolish.

Then there was the matter of Winston's "sexual appetites," as Pritchard had described them. Would a respectable newspaper print scandalous speculation? Would they detail what he'd done with the prostitute that he would never ask of Elizabeth? Newspapers had standards, didn't they? Morris could be trusted, but what about the *Daily Citizen* and the Jackson papers?

He clenched his hands around the brandy glass. His chest tightened as he imagined the stares from other parishioners on Sunday mornings. Sanctimonious hypocrites. The hell with them all! Could anyone understand, would anyone see he'd done it for love of Elizabeth, done it because she thought he was no longer attracted to her, *that* because of his damned impotence. Which had been the worst part of it all—Elizabeth believing Winston no longer loved her. How could he explain that he was afraid of losing her because he couldn't perform in bed? How would *she* react to the shame of his public judgment? He'd sooner die than lose her. Or . . . Jeremy would die.

The baneful concept occurred to him for the first time. Could he kill his only brother to protect himself? The idea had a certain appeal. He tossed back the rest of his brandy and tried to purge the notion but there it remained, drifting like a black veil across his consciousness.

Maybe he was too quick to reject the settlement offer. Twenty thousand dollars was an enormous sum, but not a devastating one. If he did settle, would Jeremy blackmail him again after losing his money on a pair of aces or a roll of the dice?

Winston sighed. The ugly thought crept into his mind again. Could he kill Jeremy? He curled his fist and slammed it on the desktop.

8

Elizabeth slipped from the bed, careful not to disturb Winston. She padded barefoot to the necessity room and looked in the mirror. Not displeased with her appearance at thirty-six, she was nevertheless concerned by frown lines forming at the corners of her mouth. Ever the optimist, she decided they were smile lines instead.

She tiptoed back through the huge master bedroom and drew the curtains tightly closed. Winston had had another restless night, tossing about and talking in his sleep. She hoped he would sleep late again as yesterday, but knowing Winston, he would wake in a matter of minutes. Six o'clock every morning, even on weekends. She was accustomed to his routine after seventeen years.

Elizabeth slipped on a robe and house shoes and let herself through the bedroom door. She walked the long upstairs hall and stopped at Andrew's room for a peek inside. He was sleeping soundly, sprawled on top of the quilt in his nightshirt. The window was open and the room a mite chilly, but she let it go.

She strode down the elliptical spiral staircase in the center of the house. Circular spiral staircases were fairly common; *Magnolia*'s elliptical design, however, was unique—there wasn't another one like it anywhere in the state, maybe the entire South.

Elizabeth reached the ground floor and looked out the rear windows. She saw Curtis crossing the south lawn to the stables. His footprints left dark tracks on the dewy grass. Curtis was an earlier riser than even Winston, usually fully dressed and ready to work by the crack of dawn.

Curtis was Elizabeth's favorite of the slaves, though she was fond of them all. She, like Winston, treated them with more propriety than other plantation owners. She felt for their plight. Bondage was a horrible condition, a belief she often mentioned to Winston. She hoped one day he would free them unconditionally. All the horrible war talk between the states would seem to make it an easy choice.

Elizabeth watched Curtis round the corner of the house. He lived in the servants' quarters on the west side of *Magnolia*. Comparatively speaking, the domestics lived as close to a normal life as slaves ever could. They worked reasonable hours, usually during the daytime. Their relatively sedentary lifestyle was a point of contention among the envious field slaves. Still, *Magnolia*'s field slaves fared better than most. They were allowed, even encouraged, to marry and form families. They were also permitted to manage an underground economy, farming small unused plots scattered about the plantation, growing corn, tomatoes, and watermelon, which they tacitly sold at the Vicksburg markets. Allowing such measured autonomy was considered dangerous by some, but Winston saw no harm in it. In fact, he directly paid his own slaves for crops grown on *Magnolia* property. Winston didn't grow watermelon and cantaloupe, but certainly enjoyed eating them, and the slaves' crops were usually superior to what he might purchase at the grocers. For their part, the slaves were happy to at least partially provide for themselves.

Elizabeth entered the kitchen. "Good morning, Lou."

"Oh. You scared me, Miss Elizabeth. Good mornin' to *you*."

"Would you make coffee for two, please? And I'd like fresh fruit for breakfast. Winston and Andrew will have their usual."

"Yessum."

"I'll be upstairs dressing." Elizabeth walked through the kitchen to the rear foyer. She glanced out the window again and could just see a brilliant yellow sun peeking through the morning mist. Such beauty, she thought, could only shine on good things. Today, would be glorious. Today was the day for an unscheduled visit with Jeremy in Jackson. Her mood improved considerably. She was finally going to *do* something for Winston.

❧

"Have a wonderful day, dear." Elizabeth beamed at Winston as he opened the front door.

Winston smiled curiously at her bright morning mood. "I'll try. What are your plans?"

She shrugged impishly. "Running errands."

Winston nodded and kissed her on the cheek. "Be careful."

❧

Winston steered his carriage along the *Magnolia* path absorbed in thought. He was obliged to visit Sam Morris who, according to Elizabeth, had walked all the way out to *Magnolia* yesterday to see him. That didn't sound like Morris; the man was as lazy as a pregnant cow. He'd mentioned some nonsense about writing a story on *Magnolia* that hadn't even fooled Elizabeth.

He had other business, including stops at the county tax assessor and the post office. And he would visit Bill Minnifield over at *Cimarron* to borrow a weaving loom. Elizabeth was making new summer clothes for the domestic slaves. Seemed like a waste of time since their current clothes weren't worn, but she was doing a good turn and Winston certainly had the cotton in abundance.

His day was full. His attention, however, was consumed by what would happen at the *end* of the day. He'd decided to see Pritchard tonight at the River Club. Though what he would say or do was unresolved. He had all day to think about it.

❧

Mary Tisbett, the prostitute, dressed in a rush to catch the early train for Vicksburg. She adjusted her corset in the hotel room mirror, and in its reflection, saw Jeremy was awake. "Sorry I disturbed you. I must hurry if I'm to catch the train."

"Yes."

"I'll bathe at the hotel in Vicksburg. No time this morning."

"Tonight's the night."

"That's right." She watched him in the mirror. His face was dour.

"You'll meet Pritchard at the hotel?"

"Unless the plan has changed."

"No."

She opened the hotel room door. "Then I'll tell you all about it tomorrow."

"Good luck." Jeremy made a poor job of smiling.

She closed the door behind her, again noting his melancholy expression. Maybe he was having misgivings about ruining his brother's life. Too late now. She shrugged and hurried downstairs.

❧

The 10:30 train arrived, and Mary Tisbett filed off with a small suitcase in hand. She wore a bright red dress with white lace embroidery and a very low bustline. She stepped from the platform onto the bustle of Levee Street and was nearly run down by a pair of oxen pulling a cart of iron ingots. The cart driver didn't call a warning, intent as he was on Mary's ample profile. She stepped back unharmed, and the man could only tip his hat open-mouthed as he rolled by.

Her second attempt on Levee Street was more successful. She crossed over to Monroe Street and made the steep climb to the Washington Hotel where she was to take a room. The man named Pritchard was to meet her just after lunch at 12:30. She hadn't asked Jeremy why she couldn't stay at her own house in town. Jeremy was paying for the hotel room, so she didn't mind. As she climbed the hill, she looked right and noted Shelly's, and above it, the River Club.

❧

When Mary answered the knock on her hotel room door, she was surprised by her own surprise. She wasn't often uncomfortable around men anymore. An experienced prostitute, she had seen all kinds—rich, poor, bright, stupid, mean, mild. Men were men. But something about this one was much different, and not altogether right. He was a giant,

Jeremy had warned her as much. He was handsome in an austere way with close-cut hair and a plain, intelligent face. He had no scars or blemishes, his wide cheeks were shaven clean, his expression was unassuming but hard. And his eyes were easily the strangest she'd ever seen.

"I'm Pritchard." He extended a large hand, which she accepted. "You must be Mary." His deep voice resonated unpleasantly.

Mary was immediately ill-at-ease with his touch. "Mary Tisbett."

He smiled, but the hardness remained. "Jeremy's description wasn't fair to you."

"Thank you. I would offer you refreshments, but under the circumstances . . ." She indicated the meager hotel room behind her.

"No matter. May I come in?" Pritchard slipped by her without waiting for an answer.

She closed the door and turned. He was close, only a couple of feet. "Excuse me." She walked around him and stood in the center of the small room. "I was with Jeremy last night. He said you had arranged everything?"

"Yes." He came closer still. Sunlight from the open window spilled on his face. "I'll meet you tonight at eight o'clock in front of a saloon called the Gin."

"I know the place." She was transfixed, certain that his eyes had changed color in the light.

"We'll go to the River Club together. Carthage must see you before he loses consciousness. You'll stay the night with him, as planned."

Mary fidgeted. A different approach had occurred to her. Now she was less sure she should mention it. This man wouldn't want changes . . .

Pritchard sensed her hesitance. "Questions?"

Mary studied her fingernails, no longer intrigued by Pritchard's face. He wasn't handsome as she had thought. "Did you allow for other contingencies?"

"Such as?"

"Winston Carthage is a very rich man. He owns half of this county."

"Not yet, he doesn't. What's your point?" Pritchard clearly saw the point.

"How much is Jeremy paying you?"

"The same as you."

"A hundred dollars?"

He nodded slowly, his jaw muscles tightening.

"I was wondering if we might not do better for ourselves if we blackmailed Winston, too?" Mary offered a conspirator's smile, and immediately felt silly for it. "Just a notion. But . . . hadn't you thought of it?"

"The first time I met Jeremy."

She laughed nervously. "Jeremy would be easy. We could tell him the plan didn't work, fabricate an excuse. We'd have his $100, plus whatever we drew from Winston." Why was he staring at her like that?

"Has Jeremy paid you?" Pritchard's mouth barely moved.

Mary folded her arms over her chest and coughed self-consciously. "Yes, but—"

"We might easier blackmail Jeremy if he wins the lawsuit. He is more susceptible than Winston, don't you think?"

Mary wanted to see the logic, to satisfy Pritchard, to stop him from staring. "I've never met Winston, but you're probably right. He must have more spine than Jeremy."

"Then we're agreed on the original plan?" There was no question in Pritchard's voice.

"Yes."

The whore had tipped her hand too early. Pritchard *did* want Winston to see her tonight before he passed out, to instill her face in his brain. He might really think he had killed her. But if she tried to blackmail Winston before the opium, anything could happen. She couldn't be allowed to see him. Stupid whore.

Mary smiled. Pritchard smiled back. He was imagining her naked and dead.

❧

Morris plodded through the streets of downtown Vicksburg, cursing the insufferable heat. As he approached his China Street office, he was surprised to see Winston Carthage out front.

"Good afternoon, Winston!"

"Hello, Sam." Winston labored down from his carriage.

"Come inside out of the sun." Morris held open the door.

Morris's office was a typical newspaperman's hovel, messy and disorganized, paper strewn everywhere. A desk in the center of the ten-foot square room was covered with periodicals, Horace Greely's *New York Tribune*, *Harper's Weekly*, and *The Farmer's Almanac*. Newspapers were stacked carelessly in a corner including copies of Morris's local competitors, the *Daily Citizen* and the *Vicksburg Whig*.

Morris offered a chair to Winston and settled behind his littered desk. "This is your first visit to my empire, is it not?" Morris' infectious smile amused his guest.

"If I'd known what I was missing, I'd have sent a cleaning crew ahead."

"Informing the masses is a dirty job. On the positive side, it's too filthy for the roaches."

"Where's your press?"

"Through the door." Morris jerked his head toward the back wall. "I have to keep it in a secure area so the public won't be tempted to make its own news."

"Very prudent."

Morris opened the top drawer of his desk and extracted a box from which he produced two slender black cigars. "Join me?" He struck a match on his desktop and lit Winston's cigar, then his own. "To what do I owe the visit?"

"My advertisement for an overseer." Winston handed him a small bit of paper. "This should do it."

"It will run in the next issue." Morris's features clouded. "I spoke with Terrance Holloway a couple of evenings ago. Terrance, he's a clerk at the jail. He mentioned you were there with your lawyer on Tuesday afternoon."

Not being a particularly good inquisitor, Morris hesitated. He could see Winston knew where this was going.

"Terrance also said you . . . well . . . you were in a rather tormented emotional condition."

"Did Terrance say it just that way, Sam?" Winston teased to avoid the question.

"What *happened*, Winston? Surely you didn't lose the lawsuit?"

"No. My lawyer talked and talked. After a time, I was simply overwhelmed by the ugliness of it all. It just came out of me. Not a very manly display." His voice softened and he gazed through Morris at the wall. "I have never properly grieved my father's death. I'm ashamed for that."

Morris winced. "Winston, I didn't mean to—"

"I know you didn't." Winston's smile was at once friendly and cheerless.

9

"Wait here, Lou." Elizabeth pointed to a bench.

"Miss Liz'beth, you shouldn't be goin' to no ho-tel by yourself. Ain't proper."

"I'll decide what's proper," she snapped.

"Yessum."

"I'm sorry to be so brusque. You're right, it isn't proper. So we shan't ever discuss this with anyone, correct?"

"Yessum."

"Good. I'll return shortly."

She climbed the hotel steps and entered a spacious and once opulent hotel lobby that was now in bad need of refurbishment. She approached the front desk.

"Mr. Jeremy Carthage, please."

The day clerk at the Edward's Hotel looked down his nose. All of Jeremy Carthage's female visitors were prostitutes. "May I say who wishes to see him?"

"Elizabeth Carthage."

"Oh . . . I see." The clerk knew the Carthage name, but his low impressions of the family were based on Jeremy. On reflection, this woman looked nothing like a whore. "You're from Vicksburg, ma'am?"

"Yes."

"Unless I'm mistaken, Mr. Carthage is out for the day. Do you care to leave a message?"

"Hello, Elizabeth."

Jeremy was standing in the doorway of the hotel bar. She turned and saw him for the first time since Charles Carthage's funeral. He appeared the same—cynically handsome, carefree, worthless. He'd gained weight, but it suited him. Winston was losing weight . . .

"Good afternoon, Jeremy." She was polite, her mouth set firmly. "What brings you to Jackson?"

"A few minutes of your time, if you can spare it."

Jeremy gestured toward the bar. "Shall we?"

"Could we speak privately?"

"Of course. My room is on the second floor."

"Don't be preposterous."

"Worried about appearances? Why would it be improper for a brother and sister to speak in private?" Jeremy emphasized "brother and sister" for the benefit of the desk clerk.

Jeremy's room? Alone? Elizabeth turned to the clerk, who quickly averted his eyes. He was the only other person in the lobby. Could she? Were it known that she'd visited a man's room unescorted—even her brother-in-law's room—her reputation would eternally suffer. Then she considered the stakes and scoffed at herself. She took a deep breath.

"Fine."

Jeremy led Elizabeth upstairs to his simple room, his home of two months. Clothes were piled in a corner, the bed unmade.

"Have a seat." He motioned to a chair near the window. "You look wonderful as always."

"Thank you." She smelled alcohol on his breath.

"Why are you here, Elizabeth?" Jeremy sank onto the bed, his feet dangling just above the wood floor.

"To make an appeal." She swallowed uneasily, annoyed by his vain expression. "Please drop your lawsuit."

"Did Winston send you?"

"Of course not."

A corner of his mouth turned up. "You came here on your own?"

She ignored the question. "You can't win. You'll get nothing."

"In that case, I'll ask again—why are you here?"

She tugged distractedly at a clasp on her pocketbook. "I don't care if he wins anymore." She cursed inwardly at her own wavering voice.

"I've offered to make a settlement, but he's been very inflexible. What else can I do?" Jeremy's voice was sing-songy by comparison.

She fought for control. "Leave him alone! First his mother died, then his father, and . . ." She put a hand to her mouth and felt tears welling. She spoke deliberately. "Don't you want to reconcile with him? He's your only family."

"Winston's stubbornness is standing in the way. And by the way, I lost *my* parents too."

"Your expression of grief was sentimental—suing your own brother. I'm sure they'd be proud."

"I cried when my parents died." The defiant lie sounded nearly truthful.

Elizabeth looked out the window wanting to believe him, knowing better. "It's not too late, Jeremy. Winston wants to forgive you, I'm sure of it." She knew instinctively that Jeremy didn't care.

"Forgive me?" Jeremy chuckled humorlessly. "When we were growing up, Winston was always the *good* son. He won the accolades and attention, he got the responsibility, he got—" Jeremy stopped abruptly.

Elizabeth leaned forward searching for his eyes. "Got me?"

He looked away. "Don't flatter yourself."

She shook her head. "I'm sorry, that wasn't fair."

"No matter." He smirked. "What's in it for me to drop the lawsuit?"

"I can't speak for Winston, but he'll be equitable."

"Like Father was equitable?"

"I can't speak for Charles either. I'm sure he acted on his best intuitions."

"And what do you think, Elizabeth? Should I have received more? Maybe if I'd fawned over Father in his old age like Winston, I'd be better off today."

She bristled. "You're hopeless, aren't you? Charles gave you a decent inheritance and you used it to pay off a loan shark. Then, out of a sense of honor, Winston offered you an additional cash settlement, and you sued him. What more could you possibly expect?"

Jeremy blanched. "He told you all that?"

"He's my husband."

Jeremy assumed his best poker face, its effect as negligible as it was at the tables. "I suppose if I dropped the suit, everything would be forgiven?"

Elizabeth sighed. "You know better. You'll have to earn his trust."

"Then what's the use? Winston will never trust me. He wants to dominate me."

Elizabeth teetered between exasperation and pity. "Are you totally irredeemable? Can't you see your own potential, for God's sake?"

"Strong language for a lady," he said through clenched teeth. He jumped from the bed and landed hard on the floor. He walked toward her. "You know, Elizabeth, your husband is not as saintly as you think."

Elizabeth had pushed too far. "Nobody is without fault."

"How charitable of you!" He leaned over her, his face clutched in anger. "Did you know, *Mrs.* Carthage, about your husband's indiscretions?"

"No . . . I . . . I should leave." She rose, but Jeremy grasped her shoulders and pushed her back into the chair.

"You're going to hear this!" He bent close, his breath simmering with liquor. "Winston, the man who would do no wrong." Jeremy laughed. "He laid with a whore, did you know that? In New Orleans, a common harlot! And do you know what else? He did it again in Vicksburg! Right under your very nose!"

"Jeremy—" She was so startled by his physical treatment, at first the words didn't register. Her eyes widened in horror. "Liar." She spoke so quietly, she almost didn't hear herself.

"Her name was Michelle Tussaunt. A buxom brunette. Did you know about Winston's secret affinity for brunettes?"

Elizabeth's self-assurance vanished.

Jeremy saw it go. "He never told you, did he?"

"When?"

"Three years ago, about the time the two of you were suffering . . . marital difficulties."

"Oh God." Elizabeth flushed in humiliation.

"Yes, I know about *that* too." He appraised her. "Although it still escapes me how any man could have such a problem with you."

"You pig."

"You hypocrite!" Jeremy's eyes gleamed. "Do you really want me to drop my suit?"

"Of course."

"How badly?" He leaned over her and placed a hand on either arm of the chair.

"Get away," she hissed.

"You could end it all, Elizabeth. One time, no more. That's my price."

"If you touch me, Winston will kill you."

He made a guttural sound. "He'll never know." He leaned in to kiss her and saw incomprehension, disappointment, and unmistakable hate on her face.

She raked a hand fiercely across his cheek. She rose from her chair to run.

He grasped her upper arms and threw her backward with accentuated rage. Her head slammed into the wall behind the chair.

Elizabeth teetered, and for the briefest instant, they stared at each other. Then her eyes fluttered upward until the whites showed. She fell heavily to the floor.

❧

Jeremy carefully laid Elizabeth on the bed. He watched closely for signs of life, but her corset was laced so tightly he couldn't tell if her chest was rising and falling. Maybe if he loosened the bindings a little, he could be sure she was alive . . .

He placed a hand on her right breast and felt a heartbeat. His hand lingered there. She was so pure and angelic with her auburn hair and perfect face.

His hand slid down to her waist.

Would she know?

As if to answer, she mumbled and her face scrunched up. Jeremy backed away from the bed and licked his dry, cracked lips. Then she was quiet again, and he came closer, the thoughts in his brain finding sustenance elsewhere. She was exquisite. Beads of perspiration sprouted at his temples. He toyed with the hem of her long silk dress. He lifted it for inspection and spied her cotton undergarments, sheer for the hot months.

He lifted the hem higher, and her legs gradually emerged, shapely and full, tightly framed by white pantylegs. The hem reached higher and with intense concentration, he surveyed what he was never meant to see. Breathlessly, head spinning, he fumbled with his trouser buttons.

❧

Elizabeth opened her eyes and saw a dirty plaster ceiling. Confused, she wondered which room in *Magnolia* could need cleaning so badly. After a moment, she knew she was not in her own home by the tacky painting on the wall. She was on a strange bed, and she was fully clothed. But she didn't feel right. She felt . . . amiss.

She turned her head to the left. Her skull pounded ferociously. The back of her scalp was tender and raised. She had to close her eyes. When they re-opened, she was startled to see Jeremy.

"Elizabeth, how do you feel?" His words were cautious and syrupy.

"Where am I?"

"You don't remember?"

"What . . . where am I?" she demanded again.

"The Edward's Hotel," he answered quickly.

She arched as if to rise, but her pulsing head drove her back down. "What happened?"

"You fell." Jeremy was close, staring into her eyes.

"Oh." Why did he look so guilty? She struggled to remember. "How—"

"You tripped over the hem of your dress. I tried to catch you."

"I tripped?" she asked.

"Quite suddenly."

"That's not right."

"You bumped your head. Sometimes that can affect one's memory."

Elizabeth looked around her. Nothing in the room was familiar. "What . . . what time is it?"

"About three-thirty."

"Then I've been here for . . .?"

"You've been unconscious for a half hour."

"A half hour! Why didn't you summon a doctor?" she demanded angrily. Her head reminded her to speak in low tones.

"It was just a bump. I thought you'd be fine."

"How did I arrive on this bed?"

"I carried you," he answered.

From her prone position, she seemed to survey her own body. Her undergarments felt bunched, slightly askew. Dismissing the unthinkable, she quietly said, "Thank you."

"I was worried for you."

"Why am I here?" Her brow furrowed.

Jeremy formed his answer carefully. "You hoped to reconcile Winston and me."

"Yes. I seem to recall . . ." But the fledgling thought drifted away. "I must go. Has the late train to Vicksburg already departed?"

"No, this is Thursday. The late train leaves at four."

"Then I have time." With a supreme effort, she righted herself on the narrow bed. She felt dizzy. And she felt something . . . wet . . . in her undergarments. The unthinkable flashed through her mind again. God, no, not that! She looked at Jeremy for the truth, but he wouldn't meet her eyes.

"You might need to see a doctor."

"I'll be fine." She slid to the floor and landed on shaky legs. Her head throbbed with the movement.

"Let me escort you to the station."

"No!" She said too quickly. "Lou is waiting for me outside."

"Lou?" Jeremy froze. "She's been down there all this time?"

She heard the fear in his voice. "I couldn't come to Jackson unescorted."

"No, you couldn't."

Elizabeth grimaced in pain. "I have to go."

Jeremy walked downstairs with her, but stopped conspicuously at the front door. With every step, her resolve strengthened. Suddenly, she turned on him. The expression on her face was a mixture of shock and loathing. "My God," she whispered. "I remember what happened."

Jeremy stammered. "Wh-what do you mean?"

"You tried to kiss me. Then you pushed me into the wall."

"Elizabeth . . ." His tone was pleading.

"You undressed me." She didn't want to believe it, but the guilt on his face was plain. Her voice was steely and cold. "If I tell Winston, you're a dead man."

"Tell him what? You fell and hit your head, that's all."

"You raped me, you contemptible bastard!" she hissed. "Drop the lawsuit, or I'll tell him."

Jeremy paled. "Tell him anything you like. You have no proof." A bead of sweat traveled down his forehead.

"I remember what you said in the room. Just the once with me and you'd drop the suit. You got what you wanted."

Jeremy's mouth fell open, but he shook his head no.

"So even about that, you were lying." She walked unevenly toward the door.

"Elizabeth, wait."

She turned. "What?"

"You can't . . . you can't make up stories and tell them to Winston. It's not like you."

Her face was drawn. "Jeremy, you'll have to wonder, won't you? Whether your next day will be your last. Winston isn't weak like you. He'll make up his mind and act. I hope you're prepared for that."

"I *can't* drop the lawsuit. It's all I have left!"

"Goodbye, Jeremy." Elizabeth wobbled unsteadily through the hotel door and nearly fell down the steps into Lou's arms.

10

The train trip from Jackson to Vicksburg was Elizabeth's rolling nightmare. She relived every hideous moment of her encounter with Jeremy. Winston and his affair with the prostitute, Jeremy's assault, it all came rushing back in clear focus. Her shock and revulsion, her fear and disillusionment, magnified her headache into the most profound discomfort she'd ever known. At times, she could barely sit straight. Her forehead and cheeks were damp with perspiration. She nearly swooned when she thought of what Jeremy had done as she lay unconscious on the bed.

She made it home safely, only because Lou was beside her. Without knowing or asking details, Lou had helped as best she could, but a headache had ultimately been beyond her caring abilities. Even so, on arriving in Vicksburg, Lou had taken her ashen-faced mistress directly to Doctor Purvis. There, Elizabeth had told the doctor a disjointed story about bumping her head in Jackson. Purvis listened in disbelief, then gave her laudanum and instructions to rest. She agreed, but swore both the doctor and Lou to secrecy, determined that if Winston ever learned the circumstances of her injury, it would be from her lips.

She now watched Winston absently pick at a dinner roll. The pain in her head had diminished somewhat, but was still evident when she moved or spoke. "How was your day?" she asked, hiding the grimace on her face. Each word echoed in her skull.

"Busy, but I accomplished a few things. Minnifield says you can use his loom next week."

"Thank you. I'll have Curtis take a cotton bale over tomorrow."

"Where were you all day?"

"Pardon?" Elizabeth felt herself flush.

"I was home at six and you weren't here."

She thought furiously, but the pain seemed to block inspiration. And she knew herself to be a poor liar. "I was in town earlier." She dared not look up from her plate.

"How is it we didn't cross paths?" Winston's face was impassive.

"I don't know."

Winston watched her for a moment, then resumed eating.

She hastened to change the subject. "Andrew was famished and had an early dinner. He's upstairs doing his math lessons."

"Good."

"I didn't get a chance to tell you yesterday. I spoke with Daddy. He said if the lawsuit drags out much longer, he'll help us financially until it's resolved."

Winston smiled, but said nothing.

His muted reaction surprised her. She ventured a question. "Had you considered settling with Jeremy?"

She had his full attention now.

"What made you ask that?"

"I was thinking. . ." She swallowed hard and ignored the pounding behind her eyes. "We could pay Jeremy off and reimburse Daddy when we received our money from escrow. You wouldn't have to worry about the lawsuit anymore. Jeremy would be gone."

Winston laughed. "You make it sound so simple. He doesn't deserve any money. Come to think of it . . ."

She watched him, sensing he'd reached some conclusion. She wondered if the story about the prostitute were true. Jeremy had no reason to lie. But it had happened three years ago. She remembered the hurt feelings between her and Winston, the mistrust and resentment that surrounded their lack of intimacy. They'd begun to drift apart, each wounded and careful. When Winston's problem had run its course, several months passed before they had put it completely behind them. If she asked him about the prostitute now, the whole thing would resurface.

He didn't need that. *She* didn't need that. Especially after today. She would be forced to tell him about her meeting with Jeremy. She was sure she couldn't do that without telling him all the details, including what Jeremy had done. Winston would kill him without a second thought. No, her honor was not worth Winston murdering his own brother. This would have to wait.

"Didn't I see your carriage at the livery next to the train station today?" His face showed no accusation or mistrust.

"My carriage? Oh, well yes, my horse threw a shoe. Lou took it there while I was . . . shopping."

Winston seemed as if he were only half-listening. For once, Elizabeth felt lucky he was preoccupied.

"Winston, let's leave here."

"What?"

"Let's go somewhere. Take a vacation for a few weeks, leave Vicksburg."

"Where would we go?"

"Atlanta is hosting a flower festival next month, I read about it in the *Citizen*."

He studied her pale face more closely. "We'd be irresponsible to leave."

"Why? The spring planting is finished and the overseers are quite competent."

"The lawsuit will be resolved soon. And we don't have money to spare just now. Are you feeling well?"

"I had a headache earlier. I'm much better." She blushed. "Wouldn't you enjoy a trip to Atlanta? Just us. They don't need you for that lawsuit." She became more forceful. "You've told them everything there is to tell. The verdict won't change because you're out of town."

Winston grinned.

"Why are you laughing?"

"I'm not laughing. I just . . . I wish *you* were my lawyer. Jeremy would end up paying *me* money." The smile died on his lips. He fidgeted with his napkin, fighting for the right words. He looked at her, his face open and vulnerable, then reached across the table and took her hands. He cupped them in his own bringing her fingertips to his lips. "I love you."

Elizabeth made a happy sound. For an instant, the pain in her head vanished.

"I have business in town this evening." He rose from the table, his eyes misty.

"Business?"

"Yes. You've helped me with an important decision."

"I have?"

"You have."

"Can't it wait until tomorrow?"

"Not really." He smiled. "I shouldn't be too late." He walked around the table and lifted her to her feet. He took her shoulders and kissed her passionately. Gradually, their lips parted, but he still held her close.

Elizabeth asked softly, "Is your business really that important?"

"Unfortunately, yes."

She held his face and they kissed again. Her head seared with pain, but she didn't care. Reluctantly, she pulled away. "Be careful."

"I will."

❧

Winston brought the carriage to a stop behind Shelly's in the circle of a weak gaslight. He took a deep breath. Upstairs, the River Club was dark. He struggled from the carriage, swearing at the ungainly walking cane. The night was warm, but he wore a jacket to conceal the big Colt holstered in his left armpit. He removed a door key from his pocket and climbed to the second floor landing. He inserted the key, and with a turn, was inside. He reached for a cup of matches and lit a lamp on the near wall.

The River Club was a haven for Vicksburg's wealthy men. They were generally hard to impress, so the proprietor didn't try. He furnished the Club with sturdy Empire furniture, and Italian carpets, but the room's feel was unassuming. Whale oil lamps provided light, and in the center of each wall, full-length mirrors were positioned to create the illusion of space and to maximize reflected light. Along the back wall a glass case was stocked with an impressive assortment of liquors.

Winston opened the windows to air the sultry room. He stretched mosquito netting across the openings and considered a drink. No, better to keep his wits. Attorney Dobbins would have a fit if he knew Winston were here. And his concerns would be justified.

Winston looked again at the liquor cabinet. A drink would settle his nerves.

❧

Mary applied rouge to her cheeks and primped one last time before the grainy mirror. Her pocket watch read 8:00. She breezed downstairs past the night attendant's leering eyes into the warm night. A five-minute walk brought her to Washington Street. Two blocks ahead, she could see the Gin.

She quickened her pace, careful not to stumble on the dirt road. No sense making a mess of her nicest outfit. In her right hand, she carried a small purse. Her dress was low-cut, blue velvet. Her face was coated with cosmetics and she had not spared the cheap perfume. Her puffed hair was secured by pink and blue ribbons. She looked very much a prostitute, despite the book under her left arm, Poe's *Tales of the Grotesque and Arabesque*. Pritchard had indicated several hours might pass before she and Winston were discovered together. Until then, Poe would be her company.

Mary was nervous but optimistic about what was to come. Pritchard had assured her the opium would merely put Winston to sleep. And with a tidy commission of one hundred dollars, she could take some time off. Especially if she squeezed a little more money from Winston. Pritchard didn't have to join her if he didn't want to, but *she* was going to try.

She stepped onto the wooden walkway fronting a row of business establishments on Washington Street: an apothecary, an optician's office, a hardware store, and on the end, the Gin. She strained to see

Pritchard. She caught the glow of a cigar and saw a figure lurking beneath the awning. She threw back her shoulders and strolled purposefully, her hard-soled shoes clattering on the walkway. She stopped a few feet short of the awning.

"Good evening, Mr. Pritchard."

"Mary." He remained in the shadows, his hat pulled low. "You brought something to read."

"Edgar Allan Poe." She struggled to see him in the dark. "Do you read, Mr. Pritchard?"

"Sometimes. Poe is too ghoulish for my tastes."

She imagined a smile on his face. "You're teasing me."

"Only a little. I've no need for scary stories."

"Oh."

The Gin's door was flung open and two drunks stumbled heavily through, trailed by various sounds of celebration.

"Evenin', m'lady." The taller of the two tipped his hat. The shorter man was quiet, his eyes glued to Mary's partially exposed breasts.

"Good evening." Her voice was flat in direct contrast to her chest.

The taller man grinned. "You goin' inside?"

"Actually, no."

"Cause if you ain't, we could use some company, right, Stan?" The shorter man nodded.

Pritchard slipped deeper into the shadows.

Mary said "I'm sorry, gentlemen, but I have a previous engagement. If you'll excuse me."

"Now hold on there! Ain't we good enough for ya? I mean, it sure looks like you're advertisin'." He stepped closer as he spoke.

"I appreciate your attention, but I'm not seeking company. Another time."

"Them's about the nicest melons I ever seen. How much?" He reached for her arm.

"Hands off!" In one quick motion, Mary extracted a thin-handled knife from her purse. She pointed it at them with two steady hands. "Maybe I wasn't clear."

The taller man eyed the blade and Mary. "Let's get outta here."

His partner protested. "We can get that blade offa her!"

"It ain't worth it, out here on the street and all. Somebody'll see. Bitch probably has the rot anyway." He was already walking away. "We can find a *real* woman at the Kangaroo." The shorter man hurried after his friend, and they were gone.

Mary silently replaced her knife.

"Very impressive." Pritchard spoke from the shadows. He had noted the knife.

"Not really." She breathed deeply. "Did Winston arrive?"

"A few minutes ago."

"Good. Shall I wait here?"

"Yes. When you see the light go on in that middle window"—he pointed to the rear of Shelly's—"come up the back staircase on the left."

"It shouldn't be long then? I seem to be drawing a crowd here."

"No."

"I'll be ready."

Winston drained his whiskey glass and sniffed the rich clubroom air—expensive cigars and oiled cowhide. He had never much cared about the River Club or its patrons. It was a pretentious waste of money for men who imagined themselves in a fine Canal Street establishment. Winston belonged because his father had been a member, and because it was a good place to discuss business. Other than that, he would just as soon drink on a park bench or in a District saloon.

As Winston contemplated resigning from the Club, heavy feet climbed the back staircase. His heart raced. A knock landed on the door before it swung open. Pritchard, solemn and huge, stood in the doorway. He had to remove his hat to step through.

When they'd first met at the lake, Winston couldn't help noticing Pritchard's extraordinary size. Now, in the enclosed room, he was simply monstrous. Winston's grip reflexively tightened on his walking cane, for once treating it as a friend. The Colt was reassuringly heavy against his chest.

"Good evening, Mr. Carthage."

"Pritchard."

Pritchard scanned the club room without comment. He offered Winston his hand. "I'm glad you came."

Winston shook the hand and felt Pritchard's strength. "Have a seat. Whiskey?"

"Thanks, no." Pritchard worked himself into an overstuffed leather chair across from Winston. A low table separated them.

"You brought the affidavit?"

Pritchard nodded.

"May I see it?"

"Of course." Pritchard removed a piece of paper from his coat pocket.

Winston scanned the single handwritten page. An official-looking notary seal and a signature stated that someone named Alfred Bierman had witnessed the testimony presented. He silently read the details of his affair with a prostitute named Michelle Tussaunt. He skimmed a paragraph describing his sexual preferences. His features transformed from neutral to angry.

"Am I to presume other copies of this exist?" Winston asked through his teeth.

"Each dated and notarized."

"Who else has seen it?"

"Mr. Bierman, Miss Tussaunt, your brother, and I."

Winston tugged at his facial hair. The details were accurate but sketchy. An odd sensation gripped him. He was reading about himself, his most intimate secrets; he knew they were true, and yet, he couldn't fully remember them, or didn't want to. The affidavit was about another person, a spineless libertine, a man without a wonderful wife. He allowed his nerves to settle before he spoke.

"Miss Tussaunt was not very discreet." Winston fingered the paper distractedly and raised his eyes to meet Pritchard's. He studied Pritchard's expressionless face and wondered vaguely about his age. Thirty? Thirty-five? "This affidavit doesn't change anything."

Pritchard might have smiled. "No?"

"Jeremy has maintained for the last eight months that he deserves half the plantation, but he resorts to extortion rather than let an impartial judge decide." Winston exhaled. "You're familiar with the details. What do you think?"

"What I think is irrelevant."

Winston tossed the affidavit on the table. "I won't pay him anything."

Pritchard's nod was slight. "Jeremy felt you might not be persuaded. I think he was relying on your desire to avoid further embarrassment to your family. Your wife—Elizabeth, is it?—comes from a prominent local family. Your son, your father's memory—he thought you might wish to spare them the disgrace of a public scandal."

Winston's eyes flashed. "Jeremy is the worst scandal my family has ever realized. He has brought more shame to our house than a hundred whores and all their sworn testimonials ever could." Winston fought to keep his voice even. "My father knew Jeremy better than anyone. He gave Jeremy every opportunity to lead a life well beyond the means of the average citizen. You wouldn't believe the things Jeremy did in return."

"You're speaking of matters which hold no value in this negotiation."

"Is that what you think, we're negotiating?"

"In a sense."

"You're wrong." It was a statement of fact, not a challenge.

"Mr. Carthage, I'm not trying to incite you."

"Of course you are."

Pritchard broke eye contact. "I'd like to reconsider your offer of a drink."

Winston's response was slow. "I'll join you."

"Allow me." Pritchard was on his feet quickly to take Winston's glass. Winston noticed Pritchard's haste, but assumed it was in deference to his game leg.

"Tell me, Pritchard. How did you come to work for my brother?"

Pritchard stood before the liquor cabinet, his back to Winston. "We were introduced by a mutual friend." He glanced out the rear window and did a double-take. Mary was delicately picking her way down the hill from the Gin. She was too early . . .

"Then you work out of Jackson?" Winston's question barely registered.

Pritchard nodded.

"And what do you think of Jeremy, Mr. Pritchard?"

"It's not for me to think anything. He's a client, no more, no less." She was almost to the alley behind the building. Half a minute, maybe less. He began counting in his head.

"You're an intelligent man. Surely you've formed an opinion of my brother."

Pritchard turned back to Winston, a glass of whiskey in each hand. His enormous shoulders were silhouetted by the yellow oil lamp. "I don't judge personalities. I have a conscience, but I also have to eat. If it eases your mind, I prefer to work for people like you." Pritchard was beside Winston, speaking down to him.

"Like me? And what kind of person am I?"

"You didn't come here to talk about yourself." Pritchard handed him a glass.

"No. I'm trying to gain some insight to your motivations."

"I'm simply an intermediary." Pritchard sat down, carefully watching Winston's glass, counting, twenty-one, twenty-two. She would be approaching the back staircase by now. When she began the climb, Pritchard would have to act.

Winston asked, "How much was Miss Tussaunt paid for her testimony?"

"Mr. Carthage, I have fiduciary responsibilities to my client."

"You sound like a lawyer. I don't suppose you'd care to tell me how much he's paying *you*."

Pritchard took a sip of his whiskey, trying to lead by example. "If you're interested in hiring me, we can discuss my fee at such time.

Otherwise . . . " Thirty-two, thirty-three, thirty-four. Did she stop in the alley?

"It's none of my business." Winston looked away for a moment. He took a long draw from his glass. "Do you appreciate irony?"

"What do you mean?" Forty-one, forty-two. Maybe she was waiting for the bedroom lamp to come on.

"I could easily afford my brother's price—when I win the lawsuit, that is. But I don't have twenty thousand dollars to spare at the moment. Besides, if I rejected ten thousand the first time, why would I agree to twenty when the outcome now seems certain?"

For only an instant, Pritchard's face showed surprise. "The first time?"

Winston chuckled. "I see he never told you he's tried this before. No, you wouldn't be here if he had."

Pritchard quietly stared. Jeremy would pay extra for that omission. But it became less important with each drop of whiskey.

Winston obliged with another sip. "Furthermore, I'll wager a copy of this affidavit exists that Jeremy doesn't know about. If I strike a deal with him, I might obligate myself to do the same with three other people, including you."

"Meaning I would coerce money from you myself?"

"Why not?" Winston emptied his glass, expecting a vigorous denial.

"Why not indeed?"

Winston squinted at Pritchard. "What's so funny?"

Pritchard and Winston both turned at the sound of footsteps on the staircase.

Winston slid a hand inside his jacket. "Who. . . " He grasped for a thought. Beads of perspiration formed on his upper lip.

The person climbing the staircase stopped halfway, as if to listen.

"Who is that?" Winston's voice was suddenly strained and whispery.

Pritchard watched in quiet fascination as the mighty Winston Carthage melted like a candle.

"It's very warm in here . . ." Winston's hand involuntarily fell from his jacket.

"Mr. Carthage, do you have any money?"

"Money? I don't . . . what did you say? Isss . . . somebody . . . at the door?" A trail of saliva snaked down Winston's chin and his head rolled sideways.

"You'll save me the trouble of searching your pockets."

Winston spoke with enormous effort. "I've got a gun." The whiskey glass to which he'd been clinging bounced to the floor.

"A gun, you say?"

"Drink . . . was . . . my drink." He clumsily groped again at his jacket, but his motor functions had essentially ceased.

"Tincture of opium," Pritchard offered. "A substantial amount, I'm afraid."

"You . . . " It was Winston's last lucid word.

❧

Mary calmly climbed the steps, though she was excited and scared inside. She was about to meet the famous Winston Carthage. She felt like she knew him already after so many of Jeremy's tirades. At the middle landing, she paused and straightened her hair, a dab more perfume from her purse. She heard a shuffling sound inside the club room. Was she too late? She climbed the remaining steps and pushed through the door. Contemporary furnishings—not bad—a glass of whiskey on a table, an empty glass on the floor. She crossed the room to an inside door and entered a narrow hallway with several more doors. The closest one, she could see, led to a privy. The second was slightly ajar.

"Come in, Mary." Pritchard sat easily in a chair inside a small bedroom. Sprawled across the bed was a sleeping man who was unmistakably Jeremy's brother.

"It's already done?" Mary's face clouded.

"It is."

"I thought you wanted him to meet me first."

"Why didn't you wait for the light?" Pritchard's eyes flashed.

"Because I thought you might do it this way. You didn't want him to talk to me after all, did you?"

Pritchard glared at her. "Help me undress him."

It took only a minute to strip Winston. Pritchard turned to Mary. "Now take off your clothes."

"Excuse me?" Mary actually felt herself blush. "This wasn't part of it," she protested. "I was only supposed to be found here with him. There was nothing about me undressing."

"Do it."

She hesitated at his brittle command, her enthusiasm suddenly gone. She fumbled with the buttons of her dress and carefully laid it on the corner of the bed. She'd disrobed in front of men hundreds of times, but this was completely different. Pritchard was watching her too closely. Her bosom strained at the ties of her corset. She unlaced the heavy undergarment and her breasts spilled forth. In another moment, she was completely nude. Feeling exposed and unattractively large, she stood motionless for a full minute.

"Well?"

Pritchard rose from his chair. "You cut a handsome figure."

She blushed again. "I don't feel that way just now."

He spoke in a husky voice. "I'd like to spend some money on you."

"You would?" Something in his eyes wasn't right.

He roughly placed a huge hand on her equally huge left breast.

She stepped backward. "We won't have time."

"I think we will."

Mary quivered as his other hand reached downward. She had to grasp his forearms for support. Her stomach was turning cartwheels.

Pritchard persuasively guided her to the bed. Winston Carthage didn't seem to mind the intrusion.

❧

Mary moaned, hoping she sounded more ecstatic than fearful. She prayed he would finish quickly. He was too big, too powerful, too forceful. She always liked some measure of control, but with him she had none.

Pritchard thrust into her again and again. He arched his back and growled deeply. He pressed her hard. She responded by wrapping her arms around his midsection. They writhed in unison, he with urgency, she with professional detachment. Next to them lay Winston, oblivious to the passion play.

Pritchard climaxed. He pushed back on his elbows and raised himself until his weight rested fully on his knees.

She looked at him—he seemed more aroused now than ever. His breath was coming in choppy bursts. His eyes were misty and strange like he was somewhere else. Then they focused on her and . . . Oh, God! She whimpered and frantically tried to lurch sideways from the bed.

Pritchard drove his right fist into her midsection. Air rushed from her lungs and she was helpless to scream. Her knees reflexively drew toward her chest. Pritchard clamped his hands around her throat and used his weight to push her back flat on the bed. She whined pitifully and flailed without effect at his rigid upper arms. Her cheeks turned crimson and her swollen tongue bulged crazily between blue lips. Tiny blood vessels exploded in the whites of her eyes.

Suddenly, she was still. The entire struggle lasted less than sixty seconds.

II

Sam Morris spent many nights, and quite a few days, in Shelly's bar. It was his favorite place to drink because it was on the riverfront near all the action. And Shelly's was a cut above most of the Levee Street gin joints where fistfights and violence were far too common. Shelly's clientele were reasonably well-behaved.

Morris hiccuped. He was mildly disappointed in himself for drinking so much. Then again, who was to care?

He lumbered from his bar stool and exited the swinging front door. He weaved around the south corner of the building looking for a good spot. He didn't normally urinate in public, but it was late and he was drunk. He noted a parked carriage behind the building. He squinted. It looked like Winston's. He wobbled closer and saw that indeed it was. Satisfied, he stood next to the horse and urinated on the ground.

"I'm sorry you had to see this," Morris chortled, but the horse was indifferent. Morris re-buttoned his trousers and aimed himself down the alley. He lurched to a stop under the club bedroom.

"Hey, Winshtun!" He watched the curtain expecting to see his friend's face pop into view. He called louder.

"Winsthun!"

The curtain didn't stir.

"Must be asleep." Morris trudged ahead then stopped again. Did Winston ever sleep in the club?

The answer took twenty seconds to wind its way through his besotted brain. No, not usually.

Morris started walking again. Then, like a dog on a leash brought to heel, he stopped, a profoundly confused look on his face.

Winston wouldn't leave his horse bridled all night would he? Son of a bitch was up there hiding out, drinking alone, not wanting company. Well, he was going to have some company whether he liked it or not.

Pritchard sat astride Mary, his eyes closed, still savoring the thrill of death and sex, when he heard Morris call from the alley. He leaped from the bed and tugged on his pants. He heard a second call, then a moment later, footsteps on the outside stairs. Pritchard tip-toed to the window.

Morris leaned into the stairs thinking he might just sleep on the Club couch if Winston permitted it. The door was unlocked and a single lamp burned on the nearest wall. He spied two drinking glasses, one on the floor, and an empty bottle of whiskey. A misplaced odor pervaded the room. Perfume? He heard a noise in the back, like someone bumping against a wall.

"Winshtun?" He staggered across the room to the hall door and stepped through. The smell of perfume intensified and a light shone from the bedroom.

An uneasy tingling traveled along his scalp as he tapped on the door. No answer. He pushed it open and peeked inside. Two naked people, a man and a woman, lay on the bed. The woman was on her back nearest the door. The man lay on his side facing her. The man *was* Winston, but the woman sure as hell wasn't Elizabeth Carthage. So that's what it was about! Winston was having an illicit affair. Morris started to retreat from the room. As he pulled the door nearly closed, he guiltily took one last look at the naked woman. She seemed familiar. Why hadn't they answered his knock? Were they even drunker than him?

Morris pushed back inside. Something wasn't right. A hollow fear gestated in his stomach. Winston's trousers were draped over the petticoat sofa and his shirt lay on the floor next to a blue dress and corset. The flaxen-haired woman didn't move. She had enormous breasts. Morris took a second, and even a third glance. Then he looked at her more closely. Her neck was bruised and hand prints were clearly visible on her skin.

"Ma'am?" Morris whispered. "Winston?" He had sobered a little.

A soft breeze raised the curtains on the open window. Morris stepped nearer and peered down to the alley where he'd stood only a moment ago. In his peripheral vision, he saw a dark figure retreating toward the street, avoiding the glare of the gaslight. Morris watched briefly, then turned back to the bed.

"Winston!" His voice was more urgent.

Neither of the bed's occupants stirred. Morris grasped Winston, who was at least breathing normally, and shook his shoulders. Nothing. He leaned over and nudged the woman on the arm. Christ, what was going on here?

On the bedstand was a small wash basin. Morris lifted it and poured a few drops of water over the woman's face. Her head twisted from side-to-side and finally her eyes blinked open.

She sat up in the bed. Morris noted her breasts were even larger than he'd thought.

"Aren't you . . ." Morris vaguely recognized the woman.

Mary looked wide-eyed around the small room. Her mouth opened, but no words issued. She coughed. The sound was strangled and painful to hear.

Morris drunkenly attempted to focus on her panic-stricken face. "What happened?"

She tried to speak, but could not. She swung her bare feet over the edge of the bed and stood, not seeming to notice her own nudity.

"You don't look too well." Morris helped her, but she sagged as she gained her feet. "You need to sit back down."

She pleaded with her eyes, but Morris wasn't sure what she sought.

"Here." Morris lifted her dress from the floor. She took it without acknowledgment.

"Your throat . . . are you hurt?"

She slipped into the dress.

"Can you talk?"

Her mouth opened, but nothing came out.

Morris jerked his head at Winston. "Is he hurt?"

She shook her head no.

"Wait. Use this." Morris, the ever-present journalist, fumbled through his coat. He produced a pad and pencil. By then, Mary had donned her shoes and was walking shakily for the door.

"Hold on a minute!" Morris rushed over and placed himself between her and the door. "You're not going anywhere."

Again, Mary's eyes were pleading.

"Write it down, Mary."

She looked surprised at hearing her own name.

"I've been to Mollie Bunch's house once or twice. We've never had the pleasure." Morris extended his hand. "I'm Sam Morris. I own the *Vicksburg Reader*."

Mary shook his hand distractedly and took the pad and pencil from the other. She scribbled and returned the pad.

She had written "He must've thought I was dead." Morris frowned. "Who thought you were dead? Winston?"

She shook her head vigorously and wrote again.

"Pritchard? The big man? Why? And how is Winston involved?"

She wrote more hurriedly.

"Jeremy Carthage? Oh come now!" Morris was rapidly sobering.

Mary scribbled a few more words and reached for the door knob.

Morris took the pad and again prevented her from leaving. "You were trying to frame Winston? For what? And why did Pritchard try to kill you?"

Mary shrugged.

"I see." But he didn't see at all. He only knew that the terror in her eyes was real. "I suppose the sheriff will make some sense of it. What's wrong with Winston? Is he drunk?"

Mary wrote "Drugged" on the pad. She wrote some more.

"You don't want me to summon the sheriff? Nonsense! A crime has been committed here."

This time Mary wrote for a full minute.

Morris read the message aloud.

"If the sheriff comes, I'll be arrested for my part in this. I was almost killed. I don't deserve more punishment. The man responsible for this is a fiend. He tried to kill me once. If he thinks I'll implicate him, he'll kill me. I don't want to die."

Morris was trying to absorb it. "Mary, this man must be brought to justice. The sheriff will protect you."

She shook her head no and seized the pad.

"He can't protect me from Pritchard. And I'm a prostitute. The fact that I was hurt won't matter. I'll be jailed. Please let me go."

Morris knew his thought processes weren't as acute as they should be. "Here, help me revive Mr. Carthage, and we'll see what he has to say."

Mary resignedly nodded.

"Good. Let's see if we—"

As Morris turned for the bed, Mary bolted out the door. Morris was too slow to stop her. A moment later, he heard her crashing down the back staircase. He stepped to the window and saw her fleeing along the same alley that Pritchard had used barely five minutes earlier. He silently hoped she chose a different direction. Morris turned his attention to Winston.

❧

"Christ, Sam, I was stupid enough for three people." Winston rubbed a palm across his scalp and winced. He was still groggy from the opium.

"What was the point in all this?"

"To frame me for a woman's murder would be my guess."

"Jeremy would do something like that?"

"I wouldn't have believed it."

"Shouldn't we . . . take some action?"

Winston was thinking slowly. "I've spoken with this man Pritchard a couple of times. He's a brute, but he's smart as hell, you can see it in his eyes. He won't allow himself to be caught—"

Winston was interrupted by the sound of heavy footsteps pounding up the back staircase. Morris and Winston both jumped.

"Who is it?" Morris whispered as he searched the room for some sort of weapon. Winston fumbled through his jacket, but Pritchard had taken his pistol.

"I don't know. The barkeep from downstairs maybe."

A moment later, a booming voice reverberated through the club.

"Anybody in here?"

Winston and Morris looked at each other.

Winston spoke. "That sounds like Burkett."

"Yes," Morris said, visibly relieved.

The Warren County Sheriff, Adam Burkett, burst into the small bedroom. He looked at the men, both of whom he knew, with a cross expression.

"Winston, Sam, what's goin' on here?"

Morris spoke first.

"Hello, Adam."

"Sam." Burkett looked sternly at Winston. "Mr. Carthage, you got a lady in here?"

"No. Why do you ask?"

Burkett, a large fleshy man, harrumphed and walked to the other side of the room. It was a short trip. He resisted the temptation to drop to his knees and search under the bed.

"Somebody banged on my door about 15 minutes ago. Left this and ran off."

He handed a piece of paper to Winston. Printed in large block letters was the message:

WINSTON CARTHAGE KILLED A WOMAN AT THE RIVER CLUB TONIGHT.

"What would you two know about that note?"

Morris began to speak, but Winston cut him off.

"Sheriff, this appears to be a ruse. I was having a late drink in the Club when Mr. Morris stopped by. As you can clearly see, I was undressing for bed when he arrived."

"Since when do you sleep here, Mr. Carthage?" Burkett rolled a thick wad of chewing tobacco from one side of his mouth to the other.

"When I drink too much like tonight."

The Sheriff wasn't an admirer of the Carthages, but couldn't see that any laws were being broken, and no dead women.

"Gentlemen, y'all have a nice evening." The sheriff stomped from the room, greatly irritated that he'd been disturbed from his sleep for no reason.

12

Jeremy rose on an elbow and peered at the nameless, snoring whore sprawled across the bed next to him. He was tempted to wake her and make her leave.

He couldn't sleep. It had been three days since Pritchard was to have hatched his plot to implicate Winston for murder. But the newspapers had carried no stories to support that outcome. He'd heard no rumors. Pritchard had not contacted him, and though they weren't scheduled to meet again until month's end, Jeremy had assumed Pritchard would somehow let him know the plan had succeeded. Was Mary really dead? Winston in jail? Jeremy simply couldn't believe it without verification. He'd been tempted to take the train to Vicksburg and see for himself, but that would've been too risky.

As if to heighten Jeremy's anxiety, his attorney had contacted him that afternoon and told him the judge would announce the lawsuit decision tomorrow morning, a decision that would almost certainly favor Winston. Would Winston be there to hear it? Jeremy squirmed and wondered if he still had time to try and bribe the judge . . .

The anonymous whore said something in her sleep. Jeremy poked her.

"Hey! Get up!"

She blinked open her eyes. "What?"

"I need some sleep, and you snore like a locomotive. Get the hell out of here."

❧

Judge Harold Permutter was a startling man to behold. He had small fierce eyes, a hook nose, and a weathered complexion. His shock-white hair covered an oversized head that was not grossly large, but generally out of proportion to his narrow shoulders. His appearance and explosive temper prompted local attorneys to dub him "Mount Harry" for his frequent eruptions.

"Bailiff, are we ready to convene these proceedings?" The judge spoke with a heavy Southern accent.

"Both parties are present, Your Honor."

"Let's get on with it then."

The bailiff called the court to order in the civil matter of Carthage versus Carthage. Judge Permutter scanned the courtroom, seemingly disappointed so few people had come to hear his judgement.

"I see both parties are present with their lawyers." The judge cleared his throat. "Gentlemen, this has been a long and protracted affair, the longest case I've ever been associated with. As such, I should caution y'all my decision is final, there will be no additional arguments proffered or heard. Course y'all can appeal, if you so desire." The judge smiled broadly through coffee-stained dentures. He was met by empty stares.

"Are there any questions before I read my decision?" No one budged. "No? For the record, this is case number one sixty-four of the Probate Docket, the matter of Carthage, Jeremy, Plaintiff, versus Carthage, Winston, Defendant. I am Judge Harold Permutter, Presiding Judge, Hinds County Probate Court, on this day, twenty-four May, eighteen fifty-eight. I find as follows."

With a loud crack, Permutter pushed his fingers forward and eight knuckles popped simultaneously. He lifted a one-page, handwritten decision from his bench. His bushy eyebrows raised ever so slightly. "Mr. Carthage . . . Mr. Winston Carthage. You, sir, are forty-six years old. And Mr. Jeremy Carthage, you're forty-one."

Both imperceptibly nodded, not sure if a question had been asked.

The judge wagged his head from side to side. "I declare, two grown men." He waved at Winston. "You probably remember the day your brother was born. And you," he turned to Jeremy, "probably idolized your older brother until you reached the age when you began to resent him." Jeremy squirmed under the judge's gaze.

"Ummm. Your Honor?"

"What, Counselor Burnside?"

"Nothing, sir."

"Good, hush up. Where was I?" Permutter frowned, then presumably reclaimed his train of thought. "I took a long time to decide this case, thinking two brothers might settle this amicably. Didn't happen though, did it?"

The judge shook his shaggy head from side to side.

"The late Mr. Charles Carthage was a very wealthy man. Upon his death, he left virtually his entire estate to the oldest surviving male Carthage, which to this old judge, sounds a lot like primogeniture as defined by the Mississippi civil code. The oldest surviving male Carthage would be you, sir." The judge flipped his gavel around and pointed its handle at Winston, then absentmindedly tapped it on the bench.

"The late Mr. Carthage had a second heir to whom he left a cash sum of ten thousand dollars. That would be you, Mr. Jeremy Carthage. These facts are indisputable. The question before this court is whether or not his will is legal and binding. If I decide the will is invalid, Mr. Charles Carthage died *intestate*, in which case, primogeniture applies anyway, making the matter of his will a moot point. The third consideration is the legality of primogeniture and whether Jeremy Carthage can challenge the general principle itself."

Permutter's bushy eyebrows shot up as if he expected someone in the court to provide the appropriate answer.

"The late Mr. Carthage wrote his will only days before his unfortunate demise. As a probate judge, I see this sorta thing from time to time. It tends to cast suspicion on the motivations of the decedent. It also brings other questions to mind such as why a wealthy man like Charles Carthage did not utilize the services of an estate attorney, or why he simply didn't sign over control of his estate to his preferred inheritor *before* his death. Those types of questions must be examined. Further, it is up to me to ascertain if the late Mr. Carthage was coerced or manipulated into behaving as he did."

Permutter paused.

"It is my personal opinion that Charles Carthage should have left more to his son Jeremy than he did."

Every face in the courtroom experienced a transformation. In the front row, Winston went white and felt dizzy. Attorney Dobbins frowned deeply while on the opposite side, Attorney Burnside was so stunned, his eye stopped twitching. Only Jeremy remained strangely stoic, his attention focused on his fingernails.

"Your Honor, if I might approach the bench—"

"Mr. Dobbins, you do *not* have permission to approach the bench. If you have somethin' on your mind, save it 'till I'm finished."

"But, sir—"

The judge cut him off. "Jeremy, if I may be so informal as to use your Christian name, you are a Carthage every bit as much as your brother. I gather you don't have the business acumen your father did, else you'd have been more involved in the daily operations of *Magnolia*. The problem is, I found no convincing evidence your father was of unsound mind or unduly coerced when he wrote this will." Dobbins held his breath and Burnside's dormant eye suddenly re-activated.

"Your attorney took more depositions and presented more evidence, if that's what you want to call it, than I ever believed possible. Very creative, Mr. Burnside, you are to be congratulated. However, the fact remains, Jeremy, you ain't got a leg to stand on." The judge winked at Winston and motioned toward his cane. "Glad I didn't have to say that about you."

"Winston Carthage appears to have acted properly in every respect." The judge looked squarely at Jeremy and his eyes thinned. "You, on the other hand, ought to be in jail. If I'd had a witness to our conversation in my chambers this mornin', that is exactly where you would be." Burnside looked at his client in sheer amazement.

"All that notwithstanding, I find in favor of the defendant, Winston Carthage. The will stands as written. My clerk will inform the estate trustee to release all assets currently in escrow to Mr. Winston Carthage. Y'all have a good day, gentlemen." The judge rose abruptly and left the courtroom.

Sam Morris observed the two brothers for their reactions. They were both subdued. Jeremy remained in his seat while his attorney stuffed papers into an attache. Across the way, Winston pumped his lawyer's hand in triumph, but his attention seemed focused on Jeremy. Even from a distance, Morris could see a glint in Winston's eyes. Morris slid back in his seat to watch their interaction.

The small, nervous man next to Jeremy—Burnside, was it?—said something quietly to his client and strolled hurriedly from the courtroom. Winston cast sideways glances at Jeremy while a reporter from the Jackson newspaper plied him with questions. Winston didn't look exceptionally happy as he pushed toward the exit. Morris could guess why. Jeremy was still alone in his chair, gazing into space. Morris decided to speak with him first.

"Mr. Carthage. Samuel Morris from the *Vicksburg Reader*." Morris extended his hand. Jeremy shook it. "I know who you are." His voice was lifeless.

"Would you care to comment on the ruling?" Morris knew it was an asinine question. It was all he could do not to ask about Pritchard and the prostitute.

"I thought my case was strong. The judge disagreed."

Morris made a note on his pad. "What exactly did the judge mean about your meeting with him in chambers this morning?"

"I have no idea. He is obviously a disturbed individual."

"You didn't attempt to bribe him?"

Jeremy looked up sharply. "I just told you, my case was strong."

"Yes, of course. What are your plans from here?"

Jeremy's face went blank again. "An excellent question."

"Has your lawyer suggested an appeal?"

"I expect not."

"Will you return to Vicksburg?"

"Why would I do that?"

"It is your home, after all."

"Not any more." Jeremy rose from his chair and Morris backed out of the way. Jeremy walked to the rear of the courtroom and stopped at the door, but didn't go through. After a moment, he turned around.

"Sam, did anything unusual happen in Vicksburg last week?" Jeremy's eyes showed interest for the first time.

"How do you mean?" Morris knew exactly what he meant.

Jeremy unsuccessfully tried to read Morris's expression. "Never mind," he said and left the courtroom.

Winston waited impatiently in the courthouse vestibule. He'd managed to extricate himself from the persistent Jackson reporter. Winston seethed. He had barely maintained his composure in the courtroom when he'd first seen Jeremy. The verdict had become almost a secondary concern, even though Judge Permutter had correctly decided the case.

The vestibule, like the courthouse, emptied quickly after the judgement, the Carthage case being the sole item on the day's docket. The door to the courtroom slowly pushed open and Jeremy passed through. He barely looked at Winston and would have continued without speaking except Winston blocked his way.

"Why did you do it?"

Jeremy stopped, his face a mask of caution. "Because Father should have treated me better. Why else?"

Winston restrained himself. "Is it worth that much to you?"

"You are taking this too personally, Winston. The lawsuit was my only recourse. I had a reasonable chance of winning, so I had to try. Even Father would have understood that."

Winston moved closer until he was only inches from his brother. "My father was the most honorable man I ever knew. *You* are a despicable aberration of nature. You're not a Carthage, not any more." He hissed the words with such passion, Jeremy shrank away.

"You denied me my inheritance and now my birthright. Go to hell."

A gruff sound slipped from Winston's lips. He raised his cane across Jeremy's chest and shoved him into a corner. Even with his bad leg, he easily overpowered his terrified brother.

"Who was she, Jeremy?" Winston's eyes narrowed to slits of enmity.

Jeremy couldn't hide his shock. "Who was who?"

"Was she a friend? A trollop you hired off the street?"

Jeremy tried to dismiss him. "I think the pressure of this has affected you."

Winston slammed a fist into his brother's belly doubling him over. He seized Jeremy's collar and straightened him.

"Did you think I wouldn't know?" He slapped Jeremy hard across the right cheek. A cut opened near the corner of Jeremy's mouth. Blood trickled down his chin to his white collar.

Jeremy had never suffered a beating at Winston's hand. Their age difference meant Winston had always had a physical advantage growing up; as adults, Jeremy had never been stupid enough to antagonize Winston. He tried to yell for help, but Winston clamped a fist around his throat.

"Your man Pritchard was most convincing," Winston snarled.

"You . . . choking me," Jeremy gasped.

Winston released his grip on Jeremy's throat, slipped an open palm under his chin, and slammed his head against the hard vestibule paneling. Jeremy slumped to the floor. Winston resisted the urge to fling him across the hall. "If you've got anything to say for yourself, say it now because we will never speak again." Spittle flew from his lips and his fists were clinched so tightly they turned white.

"I don't know anyone named Pritchard," Jeremy panted.

"Big man, gray eyes, you know him, goddamn it!"

"All right, I know him!"

"What about the woman?"

"What woman?"

"The one you meant to kill!" Winston roared as he cuffed Jeremy's head.

Jeremy fell sideways to the floor. He struggled to right himself. "Pritchard was supposed to blackmail you, that's all. He said something about a prostitute, but never gave me the details."

"You expect me to believe you?"

"You'll believe whatever you want, Winston, you always have."

Winston's rage was only exceeded by his revulsion. He knelt down until they were eyeball-to-eyeball. "Listen very closely," he hissed. "*Magnolia* now belongs to me. If you ever set foot on *my* property again, I will personally ensure your slow, painful death."

Winston straightened his jacket and limped from the courthouse into the bright May sunshine.

❧

Winston sat alone in his first-class compartment. The train was thirty minutes out of Raymond. His rage slowly diminished, but he meant what he'd said to Jeremy, every word of it.

A light rap landed on the glass window of his compartment door. Sam Morris.

"Come in."

Morris opened the door and stepped inside. He had to steady himself from the train's sway.

"Congratulations, Winston." Morris tried to estimate Winston's temperament.

"Thank you. I'm glad it's over." Winston said.

Morris slid uninvited into the seat across from Winston. "I won't take much of your time. You want to enjoy your newfound prosperity, I'm sure."

"Stay as long as you wish. I'll enjoy the company." Winston smiled. "Judge Permutter is an odd bird, wouldn't you say?"

"Yes, he is. Do you think Jeremy tried to bribe him?"

"Wouldn't surprise me."

Morris apprehensively bit his thumbnail. "Winston, I overheard your encounter with Jeremy in the vestibule."

Winston looked at Morris, then turned his gaze to the deep woods along the railroad tracks. "Insolent little bastard. I hope I never see him again."

Neither spoke as the train jarred along.

Morris cleared his throat. "You are the sole owner of *Magnolia*."

A corner of Winston's mouth lifted. "True."

"I have the opportunity for an exclusive interview with Warren County's most powerful land baron." Morris smiled. "Mr. Carthage, would you care to comment on your victory today?"

"No." Winston winked. "Did you get all that?"

The Tennessee countryside rolled slowly away as the train departed Memphis. Six days to New York City. Six days to formulate a new life and forget the disaster of the last eight months.

Jeremy disinterestedly scanned the other passengers in the coach car: cackling women on spring trips to see relatives, salesmen with sample cases, commuters traveling east. Jeremy felt the bulky valise under foot and realized it contained all his worldly possessions: three good suits, a half-dozen shirts, and a few hundred dollars from selling his carriage and horse.

He intended to start fresh in New York, even if he had to start at the bottom. New York was his favorite place, the city where the distinctions between good and bad, right and wrong, were blurred. The Deep South, with the exception of New Orleans, was stultifying; New York offered liberation.

And of course there was the matter of Pritchard. Jeremy was scheduled to meet him at the Edward's Hotel and pay for Pritchard's "work." Jeremy shuddered. If he never saw Pritchard again, it would be too soon.

He settled back in the cramped seat and closed his eyes. Six days.

❧

"Sir, he gave no forwarding address. In fact, he left with a substantial account balance unpaid. Almost three hundred dollars. We would like to know his whereabouts as well. Beyond that, I can only tell you he left on the morning of May twenty-sixth and we haven't seen or heard from him since."

Pritchard thanked the Edward's Hotel clerk and walked out to the street. He weighed his options: try to find Jeremy or ascribe the whole thing to a loss.

He'd read in the newspaper how Winston had won the lawsuit, so something had gone wrong that night. Whatever, Jeremy was surely far away by now, probably in New Orleans.

Pritchard took a deep breath to calm himself. He was not happy, not happy at all.

13

JUNE 3, 1858

Andrew wanted to look the part of a self-confident suitor, a worldly man of fourteen years. His fair skin was scrubbed and his hair freshly washed. He had trimmed and cleaned his fingernails. He wore his finest suitcoat and trousers, but they felt unsuitable for a picnic, on such a hot day. Already, perspiration streamed down the center of his back, but that could've been nerves.

He'd waited almost a year for this day, since first seeing Catherine Parker at church one dreary Sunday morning. He'd been instantly smitten and had looked forward to church every Sunday since. The fact that she was only a girl—an incredible girl, but a girl just the same—was wedged somewhere between his anxiety and longing. In his heart, he knew she was the one. Not the prearranged one as per plantation society custom. His father had never imposed that custom on him, calling arranged romances archaic. Andrew had chosen Catherine. Whether Catherine—or her father—would choose *him* was unclear. And to assume she might be attracted to him seemed hopelessly premature. The plain truth was, they had never spoken for more than a few minutes at any one time. She always seemed pleased to see him, but he knew her only superficially. She was well-mannered, bright, and had a good sense of humor. And there was something else—an impish quality that he couldn't define. She was older than he by a few months, remarkably attractive, tall and blonde, with blue eyes and the whitest teeth he'd ever seen. She spoke with a soft Southern accent, twinged with a curious inflection, an upward curl at the end of certain words almost as if they gained momentum simply being uttered from her mouth. Andrew had been told her accent came from her childhood years in Paris where her father had worked as a diplomatic attorney. Hers was like a New Orleans accent—southern, but not entirely so, and positively exotic.

The picnic was a small affair, a few local plantation owners and their families. The venue was *Magnolia*'s rear terrace where a table had been arranged with platters of sliced ham, bread, and fresh fruit. For the men, it was a chance to talk business, for the women, gossip and mint juleps, and for the youngsters, games of tag and marbles. None of these activities presently held any interest for Andrew. The Parkers were late, and he was anxious. He was dressed as an adult and tried to mingle among the men, but couldn't focus on their words. He stayed close to his father who appeared bored, though in a much better mood since the lawsuit had been decided in his favor.

"Father, could I have a word?"

Winston seemed relieved to excuse himself. "Of course."

They strolled to the food table where Andrew spoke.

"Weren't the Parkers invited?"

Winston smiled. "They'll be here."

"You're sure?"

"Quite."

Andrew fidgeted at his shirt collar. "It's too hot for a picnic."

"Then find some shade. And think pleasant thoughts. You look as if you have a splinter in your arse."

"Yes, sir." But Andrew's expression remained serious.

Winston chuckled. "I'd share a humorous story, but I see we haven't the time."

"Why not?" Andrew followed his father's eyes. The Parkers had finally arrived.

❧

"Winston, how are you?" Stephen Parker extended his hand and Winston accepted it. "And you must be Andrew. A pleasure to meet you."

"Yes, sir." Andrew wiped his palm on the back of his trousers before offering it. Catherine was standing behind her father watching the other picnic guests.

"Winston, my wife offers her regrets to you and Elizabeth. She wasn't feeling well and couldn't be here."

"We understand completely."

"In her stead, I'd like to present my daughter, Catherine."

Winston bowed at the waist and took her hand. "A pleasure, Catherine."

"Nice to meet you, Mr. Carthage." She wore a simple but elegant white dress with a high neckline and ruffled sleeves. Her smile was dazzling. "Hello, Andrew."

"Good afternoon." Andrew took her hand and bowed like his father, sure that his slippery palm felt like catfish skin. "That's a lovely dress."

"Thank you. Father bought it for me in New Orleans."

Winston spoke. "Catherine, this is your first visit to *Magnolia*?" She nodded. "Then I'm sure Andrew would be pleased to offer you a tour."

"I'd enjoy that."

Mr. Parker addressed Winston. "I'd like to pay my respects to Elizabeth."

"She's just there with the other ladies. Shall we?" They walked away.

Andrew felt abandoned.

"Could I see the house?" Catherine had taken a step closer.

The temptation to flee crossed Andrew's mind. "Inside, you mean?"

"I can already see the outside."

"That's true." Andrew flushed. "We really should have an escort if we're going inside."

"I trust your intentions." Her mouth was teasing.

"I don't know . . ."

"Let's walk around front and go in. No one will see."

"I guess so."

"If you'd rather, we could join the picnic." Her eyes indicated that was a poor alternative.

"No, no, the house is really unique."

She beamed. "Well, then." And extended her left arm.

Andrew hesitated for a moment, then grasped her elbow as if it were a precious heirloom. They strolled to the side of the house. He pointed at one of the stone turrets, explaining its origin, hoping Mr. Parker wasn't watching them.

Catherine's voice was playful. "That's interesting. Your grandfather was British?"

"Yes."

"He hosted those magnificent New Year's Eve parties?"

"Yes. Last year we skipped it because of his death. This year, my parents will re-establish the tradition."

"That's exciting. Will my family be invited?"

Andrew smiled. "I'll be sure of it."

This pleased her.

They circled to the front of the house. Andrew pointed at the ground. "This was a moat until Father filled it in."

"Why?"

Andrew shrugged. "He said mosquitoes bred in it." They climbed the steps and he opened the door for her. "The house is about twenty years old."

"You were born here?"

He nodded. "Upstairs. Where were you born?"

"New Orleans. We moved here when I was very small."

"How long did you live in Paris?"

She smiled. "Seven years. From when I was five until I was twelve."

"Did you like it?"

"It was splendid. I hope to go back someday."

They walked through the great room. Andrew pointed to his right. "That's the double parlor room. And around here is the elliptical staircase. It's supposed to be the only one in the whole state." They were standing in the rear foyer and could see the picnic through a glass-covered rear wall. "Maybe you should stay back from the windows."

"That's a lovely view." She pointed at the staircase. "Your room is up there?"

"All of the bedrooms."

"Show me."

Andrew paled.

She giggled. "I didn't mean to make you nervous. We don't have to."

Andrew glanced outside. "Your father—"

She bolted up several steps and stopped, her eyes shining. "Coming?"

"Catherine . . ."

He looked outside again. The picnickers were some distance away and probably couldn't see inside. "Maybe for just a moment." He took a step toward the staircase. She climbed higher until he could no longer see her. "Catherine?"

"Come on!"

Andrew took the steps quickly until he was beyond the window view. Then he slowed. She was already at the top leaning over the rail. "Hello down there!"

"Shhh!"

"What's wrong?"

Andrew was still climbing. "Nothing." He reached the top step and she whirled away. He followed.

"What's this?"

"My parents' room."

She poked her head inside. "It's cute. Show me the rest."

"Catherine, maybe we shouldn't—"

She grasped his hand. "What's down here?" she asked, tugging him along.

"Guest rooms."

She stopped at the end of the hall before a full-length mirror, Andrew reluctantly at her side. She scrunched closer until their shoulders touched. "I'm as tall as you."

Nothing coherent came to Andrew's mind.

"Which room is yours?"

"We already passed it. Across from my parents."

"Show me."

Andrew's heart hammered in his chest. They walked back to his room. He couldn't remember if he'd straightened it this morning like his mother had asked. "Here," he croaked.

She went inside. "I like it." She breezed across the room and stood before the window.

"Stay away from there! Someone will see you."

She turned around, a curious smile on her face. "Why would they be looking up here?" Her voice had changed.

"I don't know." Currents of sweat rolled down his back.

She came closer, close enough that he could see the tiny freckles on her nose and smell her lilac fragrance. "Am I the first girl who's been in your room?"

"Well, the slaves . . ." Dizzying emotions surged through him. Minutes ago, he had been worried about how he would present himself and if she would even talk to him. Now she was standing in his bedroom.

She reached up with her forefinger and tickled his chin. "Slaves don't count," she whispered. Their faces were inches apart. She closed her eyes.

Andrew had never kissed a girl and certainly never in his room. He hesitated, then lightly pressed his lips against hers. She responded by twisting her mouth, spreading her lips ever-so-slightly. Her tongue darted out. Startled, Andrew pulled away.

"I learned that in France," she giggled. "Did you like it?"

"It was surprising." Andrew could barely speak. His brain was intoxicated with possibilities. He felt a stirring below his belt. "I liked it though." He reached to kiss her again.

"Massa Andrew! You up there?" An angry voice called from below.

Andrew pulled away from her. "Oh god!" he whispered.

"Who is it?" Catherine's eyes shone with danger.

"Curtis."

"A slave?" She looked annoyed.

Footsteps were slowly climbing the staircase. "Come on." He pulled her into the hall just as Curtis appeared.

Curtis glared at them. "Massa Andrew, they looking for y'all down at the picnic."

"We were just coming."

Curtis surveyed Catherine. "And you know better, don't you, Missy?"

Catherine mildly protested. "We weren't doing anything—"

"Uh huh." Curtis didn't believe it.

"Curtis, please don't—"

"Go on 'fore I take a mind to tell your parents." His lips pressed together in thin displeasure. "Git!"

They scampered down the stairs.

14

SEPTEMBER 9, 1858

Jeremy stood and nervously smoothed his suit. How humiliating, he thought, to grovel for a job he didn't really want anyway. How low could a person sink? Damn Winston, this was his fault.

He strolled by the bored secretary at her desk and stood near the office window. He'd never seen a female secretary before.

He watched the mid-morning activity in Manhattan's financial district. Wagons and carriages rolled by as businessmen hurried along the sidewalks to meetings and sales appointments. The four street corners were ringed with vendors hawking bagels and pastries, hot coffee, newspapers, and shoe shines. A decrepit dog trotted down the center of Broad Street amidst the purposeful legions of capitalism, weaving through moving carriages, stopping at one point to paw an annoying flea. Jeremy watched in macabre fascination as the wheels of a wagon rolled over the cur's tail. It darted squarely into the path of a horse team. When the horses had passed, the dog was but a spot on the street.

"Sir!"

Jeremy whirled around, pale-faced. "Yes?"

"I'm sure your appointment won't be much longer, Mr. Harper."

"Thank you, Miss Coswell." He returned to his seat and watched her lift a stack of letters from the corner. One by one, she opened the letters, tossing the used envelopes into a waste basket.

Three months in New York had done little more than squander Jeremy's precious money. He'd nosed around the business district looking for a quick way to parlay his dwindling cash into a much bigger pile of cash. But all he'd learned were directions to the horse track. A string of nag losers had left him nearly broke. He *needed* a job just to eat. At least he'd fought the urge to borrow from a shyster. No sense traveling that road again until a means of repayment was assured.

"Are you staying in town, Mr. Harper?" The secretary's milky eyes danced.

"Yes." Silly crone, he thought, return to your letters.

A real job was such a thoroughly depressing concept, a point made more evident by the insipid woman before him. The standard methods of advancement in the business world were of no interest to him. Careers took too long and people expected too much. Deadlines and accountability, punctuality and loyalty—utter silliness. Jeremy was destined for privilege and determined to start near the top, not at the entry level.

He had casually asked around, stuck his head into a few businesses, made inquiries. Opportunities abounded for wharf laborers and butchers and other such vital vocations. But he couldn't, he *wouldn't*, resort to manual labor. Unfortunately, a requirement of experience was attached to the best-paying positions. He didn't *have* any work experience.

He'd begun reading the classified postings in the newspaper and noticed an uptown bank's advertisement for an assistant loan officer. A bank offered interesting possibilities. Money, and people who had money. Not a bad starting point.

"If you could excuse me." Jeremy rose, his face filled with chagrin. The secretary's smile was understanding.

Jeremy stepped from the office into a long narrow hall lit by windows at either end. He turned left and entered a stairwell. Halfway down the inside staircase, he withdrew a flask and a rumpled piece of paper from his suitcoat. On the paper was a collection of handwritten notes. These he reviewed while re-climbing the stairs to the office where he'd so long waited, stopping briefly for a needed mouthful of whiskey.

The secretary smiled again. "He'll see you now, sir."

Jeremy followed her into a posh mahogany-trimmed office.

"Mr. Harper to see you, Mr. Stanton." The secretary presented Jeremy and scurried out.

"Please have a seat, Mr. Harper."

Behind an oversized desk sat an oversized man, R. T. Stanton, president of Merchant Bank and Trade Corporation, New York City. Without rising, Stanton extended a hand. Jeremy squeezed the pudgy fingers and felt a disagreeable sense of softness, like a cow's udder. Stanton was draped in a suit which couldn't seem to keep pace with his blossoming girth. His three chins stretched from ear-to-ear forming a miniature staircase ascending to his face.

"Thank you for seeing me, Mr. Stanton." Jeremy took a seat, wishing he'd brought a pastry as a goodfaith gesture.

Stanton adjusted a pair of delicate spectacles which were disproportionate to his broad face. He sifted through a sheaf of papers, Jeremy's "resume," occasionally stopping at something that caught his interest, never spending more than a few seconds on a single item.

"Jackson Railroad Bank . . . thirteen years . . ." He looked up. "Very impressive, Mr. Harper."

Jeremy shifted slightly in his seat, expecting questions to fit his rehearsed answers.

Stanton dabbed an embroidered handkerchief across his upper lip. "Why do you want to work here?" His voice was strangely highpitched.

Jeremy nearly pulled the piece of paper from his pocket for reference. This dimwit would never notice. "New York is the best place to broaden my banking skills."

Stanton nodded vaguely.

"I've always worked in the personal loan area. My reward was in helping people through the confusion of personal finances." Jeremy winced, guiltily appreciating the disaster that was his own finances. "I think the next logical career move is to advance to commercial lending."

Stanton palmed his glistening scalp. "Why did you leave . . .," he lifted a piece of paper from the stack, ". . . Jackson?"

Jeremy had researched Mr. R. T. Stanton, knew he had recently inherited this bank from his dying father. Apparently, Stanton was perceived by the financial community as incapable of managing much more than a newsstand. On first impression, the rumors were valid.

"New York is the financial capital of the country."

Stanton considered this and could find nothing constructive to add.

"I've also heard very good things about this bank's management style."

Again, Stanton was silent. Jeremy determined it was time to seize the initiative. He rose and strolled purposefully to the office window.

"Down there, Mr. Stanton, down there is why I want to work in your bank."

Stanton raised his eyebrows, not sure if he was to come look where Jeremy pointed. The easiest thing was to remain seated, so he did. "I don't follow you," was his unintentional pun.

"The people who need the help of your bank."

"Oh, you mean the . . . customers." Stanton dubiously tugged on a pink ear.

"Yes, sir, the customers." This was too easy.

Stanton mumbled something about "a positive outlook" and snatched another piece of paper off the pile. "Virginia, New York University . . . you certainly have the right educational background." Stanton frowned and placed an index finger across two full lips.

"Something else, sir?" Jeremy's voice was innocence defined.

"You listed Jefferson Davis as a reference. Is that *the* Jefferson Davis?"

"Yes, it is."

"How do you know him?"

"In my former position, I worked with a number of the larger landowners in southwest Mississippi. Jeff and his brother Joseph own plantations in Warren County." It was true that Jeremy had once met Jefferson Davis, but beyond that, they were strangers.

"I've read articles about Senator Davis." Stanton was duly impressed. "Tell me, have you ever discussed the possibility of war with him?"

Jeremy's puzzled expression was not evident to Stanton who studied a cufflink.

"War between the North and South?"

"Of course."

Such weighty subjects rarely infringed on Jeremy's time. Politics was the dreariest of all topics. "Senator Davis is dead set against war." Jeremy figured his answer was safe.

Stanton nodded. "I agree. Maybe the politicians will find a way to avoid it." He fumbled with some papers on his desk. "Mr. Harper, MB&T could use an experienced man like you. I've yet to interview a few more people, and these references must be checked, you understand." Stanton struggled to his feet and offered his right hand.

Jeremy rose. "Certainly. Thank you for your time. I'll leave a notification address with your secretary."

"That will be fine. Good morning."

Jeremy emerged from Stanton's office and gave an address to the brainless secretary. He jaunted down two flights of stairs, smiling. The interview had been perfect—brief and short on specifics. Stanton was exactly as advertised: vacuous, indecisive, and easily manipulated.

On the ground floor, Jeremy stopped near the building's exit at a room marked 'Outgoing Correspondence'—the mail room. Inside, he found a young man of twenty or so, tall and gangly, still in the throes of acne.

"Good morning," Jeremy pronounced importantly.

"Morning, sir."

"I'm Jeremy Harper, Mr. Stanton's new executive assistant. You are...?"

"Dean Tully."

"Pleased to meet you. Mr. Stanton has made it one of my first official duties to review all his outgoing correspondence. He's asked me to personally deliver his letters and cables to the post office and telegraph office. I'll be stopping by on my way out each day to pick them up."

Dean was plainly confused, maybe even hurt. "Did I do something wrong?"

"No, nothing like that." Jeremy's voice dropped in confidence. "Miss Coswell upstairs has been careless recently with some of Mr. Stanton's important letters, addressing them incorrectly and such. He's asked me to evaluate the problem."

"Oh."

"Miss Coswell mustn't know about this. We don't want to embarrass her. Do you understand?" Jeremy squeezed Dean's shoulder.

"Yes, sir."

"Good. Then starting tomorrow, I'll drop by about four o'clock each day. Set aside any outgoing correspondence from Mr. Stanton's office, including cables."

"Yes, sir."

"Mr. Stanton will be made aware of your cooperation."

"Thank you, sir."

Mr. Albert Granger
24 October 1858
President, Jackson Railroad Bank
Jackson, Miss.

Mr. R. T. Stanton
President, Merchant Bank and Trade Corp.
New York City, New York

Dear Mr. Stanton:

Regarding your letter dated 4 October concerning Mr. Jeremy Harper, allow me to recommend him in the strongest terms possible. Mr. Harper served as a loan officer and Junior Vice President for JRB from 1844 until his resignation earlier this year. His performance was always of the highest caliber. Mr. Harper would be an asset to your bank and well-suited to the job description provided in your letter of inquiry. I'm pleased to assist you in this matter.

Sincerely,
Albert Granger

Jeremy carefully signed the letter and placed it in an envelope. The official-looking bank letterhead was the product of a precious dollar spent at a mid-town print shop. He would deliver the letter personally to Dean Tully in the MB&T mail room where it would find its way to Stanton's office. Jeremy was confident that Miss Coswell would fail to notice the lack of a postmark before she threw the envelope in the waste basket and passed the letter to Stanton.

Stanton had only sent out one inquiry, to Jeremy's mythical former employer in Jackson, the Jackson Railroad Bank. Stanton was a fool. And if that were true, there had to be a way to obtain some of his money. Jeremy would determine the surest method in due time.

Two days later, Jeremy Harper, a.k.a. Jeremy Carthage, was awarded the position of assistant loan officer for commercial accounts at Merchant Bank and Trade Corp.

Elizabeth gripped the staircase handrail in silent agony. Pain seared from the base of her skull to her crown. She sank to the steps fighting vertigo and nausea. Tears flowed down her cheeks.

The seizures always came without warning. This was the third in as many months. Ever since that day in Jackson with Jeremy . . .

Doctor Purvis had told her she was suffering the after-effects of a concussion; the headaches would run their course. Dear God, but the course was difficult.

She disjointedly clutched the rail and waited. After a time, the pain subsided to a dull pounding. She rose unsteadily and continued down the staircase. At least no one had seen this seizure. Winston had witnessed the tail-end of her last one as she lay weeping on a sofa in the great room. He'd been shocked and concerned, and it had taken all of her persuasions to convince him she was all right. But today's attack was the worst yet. She could never have convinced anyone she was well five minutes ago.

She would see the doctor again, obtain some more laudanum. But there was nothing he could do for her true agony, her awful, bitter truth.

She'd been raped, yet she could confide in no one, not her doctor, not her father, and certainly not Winston.

She reached the bottom step and was slammed again by a sharp pain in her head.

❧

"Mother?" Andrew rushed across the rear foyer. "What's wrong?"

Elizabeth's eyes fluttered in their sockets. Her face was pale and wet from tears and perspiration.

"I'm just a little flustered. I'll be fine, dear."

"You're not fine, Mother! Have you fallen?" Andrew knelt at her side.

"No, it's just a headache." She tried to smile.

"I'll be right back." Andrew raced to the kitchen. "Lou!" He and Elizabeth were alone in the house. He darted out the kitchen door, but again, no one was close. He returned to the stairwell and found his mother standing.

"See, I'm feeling much better."

Andrew wanted to her tell her she'd never looked worse, but instead said, "You should lie down."

"I will."

Andrew nodded. "Can you make it upstairs?"

"I think so. A glass of water would help."

"Yes, ma'am." He sprinted to the kitchen and returned to find her again slumped on the stairs.

"Thank you, Andrew." Elizabeth sipped at the water.

"I'm going to get Father."

"Don't worry him. I'll be all right in a few minutes."

"But, Mother—"

"I promise, it's just a headache." Her eyes were pleading.

Andrew was frantic, close to tears. "Why don't you want Father to know?" He was nearly shouting.

"Because my condition isn't serious."

She patted his face with a shaking hand.

Andrew didn't know what to say.

Elizabeth struggled to her feet.

"Let me help." Andrew took her arm.

"Thank you." She grimaced. "Promise me you won't worry your father over this."

Andrew was dumbfounded. "Yes, ma'am."

15

DECEMBER 20, 1858

Wind crashed through the trees, blowing snow into Pritchard's bearded face. He wrapped his jacket tighter, but it was inadequate for the Illinois winter. He ducked his bare head below the thin collar knowing he would find shelter before nightfall or die from exposure.

Pritchard couldn't explain what had brought him here. It certainly wasn't a compelling interest to revisit his boyhood home. He'd simply tired of the South. Two futile months in New Orleans had produced no sign of Jeremy Carthage. He'd looked in every whorehouse, saloon, and gutter. Either Carthage wasn't there or he'd learned a new lifestyle. Pritchard left New Orleans, not because he didn't like the city. It wasn't a bad place, it just wasn't his place. Crime didn't pay in a city with so many criminals.

Jeremy Carthage was a lucky man. Pritchard wasn't generally susceptible to his emotions. The rational part of his brain was merely offended by Jeremy's betrayal, by the unfulfilled business agreement. That problem had a logical solution. They would meet again someday. Pritchard couldn't be sure how or when, but he knew they would. And Jeremy would be held accountable. Blood or money. Either was fine.

DECEMBER 31, 1858

The crowd swayed like wind-blown wheat, undulating to the seven piece orchestra in *Magnolia's* huge double-parlor room. Most revelers were dressed in their finest winter attire, a Carthage party being the year's defining social event.

Winston raised a champagne glass to his lips, impressed that so many would brave a bitter winter night for his New Year's Eve party. *Magnolia*, he knew, was the inevitable attraction. But some came merely to be seen, others for the French champagne, and still others to sample the extraordinary midnight buffet.

"What a delightful party!" Elizabeth glided into the room, her eyes sparkling. She didn't look her best, but better than earlier.

"A good turnout considering the weather."

"I just checked the guest ledger. There are one hundred forty-seven people here. We only invited one hundred thirty!"

"They came to see you," Winston teased.

"You're kind, but not very persuasive."

"Did the Davis brothers arrive?"

"No."

"Pity. I was hoping to speak with Jefferson."

"About what?"

"Politics."

Elizabeth made a face. "Are you going to run for office?"

"Hardly. I wanted to ask his thoughts on secession."

"That's a depressing subject."

"Get used to it."

"You really think Mississippi will secede from the Union?"

"I hope not. Secession would be a tremendous mistake." Winston's mood instantly began to sour. "Let's talk about something more pleasant."

"Gladly."

"Did you notice Andrew?"

Elizabeth smiled. "I did. He's been keeping company with the Parker girl all night."

"She's a lovely young lady. Did you see the cuts on his chin? I made him shave this morning. He lost a lot of blood." They shared a laugh. Winston studied his wife more closely. "Has your headache improved?"

"Some." She feigned an inebriated slur. "But it could be the champagne."

"You've been on your feet all night. Why don't you rest a bit?"

"Oh, but I can't miss the midnight celebration! That's the whole point of the party."

"At least sit down for a few minutes."

"I will, I promise."

Winston watched her walk away. She'd been erratic lately, complaining of headaches, forgetful, weeping alone for no apparent reason. Her pain seemed as much internal as physical. She'd become defensive, even angry, when he'd tried to understand, to help. It was so unlike her, as if she were ashamed, hiding something. He discarded the thought and retreated to the rear terrace for a breath of air.

❧

"Are you enjoying the party?" Andrew studied Catherine's perfect face, the sweeping curls in her blonde hair lying on the swell of her breasts.

"Immensely."

He stood close to her, absorbing her flowery perfume. Around them, the party was like a grand show staged specifically for their benefit. "Where is your dance card?"

"I was saving my dances for you." She made a pouty face. "Besides, Father won't let me have one."

"I applaud your father's decision. Would you like something to drink?"

She scrunched her nose. "That punch is too tart. Champagne would be good." She whispered, "Maybe your friend Curtis could get us some."

"No, he wouldn't." Andrew dropped his voice. "But the wine is good."

Her eyes frolicked. "You've been drinking already?"

Andrew frowned, looking left and right. "Not so loud."

She tossed her head. "No one cares. They're all drinking, even some of the Methodists."

He looked at her in profile and felt his adrenaline surge. "Follow me." Andrew's boldness came from two glasses of wine. Courage sometimes had to be forced.

"Where?"

He took her hand and they slipped easily through the crowd, an attractive young couple enjoying a formal social setting. They walked through the rear foyer and outside saw Winston, alone, his back to them, staring off into the night.

"What's your father doing?"

"Probably smoking." Andrew tugged on her wrist. "The kitchen is this way."

"I'm not *hungry*, Andrew."

"Come on." They entered the kitchen, which was alive with servants preparing food trays for the party. The servants looked up, but quickly returned to their duties after a sharp glare from Andrew. They crossed through an arch that took them down a short hallway into *Magnolia*'s breakfast room.

"This is beautiful," Catherine whispered. "Light a lamp so I can see better."

"Look over there." Andrew pointed to his right through a massive bay window. Across the way, they could again see Winston on the veranda, this time from the side, smoking a cigar. "If I light a lamp, he'll see us."

"And we don't want that?"

Her hushed voice made Andrew's spine tingle. "We don't." Andrew reached beneath the breakfast table and produced a wine bottle and two glasses. "Here."

"How much have you had already?"

"Not much." He filled their glasses and raised his in a toast. "To us."

She took a tiny sip and examined him over her glass. "What about us?"

"Good question." Andrew sucked in a quick breath. "We're both fifteen now. We have to make plans."

"Oh, we do?"

Even the alcohol couldn't force him to completely expose his feelings. "I care for you," was as far as he could go.

"And?"

If she was encouraging him, he thought her far too subtle. He tried to sound offhanded. "Maybe we have a future together."

She nodded.

Was she agreeing or simply being agreeable? As much time as they'd spent together the last six months—church functions, cotillions, picnics—he still couldn't be certain what she was thinking at any given moment. It was both mysterious and frustrating. He lost his nerve. "Is your wine good?"

"It's very sweet. Makes my mouth pucker." She smiled and pursed her lips.

He understood *that.* He took her in his arms and kissed her.

The night was achingly cold, well below freezing. The gardenias and camellias were covered with burlap for protection.

Winston drew on his cigar. The chill was bracing, the night clear and windless. He exhaled and couldn't tell when the smoke stopped and his breath began.

He could have stood there all night if it meant skipping the party. He was not socially active like Elizabeth. He had a sense of humor and could talk knowledgeably on many subjects, but parties tended to make him uncomfortable. People were always more formal at parties, like they had to impress by acting a certain way. Winston didn't impress easily and had little time for people infatuated with themselves.

Despite his social reluctance, Winston was on good terms with Warren County's most influential citizen, United States Senator, Jefferson Davis. Davis was only an acquaintance really, a brilliant man, Winston's rival in some respects. They had first met many years earlier as classmates at the University of Transylvania in Lexington, Kentucky. Davis had been then, as now, an interesting, if subdued, conversationalist. Winston had hoped that tonight he might probe Davis's thoughts on the increasing possibility of Southern secession. Another time perhaps.

He drew on his cigar again. Screams erupted from inside. He checked his pocket watch. It read twenty minutes 'til twelve. What was the commotion?

He ground out his cigar and stepped inside. The band had stopped playing and a host of people had gathered around in the parlor.

"Winston!" Someone shouted his name.

He waded through the crowd and found Elizabeth lying unconscious on the floor.

16

JANUARY 1, 1859

Elizabeth's skin was a shade lighter than the sheets bunched under her chin. She'd been unconscious for ten hours. Doctor Purvis, the Carthage physician and a party guest, had stayed the night at *Magnolia*. He'd left an hour earlier saying he would return after lunch and to summon him immediately if she regained consciousness. But she remained the same lifeless form, occasionally twitching around the eyes and mouth. She had no detectable fever; the doctor had said her problem was internal.

Winston sat red-eyed on the sofa, an arm's reach away. He'd been almost as motionless as Elizabeth, watching, waiting, silently begging for a cough or a murmur, a blinking of the eyes, anything.

He rubbed a palm across his unshaven cheeks. His mouth was coarse and dry, the New Year's alcohol long since thwarted by tension. Only a dull ache remained at his temples. His thoughts wandered aimlessly, desperately grasping for hope, fearing the worst.

Elizabeth *had* to live. She was too young, too vital to die, her worldly contributions incomplete. And he was too young to live without her. He cursed himself again for not insisting she skip the party. Her headaches, which she had claimed were infrequent, were more common than she had allowed, the doctor had said as much. And Purvis knew something he wasn't telling Winston, it was in his eyes.

Winston forced himself back into the sofa cushion. The mantel clock read 10:30 A.M. He willed his eyes closed. An unwelcome sleep pierced his anxiety. Within seconds he was dreaming of Elizabeth, her face, her voice, the wonder of her existence, taken away by a cruel God. His subconscious explored possibilities his waking mind refused to consider. He slept for three hours. When he woke, the aneurism in Elizabeth's brain had ruptured. She was gone.

❧

Winston stood tall and dark beside the pastor, his face mottled and red. He felt no cold or discomfort in the wintry air. He couldn't think or reason. He was a shell, helpless as a newborn. His grief cast a pall over the entire plantation. Since her death, his sleepless nights were spent crying until dawn.

Surrounding Winston were Andrew and Elizabeth's father, her two brothers, plus a group of slaves, each of whom had known and liked Elizabeth. The gathering was deliberately small. Winston didn't want his wife's burial to become an event for the society prigs.

Elizabeth's grave in the Carthage family cemetery was next to the only other occupants, Winston's parents, Charles and Marie. A large hole had been carved from the earth to receive Elizabeth's mahogany and brass casket. Her simple marker read "Elizabeth Dearman Carthage" and beneath that, her dates of existence. In small, neatly engraved letters near the bottom of the stone was inscribed Winston's farewell: "Life and light, beauty and sweetness. God's Kingdom is enriched."

The pastor, E. H. Rutherford, was a thin, pasty man with shaggy hair and a surprising baritone. His words echoed across the rolling landscape with pious strength. He spoke for ten minutes, then stood aside and allowed the family their final moments. One by one, the Dearmans somberly dropped a handful of dirt onto Elizabeth's coffin. Andrew did the same. When it was Winston's turn, he grasped a clump of earth, and collapsed to his knees. Tears poured down his cheeks as freely as a spring shower.

"My love," he whispered, "I don't see God's plan, but He must have one. Your strength exceeded mine. You gave me a purpose and a will. You gave me our wonderful son. You gave me so much." And then he was out of words. He shuddered and a forlorn moan welled from deep inside him. The sound was so utterly sad that bowed heads lifted to see.

Winston tried to raise himself from the cold earth, but couldn't. Andrew rushed to his side, and together, they brought him to his feet.

Andrew and Winston were alone in *Magnolia*'s great room. Their faces were splotchy from a day of unchecked tears. Neither had spoken for over an hour. Finally, Andrew had to talk.

"How long did you know Mother?"

Winston took a long time to answer. "We met when she was fourteen and I was twenty-four."

"Did you like her then?"

"Instantly."

"Did she like you?"

"I'm not sure. I believe so." Winston was startled to see so clearly in Andrew's face what he always knew was true—Andrew looked exactly like his mother, the same green eyes and strawberry-blond hair, the clear fair skin.

Andrew chewed a familiar lower lip. "When did you know you would marry her?"

"I *wanted* to marry her from the time we met. Unfortunately, Mr. Dearman was less certain of my prospects."

"How do you mean?"

Winston's face changed. "He had to be sure I was right for his only daughter. He tested my resolve. I wasn't allowed to see her more than once a month at first, only on Sundays. I grew impatient, which was exactly what Mr. Dearman wanted."

"Why would he want that?"

"To measure my commitment to her, to see if I developed a wandering eye. I didn't."

"How long did you court her?"

"Three years." Winston sniffled. "But it passed like three months."

"I'm glad you were patient," mumbled Andrew.

"I really had no choice."

"Did Mother have suitors besides you?"

"Yes." Winston looked away.

"Who else?" Andrew sensed the evasion.

Winston's leather chair made a groaning noise as he shifted. "Your Uncle Jeremy."

"Really?"

"Yes, although your mother and Jeremy never got along well."

Andrew's adolescent mind formed the next logical question, logical because he'd wanted to ask it for months. "Where is Uncle Jeremy?"

"I've been told New York."

"New York City?"

Winston nodded. "A friend claimed to have seen him there."

"Is he all right?"

"I don't know, son."

"Do you hate him?"

"Hate is an extreme word."

"But you never want to see him again?"

Winston looked questioningly at Andrew. "I can't think of a situation . . . No, I don't want to see him again."

Andrew stared intently at his father's face, so temperamental over the last few days, now a blank slate on the topic of Jeremy. "What *happened*? I mean with the lawsuit and all."

Winston frowned but didn't answer.

Andrew leaned forward. "I should know. He's my uncle." He looked down. "I asked Mother about it once."

"She told me." Winston's voice softened. "You were too young."

"Am I still?"

This was not an appropriate day to discuss Jeremy. "Another time."

Andrew sagged. "Yes, sir."

A grandfather clock ticked in solitude for two heavy minutes.

"I'll tell you a better story. More uplifting than the other. About your grandfather, my father." Winston paused in thought.

Andrew waited a respectful moment. "What about Grandpa Carthage?"

"Yes, Grandpa Carthage." Winston smiled just a little and stood. "We shall do this properly. Follow me."

They went through the foyer to a small door in the rear of the kitchen. Winston opened the door and they proceeded with a lamp down a flight of steps. On the near wall was Winston's makeshift wine cellar.

"Does anything entice you?"

"Sir?"

"French or Italian. What do you prefer?"

Andrew grinned. "I can have wine?"

"Yes."

Winston had largely ignored plantation tradition which held that a father should introduce his son to sex and alcohol at some point during the son's middle-teen years. Winston's father had allowed him to drink at an early age and had arranged his first sexual encounter with a slave at the age of 16. But Winston couldn't bring himself to do the same for Andrew, always afraid his son might sink into alcoholism and lewdness—like his Uncle Jeremy.

"We'll toast your mother's memory. And don't try to pretend you've never had spirits."

"Sir?"

"I saw you at the New Year's Eve party."

"Saw what?"

"*You* and Catherine in the breakfast room."

"How did you see us?"

"There was a full moon. I was going to mention it, but then with your mother and all . . ." Winston's expression paled.

"Which of these is best?" Andrew asked.

"Hmmm? They are all splendid."

"Then you pick."

Winston scanned the upturned labels. "We'll have a Bordeaux."

"What's *Bordeaux*?"

"Bordeaux is in southwest France. The vineyards there produce the world's finest wines." Winston removed a bottle. "This will do."

Andrew followed his father back up the steps into the kitchen. Winston found a corkscrew and manipulated the stopper from its neck.

"Fetch two glasses from the crystal cabinet."

Andrew did as instructed and they returned to the great room. Winston filled their glasses and took a small sip. "Outstanding."

Andrew gulped a mouthful. "What was the story?"

Winston relaxed a bit."My father told me this, just after you were born. You'll be only the second person to hear it."

"Is it bad?" Andrew slid his hand around the base of the bottle. He refilled his glass without objection from his father.

"Some might think so, but you won't. And you should know." Winston leaned back into the sofa. "As you know, your grandparents on my side were European immigrants. Father was from England and Mother from France. They came to this country through New Orleans . . . "

17

A HALF-CENTURY EARLIER, DECEMBER 23, 1810

Charles Carthage pulled his peacoat tighter and walked carefully through the seedier section of the French Quarter. Last night's rare winter storm had left New Orleans blanketed in a shiny cover of ice. He pressed south past the restaurants and whorehouses, all quieter than usual in the frosty night. An occasional street person greeted him along the way, an underdressed Creole or a European sailor, looking for unwholesome entertainment and a kindred spirit with whom to share it.

Charles liked the Quarter, especially at night. It was reminiscent of London's Soho District, only more bawdy and frenetic. The Quarter could be dangerous, but he knew his way around. He wasn't a large man but was wiry and tough, a veteran of the London docks.

He arrived at a low-rent, one-story dive known as Drago's. He pulled open a heavy oak door and stepped into a smoky malodorous room, forty feet square with a long wooden bar along one wall. A half-dozen tables with spindly legs were scattered about. Dim light glistened from oil lamps along the walls. The room was largely empty. A few hard drinkers, mariners and roustabouts, looked up at the chilly blast of air. Charles nodded, but no one returned his courtesy. He shook off the cold and approached the bar.

The barkeep, a West Indian named Francois, huffed in from a back room with a rack of beer mugs on his shoulder.

"Hey, Charlie! What brings you out on such a night, huh?" Francois smiled toothlessly, his round brown face glistening with sweat despite the weather.

"Business, mate." Charles's lilting British accent was different—but appropriate—in a seaman's bar.

"You still clean the club on Decatur?"

"Yes." Charles winked. "I'll own the place some day. The current proprietor just doesn't know it yet." Just as I'll own this place one day, he wanted to say. "How 'bout a lager?"

"No lager. This ain't London. Beer is all." Francois placed a mug under the tap and produced a foamy, tepid draft.

Charles swallowed and winced at the weak and flavorless beer. He truly missed London's pubs. "Jules in back?"

Francois tried to hide the frown on his face. "Yes."

Charles observed this without comment. He dropped a nickel on the bar.

Francois took the money and placed it in a cash box below the counter. "Are you still keeping the books for Jules?"

Charles nodded. He was actually Jules's newest partner.

"Charlie, you work too much." Francois's curly black beard danced as he spoke. "Sometimes the money, it don' feel good in your pocket."

"Money is money, mate."

"Money ain't everything, Charlie." Francois wiped absently at the bar with a rag. "How is Mrs. Charlie doin'?"

"She's with child."

"Hey! That's great! You be thinkin' a boy or girl?"

"Either is fine. Healthy is most important."

Francois leaned over the bar, his breath smelling of sweet smoke. He was abruptly frowning again. "Charlie, why you wanna work for Jules?"

"You work for him too."

Francois nodded slowly. "Not 'cause I want to."

Charles smiled. "I have business in back. Cheers." Charles walked to a door that was nearly hidden in the rear stone wall. He rapped twice and waited. After a moment, the door swung open.

"Monsieur Car-tage, please come in." Jules Drago was the bar's owner. He was another immigrant in a city of immigrants, a Corsican, tall and dark, distinguished in an oily, knavish way. His black hair and Mediterranean features were handsomely offset by a small black goatee curled across his chin. Charles secretly envied him.

"Good evening, Jules." The door opened just wide enough for Charles to slip into a large drafty room with a low ceiling and brick walls. This was Jules's office, the center of his business enterprises. Seated at a table were three fellow Corsicans whom Charles knew as Jules's partners, now his partners too. They were all products of the New Orleans waterfront, seamen-come-ashore, tough and crude. Jules was their leader.

"Bonjour." Charles tried to sound cheerful.

"Bonjour," the partners mumbled in unison without raising their heads, their card game more interesting than the puny Brit.

Jules was more gracious. "Thank you for coming at such a late hour. You must be very tired. You are still working two jobs, no?" He asked the question without concern for Charles's hardship.

"I keep the books for the Archbishop, and yes, I still work at the Golden Star." He was, in fact, a janitor at the Golden Star cabaret.

"Mon Dieu, Charles, you will kill yourself." Jules clucked his tongue. "I'm afraid our partners will become impatient if I don't return to the whist game." He pointed at an old desk. "The ledgers are there."

"I'll get started tonight and finish tomorrow."

Jules's eyebrows pointed inward toward his nose. "We need the balances promptly. The partners are anxious to know the November profits." Jules grinned, his white teeth glittery against his swarthy skin. "I think late Christmas shopping drives their impatience."

Charles glanced at the partners seated around the table. None of them were married or had families. "I'll hurry."

"Excellent."

Charles removed his peacoat and approached the desk, carefully avoiding tin plates stacked with onion shards and garlic, horseradish and oyster shells, half-eaten clumps of bread. He pulled up a chair and selected an accounting ledger labeled "Accounts Receivable." He wearily opened it, ignoring the card game, the curses in French, and focused on the disjointed ledger entries for November. Within minutes, his weariness was overcome by excitement as he added the figures. Drago Trading Company was an importer of French perfumes, Bahamian rum, and

Chinese silk, fine products sold to local merchants and wholesalers at good prices. Drago's warehouse was somewhere down at the waterfront, though Charles had never seen it. He didn't have to—the business was doing well.

The company owned only one vessel, a two-masted schooner, the *Angelica.* The small ship didn't actually sail the long hazardous routes to France or China. Drago was primarily a re-seller of goods bought on consignment. Jules handled all purchases using connections in New York and Marseilles. He received very favorable prices which translated into handsome profit margins.

Charles was not naive. He assumed that goods obtained at such extraordinary prices were smuggled or stolen or both. It was the only explanation. But Charles could look the other way now that he shared the profits. Smuggling was a victimless crime. He could always later claim ignorance.

Charles scanned three full pages of November entries. In the far left hand column were merchandise descriptions. The center columns contained purchase prices, sales prices and quantities sold, and the far right column listed the purchasing agents. It was a simple accounting system made more difficult by the nature of the products, which were all taxed at different rates. Further, the entries were often garbled and incomplete, as his partners were functionally illiterate.

Charles toiled for an hour before he crossed an unusual entry which simply read "13." The amount owed was an enormous $150. He frowned. Further down the page was a similar entry. Perplexed, he turned back to the October receipts, and found a "12," also for $150. The number was a postscript, added after the October accounts had been balanced. The listed merchandise was a bundle of silk. Why had the number been added afterward?

He flipped back through previous months and found other examples. He noticed the purchasing agents for the numbered items were all individuals, not wholesale companies or retail merchants.

The four Corsicans were still deeply involved in the whist game. He would ask Jules about it in a private moment.

❧

At 1:00 A.M., the card game ended and the partners loudly departed, save Jules.

"Charles, we made a profit in November, no?" Jules was red-eyed and drunk. Small bits of spittle had collected at the corners of his mouth.

"So it would appear." Charles spoke hesitantly. "Jules, these numbers to the side of certain items—do they have a specific meaning?"

Jules looked over Charles' shoulder and flushed. "No, no. Those are merely reminders to me. They are unimportant."

"Reminders?"

"Do not concern yourself. They are . . . what is the word? Meaningless. The prices are critical, nothing else."

"I understand, but suppose the tax collectors make inquiries?"

"I think the tax collectors will not be so curious, eh?" Jules smiled, but his face was exacting and hard.

Charles shrugged. Bribes to tax collectors were common. "I don't mean to pry." But of course he did.

"My word is good, my business is good." He indicated the room around him. "It is not as if I flaunt my success, no?" Jules burped and a trail of mucus dribbled from his right nostril. "Damn weather has given me a cold. I should have some rum and honey. You are through here, Monsieur?"

Charles nodded.

"Good! Go home to your lovely wife."

"Yes, I'll finish and be on my way."

Jules left Charles and staggered through the door to Drago's.

Charles opened the 'Deliveries' ledger. He scanned the page of December lading and noticed that tomorrow, a shipment of French perfumes was to be picked up directly from Jules's ship on the waterfront. The entry listed a time of 10:30 P.M. Why would a perfume merchant pick up a shipment at night? Then he noticed the buyer's name: M. Bonheme. Charles flipped back to other entries with the strange numbers beside them. M. Bonheme had made a similar pickup three months ago. He was certainly selling a lot of perfume.

❧

The persistent cold spell refused to go away. Charles blew on his numb hands. Across the street, the *Angelica* was moored at a rundown pier. This was the roughest part of the New Orleans waterfront, a place where docking fees were low and a man sacrificed his life for a wrong word. The next pier over, a Belgian three-masted freighter teemed with seamen busily unloading crates. In contrast, the *Angelica's* pier was deserted.

Charles watched patiently as the *Angelica* bobbed in the muddy Mississippi. After two years on the docks of the Thames, Charles knew ships. The *Angelica* was a scruffy little boat, weather-beaten and derelict, probably unsafe for the open water. She clearly hadn't left port in months.

Charles pressed back into the shadows as a wagon rolled to a stop. Jules Drago hopped down, cloaked in a knee-length coat. He sneezed as he ambled along the dock to the *Angelica*'s berth. He crossed a short gangplank and rapped on the cabin door. To Charles's surprise, it opened and Jules stepped inside. The ship had looked completely deserted.

Five minutes later, another wagon arrived. A second man, also in a long coat, proceeded circumspectly down the icy pier. He too knocked and was allowed through the cabin door.

Frustrated, Charles stomped his cold feet. He waited five minutes and realized he would learn nothing from such a distance. He walked quietly down the pier and stopped at the gangplank. Inside the cabin, two voices argued, Jules and another voice he didn't recognize.

Charles slipped across the gangplank and stood outside the door. The voices became clearer.

"You said one hundred dollars. That's what I brought!"

"Captain Bonheme, as you can see, this merchandise is exceptional and demand is quite high. I'm afraid I must say two hundred."

"Jules, you can't expect me to have access to currency at this time of night. And I am leaving for Lafayette straight away in the morning!"

"How unfortunate. Perhaps we could reach another arrangement."

Charles spied a crack in the cabin wall. He inched his way down the slippery wooden deck, careful to counteract the boat's sway. He peered through the crack and saw Jules, who sat comfortably in a cabin chair near a pot-bellied stove. Next to him was a brutish man named Henri, a partner in the Drago Trading Company. The customer, M. Bonheme, was not in plain sight. Neither could Charles see the merchandise over which they haggled.

"What other arrangements are you speaking of?"

Jules stroked his goatee. "You are wearing an exquisite jacket. Lambs' wool, yes?"

"This jacket was a gift from my daughter. I couldn't part with it."

"Ahhh, Monsieur, some things must be sacrificed for others. I suggest you would be passing a superb opportunity." Jules reached behind him into the shadows and jerked forward.

Charles's breath caught in his throat. It was a small girl.

"I can promise you, Monsieur, she came from a village in Crete. She is a virgin, I checked myself."

Christ in Heaven! Bile rose in Charles's throat. The girl couldn't be more than twelve or thirteen. The numbers in the ledger.

Charles studied her anxiously. She was beautiful, brown-skinned and doe-eyed. Her white, ankle-length gown revealed the first hint of young breasts. Teardrops had cut clear paths across her grimy face and her lower lip trembled. Whether from cold or fear, she shivered constantly. Even through the small crack, Charles felt her terror.

M. Bonheme spoke. "You can have the jacket. But let's get on with this."

The man stepped forward to remove his jacket and Charles saw him clearly for the first time. He was in his forties, balding and overweight. Beneath his jacket, he wore the uniform of a police precinct captain.

Captain Bonheme pawed the girl, first squeezing her thin upper arms, then sliding his hands around to fondle her bottom. Her tiny cry was helpless.

Charles stepped back, his mouth dry and foul. A wave of penitence swept over him as he realized he'd helped facilitate this abomination. The feeling was deep and consuming and made his stomach roil. She was so young and defenseless. Charles had been about her age the day his parents had died in a Colchester pub fire. He thought then that nothing worse could ever befall a child. This was worse . . .

Charles clenched his teeth. How could he stop it? The three men would easily overpower him. He could find a constable, but that might take time in this part of the city. And which constable would be willing to arrest a precinct captain?

Charles silently cursed and retraced his steps down the gangplank. Behind him, the cabin door opened. Jules and Henri stepped outside to allow Captain M. Bonheme his privacy. Charles scurried away in the night, but was close enough to hear the girl's plaintive wail as Bonheme more fully inspected his purchase.

Charles could think of only one thing as he hurried through the deserted Quarter: the accounting ledgers. He would turn them over to the police. That would give them the proof they needed to believe his story. He would be implicating himself as a partner, but that was a secondary concern. He had to stop Jules, the sooner the better. And at this moment, he reasoned, Jules was at the docks. He would return to Drago's and pinch the ledgers. Francois would help.

"No, Charlie." Francois crossed his brown arms.

"I must make some ledger corrections."

"You make changes when Jules come back. I don' got an office key."

Charles watched as the bar's only other customers, two Dutch mariners, rose from a table and stumbled outside. "When will Jules return?"

"He don' say." Francois frowned. "But he usually comes back at closing. He don' trust Francois with the money."

Charles' eyes danced from spot to spot. "Francois, I really need to get in there."

"You don' look good, Charlie. Maybe you come back tomorrow when you feel better."

Charles wiped sweat from his upper lip. He couldn't come back. This was the last time he would ever set foot in Drago's.

Francois placed a glass of whiskey on the bar. "Since just you and me here, this one's free."

"Thank you." Charles took the glass and stared intently at his shaking hands. The girl's cry reverberated again and again in his head. Damnation! He'd suspected that Jules was smuggling, but couldn't have imagined human cargo. Francois had known, had even tried to warn him. Money. All for money.

"Francois, I have to get in that office."

Francois cocked his head to a side. "You learn something tonight, Charlie?"

"I did." Charles brought the whiskey to his lips and spoke in a monotone. "Few secrets among partners."

Francois stared with a mixture of curiosity and disappointment. "Partners?"

"That's right," Charles hissed with self-contempt.

"A partner should have his own key, eh, Charlie?"

"I suppose, but I don't."

"Me neither."

Charles slammed his fist in frustration and searched Francois's face, looking for an answer that wasn't there. "I'll wait then."

"For what?"

"Jules."

Francois shook his head. "Bad idea."

"I have to stop him."

"Not alone."

"All I need are the ledgers."

"Jules ain't gonna give you the ledgers."

"I'll tell him I'm taking them home for some final adjustments."

"He'll see it in your eyes, Charlie."

"I'll think of something else."

"Don' sound like much of a plan." Francois sighed. "That door ain't the only way into the office." He pointed at the ceiling. "This building has a crawl space."

Charles struck a match to an oil lamp and the rectangular office was lit by a pale glow. Against the nearest wall was the rickety wooden desk. He tugged on the top drawer. It was locked. Jules would have the key, but that didn't matter. The drawer was coming open, key or not.

Charles unsheathed an eight-inch knife Francois had given him and hacked at the cheap wood surrounding the brass lock. He would remove the whole locking mechanism if necessary. He drove the knife blade completely through the drawer's flimsy front panel. An inch-wide slit cracked open. He stabbed again and again, weakening the panel. He dropped the knife and with his palm, smashed the panel to pieces.

Charles reached inside. The ledgers were there.

Francois nervously polished a beer mug. Charlie was making a lot of noise. Lucky there were no customers . . . Customers!

Francois ran to the door, fumbling for a key in his pocket. Before he could lock it, the door opened. Jules Drago and the beastly Henri stepped inside.

"Francois, you are alone?"

"Last customers be gone about a quarter hour."

"We will close then. Lock the front door."

Francois nodded, waiting for the telltale noise from Charles that would get them both killed.

Henri went straight for the cash box behind the bar. Jules drew out a key chain from his new lambs' wool jacket and approached the office door.

"You goin' in the office?" Francois tried to keep his voice level, but failed miserably.

Jules didn't turn back. "Oui." He unlocked the door. Henri followed.

❧

Jules lit the oil lamp and quietly noticed that the glass casing was already warm. Henri sat at the table and emptied a pouch of gold coins next to a stack of currency.

Jules casually scanned the office and saw that a chair had been pulled in front of the desk. Small bits of wood littered the floor. He sat across from Henri and began to count coins. After a few moments, he spoke in a clear voice.

"You can come out, Monsieur Car-tage."

Henri looked inquisitively at his partner.

Charles slowly emerged from a crouch behind the desk.

Henri slipped a hand into his boot and extracted a long ugly knife.

Jules spoke quickly in French and Henri replaced the knife. He cocked an eyebrow at Charles. "Monsieur? Do you wish to help us count the money?"

"No, I wish to speak with you privately."

"It is a business matter?"

"Yes."

"Your behavior puzzles me. How did you enter this office?"

"If we could speak privately."

Jules made a motion to Henri, who reluctantly lifted his huge frame from the chair. He pushed past Charles and stomped through the door into Drago's. He waited just outside.

Charles inched closer to Jules. His eyes were drawn to the money on the table.

Jules indicated the pile of cash with a careless gesture. "You require Christmas money, Monsieur?" Under the table, Jules's left hand grasped the hilt of his own knife.

"No." Charles was fully to the table. He took a deep breath. "I want out."

"Out?"

"Of the business."

"What prompts such a hasty decision?"

Charles struggled to keep his face neutral. "Other commitments."

"That is most unfortunate." Jules smiled. "Must you resign your partnership? Commitments can be . . . prioritized."

"I'm afraid it's the only solution."

Jules hesitated. "Monsieur, tonight is a full moon."

Charles frowned impatiently. "You superstitious?"

"Me? No, no." Jules fingered the wiry hair on his chin. "It was cold at the waterfront, yes?"

Charles blanched. "I was . . ."

"I almost called to you as you hurried away, but felt it best not to upset my customer." The smile left Jules's face. "Why would you spy on me?"

"Because you let me involve myself in this . . . this . . ."

Jules nodded. "When you left the docks in such a hurry, I suspected you might come here." He pointed at the desk. "The ledgers, correct?"

Feeling like an idiot, Charles said nothing.

"Monsieur, what will be your share of the monthly profit?"

"The profit?" Charles gaped. "A child's life can't be reduced to money, you bastard! How do you live with yourself?"

"I live very comfortably."

"Good bloody well for you. But count me out of it!"

Jules laughed. "Monsieur, you are in New Orleans, not London. If a man pays me for a service, how can it be wrong? Some men seek to explore the mysteries of the young body, to see themselves as young. I help them. It is only business."

Charles breached the line between fear and anger. "Is that your justification? You disgust me." The words spat across the table. "Good bye, Jules!"

Jules was matter-of-fact. "I cannot allow you to make such a mistake."

"What does that mean?"

Jules coolly assessed Charles. "You are thinking of the police, no? The gendarmes are some of my best customers. The man you saw tonight—he will become the commissioner for all city police next year." He flicked his wrist off-handedly. "Why not forget what you have seen? Enjoy the money for a week or two. If you still wish to withdraw, we'll arrange it then."

Charles wasn't listening. His blue eyes sparkled with hate. "The extra numbers in the accounting ledger—children's ages?"

Jules shrugged, his voice guarded but sure. "Some men prefer older, some younger, some prefer girls, some prefer boys. Those who choose boys are my favorites. They pay well to keep their preferences a secret. I do not judge, I merely act as the middleman."

Charles shook his head in disbelief and turned to leave.

"Henri!"

The burly Corsican darted inside and slammed the door behind him. Jules spoke calmly in French.

Henri's eyes narrowed. "Oui." A grotesque grin creased his face. He bore down on Charles, his arms spread wide like a bear.

When the mountainous man was nearly upon him, Charles thrust a pointed boot directly into Henri's genitals. He screamed. Charles tried to slip around him to the door, but despite his agony, Henri swiped with a powerful arm and sent Charles tumbling back toward the center of the room.

Unhurt, Charles regained his feet. Behind him, Jules stood from the table. Only Charles's heavy breathing broke the silence.

Henri straightened at the waist with a grimace. The blow to his genitalia inevitably did its work. A thick stream of vomit poured from his mouth and formed a viscous yellow puddle on the floor. He grinned at Charles and spat.

Charles was trapped. He cursed his own stupidity.

Henri took a halting step forward, then another. Charles made a desperate decision. He spun around and dove at Jules, pounding his fists furiously into Jules's face. Many punches missed wildly, but several connected, sending the Corsican staggering backwards. Together, they crashed into the table and money sprayed in every direction.

Charles pressed the attack, but Jules recovered quickly. He hammered several short jabs into Charles's face. Charles thrust himself inside the taller man's reach and seized Jules's greasy black hair. He pulled downward, smashing Jules's nose on the top of his head.

Jules reeled away clutching his face. The force of the impact left Charles dazed, and before he could turn, Henri swarmed him from behind. Charles struggled and kicked, but Henri slipped two arms beneath his shoulders and locked ten fingers behind his neck.

"You will die, Monsieur," Henri's heavily accented English oozed into Charles' ear.

Jules moaned, his face hidden in his hands, blood and tears spilling between his fingers. He slowly dropped his hands.

"You fool." He reached to the floor and arranged a row of gold coins in his palm. He wrapped his fingers tightly and slammed a weighted fist into Charles's stomach. Charles coughed and doubled over, but Henri righted him. Jules delivered another punch to the kidney. Charles cried in agony.

"You think I care about little girls and boys? They are nothing!" Jules raked a heavy backhand across Charles's mouth, ripping a gash on his lower lip, then pummeled him repeatedly in the face. Charles slumped forward. Jules placed a hand on Charles's forehead and pushed back, exposing his neck, preparing to crush his windpipe.

Helplessly, almost mercifully, Charles drifted away, knowing the next blow would kill him. In the recesses of his mind, he heard a voice.

"Stop that." Francois stood at the door, a flintlock pistol in his right hand. "Let Charlie go."

Jules and Henri turned in unison.

"He tried to rob me," Jules offered.

"No, I don' think so." Francois surveyed the scene before him. "You do all this, Charlie? You fight like a mongoose, eh?" Francois chuckled, his normally vapid face animated.

Charles could only acknowledge with a gurgle.

Jules was thinking quickly. "We'll need a new partner, Francois."

"I don' wanna be no partner."

Jules breathed heavily, his broken nose making a whistling sound. The gold coins in his fingers clinked to the floor, several landing in a pool of blood at his feet. "Francois, that's my dueling pistol. Have you ever fired a gun?"

"Not today."

"It only fires one shot. Parlez vous?"

"Yeh, but I don' think you want to die 'cause I'll shoot you for sure. Parlez vous?"

Jules searched Francois's red-rimmed eyes. "Let him down, Henri."

Henri released Charles who dropped to the floor. His eyes were both swelled nearly shut, and he could see Francois only through a red haze.

"Cock it, Francois," Charles croaked.

Perplexed, Francois realized his mistake and pulled back the pistol's hammer. "Thank you, Charlie."

Jules took a slow step forward. If the gun wasn't cocked, it probably wasn't loaded either.

"We let him go. Now drop the gun."

"Stop or I pull this trigger."

"Francois, you've been smoking opium again, haven't you?" Jules was calm, in control.

"I smoke, I don' smoke. That no reason to kill Charlie." Francois waved the hefty pistol. "Charlie, come over this way."

Jules sprang forward. His move was fleet, but not unexpected. Francois calmly aimed and pulled the trigger.

Click! Jules froze for a split second. Pleased to find no hole in his chest, he resumed his charge. He drove Francois hard to the floor. After a brief struggle, Francois screamed in agony as Jules's knife found traction on his throat.

Henri dashed across the room, but Francois's life had already begun to slip away.

Jules rose and spat on the dying barkeep.

Charles struggled to his feet, his vision blurred, his side searing from the kidney punch. The Corsicans turned to face him.

Jules panted. "And now for you, Monsieur." He waved his knife. "First, your tongue, then your ears, and finally, your eyes."

Charles took a step backward on trembling legs. Remembering his own knife, he slid a hand into his back pocket and unsheathed it, but kept it concealed behind him. The windowless room offered no escape. His only hope was to draw them away from the door. He stepped back again and both men obliged him, Henri advancing first, Jules on his flank. Charles retreated around the overturned table until his heels touched the wall. He was cornered.

Henri approached on one side of the table, Jules the other. Henri dropped into a crouch intent that Charles not slip past him. He was so close, Charles could smell his rancid breath. Henri lunged forward.

Charles anticipated the move and stepped neatly to his left. He brought his knife up and plunged it deep into Henri's chest. The heavy man's eyes opened wide as he crashed into the wall. He tried to breathe, but instead made a rattly noise. He crumbled to the floor, slowly drowning in his own blood. Charles ripped the knife free and turned to face Jules. His battered face spread into a grisly grin. "Now it's a fair fight, mate."

With a roar, Jules thrust his knife at Charles's head. Charles ducked and brought his own knife slashing upward across Jules's chest. Jules grimaced and backed away.

Charles was low, ready for the next assault. Jules charged again, this time more cautiously.

Charles evaded the thrust, but his strength was waning. He circled the table away from the wall to the center of the room. Jules was quicker and blocked his escape. He hissed and thrust twice with his knife. Charles retreated too far and tripped over the leg of a chair, falling hard to his rump.

Jules dove for the kill, but was too slow. Charles rolled sideways and gathered his feet. With a grunt, Jules too regained his own feet and tried a wild, slashing charge. Charles fell to a knee and thrust his blade hilt-deep into Jules's side.

Jules shrieked and fell face down, his hands splayed out, knife clattering away. Panting, he reached for the handle protruding from his abdomen. Charles grabbed it first. With a deliberate, digging motion, Charles tore the knife free. Jules shrieked as perforated organs discharged into his bloodstream. Moments later, he was dead.

Charles dropped to the floor, his head spinning. He surveyed the carnage around him and fought the urge to vomit. Three dead bodies . . . Then he saw the money—gold coins and paper currency scattered everywhere. And a leather pouch. On hands and knees, he collected the coins. A deep pain pulsed in his kidney, and he had to stop and rest. Some coins he had to pick from the congealed blood, the sight of which made him dizzy. He felt his strength slipping away. When he'd collected all the coins, he scooped a few paper notes and left the rest. He rose to his feet and stopped. The reason he was here in the first place rushed back—the children. What should he do? With Jules and Henri dead, he concluded the business would cease to exist.

Across the room, Francois was bunched in the doorway, his eyes open in death, a semi-circular cavity across his throat. Charles withdrew the front door key from Francois's pocket. "Thank you, my friend," he said quietly.

Charles stepped outside and didn't notice the night air had grown colder. He was thinking that Jules's other two partners would surely search for him. He would be safe for a few hours, a day maybe. He would have to leave New Orleans.

He locked the door to Drago's and tossed the key into the gutter.

18

"Grandpa Carthage did *that*?" Andrew couldn't imagine his grandfather, the old patriarch with the odd British accent, in a death fight with Corsicans. What was a Corsican?

"He did."

"He was so small."

"But a different man in his prime, smart and tenacious."

"Did your mother know that story?"

"She spoke vaguely of it a few times. She knew part of it, but not everything. In fact, a couple of times I felt as if she was trying to gain information from me." Winston's face clouded. "Come into the study." He grabbed his cane and lumbered from the great room. Andrew followed.

Winston went to a painting on the study wall, one of his own creations, showing Brown's Lake and the magnificent magnolia tree bathed in a summer sunset. He clumsily removed the canvas and frame from the wall. Behind it was an iron safe.

Andrew was shocked. A day of revelations. "Where did that come from?"

"Father had it built years ago."

"Do you know the combination?"

Winston chuckled. "I do." He reached up and spun the combination spindle past zero and stopped at the number 10, which Andrew quietly noted. Winston unknowingly shifted his body left, blocking Andrew's view.

"How does it work?"

"Hmmm?"

"The combination." Andrew tried to sound casual.

Winston talked over his shoulder. "Left past zero, right past zero, left past zero."

"That's it?"

"Well, you must know the numbers in between."

The safe clicked open and Winston fished around inside. He removed a tattered leather pouch with a drawstring that he carried across to his large desk. Andrew glanced inside the open safe, but saw nothing in its dark recess. The door was swung fully open against the wall, so he couldn't see the combination's last number.

"Here." Winston gently loosened the drawstring and turned the pouch upside down. Two gold coins clattered onto the desktop.

Andrew was spellbound. "Are those the ones he—?"

"The very same." Winston offered one of the coins.

Andrew took the heavy, smooth gold specie and examined it in his palm. The printing denoted a U.S. five-dollar gold piece mint marked 1807. The bottom half of one coin was smeared with a dark film.

"What happened to this one?"

"That's blood."

"Whose?"

"Either Father's or the Corsicans'. He didn't know for sure." Winston paused. "Before he died, Father instructed that Jeremy and I each take one of these as a keepsake. Since your uncle is no longer here to claim his, one should belong to you."

"Which one?"

Winston shrugged with a faint smile. "They're both the same."

Andrew examined the coins. Each had a likeness of a woman's head, on one side wearing a band which read "Liberty," and an eagle on the other side surrounded by the inscription "5D. United States of America." Only one of the coins was smeared with blood.

"This one."

"I thought you might say that."

"May I take it?"

"Not just yet. We'll leave it in the safe a while longer."

"May I come and look at it sometime?"

"That would be fine. Just ask."

"Thank you."

"You're welcome."

"Father, what else is in the safe?"

"Records mostly, deeds of title, a few other items."

"May I see?"

"When the time comes."

"How big is it?" Andrew couldn't let go.

"The safe? Not very."

"Can't I look inside?"

"Some day." Winston became serious. "You mustn't tell anyone about the safe. I don't even allow the servants to dust that painting. I tell them it's my favorite and not to touch it."

"It *is* your favorite, isn't it?"

"I suppose."

"It's nice," Andrew agreed. "I won't speak of the safe, Father." *But,* Andrew said to himself, I *will* learn the combination.

"Father?"

"Yes?"

"Thank you for the story."

19

June 9, 1859

On most spring days in New York's financial district, a slender woman in a gossamer dress and a feathered sun bonnet would draw attention. The district ratio of men to women was high. Of the few women employed here, some were bright to be sure, but a significant number were beautiful ladies looking for a rich husband. The men, of course, were keenly aware of such women and not above using that situation to their advantage.

The well-dressed woman who happened along today was Sophia Anacoste Reese. Unlike most district women, she wasn't seeking a husband, and she certainly wasn't pretty. Her fine white dress and plumed bonnet did little to stir the imagination. She was thirty, a recent widow, and she maintained an account at the Merchant Bank and Trust, as had her late husband. She presented an interesting challenge few men dared to accept, a complete role reversal in the district's normal romantic structure. Men were accustomed to the pursuit of money, and when they succeeded, they became the object of attention. Their money demanded it. But Sophia was the daughter of Benjamin Anacoste, one of the wealthiest men in the country, a manufacturing baron. The district men knew her, knew of her father's empire, yet still couldn't bring themselves to court her, and by proxy, the Anacoste millions. Their disinterest went beyond her plain looks. Her strong personality intimidated most suitors.

Sophia was intelligent. She had excelled in school as a child, her cognitive skills superior to most of her classmates at an exclusive upstate girls school. She was good with numbers and facts, her mind quick and decisive. Yet despite her mental acuity, she was then, as now, unnoticeable. That fact didn't dampen her spirits; she was remarkably self-sufficient and independent. Perhaps these qualities came from the security of her father's money, or perhaps she had inherited his personality traits long before she would inherit his wealth. She was a devout Catholic. She loved the church and everything about it. Her childhood heroes, after her father, were always the priests in her diocese. In any event, she was strong-willed and self-assured, her lack of beauty less a concern to her than to a weaker woman. So, as usual, she strolled the financial district with barely a second glance from the clustered businessmen, shysters, and nobodies.

Sophia entered the MB&T lobby on Monday morning as always to withdraw her self-imposed twenty dollar weekly allowance. Her savings account, roughly four thousand dollars, was an inheritance from her late husband. In the eight years since her marriage at the late age of twenty-two, she'd not asked for nor received any money from her father.

"Good morning, Mrs. Reese," called a bored teller.

"Hello." She pulled a withdrawal slip from the stack and began her weekly ritual.

❧

Jeremy crossed the MB&T lobby on the way to his third floor office. Near the stairwell, a woman in a white dress fumbled with a writing quill and a withdrawal slip. She was plain, her eyes too big for her face, her nose thin and pinched at the end. She looked at him briefly and did a noticeable double-take. Jeremy smiled, pleased to turn a woman's head, even an ugly one.

"Excuse me, sir." Sophia spoke in a hesitant voice.

This Jeremy ignored.

"Excuse me!" Her voice rose an octave.

He couldn't ignore *that*. "Yes?"

She fidgeted, obviously with nothing to say. The paper in her hand saved her. "Could you help me with this form?"

"Ma'am, one of our tellers will gladly assist you." He pointed dismissively across the lobby.

She never looked away from his face. "Yes, but the tellers are all so busy." Her blue eyes were frank and uncomfortably perceptive.

"What seems to be the problem?" he asked. He tried to look away, but she held his gaze as she might that of an embarrassed small child.

The corners of her mouth turned up. "Was that so hard?"

Jeremy's smile was flustered. "You are Miss . . . ?"

"Mrs. Sophia Reese." She studied him for a reaction. "I've had an account, or rather my husband and I had an account here for years. Now it is only I." She passed the form with her left hand. "Where do I indicate the withdrawal amount?"

Jeremy studied the diamond cluster on her ring finger. Sophia Reese—why was the name familiar?

"Here under 'Transaction Amount.'" He was close enough to smell her perfume.

"You've been very helpful. Who are *you,* by the way?"

Jeremy extended his hand. "Jeremy Harper, Loan Officer for Commercial Accounts." He was an *assistant* loan officer, but she needn't know.

"An officer, no less." She primly allowed him to shake her hand. "To hear my father, business loans are the foundation of progress." Her odd stare was mixed with something else, an intellectual curiosity maybe.

"True enough."

"Thank you again, Mr. Harper." She turned away with a wispy smile on her lips.

Jeremy watched her advance to the teller's cage and shrugged. He wondered briefly about her money, but decided she probably didn't have enough to interest him. More importantly, he could tell that she was a complicated woman, and complicated women were essentially worthless. He climbed the stairs to his third floor office, Sophia Reese soon forgotten.

On the next Monday, a cool morning, Jeremy bounded into the MB&T building and again was confronted by Sophia Reese, in a blue sun dress and a straw hat. He regarded her from the corner of his eye. Her long brown hair was curled meticulously, her face enhanced by a touch of cosmetics. After a few drinks, he surmised, she might be passably attractive. But at 9:00 A.M., he was sober. He quickened his pace through the lobby and almost reached the stairwell.

"Mr. Harper!"

Too damn slow. "Good morning, Mrs. Reese. A pleasure to see you again." He reached for the handrail.

She fixed him with the same odd look as before. "*Please* tell me I don't have to wait in this insufferable line just to withdraw my twenty dollars."

The "insufferable line" amounted to two people. "It should only be a minute, Mrs. Reese." Jeremy placed his foot on the first step.

"When my husband was alive, he handled our financial matters." Her eyes twinkled and she still stared.

"We all must make adjustments. Part of the mourning process." Jeremy reached the second step.

"Do I appear in mourning?"

He smiled. "Not especially." The third step.

"It's been thirteen months. Not a day passes that I don't curse the late Mr. Reese for stepping off that curb. He was run down by a team of horses on Thirty-fourth Street."

"How tragic." The boob probably committed suicide. A team of horses . . . Reese . . .?

"Quite untimely."

She continued to talk, but Jeremy was climbing the stairs again. He reached the landing and bumped into Dean Tully, his former unknowing mail room accomplice.

"Talking to Mrs. Reese, sir?"

"Yes, Dean." Jeremy brushed by him.

"All that money . . ."

Jeremy stopped. "What did you say?"

"Didn't you know? Her father is Benjamin Anacoste, the industrialist."

Dean stepped aside as Jeremy rushed back down the stairs. She was still waiting in line.

"Mrs. Reese!"

"Yes?"

"Mrs. Reese, I hope you won't think me too forward, but would you be interested in lunching with me today?"

"I would, Mr. Harper."

Four Weeks Later

Jeremy sought details in the cavernous Catholic church. Flowers, a great multitude of colors and scents, lined the aisles of the nearly empty cathedral. Gray daylight filtered through the stained glass windows, rain having obscured any hope of an outdoor reception. A dozen relatives, all Anacostes of one description or another, sat primly on the bride's side. The groom's side, save Jeremy's boss, Mr. R. T. Stanton, was empty.

Jeremy had always imagined his wedding day differently, more pageantry and fanfare, a social event of note. These childhood expectations went unrealized as he grew older. Such a waste to commit to a single woman forever. Prostitutes were relatively inexpensive compared to the cost of marriage. Sophia had changed his mind. She was not beautiful, and her personality was aggressive and self-assured, traits Jeremy found unladylike. But she did have an appealing maiden name, and despite her intellect, a glaring blind spot with regard to his character.

Jeremy and Sophia's romance had been a whirlwind affair. She'd grown to love him almost immediately, her affections genuine and deep. Jeremy encouraged her though he loved her far less than he loved himself. She was a conduit to wealth, a means to an end. And she might give him a son one day, something on which, strangely, his advancing years placed greater emphasis.

In the front row of the cathedral sat Benjamin Anacoste, the bride's father, a man who measured his money in millions, an empire built on the manufacture of ball bearings, boiler plates, and steam pipe fittings. His eyes were sad and watery, his swarthy skin rough and pockmarked. He looked at Jeremy and obliged a smile that Jeremy returned.

Jeremy knew Benjamin Anacoste was sickened to be here. The old man was obviously more perceptive than his daughter with regard to Jeremy's character. Jeremy didn't really care. He was accustomed to others thinking poorly of him. He had learned to take comfort in it.

He sucked on a peppermint candy to hide the whiskey on his breath. The old bastard Anacoste didn't trust him now, but if it took a year or five years, Anacoste would come around. Jeremy would *not* be left out of a will twice.

The priest flowed into the cathedral. A pipe organ sounded.

Jeremy's lips curled into a smile.

20

July 16, 1859

The July sun was yet only warm. By noon it would blister, by three it would humble all living creatures. Sam Morris tried to keep his hand away from his face but couldn't.

"Stop it!"

"All right!"

"The rash will go away, Sam." Winston suppressed a chuckle.

"Yes, I know."

"Stop scratching it."

Morris pulled his hand away from his cheek in disgust. "A *heat* rash, the doctor said. How the hell do you cure a heat rash during the hottest month of the year?" He frowned. "I was supposed to have an engagement tonight."

"What happened?"

"I canceled."

"Because of a rash?"

"Yes." Morris was indignant.

"With whom do you no longer have an engagement?"

"The cashier from Ackerman's."

"Lovely young girl."

"She's eighteen."

"And you?"

Morris grinned. "Less than twice her age."

"It's good that you have prospects. Have you ever thought of marriage?"

"I was married once."

A smile rippled Winston's face. "Do tell."

"For two inglorious years in Huntsville. Her name was Dollynn, a lawman's daughter."

"What became of her?"

"She was a shrew in the mornings, I was a drunk at night, we just . . . didn't like each other. So I left."

"That was it?"

"Yes." Morris fought the urge to scratch. "Ten years ago. Never tried again."

"You don't mind being alone?"

"Not really."

Winston frowned. "I don't care for it at all."

"You have Andrew." Morris snapped his fingers. "I just remembered. The Widow Harris asked of you yesterday."

"Do I know her?"

"Her husband was a physician, passed away two years ago. She's very attractive."

"And?"

Morris sniffed. "And nothing. She asked of you. Take that as you please."

"I'm really not . . . it's still too soon." Winston's eyes wandered. "I wish I could think of other things, other women, business responsibilities. Whenever I'm able to distract myself for a few minutes, something always takes me back to Elizabeth."

"It's only been six months."

The air thickened with silence and humidity.

Winston forced a different subject. "I saw Andrew scolding an overseer yesterday for being careless."

"Interesting."

"He's only fifteen, but damn, he was right."

"Probably like you at that age."

"No, he's very much like his grandfather. You know he's been seeing a young lady?"

"Catherine Parker?"

"Yes."

"Are his intentions serious?"

"Hard to tell with Andrew. He doesn't speak of her often."

Morris nodded, but could stand it no longer. He raked his fingernails across the rash in exquisite agony.

"Where are you going so early?" Winston stood in his house robe on *Magnolia*'s front porch.

Andrew brought the carriage to a stop. "I'm visiting Catherine."

"For a social call?"

"Not so much. We're taking a carriage ride this morning and perhaps lunch in town afterward."

Winston frowned. "Sounds pretty damn social to me. Unescorted?"

"Is that improper?"

Winston rubbed at his unshaven cheek. "If Mr. Parker doesn't object, neither do I."

Andrew grinned. "Well, I'm off."

"Mind your manners."

"Yes, sir!"

"Where are we going?" Catherine showed Andrew her perfect teeth. Her green dress and matching sun bonnet were brilliant in the morning light. Up close, she smelled delightfully of cherry blossoms.

Andrew forced his concentration back on the road as he maneuvered through a rut. "I thought we might ride to Washington Street and watch the river."

"Watch the river do what?"

"Flow, I suppose."

"How romantic." She giggled. "Maybe we could go to that pond near your house."

"Brown's Lake? There's not much to do there but fish."

She fiddled with her skirt. "Or swim."

His mouth fell open. "What about your clothes?"

"I wouldn't want to get them wet." Her face was guileless.

"Oh." Andrew's body temperature increased measurably. "That lake water is dirty." For some reason, he couldn't stop his mouth from saying it.

"That's true." She sighed. "Let's just look at the river then."

"No! I mean, we could swim. It's certainly warm enough. But sometimes my father goes to that lake. I wouldn't want him to see you, you know . . ." Andrew felt his face flush.

"Are you all right?" She was smiling at him and patted his knee, a gesture replete with possibilities.

Andrew's blood detoured from his brain to points south. Sweat collected at his temples. "I'm fine." He pulled his suitcoat over his lap and tried to recompose himself. "Let's ride to the lake." He tried not to sound urgent.

Her lips pursed. "Never mind. I did bathe just this morning." And with that, she dismissed it.

"We'll go another time, when we know my father isn't there."

"Fine." She now seemed bored with the entire notion.

Andrew's brain swirled. What had just happened? Had they really been close to swimming naked together? And had he *talked her out of it*? It would've been dangerous. *So what?* Swimming would've almost certainly lead to other things. Was he ready for that? Not really. He needed more time to prepare. *Prepare?* How could he possibly be any more prepared? Catherine dominated his thoughts, her long supple legs, her emerging breasts, her seductive blue eyes. He often imagined her as his wife, mother to his children, mistress of *Magnolia*. He fantasized about her. He had dreams about her that ended in messy frustration. If he was not now prepared, he never would be. But what if she were toying with him, had suggested a swim merely to see his reaction?

He looked at Catherine from the corner of his eye, unable to stare directly for fear that she would see into his mind. Her untroubled faced was bathed in morning sun, oblivious to his inner turmoil.

21

November 5, 1859

"Father? Lou? Anyone?" Andrew's voice pierced the silence of the huge house. No answer. "Father?" he called again as he strolled through the great room to his father's study. "Lou?" Still no answer.

He ducked into the study, his heart beating rapidly. On the inside wall, he studied the painting of Brown's Lake and the magnolia tree, pleasant and innocuous, but with a secret. He grasped the frame and lifted it from a brass hook. The safe door gleamed. He gripped its combination spindle and turned counterclockwise once past zero to the number 10 and stopped. He frowned and turned clockwise past zero again to six, then rolled back the other way to one. The combination, 10-6-1, did not work. He began again and substituted two as the last number. And three, and four until he'd checked every possible third number through fifty-nine.

Six was not the combination's second number. The entire process had taken about fifteen minutes. Nervous and sweating, he replaced the painting. Sooner or later he would try all 59 possible second numbers until he found the correct one.

Carriage wheels rattled across the front driveway. He raced to the window and saw his father. He rechecked the painting, then ran from the study through the hall and out the back door.

DECEMBER 12, 1859

Winston scanned the newspaper headlines. Since Elizabeth's death, he had more time to follow politics, but less inclination to do so. Southerners talked of secession. Northerners debated whether to let the Southerners leave or to enforce the Constitution as they interpreted it. Opinion writers from both sides of the Mason-Dixon fired editorial volleys back and forth, their words puerile and sniping. Abolition versus slavery, states' rights versus nationalism, the rhetoric was untenable.

Southern sectionalism would ultimately be a fatal rip in the national fabric. Neither side would stand to gain, indeed both had much to lose. Thus, Winston had concluded a reasonable man should fear secession and a wise man prepare for it. But how?

22

JANUARY 2, 1860

At 9 A.M. on the year's first workday, Jeremy's chin sagged into his upraised palms. The New Year's Eve party Saturday night had lasted until almost 3AM Monday morning. A scant six hours later, he sat at his desk, his stomach foul from a two-day drinking binge.

Jeremy regarded a stack of papers on his desk with disgust—loan applications—piddling requests for a hundred dollars here, two hundred there, things he'd neglected to do before the Christmas break. The new year did not make the paperwork any more interesting and his current condition guaranteed it would remain untouched for at least another day.

A knock landed heavily on his door.

Jeremy raised his eyes in agony. "Yes?" he asked thickly.

R. T. Stanton thrust his enormous frame through the door. "Happy New Year, Jeremy. May I have a word?"

"Absolutely. Happy New Year to you, sir." It paid to be unctuous in the business world.

Stanton was dressed in a dark blue suit cheerily adorned with a red carnation on one lapel and crumbs from his morning pastry on the other. "Did you have a nice holiday?" he wheezed while negotiating his hips into a chair.

"Yes, sir, very nice. We made the round of parties."

Stanton nodded disinterestedly. "How is your lovely wife?"

"Never better. You were a newlywed once, sir." Jeremy winked.

"I do remember." Stanton forced a laughed. "Actually, I'm here to discuss business."

"Business?"

Stanton squirmed uncomfortably. "Important developments."

Jeremy was in no condition to dance with words; it was all he could do to sit straight. "Was there something specific, sir?"

Stanton's round eyes darted about, unable to rest complacently on Jeremy. "You've done a fine job since you came to work here," an assessment both men knew was ludicrous. Jeremy's laziness was rivaled only by his apathy. "I'd like to discuss your future at MB&T." Stanton exhaled as he spoke.

Jeremy's stomach churned. Was Stanton firing him? Shit, not today. "Mr. Stanton, I hope my position here—"

"How would you feel about a vice presidency?" Stanton interrupted.

Jeremy's mouth fell open. On a better day, he might've hidden his incredulity. "My position would be . . .?"

"Development of new corporate accounts." Stanton grinned cleverly.

Jeremy relaxed as the reality of his promotion became plain—the Anacoste money. "I could do that."

"That's why I think you're right for the job," Stanton gushed. "You have enviable connections. Perhaps you can develop clientele in the industrial sector."

Despite such a miserable start to his day and year, Jeremy was suddenly quite pleased. Stanton was Stanton again, the obsequious and incompetent capitalist.

"Mr. Stanton, may I be candid?"

Stanton's head bobbed up and down, his chins expanding and contracting like accordion bellows.

"I've been approached recently by . . . competitors." Jeremy clasped his fingers together and formed an arc on which rested his stubbled chin. "Like you, they've come to recognize my talents." He let this sink in, hoping he didn't have to elaborate.

"What are you saying?"

"I have many options to consider."

"Are you leaving MB&T?" Stanton's round face paled.

"I'd rather not. Are you prepared to make a competing offer in terms of compensation?"

Stanton gulped. "Let's see . . ." He tried to calculate a suitable raise in his head, but was helplessly slow with numbers. "Two hundred dollars per month."

Jeremy smiled. "That should do for now. Where will my new office be?"

❧

Crack! A spike buck two hundred feet distant dropped to the earth.

Winston lowered his rifle. "Think your father has lost his eye?"

"Luck. Pure and simple."

Winston chuckled. Andrew had already missed two shots.

They walked across a flat piece of *Magnolia* terrain to where the deer lay. Steam rose from its hide in the chilly morning air.

"Through the shoulder. Nice shot."

They field-dressed the animal for Curtis to retrieve later and began the long walk back to their wagon. Winston asked for a short rest. They sat on a fallen log near a tiny pond.

"Father, may I invite Catherine Parker to dinner Saturday night?"

"Certainly."

Andrew tossed a piece of bark into the pond. "Did I mention she might travel to Europe this summer?"

"For what purpose?"

"To study at some school in Paris."

"How nice for her."

"I don't think it's so nice," Andrew mumbled.

"Why?"

Andrew's face was suddenly glum. "I've been courting her for almost two years."

"That isn't unusual."

"We'll both be seventeen this year."

Winston nodded. "Have you discussed marriage?"

"Indirectly. She speaks around the subject when I raise it."

"Women are that way."

"Sir?"

"Distant, aloof. It's their means of controlling you." Winston chuckled.

"I don't understand."

"That is because I didn't explain anything. Let me try again." Winton rubbed a hand across his chin. "If a woman reveals her feelings too soon, you might take her for granted. She wants to be pursued, romanced."

"Father, we've done things . . ." Andrew stopped himself. "She has to know I'm devoted."

"Women have different attitudes. Perhaps she doesn't recognize your intentions. Or perhaps she's being coy." Winston shrugged.

"What should I do?"

"I haven't a notion."

Andrew made an exasperated sound. "You're not helping."

Winston laughed. "Next time, select an easier topic."

Andrew enjoyed his father's amusement which had been absent lately. "Father, you should know these things."

"Women were never meant to be understood by men. Don't blame me. God's way of teaching us humility."

They laughed together.

Winston's face slowly grew serious. "This is an area of few absolutes. If you're certain, perhaps you should take the next step."

"Propose?"

Winston raised an eyebrow. "Do you love her?"

"I do."

"Does she have other suitors?"

Andrew nodded. "One that I know of. I think she sees him to make me jealous."

"*Are* you?"

"Not really."

"Good. Jealousy is a squandered emotion. There is an alternative to proposal."

"What?"

"Find another young lady on whom to call."

Andrew considered this and shook his head. "I want Catherine."

"But Catherine doesn't know that."

"Oh." Andrew rubbed his chin much like his father.

"Show her you have options, too."

"Wouldn't that be unfair to the new girl if Catherine is my true interest?"

"Answer yourself this way: is it unfair to that other young man that Catherine is seeing you? Does he feel manipulated?"

"I have no idea."

"I doubt he feels anything but pleased that a beautiful young lady would see him, regardless of the circumstances."

"Such logic doesn't apply to me." Andrew grinned. "I'm not a beautiful young lady."

"You're an eligible young man."

"I don't know . . ."

"You shouldn't rest all of your expectations on Catherine, especially if she is hesitant about committing to you."

"Yes, sir."

"Young women—and young men—don't always know what they want. Give her a little more time, but don't wait forever."

They drifted into silence.

"My damn leg is stiffening." Winston painfully straightened it. "We had better go."

"Yes, sir."

"We must do this again sometime."

Andrew helped Winston to his feet. "I'd really enjoy that."

Winston hated to read newspapers anymore. Each day seemed to bring more ominous news than the previous. Politics the most depressing of all topics, was becoming a farce, a free-for-all dominated by emotions and hatred. His Democratic party, was fragmenting, feeding on itself like a wounded wolf. And the issues became increasingly stark: secession or unity, slavery or abolition, peace or war. Never had an upcoming election seemed more important.

❧

From the *Vicksburg Reader*, May 4, 1860:

The national Democratic Convention in Charleston, South Carolina adjourned yesterday after failing to nominate a presidential candidate for the November election. The presumed nominee, Illinois Senator Stephen A. Douglas, was unsuccessful in garnering sufficient votes to secure the nomination. His failure was generally blamed on his "popular sovereignty" policy in which he expressed belief that newly formed states west of the Mississippi River should be allowed to decide for themselves the issue of slavery.

Reportedly, 57 different ballots were cast, but Douglas failed to gain the required two-thirds majority on any ballot. Convention delegates agreed to reconvene in Baltimore a month hence.

From the *Vicksburg Reader*, May 19, 1860:

The Republican Party nominated Abraham Lincoln as its presidential candidate for the November election.

From the *Vicksburg Reader*, June 25, 1860:

The Democratic party's second convention ended yesterday when southern delegates walked out in protest over repeated attempts to nominate Senator Stephen Douglas. In the southerners' absence, northern delegates promptly nominated Douglas anyway. Southern delegates met separately and nominated their own candidate, Kentuckian John C. Breckinridge, whose pro-slavery views are far more aggressive than those of Douglas. For the first time in modern history, the Democrats will field two candidates, both of whom have vowed to campaign extensively. Their primary opposition in the November election will be Constitutional Union Party candidate, John Bell of Tennessee, and Republican candidate, Abraham Lincoln of Illinois.

23

July 22, 1860

Andrew could hardly stand the anticipation. Today was the day. Their relationship would finally proceed to the next step, he was sure of it. She had written him a note and given it to him after church as she often did, asking if they might meet Monday afternoon. Such a request might seem innocent to a casual observer, but whenever they met secretly, romance was an assumed part of their itinerary. And most recently, she was allowing him to do things, to take small liberties, to touch her in ways that had clear meaning.

Andrew squirmed in the carriage seat to counteract his strained trousers. He was ready. More than ready, he was primed. And it wouldn't be inappropriate or scandalous. They would be married soon enough; that was something they had discussed, though Andrew hadn't formally asked for her hand. But even if he asked her today—and maybe he would—they couldn't possibly be married anytime soon with all the planning required. He couldn't wait. He didn't think she could, either.

He sat in his wagon at their regular meeting place, a street corner in town several blocks from her house. He wondered if she would bring a change of clothes. They had never actually taken that swim at Brown's Lake she'd once promised him.

Andrew leapt to the ground and waited.

A minute later, Catherine arrived, on time as usual. She wore a red silk dress with white ruffles at the sleeve-ends and a high, white-laced collar. Her hair was pinned with pink ribbons and she walked beneath a paisley parasol. The dazzling array of colors was typical for her.

"Hello!"

"Good day, Andrew." She smiled at him. "Is that a new suitcoat?"

"It is." He took her white-gloved hand and helped her onto the carriage. "You look magnificent."

"Thank you." She removed a glove and tested the carriage seat with her hand. It was hot from the morning sun.

"Sit where I was sitting. It's not as hot."

"Ever the gentleman."

Something in the way she said that made Andrew know their moment was near. He sat beside her and lifted the reins.

"Where shall we go?"

"Could we ride downtown? I need to collect a case that Daddy bought for me."

Andrew shrugged. "Easy enough. What kind of case?"

"Oh, just a carrying case, for clothes." She didn't look at him.

"Like a trunk?"

"I suppose."

Andrew twirled this thought in his mind. "Do you have any other errands?"

"No, just the one."

Andrew felt a gnawing uneasiness. She was being distant, which wasn't uncommon, but today was supposed to be special, or at least he'd convinced himself it would be.

"Why do you need a trunk?"

Andrew scratched his nose and regarded the safe. Twenty-eight was the first number to try, almost halfway through all 59 possible second numbers. Two weeks ago, 25, 26, and 27 had proven fruitless. Today, he hoped to reach 30 without interruption. He was in a sour mood. Maybe if the safe opened, his day would improve.

He entered the combination 10-28-1 and tugged downward on the horizontal locking bar. Nothing. He repeated with two, three, and four as the third number. Still nothing. He stopped to stretch his fingers. The tumbler was poorly oiled or something making it very difficult to turn. His fingers and wrist were always sore afterwards.

An hour later, he completed 10-30-59 and the lock bar did not release. Three complete sets of numbers had been eliminated. He replaced the painting and walked upstairs through the empty and miserably hot house to his bedroom. He peeled off his sticky shirt,then his trousers.

Andrew observed his nudity in the full length mirror. He would be seventeen in November, his five-foot-nine, 145-pound body nearly full grown. He didn't like his reflection. His hair was that awful reddish-blonde color and his arms appeared spindly and weak. He longed to be taller, more muscular, like his father. His sparse chest hairs seemed lonely and reflected his current state of mind.

Damn her! Who did she think she was? A year. Nobody went to Paris for a whole year. She said her father was making her go; he wanted her out of the country until talk of secession and war subsided. She would be safer there.

Their day together had ended on a poor note; Andrew was unable to hide his disappointment. She had taken it in stride, implying their relationship could begin again when she returned.

Without thinking, Andrew fondled himself. He closed his eyes in bitter irony and imagined Catherine, who had once stood on this very spot and kissed him with her open mouth. Immersed in self-seduction, he was oblivious to quietly approaching footsteps.

Weekday mornings were Lou's quiet time; Winston and Andrew were usually off somewhere on the plantation. Curtis wandered around, but rarely came inside.

Lou hummed a slave melody to herself, a sad old song made brighter by her pleasant voice. She carried a stack of clean sheets and stopped outside Andrew's bedroom door, unaware he'd come home an hour earlier. She opened the door and was startled to see Andrew, tensely nude, eyes closed, his right hand clutching his . . . The sheets tumbled from her arms to the floor.

Andrew's eyes snapped open in horrible recognition.

"Massa Andrew, I didn't know . . ."

Andrew was too mortified to move or speak; his fair skin turned an absurd shade of red. His hand slipped to his side, but his penis pointed at her like a weapon before slowly dropping its aim. The range of emotions he was experiencing was not unlike his worst nightmare. Without warning, something stirred, something untamed and visceral. Suddenly he was virile and desirable.

Lou watched Andrew's transformation from shock to shame to lust occur in rapid succession. She bent and scooped the sheets from the floor. Her loose-fitting work blouse fluttered free from her neck allowing Andrew the slightest hint of cleavage.

The next moment was profoundly important for Andrew. It all became clear to him—Lou was the deliverer, the one who would show him the way. He stepped toward her hesitantly, his manhood again nearing full attention.

Lou was three years Andrew's senior and a longtime *Magnolia* domestic. She knew Andrew, but the look she saw on his face was so different from any she'd ever seen—confused, aroused, completely *lost*—her reaction was unfortunate, but natural. She brought a hand to her mouth and giggled. And she giggled again. Then she quickly backed from the room. Andrew stared stupidly as the door closed. Her footsteps retreated down the hall, but her giggle became a clear laugh.

Andrew glumly opened his bedroom door and peeked both ways. Three agonizing hours had passed since his confrontation with Lou. Leaving the door unlatched had been unthinkably careless. Lou was just a slave, but she now knew his ultimate shame. She'd laughed. She had read his thoughts and *laughed*. And she was a house servant, there to laugh at him every day.

Andrew slipped into the long upstairs hallway and hastened for the stairs. He looked down through the center of the elliptical staircase and cautiously placed a foot on the first step. It creaked under his weight. Slowly, he reached his toe for the second step. Again the wood protested with a loud creak. He held his breath and charged down the staircase. At the bottom, he raced for the back door. He grasped the handle and pulled it open—and there was Lou, her hand on the other side of the knob, her free arm loaded with a basket of eggs.

Andrew stuttered an unintelligible word and stepped backward. Lou intently studied the egg shells for cracks.

"Massa Andrew." She didn't look up.

Andrew's mouth abandoned him. "Uhhh . . . the eggs . . ."

Lou strove for a neutral tone. "Massa Andrew, I'm real sorry I bust in your room like that." She refused to meet his eye which, in a later moment, he would appreciate.

"Well . . . it's not uhhh . . ." Helpless retreat was his only option. He spun and darted up the staircase.

Lou sighed and carried her eggs to the kitchen.

Andrew opened the large cedar chest at the foot of his bed. This time his bedroom door was securely locked. He dug through a pile of books to a volume near the bottom. This he lifted and turned to the middle where a half-dozen loose pages were tucked away, torn from another book he'd read a year ago, a book about sex.

He scanned the first few pages and stopped. Why arouse himself again? He tossed the pages away. Ready or not, he had to become a man.

Sam Morris blew on his cup of morning coffee and studied the latest edition of his chief competitor, the *Guardian*. Its new editor, an opinionated blowhard, was advocating use of public funds to address the "fallen ladies," the motley assortment of prostitutes who resided at 15 China Street and other District flop houses, and of course, at the Kangaroo. These ladies, the editor blithely asserted, were the product of the city's inaction on prostitution and gambling among the itinerants who passed through town. The itinerants, he wrote, "leave behind the dregs of their maladies. Surely a cosmopolitan city can erase the stench of gambling and its progeny—prostitution, profanity, drunkenness, and human debasement."

Morris snorted. Gambling had been a Vicksburg fixture for decades, and as for prostitution, why would Vicksburg be different from any other river city?

Morris himself was no stranger to Vicksburg's houses of ill fame. A man had certain needs, particularly a single man with no immediate romantic prospects. But for the moment, Morris found himself thinking of the Kangaroo.

The original Kangaroo had been located then, as now, near Glass Bayou just north of town. It had been established in the 1820s—shortly after Vicksburg's emergence as a city of commerce—first as a whorehouse, then a saloon, and finally a gambler's refuge.

Vicksburg's reputable citizens tolerated the Kangaroo until it encroached on their lives, as in 1835 when, during a Fourth of July picnic, a drunken Kangaroo rowdy interrupted the town's celebration with outrageous and lewd behavior. He was promptly arrested, but just as promptly released on bail, whereby he returned to the picnic brandishing a gun and a knife. The picnickers subdued him, and he was publicly tarred and feathered. The incident might have been forgotten, but the man's cohorts from the Kangaroo, "the gamblers," mistakenly vowed revenge. Public outrage, first at the picnic disruption, and later at the veiled threat from the gamblers, reached a critical level. Two days passed before an *ad hoc* group calling themselves the Anti-Gambling Society descended on the Kangaroo. Their intent was to roust the gamblers; the gamblers were just as determined to stay. A bloody riot left six people dead, including the Society leader, a prominent city doctor.

Morris shrugged. Did the *Guardian* editor think he would tilt

Vicksburg's moral balance with a few irate sentences? On the other hand, a serious investigation of the problems might reveal substantial solutions. Morris knew where to start. He would write a story on the latter-day Kangaroo.

24

July 30, 1860

Morris tied the laces on his oversized leather shoes. He straightened in the full length mirror and saw a ten-year-old hat, a tattered shirt, and worn cotton trousers. A three-day growth of brown whiskers shadowed his face.

He grabbed a knapsack with a clean change of clothes and left his small house. After a short walk, he was beyond the city limits on Jackson Road, thankfully not passing anyone who might see his slovenly state. Five minutes further brought him to a fork in the road. He turned right, his anxiety rising with every step. The Kangaroo was not a terribly safe place, particularly for the uninitiated.

Morris pressed ahead. He sweated profusely, occasionally passing a hand over his brow to keep the drips from his eyes. His feet squished in the oversized shoes, and his scruffy shirt was soon soaked through from armpits to waistline.

Jackson Road wound up, down, around, and through the thick woods north of Vicksburg. The road was in fair shape, the wagon wheel ruts as yet not too deep, thanks to a dry spring. Morris stopped briefly and deposited his knapsack behind a tree. He trudged on until he rounded a small curve and was confronted by seven or eight buildings along either side of the road. Each was poorly constructed, in need of paint, but otherwise unexceptional.

He spied a small black boy who sat in front of a rundown stable. The boy appeared to be minding a group of horses tied to a rail. His face was stern and full of responsibility.

"Afternoon!" Morris ambled lazily over to him.

The boy cocked his head sideways. He was maybe ten or eleven with close-cut hair and a flawless brown complexion. He chewed on a reed that rolled from one side of his mouth to the other.

"Whatchoo want?"

"Uhhh . . . well." Morris blanked. What *did* he want? "I'm here to have fun." The words sounded ridiculous, even to him. Luckily, the street was empty save the boy.

Two sharp brown eyes examined Morris's loose trousers, floppy shoes, and a shirt too tight across the middle.

"You in the right place for fun," the boy said.

Morris smiled. "Are you watching these horses?"

"Thass right."

"Very commendable, an honest man's work."

"Yassa." The boy's expression was unmoved.

"Where are their owners?"

"They's aroun'."

"I see. Well, remain vigilant." Morris turned to walk away.

"You here to see the ladies?"

Morris stopped. "I might be. What would you know about that?"

"Black or white?"

Morris laughed despite himself. "White, I suppose."

"You new 'round here, ain't you?"

"What makes you so sure?" Morris wondered if the cheeky little boy was a slave or free.

"I knows the reg'lars and you ain't no reg'lar. And you ain't wearin' your own clothes." He pointed at Morris' feet. "Them shoes ain't never fit you."

"I received these from the public mission in Vicksburg. Indigents like myself are eligible for community charity."

"Indi-gen? Whass that?"

"An *indigent* is a person lacking the basic necessities of life."

"Oh." The corners of the boy's mouth turned up. "If you indi-gen, how come you too fat for your shirt?"

Morris patted his stomach. "I have a glandular condition." My glands, he thought, adore cornbread and mashed potatoes.

The boy nodded. "Them glans is bad. My Daddy had one of them glans."

"If he didn't have glands, he'd be dead."

"He is dead."

"Oh . . . I'm sorry, how did you lose him?"

"He ain't lost. He's in a patch of ground 'bout a mile from here."

"No, I mean how did he die?"

"Got shot over a bottle of whiskey. White man shot him right over there." He pointed at a clump of woods. The boy's wide eyes roamed over Morris. "He liked to have fun too."

"My name is Sam. Who are you?"

"Why you wanna know?"

"Never hurts to know a person's name. You might be a subscriber someday."

"A what?"

"Nothing. Wishful thinking."

"I knows whatchoo thinkin'." The boy stuck his chest out. "My daddy was free. That makes me free."

"It certainly does, and believe me, I'm happy for you."

After a moment, the boy said, "My name's Rufus."

"A pleasure, Rufus. Do you live around here?"

"I live at the ho-tel."

"Hotel?"

"Yep. Up the street. Got my own mattress."

"Congratulations, Rufus. May I ask a question."

"Ax."

"What? Oh, yes. Where is the Kangaroo?"

"Right there."

Morris followed the boy's pointed finger across the street to a run-down two-story building. "Kangeroo" was misspelled in squiggly black letters above the door. The famous Kangaroo—the notorious house of prostitution and gambling, its legend exceeded only by the bawdy Natchez Under-the-Hill district seventy miles south. Morris wished he could've seen this place twenty years ago at its peak.

"So that's the Kangaroo," Morris mused aloud. "Are they open?"

"Roo don' never close."

"What might I expect to find inside?" Morris experienced a wave of apprehension.

"Card games and drankin'."

"What about ladies?"

"Naw, you gotta wait for that."

"Why would—?"

"They got the cleanest whiskey. Card games is mostly honest. But the ladies at the Roo is best. You gots to have money for the Roo ladies."

"Well, thank you for your help, Rufus."

Rufus nodded solemnly. "Be careful."

Morris smiled. "You have my word."

The Kangaroo was a two-story clapboard building, its roof crowned with tin sheets and a heavy layer of tar. The warped green walls badly needed paint and the building's foundation seemed tilted to the left. The ground-floor windows were covered with black blankets from the inside. Glasses jingled and cheap cigars thickened the heavy July air. The swinging front door was adorned by a rendering of a kangaroo, a beer mug in its paw, an ace of spades protruding from its pouch. Morris' sweaty palm landed on the kangaroo's face as he pushed through.

The inside of the Kangaroo was as drab as the outside. The air was smoky and torrid. The low plaster ceiling was crusted with grime, beer stains, and whale oil residue. Gamblers, drunks, transients, at least two dozen men, black and white, were scattered around the large ground floor. This was, Morris knew, the only place for miles where a black man might drink in peace. Warren County was home to a very few free blacks. Morris assumed he was looking at the majority of them. Women, of any color, were conspicuously absent.

To the right were men clustered around two card tables, to the left, a long and crowded bar. Conversation was subdued and the ubiquitous aromas of body odor and cheap alcohol mingled disagreeably. Morris stepped self-consciously to the bar.

An enormous black man poured drinks. He was bald-headed, with thick curly sideburns extending from the tops of his ears to the base of his chin. His full chest was barely contained in his thin, cotton shirt, his smile a dazzling array of white teeth. Morris tried to squeeze himself between two patrons. One of the two, an ugly, mush-mouthed man, resented the intrusion.

"Watch it, you little prick."

Morris was too startled to speak.

"Easy, Billy." The barkeep's mellifluous voice soothed. His teeth flashed again. "I'm Calvin."

"I'm Sam," managed Morris.

"I'm Sam," mimicked Billy. The drunks within earshot chuckled.

Morris stepped back. "Have I offended you, sir?"

"You're working on it," snarled Billy.

"I'll find another place." Morris moved further down the bar and found an open spot.

"This your first time in the Roo?" Calvin appeared, his face a friendly oasis.

"Well, yes, as a matter of fact . . ." Morris followed Calvin's eyes to the door where a young man, a *very* young man, had just entered. He was slight, dressed in work trousers, a cotton shirt, heavy boots. He tried to slide unobtrusively along the wall and blend with the regulars. Every pair of eyes in the room followed his uneasy progress.

Morris turned back to Calvin, appreciative of the boy's discomfort, but more interested in his current mission. "As I was saying, this is my first time in your establishment."

Calvin's laugh was deep and resonant. "Ain't my place. I just work here. What can I get ya, Sam?"

Morris's answer was interrupted by a commotion at the door. Several men jostled each other around the young newcomer. The Kangaroo became silent. Even the gamblers turned in their chairs to watch.

"I was here first, goddammit!" spoke mush-mouthed Billy. Slowly, the other men backed away and returned to their seats.

The young man squirmed miserably at all the attention. Nobody spoke. Sam Morris stared for a moment, then pulled his shirt collar high around his face.

Billy dropped his voice. "Whatcha after, young fella?"

"Uhhh . . ."

"Whiskey?"

". . . mistake . . ." Andrew Carthage tried to slide back to the door, but Billy's arm came up and stopped him.

"A card game? Did you come to play cards?" Billy leaned in close.

Andrew shook his head no. "I was . . . ummm . . . Aren't there women?"

Billy leered through brown teeth. "They're upstairs sleepin' so's they can work at night."

"Oh." Andrew had difficulty meeting the man's eye.

"If it's ladies you're after, I can help," Billy said.

Conversations resumed around the saloon; the boy was Billy's now.

"How can you help?"

Billy ignored the question and studied Andrew's clothes. "What you got by way of money?"

"Uhhh . . ." Andrew quietly wished he'd brought Curtis along.

❧

Across the room, Morris struggled vainly to hear their conversation. Frustrated, he leaned over the bar. "Calvin, do you know that young man?"

The bar keep squinted at Andrew. "Naw, he ain't been here before. Must be the day for newcomers." He chuckled.

"That character Billy is trouble."

"Sam, look after your own self."

"But—"

"Billy ain't gonna hurt him. Not with this many people sees 'em together. He just wants that boy's money is all. Why you interested, Sam?"

"No reason. The boy is so young."

"Forget it. Let me know when you decide what you want." Calvin silently moved away.

Andrew was fishing in his pockets. He discreetly showed something to Billy who dashed up a staircase along the back wall. Half-a-minute later, Billy returned, grinning through his deformed lips and whispering into Andrew's ear. Andrew appeared dazed and said nothing.

Morris saw no valid reason to intervene. Andrew was trying to buy a woman. That wasn't the worst thing in the world. But why had he come here when 15 China Street was so much closer and more accessible? And cleaner. Didn't matter. Morris was content to let Andrew conclude whatever transaction he had arranged with Billy.

❧

Andrew tried to step back from Billy's consuming body odor. He held the ten dollar note tightly in his right hand, wanting to be certain everything was arranged first.

"She'll be right down." Billy's face was disturbing, though he didn't mean it to be.

Andrew nodded. "Where will we go?"

Billy cackled. "Right up them stairs. First time?"

Andrew muttered a non-response. A moment later, the Kangaroo quieted. Andrew looked up. At the top of the stairs, one of the Kangaroo's finest had appeared. He gulped.

The prostitute was dressed in a once-elegant dress, now too old to be glamorous. Her blondish hair was pinned atop her head. She was of average height and weight, mid-twenties, a pretty face. Her eyes were bleary and dull.

The Kangaroo regulars were unaccustomed to the appearance of a lady during daylight hours. Some whistled, others called out lewd invitations for her to sit in various places and on certain faces. She barely noticed. She scanned the room and her eyes settled on the terrified teenager. She winked. The boy was numbly unresponsive.

Morris looked up at the prostitute. He was attracted to her enormous breasts, then her face . . .

The prostitute extended her index finger and beckoned Andrew. The catcalls intensified. Andrew's feet were rooted to the floor. Billy poked him in the arm.

"That's ten dollars, boy. She'll put you right." Billy held out a grimy hand.

Andrew prepared to turn over the note, but was stopped by a loud voice above the din.

"Andrew, how are you, my boy!"

Confused, Andrew sought the source of the greeting. A hand waved at him.

"What brings you out here?"

Andrew's mouth fell open. "Mr. Morris?"

Morris looked up again and made eye contact with the prostitute. Her face registered recognition. They stared at each other for a long moment. Then she stepped away from the stair rail and disappeared into an upstairs hallway.

"Hey, Mary! Where ya goin'?" Billy bounded up the steps, throwing a furious glance at Morris, not sure what he'd done.

Morris approached Andrew. "Shall we go?"

"Sir?"

"I am walking back to town. Care to join me?"

"I . . ." Andrew scuffed a toe against the planks under foot. "Yes, sir." He shoved the ten dollar bill back in his pocket.

Morris placed a hand in the small of Andrew's back and guided him toward the door.

"You!" Billy was charging back down the stairs.

Rufus watched the disturbance in front of the Roo. A small crowd was gathered around two men, Billy and the new fellow, Sam, the tenderfoot. He couldn't quite hear everything being said, but a fight appeared likely.

"Whatchoo go and do, Sam?" Rufus spoke quietly to himself. "Billy ain't nobody to mess with." Rufus the free man—and that would become his name in later years, Rufus Freeman—raised his eleven-year-old bottom from the milking stool.

"Sam, I told you to be careful. You mo' trouble than you's worth."

"I was just looking out for the young man. Friend of the family." Morris was delaying, preparing himself, trying to remember every lesson he'd ever learned from his infrequent boyhood fights. "Billy, I assume you're a reasonable man. What's the sense in fighting?"

On the porch steps, Andrew helplessly watched.

Billy grinned, his brown teeth vivid in the daylight. "You just cost me five dollars, peckerwood. You shouldn't take money from a hungry man."

"That's true. But the Warren County sheriff is a close friend—" Morris's words were truncated by Billy's right fist. He rocked back on his heels, but didn't fall. A cut on his lower lip instantly dribbled blood. Slowly he overcame the shock and raised his hands in a defensive posture. Billy laughed.

"Anybody takin' odds on this fight? I gotta get my money back."

Billy turned left to address the crowd. Morris bunched his right arm and aimed a sweeping blow that Billy easily dodged. He countered with a sharp right hand to Morris's chin, buckling his knees and sending him to the ground. The crowd erupted in cheers.

Andrew moved to help, but two strong hands from behind held him fast.

Morris tried to regroup. Two punches, he thought, two lousy punches and he was eating dirt. He raised himself and stepped back.

Billy advanced with his hands at his sides. He feinted a punch that sent Morris scurrying backward. The crowd hooted. He advanced again and this time threw the punch. Morris awkwardly ducked away and was grazed on his left cheek. Morris bobbed left then right, waiting, measuring Billy's tactics. Billy feinted, then threw a straight right hand that missed Morris altogether. Frustrated, Billy drove in and punched hard, but Morris twisted away.

One of the spectators raised a derisive cheer for Morris. Billy stalked more deliberately. He weaved in and punched, and again Morris dodged. This time, however, Morris countered with a looping left uppercut, a desperation blow that landed squarely on Billy's nose. Billy stiffened and almost went down.

Morris edged backward, amazed at himself.

The crowd was reduced to silent shock. Then a lone whistle echoed and the crowd was cheering again, many now rooting for Morris. Billy rubbed a palm across his nostrils. It came away bloody. He snarled and his eyes became beady slits.

Morris was sure right then and there, he would never see a face as grotesque and hostile. He weighed his limited options—run or seek a truce—when a diminutive yell was heard.

"Fire!" All heads turned north to see Rufus skipping down the street. "Fire at the ho-tel!" A thin wisp of smoke drifted from the last building on the left one hundred yards away.

Fire is the greatest enemy of a shanty town, its thirst for dry wood unquenchable, its devastation absolute. The "hotel" to which Rufus referred was a run-down dwelling with ratty mattresses on the floor where many transients slept, the home most would never know. Several wooden buildings were closely adjacent to the hotel. If the wind blew wrong, fire would consume the entire district in minutes.

The listless crowd sprang to action. Cries of "Fire!" and then "Buckets!" sounded. The fight was forgotten as the crowd charged north, buckets in hand. More men poured from the Kangaroo to help. The upstairs curtains pulled open, and Mary looked out to assess the noise. Six feet separated Morris and Billy, who now stood alone, save Rufus and Andrew.

"We ain't done." Billy's guttural voice made Morris cringe.

"I think you *are* done." Andrew stepped off the porch, his words braver than his heart, but unwilling to let Mr. Morris take more punishment on his behalf.

Billy eyed the unlikely pair, Morris, his lower lip puffy and bleeding, and the fair-haired virgin.

"Don't show yourself around here again." Billy pointed a crooked finger at Andrew. "You either, boy." He reluctantly turned and trotted toward the hotel where he was a current tenant.

Andrew and Morris watched him retreat.

Rufus was tugging on Morris's arm. "Get on outta here, Sam."

Morris didn't understand. "What . . .?"

"That ain't no real fire. Just some old rags I put a spark to. You best be gone before they come back!"

"You created a distraction?"

Rufus pushed Sam. "Right, a dis-faction. Now go!"

"Come on, Mr. Morris." Andrew pulled on his sleeve. They took off at a quick pace. By the time Morris turned to thank the little boy, Rufus was gone.

❧

A mile from the Kangaroo in the deep woods along Jackson Road, Morris stopped abruptly. He slipped behind a tree and reappeared a moment later with a knapsack. He changed out of his old clothes, talking as he did. "What were you doing up there, Andrew?"

Andrew was startled to see Morris stripped to his underwear in the middle of a public road.

"Andrew?"

"What? Oh." Andrew's eyes were at first evasive, then he frowned. "Maybe I was there for the same thing as you, Mr. Morris."

"Don't get pissy with me, young man." Morris sighed. "Andrew, you could get killed in a place like that." His swollen lower lip dripped a spot of blood as he spoke.

"Or beat up."

"That, too." Morris hesitated. "After today, we won't speak of this incident again."

"Yes, sir."

"Good man." Morris cinched his trousers.

"Did you know her?"

Morris stopped in the road. "Who?"

"That prostitute."

"I don't recall. Why?"

"It seemed you knew her."

"She might've worked at Mollie's for a while." Morris had always wondered what had happened to Mary after that night at the River Club. She'd vanished from Mollie's house at 15 China. She'd obviously come to the Kangaroo. Once a whore . . .

"Let's talk about this little problem you're having."

"Problem?"

"Sex."

"I just . . . grew tired of waiting." Andrew kicked at a rock. "The girl I've been courting told me last week that she's going away to Europe for a year, maybe longer."

"That's a shame. Andrew, you know about Mollie's house right?"

"Yes. sir."

"Why didn't you go there?"

"Because her place is in the middle of town. Somebody might see me and then Father would learn of it. He'd be disappointed."

"That's commendable, I suppose." Morris pursed his lips. "You're at a difficult age, but let me tell you about prostitutes, Andrew, from someone who knows. Once you resort to that means of gratification, the habit becomes hard to break. Just ask your Uncle Jeremy." Morris was talking very fast, unable to suppress the adrenaline that still surged through him. He'd acquitted himself pretty damn well with Billy . . .

"I know all that."

"Good. Now we all do things for which we are later sorry. Do you know of the rot?" Andrew did not look at him. "If not, don't learn the hard way. Oooh, that was a horrible pun! Anyway . . ."

Morris clinched and unclinched the swollen knuckles of his left hand, the ache there enormously pleasing.

25

JULY 31, 1860

Milton Green peered intently across his desk. Green was sixty-three and silver-headed, a banker and a gentleman, respected in the business community. He spoke with an easy Southern charm that drew attention away from his quick mind. "What are your intentions, Winston?"

"I want to protect *Magnolia*. And, of course, I want to provide for Andrew."

"Protect *Magnolia* from what?"

"War."

Green frowned in mild disbelief. "That would be bad, I suppose. How would it affect *Magnolia*?"

"The South will lose."

Green's frown deepened. "I see." Which he obviously did not.

"We'll be ripped apart. In the end, the North will dominate us." Winston said this so certainly, Green shrank back in his chair.

"How do you aim to protect yourself?"

"You tell me."

Green stared for a moment, appreciating Winston's directness. "Several alternatives come to mind."

"I'm listening."

"I assume you wish to protect your cash."

Winston nodded. "But I don't want my actions to be public knowledge." Winston searched Green's face for understanding. "People might not accept my lack of confidence in the South's future."

"No one would fault you for guarding your own interests."

"If the secessionists found out, I'd be publicly defamed."

Green chuckled. "You don't give a damn about being defamed, Winston."

"It's not that simple. Better to keep it quiet, Milton."

Green shrugged. "How much money is involved here?"

Winston wasn't yet clear on the amount. "Say fifty thousand dollars."

Green shifted in his chair but his expression remained even. "You'll be making a substantial commitment to your theory."

"What's the worst that could happen? If war never comes, then my money will be safe anyway. As long as your advice is sound."

"Well then," Green smiled, "I know my margin for error." He strummed his fingers on the desktop. "You could invest in a company, but by definition you would lose your anonymity. Ownership of stocks and corporate bonds is public information."

Winston nodded. "I was thinking of privately held companies."

"That's a reasonable alternative, but it carries some risks. Who's to say that company won't be adversely affected by a war? You'd have to select carefully."

Winston waited.

"Or you could transfer your cash to a Northern bank." Green's displeasure with that idea was plain.

"Would a Northern bank be safe?"

"Safer than a Southern bank, if you're right about this."

"I'd like to be wrong."

Green lightly placed his hands palms down on the desk. "Winston, your family's money has been here a very long time."

"No reflection on you, Milton."

Green was already nodding. "That's the last I'll say of it. You can always change your mind."

"Yes." Winston's expression was neutral. "What other options do I have?"

"Overseas. Swiss or Luxembourg banks. Very discreet, very safe. The problem there lies in the fact that your money is not readily accessible."

"In a war, that might not be bad."

"Why?"

"If they can't find my money, they can't take it from me."

"This war hasn't even been fought, and you've already concluded that private assets will be seized?"

Winston's silence was his answer.

"You paint a grim picture."

"You've seen my paintings." Winston smiled.

Green counted off on his fingers. "European banks are an option. Gold would be a viable investment, but you'd have a storage problem. Real estate is always attractive, but where would you buy?" Green hesitated. "There is another alternative . . . rather ironic really." He reached for a piece of paper.

AUGUST 10, 1860

The New Orleans air was dense enough to smell, like an indeterminate swamp odor. The afternoon heat was onerous and penetrating. Winston tried to think cool thoughts. It didn't work. His mistrust of the newfangled streetcars and the fact that he couldn't find a taxi carriage meant he walked. He'd only been a few blocks, but his shirt was heavy with sweat. He dared not remove his jacket, not with the envelope inside. He wasn't nervous, which was odd considering his burden. He shouldn't have taken such a risk, he knew that. But he'd come this far. He was committed. And he was nearing his destination.

Finally he saw it—the New Iberia Bank on St. Charles Avenue. With a sigh of relief, he entered the stylish ground-floor double doors and was greeted by a tall, overdressed man of forty with small dark eyes and an amicable face.

"Mr. Carthage! Good afternoon, I'm Pierre Robinette, the office manager." He spoke with a lilting Cajun accent. "Two o'clock, right on time." Robinette's immaculate appearance was hampered by a missing front tooth.

"Winston Carthage. My pleasure." Winston extended a sweaty palm. Robinette pumped it firmly.

"You had a good trip from Vicksburg?"

"Yes, but I wasn't expecting the heat."

Robinette raised his palms. "New Orleans in August. Can I offer you a drink, something cool?"

"Yes, please."

Winston was ushered into a small, functional office. Robinette returned a moment later with two glasses of tea. They took seats opposite each other.

"Mr. Green wired me last week. He asked my help on a matter he was unable to address himself."

"That's correct."

"Mr. Green didn't specify the nature of your business."

"That was at my request." Winston took a sip, his features as cloudy as the tea. "I wish to purchase U.S. government bearer's bonds."

Robinette smiled at something so ordinary. "Easily done. In what amount?"

"What denominations are available?"

"Bearer bonds are issued in denominations of one hundred, one thousand, and five thousand dollars. The interest paid depends on the amount, higher amounts naturally paying somewhat higher rates."

"And what is the procedure for purchasing these bonds?"

"What amount had you intended to purchase?"

"You answered my question with a question."

"Forgive my impertinence. Typically, bonds are purchased with cash and a receipt is generated by the selling institution. The receipt is forwarded to the U.S. Department of Treasury and from there I can't imagine what happens to it." Robinette absently rearranged small items on his desk as he spoke. "A unique feature of bearer bonds is that they can be redeemed by anyone, not just the purchaser. In other words, he who presents the bonds may redeem them, no questions asked."

Winston knew the answer to his next question, but asked it anyway. "What if I wish to purchase these bonds anonymously?"

Robinette frowned. The expression looked out of place on him. "Strangely, sir, the Treasury requires to know exactly who purchases the bonds, but doesn't care in the least who redeems them."

"How might we circumvent that requirement, Mr. Robinette?"

Robinette's Cajun accent vanished. "This bank didn't earn its reputation through disdain for the law."

"Very well." Winston rose to leave.

Robinette was startled by Winston's abruptness. "Mr. Carthage, before you go, allow me to ask a question that might be constructive."

Winston reached for the knob but didn't turn it.

"Would this relate to a certain lawsuit a couple of years ago?"

Winston slowly took his hand from the knob. "The lawsuit to which you refer is irrelevant. No liens are pending against me."

"Mr. Carthage, if your name is submitted to the Treasury as a bond purchaser, no one need know except you, me, and a faceless government clerk."

"It's you I'm worried about."

Robinette's incessant smile again found reason to cease. His dark complexion went darker. All pretense of civility vanished. "If you don't trust me, why are you here?"

"Banks tend to specialize in confidential transactions."

"This matter will be handled entirely by me, no one else. That's all I can do."

The response appropriate, Winston slowly retook his seat. From his jacket, he tossed a bulging envelope onto Robinette's desk.

"Let's do business."

26

September 1, 1860

Winston sat with Morris on the front porch of Morris's modest Adams Street home. He exhaled a stream of cigar smoke into the damp afternoon air and turned slightly in his chair.

"I received an unusual letter yesterday."

"From whom?"

"A woman named Sophia Harper of New York City. She wrote to ask if I knew a man named Jeremy Harper."

"So?"

"She thinks he is my brother."

Morris sat straighter. "Sophia *Harper*?"

"His wife."

"Incredible. Why is he using an assumed name?"

"He's hiding from me or someone else. But it's him."

"You're certain?"

"Yes."

"Why did she write you?"

"She wants to learn about her husband."

"Seems she already knows."

"She wants me to write her back."

"Will you?"

Winston shook his head. "Jeremy is no longer my problem."

"How did she find you?"

"Private detectives."

"Fascinating."

A hint of concern crept onto Winston's face. "Her letter said that

Jeremy has taken to gambling again, drinking, carousing. The usual."

"What could you do even if you were inclined to help her?"

"Nothing really."

"New York is a world away." Morris was thinking aloud. "Private detectives . . . sort of like private policemen."

"Do you remember Pritchard?"

Morris nodded. "Hard to forget."

"He claimed to be a private detective."

"Oh." Morris squirmed. "Not to change the subject, but Pritchard's name is coincidental."

"How so?"

"When did you last speak with Andrew?"

"This morning. Why?"

"No, I mean when was the last time you *really* spoke with him, man-to-man?"

"I don't understand, Sam."

Morris removed the stogie from his mouth and held it before his face. Tiny smoke ringlets curled away from the end.

"You can't repeat this."

"What?" Winston smiled.

"A few weeks ago, I went to the Kangaroo."

"Really." Winston leered.

"Stop it. I was writing a story. Andrew was there, too."

"At the Kangaroo? Why?"

Morris recounted the entire incident, then said, "The prostitute Andrew was arranging business with was the same one Pritchard hired to frame you at the River Club. Her name is Mary Tisbett."

Winston's hand was clamped around the cigar in his mouth, covering his expression. "Are you certain?"

"Positive. She recognized me."

"Did you speak?"

"I did, but she ran away." Morris bit his lower lip. "Winston, Andrew is a fine young man."

"I agree."

"If he were anybody else's son, I wouldn't have mentioned it. But if something happened because I neglected to tell you . . ."

"You did the right thing. And I won't mention it to Andrew. His girlfriend is going to Europe for a year. That might explain his frustration."

"He told me. Must be difficult for him."

"He was on the verge of proposing."

"He still could."

"Waiting a year would require patience he probably doesn't have. He's at that age." Winston ground out his cigar. "He should've experienced certain things by now. I've been neglecting my fatherly duties."

"Without Elizabeth . . ."

"I can't use that excuse forever. He'll be seventeen soon."

27

SEPTEMBER 18, 1860

Winston had seen alcoholism kill good men, the measles and yellow fever ravage entire families, but he'd never seen an illness as pernicious and destabilizing as Southern secessionism. Normally hospitable and generous men who prayed on Sundays transformed into yattering idiots at the thought of separation from the United States. Fortunately, Vicksburg was not completely overrun with secessionists; in fact, the city was disproportionately pro-Union compared to other parts of the state. But secessionists were louder, and they made Winston nervous.

Turnout for the public debate was impressive, at least two hundred people. The secessionist speaker addressed the crowd. "If we allow the United States government to impose its morals on our citizens, we may as well paint our faces black, because we'll be slaves as surely as any other!"

Half the crowd burst into cheers while the other half was self-consciously quiet.

The Unionist speaker waited for the eruption to die. "What my opponent fails to acknowledge is that we all subjugate part of our personal freedoms in the name of democracy." He was interrupted by a smattering of boos. "We will wither and die as a state if we secede from the Union."

A lackluster cheer rose from the Unionists. Winston rolled his eyes. The Unionist made valid and utterly passionless arguments.

"Never underestimate the power of the government to tax your pocketbook *and* your liberty. Southerners are by nature a self-reliant people. The abolitionists are bound to deprive us of our sovereign right of self-determination!"

Another roar from the secessionists. The bespectacled Unionist eyed his opponent, but was stared down. Winston wondered why Sam Morris, an eloquent Unionist, wasn't here to speak.

The secessionist was emboldened. "What truly frightens me is abolition. What will we do if the slaves are freed? Who'll pick the cotton? Who'll clean the streets? How will we protect our women from those libidinous savages?" This brought a momentous roar of approval.

The Unionist tried to slow his opponent's momentum. "Your fears are unwarranted! The black man is no more a threat than . . ."

His point was lost in the unified chant of the secessionists. "States' rights! States' rights! States' rights!" Even some of the Unionists were swept up in the enthusiasm.

Winston could stomach no more. He estimated not one in ten of the secessionists owned, had *ever* owned, a slave. Most of these fools endured lives little better than slaves themselves, which at least partly explained their fear of abolition. They were small farmers, textile workers, and unskilled laborers. Free workplace competition with blacks would make their lives more difficult. Winston wanted to stand and shout at them, but instead left the hall in quiet disgust.

Sam Morris pulled his hat low over his eyes and quietly watched Winston leave. He felt like a coward. He'd been asked to speak at the debate, but had declined for health reasons. He was in no mood to be hurt. The secessionists were fanatical. No, he would offer his thoughts behind the thin cloak of the editorial page rather than in public oration for all to hear. Safer that way.

Andrew stretched his legs and took a deep breath to ease the tension in his chest and throat. He was alone in the house, but his father would return soon from the political meeting.

He gazed at the cold safe. Serious doubts were emerging a year and a half since he'd first seen Winston open it. What if he'd misread 10 as the first number of the combination? What if he'd misunderstood how the combination worked? All this time would have been wasted. His birthday was in a few weeks. Rooting around in his father's private papers seemed undignified for a seventeen-year-old. His father trusted him. He shouldn't be doing what he was doing. If he ever did open the safe, it would be his secret. He sighed and stepped closer to the wall. The next number in sequence was 48. He spun the dial to ten, spun it again to 48, and back again to one. Nothing. He tried two, three, four, and five. Still nothing. Six through 29 were unsuccessful. When he completed the combination 10-48-30, a click sounded behind the safe door. Slowly, reverentially, he reached for the locking bar and pulled. The bar turned downward. He tugged and the door swung open.

After thousands of combination attempts, he was finally in. He stared for a full minute. Guilt crept into his consciousness. Should he close it without looking inside? The thought was briskly dismissed.

He grabbed the lamp from his father's desk and brought it closer to the opening. He first saw the leather pouch with its gold coins. Under the pouch was a small stack of papers and a large envelope. He hesitated. Well?

He grabbed the stack and carried it to the desk. He began to thumb through the papers. On top was a deed of title to the *Magnolia* property, all three thousand acres of it. Boring. Under that was a Vicksburg Land Bank statement signed by Mr. Milton Green. Better. He scanned the page and from the various columns determined Winston had eleven thousand dollars on deposit. Andrew would have guessed higher.

Underneath the bank statement was a confusing document, a notice from the Jackson Mercantile Bank which stated an escrow account had been cleared for release to Mr. Winston Carthage of Vicksburg. He read further and discovered the notice listed a long string of assets including land, slaves, farm equipment, and most interestingly, eighty-nine thousand dollars in cash, which officially belonged to Winston Carthage. Andrew saw the date, May 29, 1858, and the scrawled signature of Judge

Harold Permutter, and realized he was looking at his father's inheritance, spoils of the lawsuit between him and Uncle Jeremy.

The large clock in the corner tolled the half hour—9:30 P.M. Andrew regarded the remaining stack of items. His father would be traveling home by now. Should he continue until he'd seen everything or close the safe and come back when he had more time?

He lifted several loose papers from the stack and frowned. Something wasn't right. What was it? One piece of paper listed the names and addresses of *Magnolia*'s primary customers, another summarized *Magnolia*'s agricultural output of the last five years. There were other even less interesting documents. Something was missing . . . but what?

He flipped back until he reached the settlement statement. Of course. The money! What had Father done with eighty-nine thousand dollars? It wasn't in his bank account. He hadn't bought any land.

As he went to replace the stack of papers, he noticed a final item he'd missed previously: a large brown envelope pushed all the way to the back. He carried it to the desk. It was six by ten inches, with no address or writing of any kind. He tried to slide a finger under the flap, but the envelope had been sealed by wax. Damn! He flipped it over and could see no other way in than through the flap. Then he spied the red candle on Winston's desk. The envelope wax was red.

He pulled a letter opener from the desk and slid it into the hard wax. In a moment, he was through the seal and the flap was open. Breathlessly, he reached inside and drew out a thick stack of paper. On top was something called a United States Bearer Bond in the amount of five thousand dollars. He counted the stack. Twenty bonds total, each worth five thousand dollars. Andrew gasped—one hundred thousand dollars. So this was where Father had put the money! Why bearer bonds? What *was* a bearer bond?

Andrew held an embossed bond up to the lamp light. It was printed on a thick, rough sheet of parchment, the blue ink raised and impressive. The date was August 1860, barely a month ago. Could bearer bonds be bought in Vicksburg? Why was Father putting his money into U.S. government bonds?

He would dwell on it later. Father would be home any minute. He carefully lit the red candle and resealed the envelope, then replaced it in the safe. As he hung the magnolia tree painting over the safe, he was brimming with questions he dared not ask.

NOVEMBER 9, 1860

Morris glumly read the election returns. John Bell, the pro-Union candidate for president of the United States, had won a significant majority of Warren County's votes—that made Morris proud. However, John C. Breckinridge, the sitting U.S. Vice President and friend of the South, had carried the remainder of Mississippi in a landslide. Neither of the northern candidates, Republican Abraham Lincoln, or Northern Democrat Stephen Douglas, had received a single vote, which mattered little since Lincoln would be the next president.

Morris poured half a glass of sherry. Half-empty, he reasoned, was the pessimistic assessment, but an optimist was simply a pessimist who didn't know all the facts. He shrugged and filled the glass.

"Mississippi will secede from the United States."

"We probably won't be the first state to do so, but I agree." Winston sipped his sherry. "War will follow."

"God help us."

28

From the *Vicksburg Reader*, Friday, January 10, 1861

Jackson—Delegates to the State Special Convention voted overwhelmingly yesterday to secede from the United States. Warren County's Delegates, Walker Brooke and J. Shall Yerger, spoke in opposition to the measure. Their arguments were in vain, however, as the final vote was 83-17 favoring secession. Brook and Yerger signed the secession initiative in a gesture intended to symbolize unity with all Mississippians.

Rumors have begun to surface that Mississippi will join South Carolina, the first state to secede, in a new confederation. Other states, including Alabama and Louisiana, have scheduled votes on the secession issue and are also expected to join the confederation.

February 15, 1861

The new Warren County Courthouse stood on a hill in the heart of downtown Vicksburg, on the site of the original burned-down courthouse, facing Cherry Street to the east, Monroe Street and the Mississippi River beyond to the west. Dedicated barely two months earlier, the stately edifice was a marvel of engineering and architecture, one hundred and twenty-two feet on its sides, eighty feet tall, erected precisely as designed by the Weldon Brothers of Natchez. Each building face was fronted by massive brick-and-mortar pillars bracing a railed portico. On top, a clock tower supported a giant bell and cupola. Simple yet magnificent, the Courthouse gracefully dominated downtown Vicksburg, formidable and protective of its quaint surroundings.

On this chilly winter day, Sam Morris proudly viewed the building and thought it worthy of a poem. But poems were hard to come by any more—secession and talk of war ensured that.

The Courthouse's final cost, almost one hundred thousand dollars, seemed grossly expensive. Morris had written more than a few editorials to that effect. But today was special, and for this brief moment in history, the gathered crowd was willing to suffer the outrage of higher taxes for its existence.

Morris was among perhaps two thousand other county residents who watched and listened in awe as Jefferson Davis spoke from the steps of *their* courthouse. Davis was President-elect of the fledgling Confederate States of America. He was en route to Montgomery, Alabama, the new Confederate capitol. The Confederacy had been a whirlwind creation of only a few weeks, whereby six states had joined South Carolina's secession from the Union. Even now, delegates from South Carolina, Mississippi, Florida, Alabama, Georgia, Louisiana, and Texas met in Montgomery to form a new government. Their first order of business had been to construct a constitution, followed by Davis's election as provisional president.

Davis's farewell speech was being well-received by his Warren County neighbors, and they, to a person, would have denied ever questioning the need for such a majestic courthouse. He was occasionally interrupted by boisterous hurrahs from the admiring crowd. A colorful array of fireworks exploded over the river and confetti streamed through the air to the sound of the Vicksburg Auxiliary Orchestra. This was a crystal-clear political lesson, Morris thought, of how to shape one's image to fit the situation. Jeff Davis was an aristocrat, a wealthy planter, a Mexican-American War hero, a highly esteemed United States Senator, exceptionally smart—hardly the qualities of a seditious man. Yet there he stood, persuading, offering succor, urging the people to accept him in his first public speech since achieving his new country's highest office. And although the speech was lightly sprinkled with political rhetoric, the crowd knew only that Davis was their leader, the rebellion was righteous, and their courthouse provided a damn fine backdrop for a speech.

Morris couldn't help but smile. How much of his own speech did Davis believe? Did it matter?

Davis concluded his remarks and the crowd cheered madly. Even the Unionist Morris found himself clapping.

FEBRUARY 17, 1861

For the first time in years it seemed, Winston laughed out loud. He twirled the fanciful invitation in his fingers. Absolutely hilarious. He had been summoned to the George Washington's Birthday Ball. Every year, the able-bodied ladies of the Mollie Bunch House at 15 China Street held what was essentially the winter jamboree of prostitution. Normal service charges were waived for regulars, and special introductory prices were offered to first-timers. The event was an annual uproar since so many found it inappropriate to equate whores with the greatest man in American history. But, Winston chortled, they were officially no longer Americans, so the insult was meaningless. And he loved Mollie's cheekiness, sending the invitations only days after President Davis's visit to Vicksburg. He wondered with a chuckle if others in town had received similar postings.

"You *have* to go, Winston."

"The hell I do."

"You'd enjoy yourself."

"Doing what?"

"Dare I suggest—"

Winston glowered. "You may *not* suggest."

"Why? You're a grown man, unattached."

Winston's mouth set. "It's too soon."

"I don't mean to be insensitive, but it's been two years. How long must you wait?"

"For as long as my conscience tells me!" Winston grimaced. "I didn't mean it like that."

"Sorry I brought it up."

"Don't let me stop you from going."

"You won't." Morris grinned. "I never miss Mollie's Ball. She serves free liquor. In fact, last year I was too inebriated to avail myself of the other attractions." His eyebrows danced. "Big mistake."

"Perhaps I can participate vicariously through your exploits."

"Vicariously, huh? That's not such a bad idea."

"What's not?"

"You could go as an observer. Partake of the food and drink."

Winston made an exasperated face.

"Why not?"

"I don't know . . ."

"Then you can't think of a reason?"

"Not really."

"Wonderful! We'll go together."

FEBRUARY 22, 1861

Winston's frock coat was dusty from disuse, but by 9 P.M., Lou's magic had made it presentable. Curtis, dressed splendidly in his chauffeur's suit, gathered Winston in the carriage.

The ride to town was cold, but Winston tried to be positive. This could be enjoyable, as long as his trousers remained on. The hell with what people thought. He would drink some whiskey and perhaps meet the infamous Madame Bunch.

Morris waited anxiously on his front porch as Winston and Curtis arrived. He climbed into the carriage. "You said nine o'clock. It's nearly ten!"

"Relax."

"All right, but if I miss anything, you'll never hear the end of it."

15 China Street was a narrow, three-story brick building fronted by a picket fence and a tiny front lawn. It was a somewhat plain building considering its expansive reputation.

Curtis reined the horse to a stop. Music and laughing women could be heard inside. Morris jumped to the ground and Winston, fancy cane in hand, followed him through the front door. Curtis stayed behind to mind the carriage.

The bottom floor of 15 China Street was a merchandise warehouse, a utilitarian place of business crowded with boxes, stacks of cloth, and office furniture. Morris, however, negotiated through this outer facade of respectability to an obscure staircase that transformed a drab commercial establishment into a bawdy bordello.

They climbed the stairs to the second floor and entered what was essentially a giant ballroom, long and narrow. Bright colors and sounds assaulted their senses. Streamers and balloons hung from the ceiling and a roaring yellow fire warmed the room. A brass band played catchy modern tunes. Anxious men dressed in expensive suits dotted the floor. It might have been a cotillion or a society ball. Except for the ladies . . .

Mollie's ladies bustled about in lavish silk gowns and decadently low bustlines, flowery hoop skirts, and frilly petticoats. Some wore silly wigs and comical masks over their faces. Others were dressed in coquettish sun bonnets and pantalets. They flitted among the men, laughing, chatting, leaving suggestive hints and alluring scents. This was their night, easily their most profitable of the year. They were allowed more latitude to drink and dance, to coax and pamper, to do whatever necessary for the highest gratuities. On this night, Mollie allowed her ladies to keep all regular proceeds and customers were encouraged to tip generously. Even though most men came only for food and drink, to see and be seen at the city's most scandalous soirée, the heaviest drinkers won the ladies and usually tipped quite well.

Stone-faced, Winston wondered why he was here. Morris had no such problem.

"Let's find a drink."

"How does she get away with this?" Winston's eyebrows furrowed inward.

"With what?"

"Prostitution is illegal."

"What's your point?"

Winston sighed. "I shouldn't be too judgmental."

"Why stop now?" Morris grinned. "I'm joking. The bar is over there."

They approached a long bar where slaves in white coats served liquor and a stunning variety of food. Morris ordered two whiskeys and surveyed the room. The ladies were especially luscious this year. He was due.

"Winston, if you'll excuse me, I'm going to stroll around a bit."

"Degenerate."

Morris left Winston scowling near the bar. He crossed the room, focused on two large, barely-contained breasts. The lady in question wore a paper mask with a crude likeness of Martha Washington sketched on the front.

"Good evening, Martha."

She silently curtsied.

"Or should I call you Mary?"

Behind the mask, her eyes showed no surprise. "How did you know?" Her voice was abnormally husky and coarse.

"Your bounty is unmistakable."

"I'm flattered."

Morris offered his hand. "Sam Morris."

"Yes." She shook it. Her body language was tense.

"You're working for Mollie again?"

"Temporarily."

"Oh." Morris took a long drink of whiskey and dropped his voice. "Do you remember a day last summer, at the Kangaroo . . ."

"I remember."

"Why did you run away?"

She looked at him, but Morris had no idea of her expression. She breathed deeply and lifted her shoulders. "You called out to me. Why?"

"Because of the boy . . . the young man you were about to conduct business with."

"I wasn't going to hurt him. What was he to you?"

Morris spoke so others couldn't hear. "He was Winston Carthage's son."

After a moment, "Oh," was all she said.

"Might have been a troublesome situation."

"Should I thank you?"

Her sarcasm annoyed Morris. He'd nearly been beaten to a pulp that day. "Maybe you *should* thank me."

She huffed. "Maybe so."

"Next time, I'll stay clear."

"Good."

Morris chuckled humorlessly. "You have a winning personality, Mary. It should carry you far in this profession. Good night."

"Wait, Mr. Morris."

Morris stopped.

Her head dropped. "I didn't want to see you that day or any other. Nothing personal, it's just that some things . . . I don't like to think about. You reminded me of that night at the club." Her hand went instinctively to her throat.

Morris nodded. "Must have been a horrible experience for you."

"I was so scared that man Pritchard would come after me, I moved out of my house."

"Why did you go to the Kangaroo? I mean, it's not that far from town. If he'd been looking for you, he'd have found you there eventually."

She brushed a hand at her hair. "I was assuming he thought I was dead."

"You were lucky."

Her eyes flashed. "He nearly killed me and permanently damaged my throat. I'll talk this way the rest of my life. Does that sound lucky?"

"I apologize."

She fidgeted with her hands. "That was another reason I went to the Kangaroo. My voice was really bad at first. I could barely speak. Mollie said I was scaring away customers."

A drunken couple danced close by, then teetered away.

"Why are you here now?"

"Mollie needed extra help for the Ball. I'll make good money for one night."

Morris shook his head. "It's a living."

"Not lately."

"You've been out of work?"

"That day at the Kangaroo—when you and the boy were there—was my last. I couldn't stand it any more. I had some money saved. I moved into a boarding house."

"But now you're here again."

"It's what I know."

Morris was growing depressed. "Mary, the pleasure has been distinct."

She grabbed his arm. "Don't go."

"Why?"

"Whatever happened to him?"

"You mean . . . ?"

"Pritchard."

Morris hesitated, noting the latent fear in her eyes. "He must've left town. He was never seen again. I think Winston hired some men to track him down, but they never found him."

"Oh." She blinked several times. "I guess I overreacted."

"Not really."

Mary fidgeted some more. "I was glad Winston won that lawsuit."

Morris wondered if she meant it. "Me, too." He tugged at his bow tie. "Speaking of Winston, you might want to avoid that side of the room."

"He's here?"

Morris pointed. "By the bar."

"I see him."

Morris bowed. "Then I'll take my leave. Have a good evening, Mary."

"Bye."

This time, Morris thought she was smiling behind her mask.

Winston finished his second glass of whiskey. The Ball had become more animated. Men were loosening up, talking louder, drinking more, fondling the women.

Morris had to shout above the din. "Are you enjoying yourself?"

"Marginally," Winston replied.

"Don't feel guilty."

"Don't act like my mother."

Morris laughed. "That's the spirit."

"This band keeps playing the same song, over and over."

Morris was staring at a brunette. "I rather like this tune."

"It's making me nauseous. I'm going outside for a cigar. Join me?"

"You go ahead."

Cane in hand, Winston maneuvered through the crowd, down the staircase, and out the front door. He lit a cigar from the candle arrangement on the porch. He could see Curtis on the street, dutifully tending the carriage, and decided to join him.

"Helluva night, wouldn't you say?" Winston climbed aboard.

"Yassa."

"Andrew would've enjoyed this night more than me. In fact—"

When they first heard the noise, it was low, like parishioners chatting before church. Then it came closer, growing more intense. Furious voices filled the air. Suddenly, a riotous amalgam of humanity rounded the Cherry Street corner trundling two fire engines before them. On spying Mollie's brightly decorated house, engine bells screeched and their noise grew to a deafening roar.

Winston thought Mollie's house was actually on fire. But he saw no smoke, heard no screams of terror. He watched the approaching mob more closely and realized the truth—Mollie had simply pushed the city's good graces too far this time. Every priest, every layman, politician, banker, and businessman had received a glossy Ball invitation. The subject of prostitution had been thrust uncomfortably into plain view, and Vicksburg's religious leaders had been none too happy. This mob was their reaction, their statement that depravity had reached its limit. Their mission was obvious: destroy 15 China Street for good.

The mob descended with a vengeance, two hundred strong, teeming around Winston's carriage like a stirred-up mound of ants, men with torches and tar buckets, axes and pry-bars, uniformly incensed. They barely noticed Winston and Curtis who sat, mouths agape, not moving in awe of the furious crowd.

Axes shattered the front door, and the mob charged inside. Most had never set foot in 15 China Street before that moment and were surprised to discover themselves amidst a dry goods warehouse. A few knew the way, and they careened up the center staircase to the ballroom. Once inside, many were secretly fascinated to actually see the source of so many rumors and bawdy stories. But the mob mentality was not admiring and the destruction began. Sofas were broken apart, paintings and drapes ripped from walls, food tables upturned. Mollie's customers, who were fortunate to have not yet begun their serious business with the ladies, were hauled by their scruffs to the front yard.

The mob's original plan was to torch Mollie's house. But cooler heads had pointed out that her building was brick, making it difficult to burn, and more importantly, a deliberate fire might spread to other buildings. A belated compromise was reached. Doors and windows were thrown wide open. The fire engine pumps were primed and 15 China Street was deluged with water.

Winston watched at first in sad fascination; then he remembered Morris was still inside.

"Curtis, I'll be right back."

"You ain't goin' up in there, is you?"

"Mr. Morris could probably use some help."

"Massa Winston, you ain't got no call to—"

Before Winston could move, Morris was dragged out the front door and dumped on the ground. He clung to a prostitute who fell with him. Both were soaking wet in the frigid night air. Several men stood poised with a bucket of steaming tar and a pillowcase of feathers. Morris was being disrobed while the prostitute was held fast.

Winston snatched the carriage reins from Curtis. "Heeya!"

The horse paused, then charged ahead, straight through the white picket fence. People dove right and left to avoid being trampled. The carriage wheels dug wide ruts in Mollie's winter grass as Winston yanked to a stop inches from those holding Morris. They leaped back as one.

"Will you join me, Mr. Morris?"

Morris tugged his shirt free from a man who'd just peeled it from him.

"Yes, I will. This young lady has asked if we might drop her at home."

"My pleasure."

The shirt man found his courage. "You ain't goin' nowhere, fornicator." He grabbed Morris around the throat and tried to push him back down.

Winston withdrew his Colt and pointed it skyward. A shot thundered. Then the pistol was aimed at the angry mobster. The front yard went silent. Scores of people ceased their acts of random destruction. Morris helped the lady to her feet.

Winston's carriage clattered east away from 15 China Street. Morris and the lady shivered on the rear seat beneath an old wool blanket. They were far enough away to be safe, but could still hear the mob, which had resumed its destruction after Winston's abrupt departure.

"Curtis, please drop me here." Morris's breath vaporized in the cold night.

Winston turned. "Your house is three blocks yet."

Morris grinned, "I'm going back."

"If you have a death wish, lie down in the road and Curtis will run you over."

Morris laughed. "I'm a newspaperman and that was a riot."

"Your point being?"

"I must cover the story."

"Haven't you seen enough already? You're soaking wet. You'll catch your death."

"I have a spare suit in my office. It's just a block over." Morris hopped to the ground.

The lady murmured something that Winston couldn't quite understand.

"He'll take you home," Morris reassured her. "Oh, Winston, allow me to introduce . . . Martha."

Winston doffed his hat. "Ma'am."

She grumbled. Winston still couldn't understand her.

"I'm sorry?"

Morris spoke. "She lives at the boarding house, corner of East Street and Fourth North."

"We'll take her there."

"Thank you, Winston. For everything. Good night!" Morris trotted away.

"Good night . . . you moron," Winston muttered. "Curtis, let's get this young lady home before she freezes."

"Yassa."

Mary curled the wool blanket uncertainly around her face. In a few short minutes, they reached her boarding house. She mumbled thanks to Winston and ran inside before he could even see her to the door.

❧

From the *Vicksburg Reader*, February 23, 1861

A crowd of several hundred people descended on the George Washington's Birthday Ball last night at 15 China Street. Fire hoses were turned on the house, and many party-goers were tarred and feathered. The proprietor, Mollie Bunch, is said to be considering legal recourse since the mob used city-owned fire engines to destroy not only her place of business, but also her private residence on South Street.

Madame Bunch was not the mob's only target. Tavern owner Pat Gorman, another long-time thorn in the side of local civic and religious groups, also felt their wrath. Conversely, Mr. Gorman did not accept the assault on his property graciously. Violence erupted and at least one citizen was killed by a gunshot during the melee . . .

29

May 19, 1861

Andrew folded the worn newspaper article and placed it in his pocket. He'd read it a dozen times. It described the first engagement in the War Between the States, as it was being called. On April 15, members of the South Carolina Militia had fired on U.S. troops stationed at Fort Sumter, South Carolina. The Southerners, commanded by a man named Beauregard, had taken the fort, though the battle itself had accomplished little. No casualties had been reported on either side. Some one hundred Yankee prisoners had been captured, but they'd eventually been allowed to leave on U.S. merchant ships. Fort Sumter, formerly a U.S. military installation, was now in Southern hands. That was the most significant result of the skirmish. The Confederate States of America—Andrew liked the name—had officially attacked an outpost of the U.S. government.

Andrew also liked that he was on the Rebels' side. At least he *wanted* to be. He watched wistfully from across the street as thirty-five soldiers climbed aboard the morning train, dressed resplendently in the gray tunics of the Warren Light Artillery. Captain Charles Swett commanded the company, having administered the oath of allegiance to his conscripts only days earlier. They were bound to fight Yankees in the faraway state of Kentucky under God's watchful eye.

Andrew longed to be among them. He'd received a letter a few weeks earlier from Catherine Parker, the first she'd sent in several months. She was doing well in Paris, studying, attending Consulate parties, touring the countryside. She mentioned a young Frenchman, an architect with the city's central planning board. They were to be married in the fall.

Andrew had immediately tried to enlist in the Confederate army, but Winston, recognizing an impulsive broken heart, had forbidden it until Andrew's eighteenth birthday.

Andrew couldn't understand his father's decision. What difference did a few months make? Many seventeen-year-olds were on the very train he now watched leave. He'd considered running away to Satartia or Natchez to enlist, but decided in the end to accept his father's edict. He could last six more months. He'd lasted a year waiting for Catherine. He only hoped the war would last, too. To hell with Catherine Parker.

From the *Vicksburg Reader*, July 22, 1861

> In a bold engagement yesterday on the Virginia dell, the Confederate army lambasted Union troops at a place known as Manassas Junction some 25 miles west of Washington City. The Rebels, under the able command of General Beauregard, repelled General McDowell's advancing Yankees. Casualty figures are unreliable as yet, but estimates place the Yankee dead at nearly 3,000 and Rebel losses approximately half that.
>
> It has been reported that Union politicians rode in carriages from Washington City to the battlefield to witness the certain Rebel rout, but were seen in hasty retreat when fortunes turned against the Yankees.

Jeremy Carthage lifted his card from the green velvet table-top. Slowly, he turned the edge and saw the seven of hearts. With practiced ease, he laid his cards on the table and waited for his opportunity to bet.

The player to his right, a crusty septuagenarian, tossed a twenty-five dollar chip into the pot.

"Quarter to you, Harper."

Jeremy evaluated the bet and the bettor—the old man was cavalier, a bluffer who bet a pair of sixes like a royal flush.

"Plus a hundred." Jeremy spoke smoothly, his voice low and as noticeable as anything he'd said all night.

The raise affected all eyebrows around the table. To Jeremy's left, a druggist from Queens tossed his hand away. And the next player and the next, back to the old man.

"A hundred to me?" He fingered a stack of black chips before him. "Your hundred, plus two more." Three blacks rolled into the pot.

Jeremy's heart raced. "I'll see your two hundred, and three more."

The other players sat straighter at the thousand-dollar pot.

"Well . . ." The old man stroked his chips in thought, seeming to enjoy the moment. "Can I raise again?" he asked.

"That's three already," offered a resigned player.

The pit in Jeremy's stomach widened to a chasm. Raise again? What was . . . ? Suddenly Jeremy reached a hand into the pot.

"I made a mistake—"

Before he could withdraw any chips, no less than three other hands crashed onto his.

"A bet is a bet!" was the druggist's simple admonition.

"I thought . . . we had a table maximum. You know, a hundred was the most . . ." Jeremy stared balefully at the other players. None cared for him. None were in a compassionate mood.

The old man didn't bother to look at Jeremy. "I reckon I'll just call then." He pushed three more black chips into the pot and revealed his hand—a queen-high straight. Slowly, he turned to Jeremy, his craggy face awash in fulfillment.

Jeremy blanched. It couldn't have happened that way . . .

"Well, Harper?" The old man understood Jeremy's expression better than anyone at the table.

"If you'll excuse me," Jeremy whispered, rising from the table. His ten-high straight remained face down. Most of what had remained in Sophia's bank account was on the table. He stumbled from the club without speaking again.

❧

"There you are, Mrs. Harper." The bank teller passed a sheet of paper to Sophia who scrutinized it for an instant.

"This is wrong."

"I beg your pardon?"

"My account balance. It's wrong."

"I'm sorry. Let me check again for you."

Sophia shuddered. Most of her money was gone; Jeremy was the only person with access to it.

The teller returned two minutes later with a sheepish grin on his face. "Mrs. Harper, you were right. I neglected to include a five hundred dollar withdrawal from yesterday. Your current account balance is now six hundred twelve dollars." He noticed Sophia's unfocused look. "I could check again if you like."

"No, thank you," she replied softly. Almost three thousand and four hundred dollars without so much as a word of explanation. She stepped back and looked down at her hands which, she realized, were tightly balled fists. She whirled around and stormed up to Jeremy's third floor office where she found him sitting in front of the window, his feet propped on the sill.

"Good morning, dear." He scrambled to sit up.

"Did you lose at cards again?" Her face was tightly controlled.

"What are you talking about?"

"Over three thousand dollars. My money. Gone."

Jeremy had been waiting for this since he'd first raided her account. "That money was used to repay a loan I secured with the bank before we were married."

"Do shut up, Jeremy. I know about that gambling club of yours. And I also know you're not a good card player; you couldn't be, you lie too poorly."

"Dear, I just told you where the money went. Now if you'd like, I'll *pay* the money back to our account."

Sophia's lips thinned. She would not be put off. She crossed the room and stood next to him, hands on hips, elbows flared wide. "If you take any more of *my* money, I'll have you arrested."

"We hold that account jointly."

"I'm not talking about that! I'll have them raid your club. Only, I'll wait until I know you're there. Have you ever been to jail, Jeremy? I'm sure you'd fit right in." Her voice was loud.

Jeremy squirmed. "We'll talk about this at home."

"We have nothing to talk about. Stop gambling. Stop drinking. Stop whoring!"

Jeremy stood and faced his wife. He spoke in a hoarse whisper. "Get out of here or I swear to God I'll throw you out."

Sophia didn't flinch. "If you touch me, you'll regret it the rest of your life."

"We'll talk when I come home." His tone was quiet, submissive.

"Yes, we will." She stormed from the office.

Jeremy reached into a desk drawer and poured a glass of whiskey. The time was 9:45 AM.

30

October 25, 1861

The town hall meeting had been called to discuss Vicksburg's defensive posture. Should fortresses and breastworks be built? And what of the city's five hundred-man garrison? Was it adequate? Would Vicksburg ever *really* be attacked? These were legitimate questions, but after a short while, the answers began to fall into patterns, weasel-worded political dodges which invariably prompted someone or other from the crowd to opine on the war itself.

Winston was a specially invited guest to the meeting, one of five panelists who'd been given a table alongside the councilmen. He was quite thankful that, to this point, he hadn't been asked to speak, nor had any questions been directed his way. Enthusiasm for the fight didn't reside in him. Others displayed patriotism so easily, automatically. He was pragmatic. His emotional attachment to the South was in stark contrast to his fear of war. He could define no objective that would justify war, no moral or economic spoils worth obtaining at such a price. Still, he was a citizen of the Confederacy, and his country was in crisis. The source of the crisis wasn't relevant. He couldn't change reality. He couldn't surrender on the Confederacy's behalf or seek an audience with Abraham Lincoln.

What presently mattered most to Winston was that Andrew would be joining the Confederate army in three weeks. Winston couldn't stop that. Andrew was committed. And though the shooting war had yet to find Vicksburg and maybe never would, Andrew was leaving, as hundreds of Warren County men already had, men who even now fought in other parts of the country. Casualty lists posted weekly at the county clerk's office were, so far, often blank. That would change.

Presently, no armies threatened Vicksburg and the sounds of death were far away. Which explained the meeting's powerful mood, the sentiments of unity which, Winston had to admit, were contagious—to a point. The nationalistic motifs were well rehearsed—states' rights, economic self-determination, tariffs and, of course, slavery.

Large plantation owners, including Winston, had offered free slave labor for construction of Vicksburg's defenses. Winston's loyalty was shallow. Others were even more disingenuous. They knew too much money was invested in slavery to tolerate outright abolition, and "sacrifice" was better endured earlier than later. Supply and demand, the status quo, these were more powerful than nationalism or states' rights. Patriotism, whether real or contrived, had carried the day. War fervor was being duly promoted. Winston was *very* glad he hadn't been asked to speak.

Sam Morris watched Winston's muted performance with a mixture of curiosity and admiration. His friendship with Winston was misunderstood, but well-known, as were his views of the war.

Morris and other newspapermen were responsible for many questions from the floor. But Morris, like Winston, was adapting; he couldn't sell many pro-Union newspapers in the Confederacy. He avoided branding himself a hypocrite with good old-fashioned realism. He was a Southerner and should act like one. That didn't dissuade him from making a pointed inquiry.

"I'd like to address a question to the panelists." Morris stood and had the room's attention. "What will happen to the slaves if we win this war? Will they remain slaves forever?"

Disapproving groans sounded from all around. Someone shouted.

"How old are you, Morris?"

Morris turned, bewildered. "I'm thirty-four in December."

A second angry voice asked, "Why the hell ain't you in uniform?"

Others murmured concurrence.

"Because I . . ." Morris reddened. It was not an unusual question, and one for which he had no answer.

"I believe the original topic was slaves," Winston boomed over the growing din. "Mr. Morris, we will do with our slaves as we choose. But I envision a day when slaves will be paid wages."

The eruption was immediate. A barrage of questions were hurled at Winston from every direction. Winston listened patiently and answered each question. Forgotten by the crowd, Morris sank to his chair.

31

November 26, 1861

"I'll write as often as time allows." Andrew shifted the heavy bag to his left hand and extended the other.

"Please do." Winston's tone obscured his true emotions. Andrew needed confidence and support, not a blubbering sendoff in front of fellow soldiers.

Andrew's eyes sparkled with excitement. "Lieutenant Reaves says our first assignment will be to join the main company at Fort Pickens near Pensacola. I've never been to Florida. I've never been *anywhere*." He wore the gray uniform of the Hill City Cadets.

Winston smiled. "Remember to heed your officers. They are selected for their leadership qualities. And don't think you must win the war individually."

"Yes, sir."

"People are dying. Violent death can be astonishing to the senses."

"Yes, sir." Andrew paused. "Have you seen violent death?"

"I have."

"But not in a war, right?"

"In a riot. A long time ago at the Kangaroo. You've heard the story." Winston frowned. "My only opportunity to fight was in the Mexican war. Father wouldn't let me. He threatened to disinherit me if I enlisted, saying I was too important to the operation of *Magnolia*." Winston clasped his hands together. "I could make the same argument with you."

"That I'm too important to *Magnolia* or that you'll disinherit me?"

"If you don't want to go, it's not too late."

"Father!"

"Just making sure. Did the Captain indicate the length of your first assignment?"

"Six months before furlough." Andrew hesitated, his eyes mischievous. "Father, I've always meant to ask you . . . I mean we've never really had a political discussion." A corner of his mouth turned up in a wry smile. "Are you a Unionist?"

Winston chuckled. "Why ask now?"

Andrew shrugged, studying his father.

"I support the war effort, son."

Andrew tried, but failed, to interpret Winston's face. "Then you're an unabashed Confederate?"

"What do you think?"

"I think you're smarter than most folks in this town."

"I"m not sure what that means, but thank you."

"Ten, forty-eight, thirty," Andrew said innocently.

Winston's face was blank. "Pardon me?"

Andrew fidgeted and lost his courage. "Nothing."

Winston cleared his throat. "Are you nervous?"

"More worried than nervous."

"That's normal under the circumstances." Winston stepped closer. "Worried about what exactly?"

"I don't know. My convictions."

"The war?"

"Nah . . . I mean, no, sir." Andrew squirmed. "No matter the central issue, whether it's slavery or . . . or whatever, we can't let people in New York or Massachusetts tell us how to live. Right?"

"That's a compelling argument."

"Then it *is* more than just about slavery, isn't it?"

"I think both sides have valid concerns. But I despise the path we've chosen."

"What else was there to do? The politicians have been arguing for years."

"I'm not saying the other side is right either. The thing is that you and I didn't start this war, but if the Confederacy loses, so will we."

"Yes, sir, I see that." Andrew nodded. "But I wouldn't fight a war only to preserve slavery."

"No."

"Then could you excuse me a moment?"

Winston nodded. "Of course."

Andrew set his bag on the ground and approached the family carriage waiting on Levee Street.

"Bye, Curtis."

Curtis mumbled. "You be careful."

"I will. Look after Father while I'm gone?"

"We'll look after each other."

"Yes." Andrew extended his right hand.

Curtis hesitated, then shook it. "Bye, Andrew."

Andrew smiled broadly and turned back to his father.

"I should get on the train."

Winston clapped Andrew's shoulder. "You'll return in May to a hero's welcome."

"Yes, sir." Andrew shuffled his feet. "Father, if something should happen to either of us while I'm away . . ."

"Nothing will happen." Winston's confidence was forced. "We'll see each other in six months, I know it."

Andrew threw his shoulders back and exhaled. "I don't want to be . . . you know, maudlin but . . . I love you, Father."

Winston's heart nearly burst. "I love you too, son."

Their long hug was interrupted by a piercing squeal from the train whistle.

"Goodbye."

"Take care, Andrew."

Andrew hoisted the bag to his shoulder and climbed the depot steps. He waved.

Winston brushed a tear from his cheek as the train pulled away.

❧

Only a few hours had passed, but Winston was already struggling with Andrew's absence. He sipped at his whiskey, trying to remain positive. Andrew was just a boy, really. He should be courting girls, studying, enjoying his youth. At least he was smart. Not everyone could've figured out the safe combination.

Winston removed the magnolia tree painting from the wall. He opened the safe, using Andrew's recited numbers, and extracted the brown envelope. He studied its seal. The wax was two different shades of red. Andrew had discovered the bearer bonds. That was what he'd wanted to say.

Winston cracked the seal. The bonds were all inside, as he knew they would be.

❧

December 28, 1861

Dear Father,

Merry Christmas! I hope your holiday was joyous. Mine was spent here with the fellows on the Gulf Coast. As you know, the Hill City Cadets were ordered to Fort Barrancas at Pensacola, an outpost formerly occupied by the Yankees. We're now a part of the 9th Mississippi Infantry Regiment. We've been playing cat-and-mouse with the Yankees stationed south of here. They are holed up in Fort Pickens on an island across the harbor from us. We occasionally lob artillery shells at each other, but otherwise, there have been no engagements worthy of mention. In any event, rumor has it that we will abandon our position here and move north into Tennessee. I don't know the truth of our future, but we are primed. We drill every day and have become quite proficient in basic military skills. We long to test those skills. Military life is not as I expected. We have much free time, in fact, many are bored to distraction. I'm not among them. I will write again soon.

Love,
Andrew

32

It is not only necessary to have troops enough to hold New Orleans, but we must be able to proceed at once toward Vicksburg, which is the key to all that country watered by the Mississippi and its tributaries. If the Confederates once fortify the neighboring hills, they will be able to hold that point for an indefinite time, and it will require a large force to dislodge them. The war can never be brought to a close until that key [Vicksburg] is in our pocket. — Abraham Lincoln, 1862

"And as you can see, this position controls the river bend." The Confederate colonel gestured proudly at the emplaced cannons frowning down on the Mississippi River. "DeSoto's Point belongs to us, Mr. Morris."

Morris slowly assimilated the view—DeSoto's Point, the horseshoe isthmus formed by the southbound river as it made a sudden turn north, then south again, was named for the explorer credited with discovering the Mississippi. Morris scoffed that someone had discovered the largest river in North America, as if it would have lain hidden forever without his insights. Indians had named the river, *not* DeSoto. In any event, some versions of history said DeSoto had once camped there.

"Colonel, you have prepared admirably." Morris stepped away from the huge guns and strolled along the hillcrest, divining words for an editorial about Vicksburg's defenses. The intense colonel was his guide.

This was indeed a commanding position high above the river. Passing vessels would be vulnerable to withering fire while negotiating the sharp turn. The cannon emplacements were virtually unassailable by land or water and, not coincidentally, located on an old Spanish settlement known as Fort Nogales. These days it was called Fort Hill.

"Would you like a demonstration?"

Morris was surprised to find the colonel following him closely. Inspections were apparently serious business.

"A demonstration?"

"The cannons, sir."

"Call me Sam."

The colonel found such informalities undignified. "We can fire a round if you wish."

"That won't be necessary." Morris hoped these cannons would never be fired at all. Realistically, Vicksburg's bluffs controlled passage on the lower Mississippi River, and Fort Hill was now perhaps the single most important riverfront real estate between St. Louis and New Orleans.

An uneasiness drifted up Morris's spine. He could see it so clearly. The Yankees could not allow Vicksburg to remain unchallenged.

March 9, 1862

Dear Andrew,

Greetings from Warren County. If what I've read of your company's activities is accurate, you are somewhere in Tennessee by now.

You wouldn't recognize Vicksburg. A long line of breastworks now runs in a semicircle from the river north of town around to the south. I provided 20 slaves to aid in the construction for a month or so. Beyond that, my contributions to the Cause have been inconspicuous.

Which leads to my next bit of news. Do you remember the militia group formed about a year ago to aid in Vicksburg's defense? The Old Guard? It is a droll bunch, approximately 50 strong, merchants, physicians, lawyers, the worst fighting unit you could ever imagine. They are a public morale group, nothing more. They invited me to join last summer and, as you might recall, I politely declined, citing my infirmity. I didn't think about it again until several weeks ago when I ran into Jasper Boone, the butcher. He is a rabid Guardsman and asked if I would reconsider my decision to join. I said no and made to go about my business. He suggested that if I wouldn't serve in uniform, perhaps I should provide greater financial support to the Cause. I was in a poor humor that day and asked how much of *his* money was invested in the Confederacy. He mentioned me being the wealthiest man in the county and I replied that he was perhaps the stupidest (he took offense). Our conversation became a shouting match. Jasper seized my lapels, challenging my person. The nitwit obviously didn't see my cane.

When Jasper regained consciousness, he filed assault charges against me. The new sheriff is himself a Guardsman, so I was arrested and spent the night in jail. It was a distinct experience—thieves, rustlers, drunks. Fortunately, my cane accompanied me to jail, and we endured the night without incident. The following day, Jasper and I were brought before Judge Mills, who is not a Guardsman. Perhaps Jasper was still addleminded from the caning for he concocted a thoroughly ridiculous story. Judge Mills put several questions to him, and he was hardly coherent. Charges against me were dropped, and I never had to speak a word in my own defense. Anyway, that is my sordid criminal history. My standing in the city's hierarchy has been somewhat diminished. Fortunately, I do not care.

Magnolia is operating quite well, all things considered. The overseers are doing a fine job. (They hope to avoid conscription when the Confederate legislature votes for mandatory military service.) I've resumed my painting hobby in earnest. I've really not much else to do. I go to Brown's Lake with an easel and a lunch basket. It is a soothing way to spend one's day. The place is quiet now. I wish you were here to enjoy it with me.

You probably have demands on your time, so I won't keep you longer. Take care in all you do. We will see each other soon.

Love,

Father

33

April 1, 1862

Dear Father,

I received your letter and am just finding time to respond. We have been marching steadily and believe it or not, we are back on Mississippi soil near Corinth. Normally I wouldn't reveal our troop movements in a letter, but our location is no secret to the Yankees. They have been following us. Our commanding general, Albert Sidney Johnston, is in a constant maneuvering engagement with the Yankee general, Ulysses Grant. Grant hopes to smash us, but cannot since his army is roughly equal in size to ours, and we would prevail in a straight fight. So he sits and waits for reinforcements just across the state line in Tennessee at a place called Pittsburg Landing. Rumor has it he wants to move south to Vicksburg. If true, he will have to come through me and the Hill City Cadets first.

So here we sit. Only twenty miles of lowland separate us from the Yankees. Our concern is that when Grant's reinforcements arrive, we will be so badly outnumbered, we will have to quit Corinth. I have mixed feelings about such action: I would hate to yield to Grant, but it is distinctly possible that we might retreat south and take up a defensive position around Vicksburg.

I must go now. Please continue to write me, Father. Your letters are a welcome relief from the privations of soldiering.

Love,

Andrew

Andrew didn't say everything he might have. It was true that Grant's army awaited reinforcements and would probably attack upon their arrival. Rumor had it General Johnston was preparing to take the only action available to him short of a full-scale retreat: he would mount a surprise attack against Grant and prevent unification of the converging Yankee armies. It was a bold and dangerous move, one that might turn the entire war in the West. As Andrew signed the letter, he mulled the most pressing rumor currently being circulated: an attack could be ordered as soon as tomorrow. It would be his first real combat.

APRIL 6, 1862

Andrew shuffled quietly through the thick underbrush. He had been marching since 4:00 A.M., almost four miles altogether. The battle had not even been joined and already he was fatigued. But the prospect of combat was a powerful motivator. He and his companions spoiled for the fight. And a fight they would get. Scouting reports indicated that Grant's army was bivouacked a short distance from Pittsburg Landing, near a tiny church called Shiloh.

As dawn broke, Yankee soldiers tranquilly enjoyed their Sunday morning breakfast. Others slept in their tents. Two days of rain had passed. The woods around the Shiloh church were thick and protective, the terrain desolate and unfriendly to intruders. They felt reasonably at ease.

At 6:00, their peace was shattered by a swell of Confederate soldiers roaring from the woods. The Yankees barely had time to grab up their weapons before they were assailed by lead shot and fixed bayonets. Within moments, the first Rebel wave, including Andrew Carthage, surged through the Yankee camps sending bluecoats in frantic retreat. Hastily abandoned coffee pots gurgled over campfires and the rich smell of bacon filled the air. Hungry Confederates broke off their pursuit in favor of the cooked breakfasts. Having marched for hours on little food they couldn't ignore the succulent plunder. Frustrated Rebel officers had to urge their men away from the feast and back into battle. The officers were excited. A stunning Confederate victory seemed within grasp.

❧

Andrew fired his .54 caliber "Mississippi" percussion rifle at a fleeing Yankee figure and ducked behind a fallen log to reload. He yanked a paper cartridge from his cartridge box and bit off the end. The cartridge, about the size of his thumb, was filled with gunpowder, and at its bottom was a lead "minie" ball. He poured the powder and ball directly into the barrel, then used his ramrod to tamp them deeply into the rifle's breech. He half-cocked the hammer and withdrew a tiny fulminate-of-mercury percussion cap, placing it on the rifle's nipple. He fully cocked the hammer and was ready to fire. The entire process had taken twenty seconds.

Andrew had fired his gun countless times, but could not say for certain that he had killed anyone, always lowering his gaze to reload before his mind lingered on the question. The man in his rifle sight was an enemy and couldn't be given consideration.

The reality of combat vaulted his adrenaline. This was war, exhilarating, terrifying. And he was troubled by their assault. The 9th Mississippi was supposed to prevent the Yankee left from retreating to the nearby Tennessee River. Only, the Yankee left was firm; the Yankee *right* was dropping back, shooting and running, collapsing toward the river. Every foot of land on the left was captured at a tall price. Dead soldiers from both sides littered the battlefield like play dolls. War whoops and screeches of pain echoed through the woods. And just as Andrew's senses adjusted to the clamor of battle came the most frightful of all orders—the bayonet charge.

Andrew nervously tested the rusty blade of his twelve-inch steel bayonet. He'd used it to roast pieces of beef over an open fire, he'd thrown it at trees—but he'd never thrust it at a live human being. The ragged Yankee line was close, less than one hundred yards away. And the blue-bellies had found good cover under felled trees, behind dirt mounds and thick underbrush. The Rebels would have to cover an open field to reach them.

At a shouted command, soldiers to Andrew's right and left charged from their positions. Andrew leapt forward with them. After a few paces, many stopped and fired at the indistinct Yankee lines. Andrew ran ahead in the confusion, weaving across the field with his shoulders low. Halfway to the Yankee line, he dropped to a knee and fired. He rolled to the ground, reloaded, and sprang for another charge.

The Yankees were unprepared for such a maniacal onslaught. They fell back as the lead elements of the Rebel charge neared their positions. They retreated even further into the thick woods before their officers called for a rally. With much shouted encouragement, the Yankees responded by mounting a counter-charge.

In a matter of only a few moments, the Rebels succumbed to two prevalent problems—poor organization and fatigue. Their commanding officers were not battle-tested, and the soldiers had eaten little on their march. The counterattack sent them retreating toward their original lines, through a maze of dead soldiers as the Yankees pressed from behind.

Andrew crouched low and ran past what had been enemy positions only moments earlier. As he neared the open field, a seemingly dead Yankee soldier reached up and grasped his foot. So strong was his grip, Andrew fell face first to the loamy dirt, narrowly missing his own bayonet blade. Terrified, Andrew turned on his attacker and raised his rifle in defense.

"Help." The Yankee's whisper was horrible. A private by uniform, only a gaping cavity remained of his left eye. Deep red blood flowed from upper torso wounds.

Andrew tried to draw his foot away. The man gripped tighter. Andrew pulled back and the Yankee dragged with him. Andrew tried to pry his fingers loose. Failing that, he crashed the butt of his rifle into the man's wrist. With an expulsion of air, the Yankee released his grip.

"Please! They'll try to save me."

Andrew looked back startled by the nearness of the Yankees. Most of his comrades had crossed the grass field to their old positions. Many now shouted for him to hurry.

"I'm already dead." The Yankee's facial fissure contorted and blood pumped freely.

Andrew rose to a crouch. "God forgive me." His bayonet split the man's heart.

Just after two o'clock, Fate intruded on the pitched battle of Shiloh. General Johnston, architect of the Confederate surprise attack, was struck in his right leg by a stray bullet. Johnston had suffered a wound in the same leg during the Mexican-American war, leaving him permanently nerve-damaged. He didn't feel the Yankee ball, which severed an artery below his kneecap. Less than an hour later, Johnston died from blood loss, his wound undetected, the tourniquet in his pocket untouched. The Rebel advance stalled.

Andrew was beyond tired. The hellish day that had started so long ago was over. Exhausted men lay in clusters all around him, some wounded, others like Andrew, trying to absorb the day's events. Andrew had killed his first Yankee, a man missing half his face. That face. The battle had raged on, though Andrew wasn't sure of his part in it. He wasn't even sure if he had killed again. He could only remember that face.

The Yankee soldier would have surely died. Andrew had seen such wounds before. A quick death was lucky. Andrew had given the Yankee faster peace. Like shooting a lame horse. The right thing to do.

Andrew shivered beneath his blanket, older, not wanting to be. He fixed on the stars, trying not to see the face in them. He thought of his father, *Magnolia*. He slept.

❧

The second day of Shiloh was a rout. The Union army had seemingly multiplied overnight and with fresh troops came momentum. The disorganized Confederates were driven from the field and sent in a headlong retreat back to Mississippi. Fearing General Grant's army would pursue them, the young and inexperienced Rebel troops rushed for the relative safety of Corinth twenty miles south. Their problems, however, were many. Thousands of wounded had to be withdrawn from the field by any means available. They had precious few ambulance wagons, and those that existed were filled to overflowing. April rains had returned, making many of the roads and trails impassable. Food was scarce and the two-day walk to Corinth forced soldiers to forage for subsistence.

Andrew Carthage slogged alongside a makeshift road that cut through the thick landscape. Draped over his shoulder was the arm of a fellow Hill City Cadet, a heavy-set man named Simmons suffering a severe thigh wound. A tourniquet had slowed his blood loss, but Andrew feared Simmons would lose his leg, or worse. Simmons had fallen late on the second day and Andrew, being closest, had helped him.

They were, at best, only halfway to Corinth. Simmons was in severe pain and becoming feverish. They occasionally met other fleeing troops, but the horror of Shiloh had cast a collective pall over them. Conversation was scarce, visceral fear plentiful. Grant could be right behind them.

In late afternoon's gray dusk, Andrew looked skyward and saw no break in the rain. He was soaked through and had never been so tired. He would have to stop soon, find a dry spot for the night where Simmons might stay warm. It was then he heard the clatter of an approaching wagon. They hadn't encountered other soldiers in some time. Andrew sensed he was toward the rear of the long and disparate Rebel retreat. He guided Simmons into a thicket of trees off the road. Whoever approached was in a hurry.

The wagon emerged fifty yards away. Andrew strained for a better look. It was an ambulance wagon filled with wounded troops; its driver sat on the buckboard, hunched over in a cape against the rain, urging a single horse forward. Andrew whispered to Simmons and they came from their hiding place to stand in the road. As the wagon drew closer, Andrew waved with his free hand, but it didn't slow. When it was nearly upon them, Andrew had to push Simmons out of the way.

"Fool!"

The wagon ground to a halt a few yards past them and gently rocked on its wheels. As they shuffled closer, rainwater and blood dripped from the wagon's rear. The wagon was full, ten men at least, stacked atop each other. Andrew wondered how the horse managed such a load.

"I have a man here," Andrew called to the driver.

"No room. Sorry." A female voice.

He was too tired to be surprised. "He won't last the night in these conditions."

She nodded toward her cargo, her face hidden beneath the cape. "Neither will they unless I get them to Corinth. Your man has made it this far, he'll make it farther."

Andrew ground his teeth. "You have room for another!"

"No. My horse is already struggling with inclines. If she gives out, these men will perish," she snapped.

Neither spoke. Andrew tried to see her face but the rain was too strong. "I don't give a damn about your horse." Andrew began to lift Simmons over the side. He stopped at a sound. The faceless woman aimed a small pistol at him.

"Don't," she said, "or you'll be worse than your companion."

Andrew strained to see her eyes, her mouth, anything he could remember. "You bitch."

She didn't flinch. "Good luck." She clicked her tongue and the horse tugged slowly ahead, then gained momentum.

A day later, near dusk, Andrew stumbled into Corinth, so tired he nearly dropped where he stood. He asked directions and found a livery stable that had been converted to a hospital. There he left Simmons and staggered back into the street.

Corinth was in a state of stunned turmoil. Soldiers milled about unwilling or unable to locate their units. Wounded arrived in wagons, on horses, in the arms of other soldiers, from every direction. Makeshift hospitals dotted the city, in churches, places of business, citizens' homes, anywhere a few men could be attended. Andrew found the discord comforting. He did not have to immediately report to wherever the Hill City Cadets had established camp in this sea of confusion. He wanted to eat and then sleep, and do both to excess. He could return to being a soldier tomorrow or the next day. He would scavenge a meal and find a quiet place to sleep.

34

The rains had finally stopped. Andrew couldn't remember when he'd last been completely dry, but when he woke, his clothes were several pounds lighter. He rose from the wooden planks where he'd slept—someone's front porch—and stretched. Two days of being another man's leg had taken its toll. His back and neck were sore, his feet blistered, his skin chafed raw from the wet clothes.

Corinth was more settled in the early morning. Giant puddles of water covered the streets. Few soldiers were about. Encampments had sprung up outside of town as the fragmented Confederate army tried to regain a semblance of organization. Soldiers moved north to help fortify Corinth's entrenchments against a Yankee attack. Andrew didn't believe an attack was imminent. The second day of Shiloh had seen a Yankee resurgence, but it was a counterattack, not a thrust to destroy the Confederate army. If Grant was coming, he wouldn't have waited three days. The Yankees were probably regrouping at Pittsburg Landing in a scene very similar to Corinth. Such was his rationalization for laziness. He was too exhausted for digging breastworks right away. Today, he would visit Simmons, scrounge a good meal or two, and rest. His short and unofficial leave of absence would end soon enough.

By midday, Andrew had seen all there was of Corinth. He was bored and hungry. As he wandered a muddy, nameless street, he passed a group of officers who surrounded a wagon. A woman—a remarkably striking woman—listened as a Confederate colonel explained the army's need for her horse and wagon.

"Colonel, you have no claim to this wagon. I won't give it to you."

Without noticing, Andrew strolled ankle-deep into puddle. That voice . . .

"Miss, you don't fully comprehend our situation. We—"

"Colonel! I drove this very wagon twice to Pittsburg Landing. I brought back twenty-three wounded men all told. I've since learned twenty-two are alive and expected to recover. Don't *tell* me I lack comprehension!"

The colonel retreated a few paces to consult with his fellow officers. Andrew recognized the wagon, the unmistakable voice, but this was wrong. The woman who had left him on the trail was a bitter old hag, a mule-faced whore hiding her shameful countenance behind a cape, trading wounded for gold. But this woman had volunteered, had brought on herself the pain of seeing things a woman should never see. And her face . . . was like a window to Heaven, high cheeks, full lips, a perfect nose. She was presently frowning, but Andrew knew it was unnatural for her. This was a woman who liked to laugh and smile. How could such an exquisitely beautiful woman have threatened his life? He stared far too long. She turned his way and seemed not to recognize him. She returned her attention to the colonel.

"I *will* be going now, sir."

"Ma'am, I have orders."

"Clear a path, Colonel." She cropped the horse and trotted straight through the startled officers. For an instant, she looked back at Andrew, then turned a corner and was gone.

"Sir, what is today?" Andrew asked a passing elderly gentleman.

"The thirteenth."

"What day of the week?"

The man snorted, "Sunday," and kept walking.

Sunday. He had lost a day somewhere. He had officially been away from his company for three days. They probably thought him dead. Or maybe lost. Occasional stragglers still arrived from Pittsburg Landing.

He determined to remain lost for one more day. And one more day of living on the local economy was all he could afford. He knew the Hill City Cadets had bivouacked north of Corinth and were presently helping construct outer defense works. But Andrew was fully convinced that Grant would not attack Corinth soon. So he considered himself expendable.

He walked the same streets he'd walked for three days, only now he looked for a house of worship. The churches all seemed to have been converted to hospitals. When he reached the outskirts of town, he retraced his steps. He neared a small house just as the front door opened. From it walked a woman, *the* woman. She pulled the door closed and fiddled with a sun bonnet. Again, he was astounded by her beauty. She wore a black cotton dress and her shoulder-length brunette hair disappeared beneath the bonnet. She was short, under five feet, and slim. She looked to be of Andrew's age, give or take a year. She stepped from the front porch, making the briefest eye contact.

"Staring is impolite." Her voice was much softer than when she'd spoken on the trail, a Sunday school teacher's voice or a librarian.

Andrew hesitated, searching for the anger of their first meeting. "Threatening a man with a gun is equally impolite."

She nodded. "It *is* you. You passed the house earlier. And in the street when they attempted to confiscate my wagon." Her expression was direct, neutral. "Are you following me?"

"I am not." Andrew's mouth turned down. "I was considering an apology for what I said to you on the trail."

"Your friend lived?"

Andrew turned away from her. To look at her clouded his thoughts. "Simmons lost his leg but is expected to live."

She watched him and spoke. "Had he boarded my wagon, we might still be stranded out there with one dead horse and many dead soldiers."

"That was not your decision to make."

Her eyes—calm before—quickened, but she didn't respond.

Andrew shifted from one foot to the other. "I hoped to attend a service this morning, but the churches are filled with wounded soldiers."

"You don't strike me as a churchgoer."

"And why is that?"

"You cannot contain your vulgarity," she said.

"You left us to die." Andrew stopped, feeling like a dullard for antagonizing her.

She fidgeted with a pair of gloves. "Good day to you."

"Is this your house?"

"No."

"Whose then?"

"A friend."

"Your husband is away?"

She shook her head at him, her tone derisive. "That's the clumsiest attempt I've yet heard to learn my marital status."

Andrew couldn't argue since she was right. "Forgive my presumption. Good morning." He strolled away as casually as his pride would allow.

"There is a church service in Iuka," she called after him.

He wheeled around. "And where is that?"

"About twenty miles east of here."

Andrew's chest heaved. "Thank you, but I can't walk twenty miles. Why are you smiling?"

She hesitated. "I'm going that way. That is, if they will allow me to leave this city with my wagon."

"And?"

"What is your faith?"

"I currently have no preferences."

"Iuka has a nice Baptist church."

"Will I arrive in time for the service?"

She nodded. "It is at five o'clock. That is where I worship. Iuka is my home."

They passed through the Confederate picket lines east of Corinth without incident. Andrew told the sentries he'd been ordered to search for wayward soldiers who might've been lost trying to find Corinth. The sentries stared long at the lady beside him, but didn't ask to see written orders. As they passed, one of the sentries winked at him.

They rode in silence, she trying to keep the wagon from bogging down in the mud, he thinking how divine she was.

"How long is the trip?"

"Three hours if we're lucky."

That was good. "Perhaps you could tell me your name."

"Emily."

"Emily what?"

Her shoulders tensed. "Emily."

"As you wish. I'm Andrew."

"Pleasure."

"Likewise."

Long minutes passed without a word, though Andrew wanted to hear her talk. Her voice had a low harmonic quality, soft and clear.

Her eyes settled on him. "Why are you so insistent on going to church?"

Andrew took a breath. "Personal reasons."

"Such as?"

He leaned back in the seat, kneading his hands together. He didn't want to discuss himself. He wanted to hear the laugh that accompanied her voice. "I haven't been to a proper service in a long time."

"Does your company have a chaplain?"

Andrew gazed at the horizon. "Easter came and went. Just another Sunday."

She watched him closely. "What else?"

"Nothing."

"I don't mind listening as long as you're not too personal."

"What troubles me is very personal." He shifted. "At Pittsburg Landing . . . I killed a man."

She looked ahead. "Your first?"

"Yes."

"But he was trying to kill you, too."

Andrew shook his head. "He was mortally wounded. He begged me to kill him."

She searched his face. "That must've been dreadful."

"Dreadful, yes," he said. And a dreadful topic of conversation. "It's a glorious morning."

"Quite."

"How much further?"

"Ten miles or so." She brushed at a fly buzzing her head. "You're staring at me again."

"Again?"

"You have been since we left Corinth."

"Soldier's prerogative."

"I am uncomfortable. Please stop." Emily self-consciously adjusted her bonnet. "If you won't stop, then you must handle the reins."

He took them from her. "You never told me about your husband."

"And I shan't."

"Then you *are* married."

Her face noticeably paled. "Leave it be please."

"Myself, I've never been married, though I was engaged once. Engaged is the wrong word. Promised is more—"

"I'm a widow," she said abruptly. "My husband was killed at Fort Henry." Her mouth turned down.

"I am sorry for your loss—"

"That's kind but unnecessary. He is two months gone, and I have begun to accept it."

Andrew was losing count of how many times he had said the wrong thing to her.

"Tell me about Iuka."

She reluctantly smiled. "I actually live outside of Iuka. We will pass my home shortly."

Her smile was warmer than the sun. "Are your parents there?"

"Father passed away many years ago. My husband and I lived with Mother before he enlisted."

With each word she spoke, Andrew's enchantment grew.

They stepped into the cool evening with a handful of other Baptists, almost all women save a pair of elderly gentlemen. Andrew's presence with the recently widowed Emily had drawn stares and whispers, but she had paid them no mind. She allowed Andrew to take her arm and lead her down the church steps.

"That was a bracing service."

Emily nodded. "Was it like your own church?"

"Similar. I am Presbyterian."

"You never told me where your home is."

"Didn't I? I felt I talked all afternoon. I am from Vicksburg."

"You did talk all afternoon." She smiled. "And what do you do in Vicksburg?"

"Farming."

"I fail to imagine you as a farmer. You are wealthy."

"My father is wealthy. He has a large plantation. How could you tell?"

She laughed for the first time and his heart danced. "Money isn't difficult to spot," she said lightly. "You carry yourself differently from other soldiers."

"I hope that's a compliment."

"It is not an insult," she said. "Your education, the quality of your uniform, your manner of speech."

"Is there anything else about myself I should know?"

"You are about to step in a pile of horse dung."

Andrew avoided the dung. "I saw it."

"As you saw that puddle in Corinth?" She didn't look at him. "You're staring again."

"Forgive me." They reached her wagon and he helped her climb up.

She seemed to hesitate before speaking. "Would you like to see our home? Mother will feed you."

Andrew beamed. "That would be nice." Then his face was puzzled. "Did we pass your house coming from Corinth?"

"Yes."

"Why didn't you point it out?"

She laughed again. "I chose not to interrupt your soliloquy. I know everything about your first six months of military service, your political inclinations, and your taste in food."

Andrew laughed with her. "It's coming back to me."

"My house is a few miles from here. We should go while there's light."

They rumbled west out of Iuka into the evening sunset. Just as darkness enveloped them, she stopped at a small house. A sign out front read "Gardner" in the moonlight.

"A charming house, Emily Gardner."

"My married name is Broomfield." She flashed an easy smile. "If you're taken with the house, perhaps you would like to buy it."

Andrew hopped to the ground and held out his hand for her. "You are selling?"

"Mother and I can't make much of a living here. We only have twelve acres, mostly bottom land."

"Where will you go?"

"We haven't decided. Finding a purchaser will be difficult. War has lessened the demand for worthless real estate." She stepped through a small gate. "Mother doesn't appear to be home."

They approached the front door. Emily knocked to no answer. She opened the door, and they stepped inside. Emily went to a small table and lit an oil lamp. There she found a note.

"Mother is staying with a friend for a few days. She wasn't sure when I would return and does not like to be here by herself."

Andrew's eyes were roaming the modest but comfortably furnished house. "You shouldn't be either."

"I'll prepare something to eat."

"Then what?"

Her arms crossed her chest. "Then you will leave."

Andrew spoke too quickly. "Is there a place I could—"

"No, not at all." She was firm.

"I have grown accustomed to sleeping on porches."

"Andrew, I have created enough scandal for one day. If someone were to pass by and see you . . ." She left the thought unfinished.

"Of course. I will start back to Corinth after we eat. I can sleep along the road."

"You will be two days walking back to Corinth." She paused, thinking. "We have a barn. You could sleep there."

"That would be helpful."

"And I will take you halfway to Corinth tomorrow."

Andrew couldn't believe his good fortune. He would spend another day with her.

❧

Their return trip the next day progressed too quickly. Andrew urged a wagon wheel to break or the horse to lose a shoe. Anything to extend their time together. He wanted to spend the rest of the week with her, the whole damn month. She was the most mesmerizing woman he had ever met, beautiful and self-reliant, smart and feminine. He tried to remember the traits he'd once found attractive in Catherine Parker—her untouchable beauty, her delicate mannerisms, her social station. She was a flower to be admired and never owned, a chaste tease. Emily was equally attractive, maybe more so, but knew her own mind and was at ease with herself, not the kind to encourage a man then dash his hopes for the sheer spirit of it.

"Please stop for a few minutes." He *had* to do something.

"We're almost to the halfway point."

Andrew squirmed in his seat. "Please."

She reined in the horse. She looked at her hands, then at him. "Andrew, I appreciate your attention, but I am a very recent widow."

"I didn't mean to be overbearing." Andrew's mouth ticked. "How long were you married?"

"Why?"

"Curiosity."

She set the wagon moving again. There was a hint of doubt on her face, as if she were judging the propriety of his question. "Nine months."

Andrew nodded. "Were you sweethearts before?"

"Sweethearts." Her dimples appeared. "A winsome word."

"Pick a better one."

"I know what you are asking. Our relationship was very short. My husband courted me for six months. He was new to town, and I had few suitors." Her voice trembled. "But I did love him."

"I never meant to imply otherwise." *Again* he had said the wrong thing.

She turned away. "Walk from here."

His heart shrank. "If that is what you want."

"It is."

He climbed from the buckboard. "Will you be in Corinth again?"

She turned the wagon around quickly. "I think not."

Andrew felt a sense of panic. "That is twice!" he called to her.

She looked over her shoulder. "Twice?"

"You've left me in the middle of nowhere."

Her smile was faint. "Good-bye."

35

April 11, 1862

Winston had read of the awful battle of Shiloh, how the first day belonged to the Rebels, and the second to the reinforced Yankees. The Rebels had been forced from Tennessee back to Corinth, their starting point, not destroyed but defeated nonetheless. In ground won or lost, the battle was a draw, as if it never occurred, twenty-three thousand dead, wounded, or missing men notwithstanding.

Winston heard speculation among local war-watchers that the Yankee command staff was upset with General Grant for falling victim to a surprise attack. Winston had little to contribute to these discussions except that it now seemed Grant, whose ultimate destination had always been Vicksburg, would be delayed.

Winston was far more interested in Shiloh's casualties. Andrew had not been listed among the dead, but for the first time in the year-long war, the list was long. Andrew might have been wounded.

Winston was there when the ambulance train arrived from north Mississippi bringing wounded soldiers home to Vicksburg. For hours, it discharged an awful cargo. The handful of corpses being trundled from the train hadn't died in battle—they were the severely wounded who had perished during the long ride home. Those killed in combat had been abandoned where they fell, later to be buried in mass graves by the Yankees.

Winston held his breath, praying Andrew would not be among the fifty wounded as they were taken to makeshift hospitals all over the city. The process was excruciating. Winston clumped around the platform, generally making a nuisance of himself, not being allowed into the rail cars. Finally, a blood-soaked orderly stuck his head from a window.

"Three left. Where they goin'?" he shouted to no one in particular.

Winston used this distraction to squeeze into the last car. Rows of seats had been removed so that more wounded could fit inside. He stopped abruptly. The three-day trip from Corinth had required medical attention be administered en route. The wooden floor was stained with blood, some of it days old, some fresh. Bits of pink tissue were scattered underfoot like snails on a damp morning. Severed limbs lay stacked on thick sheets of butcher's paper, legs in one pile, arms in the other, a macabre sense of order.

An orderly tugged on Winston's sleeve.

"We usually chuck the arms and legs out the door as we go. We was busy today. Didn't have no chance to be rid of 'em."

Winston stepped fully into the car. He came closer to see the three remaining soldiers. None was Andrew. The last one at whom he looked was a private, a young man who'd once clerked at the Vicksburg Land Bank. He was bare-chested and pale, his right leg ending in a tourniquet at mid-thigh. His eyes were drawn to Winston. He nodded downward.

"Took it off this morning. Over in that pile."

"I am sorry for your loss." Winston tried to turn away.

The private snapped. "You're just happy I ain't Andrew."

Winston stopped. "You know of my son?"

"I was a Hill City Cadet."

Winston came closer. "How is he?"

The forlorn private wanted no part of a normal conversation. "Woke up this morning, my leg was startin' to turn. Smelled like an old piss pot, kinda yellow-lookin'. Didn't hurt much. That was all them orderlies needed to hear. They sawed it off." He snapped his fingers.

A loud fly buzzed into the car and landed unceremoniously on the private's stump. It crawled along the sticky red bandage and settled on a choice spot.

"I don't mean to be unsympathetic. About Andrew . . . ?" Winston shifted positions and his cane struck the floor.

"Say, there's an idea!" The private's grim face brightened. "I'll need a cane. I know what I'll use too."

Winston sighed.

"My leg! Yeah, they cut it off real clean. I can keep the foot, attach a piece of wood to the bone." He pointed. "Grab my leg 'fore they throw it away."

"Listen to me."

"Hell, I can put a shoe on it, some dressy socks."

"Listen to me!" Winston shouted above the startled soldier. "*What about my son?*"

The private's face reddened and he spoke haltingly. "I saw Andrew the second day. He was helping a man named Simmons, leg-shot like me. Andrew brought him all the way back to Corinth. Simmons got an infection. Died yesterday. He's in one of them boxes." The private's voice dropped to a whisper. "Weren't Andrew's fault."

Winston turned to leave.

"Mr. Carthage." The private swallowed. "Sorry I acted an ass."

Winston's face was unchanged. "I shouldn't have yelled."

The private blinked several times. A solitary tear streaked down his cheek. "I don't know what I'm gonna do."

Winston was too emotionally unsettled for consolation. "You will survive."

"Ain't sayin' much."

"You might not think so now. As each day passes, you will adjust."

"How do you know?"

Winston thought. "Because you have a purpose."

The private's face was questioning.

"You must make a cane." Winston smiled. "Do you have a family?"

The private took a deep breath and exhaled. "My parents. Two sisters."

"Remember that when you pray."

The Baptist service concluded, and Emily rose from her pew. She stepped into the aisle and waited for her mother. From the corner of her eye she spotted a uniform. Andrew. She felt herself smiling and pinched her own thigh to fight it. All week long, her mother had berated her for the stories of her praying with a soldier. Emily at first had felt shamed, but on examination, it was her mother's shame she was experiencing, not her own. With each day, she'd felt an increasing sense of loss and by Sunday could no longer deny she missed Andrew's crooked smile and smart green eyes. While riding to church—in her nicest dress, and it wasn't black—she realized she didn't just want to see him again, she would find a reason to go to Corinth if he didn't appear.

"Hello, Emily."

"Andrew." She indicated the older woman beside her. "This is my mother, Jane Gardner."

"How do you do, ma'am?"

Mrs. Gardner looked back and forth between them. "Fine." She brushed past.

"Did I say something wrong?"

Emily shook her head. "Outside."

They stepped into the twilight. Mrs. Gardner was walking rapidly away from church. The other parishioners, mostly women, watched with unabashed curiosity.

"Mother?" Emily called after her. "The wagon is in back."

"I'll see to myself, thank you."

"Was that about me?" Andrew asked.

Men could be so dim. Emily strode hastily around back to her wagon. She stopped. "You shouldn't have come here." She felt hypocritical for saying what was directly opposite her heart. But she *had* to say it, she couldn't be chasing a soldier. Not even a handsome, polite, well-bred, quick-witted, enthusiastic, hopelessly romantic soldier. She wasn't a little girl anymore, she shouldn't be infatuated so easily, and that's all this could be, an infatuation. They were practically strangers. It just wasn't right.

"Religious freedom is alive in Iuka."

"Don't be smart. Mother had to endure a thousand questions from those women about her widowed daughter attending church with a soldier."

"You invited me."

"I didn't invite you today. How did you arrive here anyway?"

"On back of a hay wagon."

"Have you completely abandoned the Confederate army?"

"I reported to my company last Sunday night. See these blisters? I've been digging breastworks for six days. And thinking of you."

"Concentrate on the former and forget the latter."

"I went to Corinth every day to see if you might be there."

Emily watched him talk. His eyes were so optimistic. "I had no business there."

Andrew nodded. "I'm sorry to have embarrassed your mother. Perhaps if I spoke with her, she wouldn't be so angry."

"You will *not* speak with her."

"As you wish."

"I'm going home. Good evening, Andrew."

Andrew's face fell. "Could you take me halfway to Corinth again?"

"No, and you can't stay in our barn tonight either."

"I could pay you."

She sighed inwardly. He *was* a romantic, but he veered from it too often. Her eyes narrowed. "Why are you here, Andrew?"

"I couldn't bear another day without seeing you."

That was marginally better. "Did you come here last week for church or just to be with me?"

"Both." He blushed. "More you than church."

"*Are* you a religious person?"

"I sincerely wanted to attend church. With you it was more meaningful."

Hard as she tried, she could find nothing wrong in that statement. "I will take you halfway tomorrow if you promise not to return next week."

"I can't make that promise."

She made an exasperated sound. "You'll have to sleep somewhere else tonight. Mother won't stand for you being in our barn."

"I'll sleep beneath the stars. My dreams will be sweet."

Emily had chosen a comfortable, green plaid dress for the wagon ride. It was, she knew, a dress that accentuated her bosom and clung more tightly than her others. She felt silly for wearing it, but then, Andrew Carthage made her feel silly. He told awful jokes and his advances could be embarrassingly clumsy. But he was sweet and trying to win her heart. He was succeeding.

Emily's mother had told her she was abandoning her reputation for a transient soldier, and she wasn't mature enough to recognize Andrew's intentions. Emily had rushed from the house, leaving her mother in a fury.

"We'll never beat those storm clouds." Andrew almost sounded happy.

They bounced along the road that had only begun to dry out from last week's rains.

She felt him staring, but wasn't uncomfortable as before.

Andrew scooted closer to her on the seat. "I'm going to kiss you."

"You will not."

"I can't stop myself."

She couldn't, not so soon. And she never wanted anything more in her life.

He saw her doubts and took the initiative. "I don't have anyone back home."

"That wasn't—"

He shook his head. "You think I will run away. You think I am unprincipled. Is that what you think?"

"You've known me for a week, Andrew."

"This has never happened to me, though the opportunities were there."

"Maybe this is your time to be like other soldiers."

"No," he said. He took her hands. She pulled free. "I've never felt so strongly about a woman, war or no war. I thought I did once, but I was younger, more emotional."

She tried not to look at him. "Andrew, you *will* be leaving eventually." She was shaking her head. Her eyes were misty. "You are lonely and I am vulnerable."

A corner of his mouth pulled up. "There isn't a man alive who could take advantage of you."

"You overestimate my will."

He took the reins from her and stopped the wagon. He placed a finger beneath her chin and turned her face to him. He kissed her. She squirmed away, drawing back against the seat. He kissed her again, more deliberately. Her hands stopped pushing him away. She kissed him back. A storm cloud burst overhead and the rain fell.

❧

"There! Under those trees!" Andrew shouted.

Emily pulled the wagon beneath a cluster of oak trees as the spring rain fell in sheets. The trees provided some shelter, but not before her dress was soaked.

"This has been the wettest April I can remember." Emily stood on the buckboard and removed her bonnet, shaking off moisture. Her hair fell free and streaks of water dotted her tan skin. Her wet dress clung to her breasts. Embarrassed, she turned away from him.

He was smiling. "We will have to wait."

"It's only a thunderstorm."

"Why don't you sit?"

She sank to the seat nervously and looked at him. "Don't be thinking—"

He grasped her shoulders and she quivered. Their eyes locked for a long instant, and he kissed her. Her lips and mouth yielded to his. He wrapped his arms around her. She was warm and supple. Her scent flashed imperative signals to his brain. He fumbled with her dress, uncertain and urgent.

"Wait!" Breathlessly, she stood again. Andrew thought she might jump to the ground and run. Instead, she slowly unclasped her buttons. She pulled the dress free from her shoulders and it slid to her ankles. She unbuttoned her petticoat and her undergarments slowly fell away. Her breasts were exposed in the chilly wet air, then her stomach, until finally she was nude.

Entranced, Andrew jumped to the ground, unable to look away. She offered her hand and Andrew drew her from the buckboard into his arms. He set her down and ripped his jacket free, tossing it onto a pile of wet leaves. He fell trying to remove his boots. Emily giggled. Moments later, he was as naked as she. They stood apart, barely separated.

Andrew stepped closer. Her face was dripping wet, her eyes wild and alive. "God, you're beautiful," he whispered above the heavy raindrops.

In a gentle but demanding motion, he swept her to him and they sank to the ground, their bodies meshed like vines. They writhed and explored and every inhibition fell away.

Andrew's first love was meant to be here, with this woman in this place. Nothing else could've compared.

She moaned insistently beneath him, matching his rhythm, creating her own. The rain fell harder, drenching them with clear warm water as if the heavens had opened to applaud their union.

❧

Emily brought her wagon to a halt. They saw the Confederate picket line a mile distant. The rains had passed and a brilliant late afternoon sun set before them.

"Is this close enough?"

"Yes." Andrew took her hands. "I should be off duty next Saturday. Shall I come to Iuka?"

"How will you get there?"

"Fly, if I must."

She seized his hands. "Seriously."

"I will find a way." Andrew drank in her freshness like a sweet ale. Her face was a stunning reflection of the sun. Damn, but he *would* fly.

"I have the wagon. I will come to Corinth."

"What about your mother?"

She made a face. "Mother will adjust herself to this."

"I wish I could've met her."

"Oh, yes," she said. "Mother is really a fine person." She wanted to say more but stopped.

"I will have another chance." Andrew looked at her and imagined her his wife, the next matron of *Magnolia*. He had once thought of Catherine Parker the same way . . .

"Why are you smiling?" she asked.

"The silly notions of a boy."

Her head cocked. "You?"

"Me."

She smiled with him and he could no longer remember Catherine Parker's face. "Have you been to Vicksburg?"

"Never."

"It is a beautiful city with hills and a grand view of the river and gorgeous architecture and quite wonderful people."

"I should like to see it."

"Then you will." They lapsed into a comfortable silence, staring at each other without awareness.

"You had better go." Emily straightened.

"I will meet you here at noon on Saturday. Will you be safe riding home alone?"

"I have my pistol." Her long lashes danced.

They kissed, and it was familiar and perfect.

36

April 27, 1862

A panoply of evening stars filled the sky. Emily felt she could reach out and capture one like a firefly. She nestled comfortably into Andrew's shoulder. They sat in her wagon a mile south of Corinth. The week since they had seen each other had seemed an eternity. They had ridden and talked and held hands until dusk settled. Then they had pulled the wagon into a thicket and made torrid love.

Emily twirled her fingernails across his chest and he shivered.

"Goose bumps?"

"Yes. Aren't you cold?"

"A little." But she was secure in his arms. "What are you thinking?"

"How pretty spring can be." His eyes were absent their usual optimism.

"What else?"

Andrew sighed. "We received word the Yankees are advancing on Corinth."

"Where?"

"From the north. They are trying to finish what they could not at Pittsburg Landing."

The glow of their lovemaking faded from Emily's face. "What will happen?"

"I don't know."

"Will you have to leave?"

Andrew slowly responded. "Retreat is one alternative. The other is to fight. Only the Yankees are approaching with quite a large army. General Beauregard's intentions are unclear."

Emily became silent. Her fears rushed back, fear of becoming involved with Andrew, fear of giving her heart again so soon, fear of losing him. Would life be so cruel? To take two wonderful men from her in the span of a few months?

"This day had to come," she said with false strength.

Andrew pulled her closer. "Nothing has happened yet. The Yankees are still a few miles away. But I think . . . if they come any closer, you should not try to return to Corinth until this is settled. The sentries probably wouldn't allow you through anyway."

"For how long?" It was an answerless question, she knew.

He shrugged. "A week. A month."

"And then what?" Her heart pounded in her throat.

He kissed her and his eyes willed her to listen. "Emily, whatever happens, we will be together afterward."

"I believe you." She held his face tightly. "But we must make the most of our time together."

They made love, for hours it seemed, and collapsed together in bittersweet exhaustion.

❧

The Union army under General Henry Halleck had completed its creeping, three-week march from Pittsburg Landing to Corinth. Halleck's intention was to defeat Confederate General Beauregard and capture the vital rail center at Corinth. By May 25, Halleck's large army was positioned around Corinth and a bombardment ensued. On May 29, Beauregard withdrew his Confederate troops rather than fight an unwinnable battle. By May 30, his entire army, including the Hill City Cadets, had evacuated Corinth and moved south to Tupelo.

37

The Mississippi River is the backbone of the rebellion; it is the key to the whole situation. While the Confederates hold it, they can obtain supplies of all kinds, and it is a barrier against our forces."

—Abraham Lincoln, 1862

MAY 15, 1862

The war was coming to Vicksburg. Morris knew he shouldn't be surprised, but was anyway. A Yankee fleet, under the command of Admiral Farragut, was moving up the Mississippi River. It was the same fleet that had captured, in succession, New Orleans, Baton Rouge, and Natchez. Vicksburg was next in its path. Sometimes, Morris thought, reporting the news is a dismal job indeed.

❧

From the *Vicksburg Reader*, May 19, 1862:

> Admiral Farragut's fleet steamed within view of Vicksburg Sunday afternoon. The warships dropped anchor down river and sent an emissary under cover of white flag to the city docks to deliver surrender terms. Vicksburg's military governor, James L. Autry, responded thusly:
>
> "Mississippians do not know, and refuse to learn, how to surrender. If Commodore Farragut can teach them, let him come and try."

May 27, 1862

Winston paced the floor of his master bedroom. Farragut's ships had launched a massive bombardment. Yankee shells pummeled Vicksburg. From his window, Winston could see much of Vicksburg three miles away. *Magnolia* was south and east, beyond the range of Yankee shells.

The ground rumbled as a giant bomb exploded in the south part of town. A wall of earth and debris rose above the tree line. Winston momentarily reassessed his position. Yankee shells probably *could* reach here from the river. What if their aim was poor? What if a drunken Yankee gunner fired indiscriminately?

Winston snorted at himself. The poor townspeople were the ones to be worried. The Yankees were using mortars, guns that dropped shells almost vertically downward. Few places were safe. Some desperate souls had begun to construct caves in Vicksburg's many hillsides. People were living in them. *That* was miserable.

From the *Vicksburg Reader*, June 8, 1862

> Yesterday, the Confederate River Defense officially surrendered the port of Memphis to Union forces. The fall of New Orleans and Memphis in close succession now leaves Vicksburg as the largest Mississippi River port still in the Confederate fold.

July 15, 1862

Morris was animated. "I watched it all from Fort Hill."

"Watched what?" Winston asked.

"The CSS *Arkansas*."

"What is that?" Winston's monotone conveyed disinterest.

"You don't know?"

"I assume it is a ship."

"An ironclad."

"And?"

Morris stared dully at his friend. "Never mind."

"No, tell me."

"Are you sure?" Morris needed no further prompting. "A fascinating story. The *Arkansas* was being constructed up in Yazoo City so the Yankees wouldn't find her. A captain named Isaac Brown was ordered to take her out on the river and face Farragut." Morris frowned. "You've heard no talk of this? Some have been waiting all summer for the *Arkansas* to arrive."

"I might have heard it mentioned."

Morris shook his head. "You must be the only person in a fifty-mile radius not following the war."

Winston was impassive. "I follow a different part of the war."

"Oh." Morris nodded. "As I was saying, Captain Brown and his crew finally completed the *Arkansas* a couple of days ago and steamed down the Yazoo to the Mississippi." Morris beamed. "On her maiden voyage, the *Arkansas* encountered three of Farragut's warships in a river channel."

"What happened?"

"Captain Brown attacked."

Winston's eyebrows lifted slightly. "A brave man. One ship against three."

"Damn right. He crippled one of the Yankee boats and sent the other two running!"

"That *is* an interesting story."

"No need for sarcasm, Winston. Besides, there is more. After whipping the Yanks in the channel, Brown brought the *Arkansas* out into the main river. Guess what he found?"

"Farragut's fleet?"

Morris looked surprised. "Exactly. Farragut's entire fleet. Sloops, rams, ironclads, close to forty ships."

Winston was more attentive. "And?"

"That crazy bastard Brown attacked! Can you imagine? Guns blazing, one boat against forty!"

"Was the *Arkansas* sunk?"

"Hardly! She laid a passel of damage on the Yanks. Their boats were too close together." Morris chuckled. "When they shot at the *Arkansas*, often as not, they hit each other. She blasted straight through. She's at the Vicksburg dock this very minute. Lost much of her crew though."

"Captain Brown is an estimable man."

Morris nodded. "See the excitement you miss by living this far out?"

"Yes, but not a single Yankee bomb has struck my property. That pleases me."

Winston appraised his friend. "You've become quite a military enthusiast."

"I must be." Morris grinned. "I don't have five thousand dollars to buy a substitute soldier. And as long as the *Reader* remains patriotic, the Old Guard won't raise too much hell about me ignoring the mandatory enlistment edict."

"Clever."

"Common, really."

"I suppose."

"Have you noticed how many former Unionists are now patriots?"

A smile tugged Winston's mouth. "You are presumably not including me in that group."

"Winston, you've always wanted the best for your country. The United States was once your country, and you wanted to preserve it."

"And now?"

Morris laughed. "I cannot deduce your thoughts."

Winston studied *Magnolia*'s front lawn. "Actually, I am thinking of freeing my slaves."

Morris considered his friend's rapidly aging face. "Excellent. Why now?"

"It is the right thing to do. And I am weary of the whole goddamn affair, slavery, states' rights, war, your story about the *Arkansas* notwithstanding."

Morris leaned forward. "What of your fall harvest?"

Winston thumped his cane on the floor. "Hang the harvest! I've no customers anyway."

Morris blinked.

"Sorry, Sam."

"Think nothing of it."

"The Confederate government feels it has a claim to my crops. If I don't harvest, they'll have nothing to claim."

"Winston, you might want to reconsider—"

"Why?" His voice was harsh.

"You know why," Morris shot back. "Some in this town would report you as a traitor."

"They can call me what they please."

"You could be arrested."

"Fine. Let Jeff Davis execute the warrant."

"Winston, for God's sake, listen to yourself!"

"Listen to *you* lecturing *me* on Confederate fealty."

"At least I'm not whining like a child."

Winston said nothing.

"You can't just let your crops die on the vine. Contract with a yeoman farmer."

"And be paid in Confederate money?"

"It is the currency of—"

"It is the currency of foolishness!"

Morris frowned. "You're not thinking."

"With the war this close . . ." Winston looked down and his hands trembled. "I just want to see Andrew again."

"Winston." Morris hesitated. "Andrew endured Pittsburg Landing or Shiloh or whatever the hell they call it. He is a survivor. He will come home when this ends. Do you want him returning to a bankrupt plantation?"

"Places like *Magnolia* won't exist after the war."

"But that doesn't mean he must start over. You will still own three thousand acres of prime land."

Winston turned his head away.

Morris sensed he was fighting tears.

Winston coughed. "You are right. I will harvest."

From the *Vicksburg Reader*, July 24, 1862

The Union fleet ceased its shelling campaign and withdrew from Vicksburg yesterday. Admiral Farragut is rumored to be relocating to Baton Rouge after realizing that Vicksburg could not be vanquished through arbitrary naval bombardment.

From the *Vicksburg Reader*, August 6, 1862

A final note has been struck on the short and gallant life of the *CSS Arkansas*. The ironclad which single-handedly defied Admiral Farragut's Yankee fleet last month met a fiery end yesterday near Baton Rouge. Reports indicate the *Arkansas* lost steam power as she raced downriver to join a Confederate assault on Yankee vessels in Baton Rouge. She fell adrift and became stranded against the shoreline where she was discovered by a Yankee ram boat. Her crew had no choice but to abandon ship and, to prevent her seizure, set the *Arkansas* ablaze. Moments later, she exploded.

Emily tore open the letter. It had arrived a week earlier, but she hadn't wanted to read it. She was waiting to be more certain of her physical condition. Nausea had become a daily routine. Her frequent, often irrational, mood swings were noticeable, especially to her mother. She took a deep breath and read even as tears rolled down her cheeks.

July 17, 1862

Dearest Emily —

You undoubtedly learned of our hasty departure from Corinth. It pains the depths of my soul that I had no time to give you a proper farewell. Every step of our march was a step further from you. I pondered desertion, forsaking this war and its sorrowful litany. But desertion is a coward's act, even for the noblest intentions. I cannot have you think me a coward. I will fight. I will kill again if I must, begging God's forgiveness. But this war cannot have my essence. That belongs to you.

Our retreat took us to Tupelo, where we've been ever since. Rumor has it we are leaving soon, but to where I don't know. Rumors in the army can be as false as they are numerous.

I love you, Emily. That is a plain fact. Our last night together is a cherished memory that sustains me. I would give all that I have, or will ever have, to see your fair smile again. You must accept my vow: I will return for you. Be safe and think of me until that day arrives.

Love,
Andrew

38

AUGUST 15, 1862

"Mr. Pritchard, I assume you are familiar with the sentencing phase of a criminal trial. You are guilty and owe a sizeable debt to the state of Illinois." The judge frowned down his nose at the shackled prisoner. "I have some discretion as to how you repay that debt. State Prison is one option." The judge stopped, perhaps expecting a plea for mercy.

Pritchard yawned. His eighteen-month crime spree was ended. With no guiding objectives, other than to steal money, have women, and perhaps incite mayhem, he had wandered through Illinois and Indiana, robbing, burglarizing, raping, killing. His crimes had been random, his victims anonymous. As such, the law had remained ignorant of him until he'd been caught in a wealthy man's home in Springfield, Illinois, by a crowd of constables. How they came to be there he would never know, but they'd had a time subduing him.

"You possess a disturbingly violent nature, suited for a long stay in a penal facility. Have you been arrested before?"

"No."

"Why do I not believe you?"

Pritchard didn't answer.

"Your criminal past, or lack thereof, doesn't concern me, I simply felt obliged to ask. Your actions in my jurisdiction are all that matter."

Pritchard yawned again.

"However, I think your *tendencies* might be useful in a capacity more suitable than mauling lawmen. You stand convicted of criminal trespassing, resisting arrest, and five counts of assault on a constable. You are hereby sentenced to two years' service in the Army of Illinois."

Pritchard disinterestedly scratched the lower part of his back with his cuffed hands, though he was not disinterested at all.

"Why the army?"

"Why not? Twenty-four months instead of ten years in jail—that is a bargain."

The Army was pleasing to Pritchard, but the judge shouldn't know. "What will be my rank?"

"Private. You may appeal your sentence, but that will take months, and I am instructing your sentence to begin immediately. Today."

"I have no choice?"

"Not really."

"Then I accept."

"Gracious of you. By the way, the Army shoots deserters." The judge smiled broadly. "The state has a new soldier, the taxpayers are spared the burden of incarceration, and you earn a reduced sentence that will pay rehabilitative benefits."

"If you survive the war, your debt will be settled. I have instructed that your Army salary be garnished until the constables' medical bills are paid." The judge handed a sentence decree to the bailiff. "Escort Mr. Pritchard to the 81st Illinois Infantry recruiting office. Be sure the officer in charge sees this. If the Army does not want Mr. Pritchard, we will find him a jail cell."

November 17, 1862

Dear Father,

It is many months since I last wrote. Did you have a good fall harvest? What of *Magnolia*? Did you fare well during Farragut's assault last summer? Vicksburg's stolid defense was all the talk.

I write today from northeast Tennessee. As you know, my company fought at Pittsburg Landing (Shiloh to the Yankees) last spring. From there, we retreated to Corinth, then retreated further to Tupelo. Our army was assigned a new commander, General Braxton Bragg, who led us on a circuitous route by rail through Mobile and Atlanta before arriving in Chattanooga, Tennessee, in August. From there we marched north into Kentucky. In October, however, our advance stalled at a place called Perryville and we retreated back to Tennessee.

Good news of a sort. After the Perryville engagement, I was brevetted to Lieutenant for exemplary leadership in battle. I accepted the rank, though such field promotions are common. I am now Lt. Carthage, but my pay is no higher, my duties are the same, and so is the war.

I applied for a Christmas furlough, but none will be granted unless we are close to a soldier's hometown. I am resigned to spending the Yule with my comrades.

We experienced an early snowstorm yesterday. Everything was white and beautiful for a time, but we were forced to relocate and found our movements greatly hampered. The thought of an entire winter in such conditions makes me long for the temperance of home.

I hope to see you at Christmas, but if not, have a wonderful season.

Love,

Andrew

Andrew leaned against his bed roll and stared at the dark mountain sky. There were so many things he wanted to say, but dared not in a letter. Rumor had it that prying eyes read outgoing mail to assess troop morale. If he could, he would've told his father he had fallen desperately in love with a woman from Iuka, and his heart ached because he had written her five times without response. And he would've opined that the war was being lost by timid generals and poor organization. He would've asked about the bearer bonds and what his father was doing to ensure their safety. But none of these subjects belonged in a letter.

39

Since Shiloh, Ulysses Grant's army had done little except guard railroads in west Tennessee. It was a punishment of sorts for his failings at Shiloh, but as Fall approached, he was given permission to mount a southern offensive on Vicksburg. His overland attack through central Mississippi would be coordinated with General Tecumseh Sherman, who would bring another army down the Mississippi River from Memphis. Grant's advance was a ruse designed to lure the Confederate garrison at Vicksburg away from its fortified position. In the meantime, Sherman would slip unnoticed down the Mississippi and attack a much-depleted force at Vicksburg.

In late November, Grant moved south, hoping to draw the Confederate army north to Grenada. At the same time, Sherman was preparing to move downriver from Memphis with an army strengthened by new recruits from Illinois.

November 30, 1862

Private Gaylord Pritchard stepped from a transport boat onto the crowded Memphis docks. He and twenty-four others in his company had been ordered to assemble for immediate assignment in Sherman's army.

Pritchard's only concern as he made his way along the dock was that he found himself in a war zone. After weeks of training in Illinois, the unavoidable truth was that the Union army expected him to fight. No expectation could be less accurate. War offered too many uncertainties and indiscriminate opportunities to die. Pritchard would have none of it.

On the outskirts of the Union's base camp in Memphis was a shanty bar, the Cotton Top. It existed solely at the Union army's discretion. The owner, a one-legged ex-Confederate, was permitted to sell watered-down liquor to occupying soldiers, his only fee, a weekly bribe to the Union Provost Marshal, the military equivalent of a sheriff. The Cotton Top's customers were off-duty Union soldiers and the owner earned enough money to supply himself with morphine for his lingering war wound.

The bar catered to officers and enlisted men alike. Among them was Pritchard, absent without permission from his just-arrived company. Many soldiers had slipped away from camp at sundown after the long, wearisome boat ride from Illinois.

Pritchard sat quietly on a stool wondering if his time might be better spent with a prostitute than a roomful of drunks. His attention was drawn to a nearby table where a beefy major sat.

"Ain't been this far south my whole damn life," the major said to the inebriated sergeant with whom he shared the table. The sergeant nodded indifferently and rose for another beer.

The major sipped his whiskey and winced. "Christ! Rebs don't need guns, this poison will kill us! Worst I ever swallowed." He glanced at Pritchard. "Know what I mean?"

Pritchard smiled in the dim light. "I have had better."

"Goddamn right. What's your name, Private?"

"Pritchard."

The major spun his chair around. "Butler here. Where you from, Pritchard?"

"Illinois."

"Never been there neither. Pennsylvania is home for me. Been in uniform since this war started. You?"

"Just joined."

"Good for you. Let me tell you somethin'." Butler's voice dropped drunkenly low. "The infantry and cavalry are for idiots. Get ya killed. Year-and-a-half and I ain't never fired a weapon."

"How is that?"

"I'm with the Provost's office. Least I will be when I report tomorrow. New assignment. I've been in Washington since this thing started. Pissed off my commanding officer, and he sent me here. Bastard." Butler scowled and emptied his whiskey.

"You've never served in Sherman's army?"

"Never served in any fighting army."

"What do you do?"

Butler grinned. "Routine duties—set up check points, feed and house prisoners. I work for the general staff. Pay stinks, but no Rebel has ever had me in his rifle sight."

"You don't know anyone in this army?"

Butler shook his head. "Wouldn't know my commandin' officer if he walked up and slid his willy in my ear."

Pritchard laughed. "Any family in these parts?"

Butler belched. "No. I was married, but my wife left me for a bookkeeper. A *bookkeeper!* He was stealin' money from his boss. They moved to Paraguay." Butler raised his glass. "Don't matter. I make friends easy." He teetered on his chair and nearly fell. "Say, Private Pritchard, come have a drink!"

❧

Two hours later, Major Butler stumbled onto the street and aimed for his hotel. His eyes were bloodshot and he careened from one side of the empty street to the other. Barely a block from his hotel, he staggered past a dark alley, and his life abruptly ended.

Major Butler was discovered the next day, his neck broken, his face obliterated by a heavy object. He was found in a private's uniform with papers bearing the name Gaylord Pritchard, late of Illinois.

A new Major Butler reported as ordered to the Provost Marshal's office.

On 19 December, for the second time in seven months, Ulysses Grant was surprised by an opposing general. A roving Confederate cavalry detachment under General Earl Van Dorn swept in behind Grant and destroyed his supply base as he moved through central Mississippi. Grant was forced to retreat to Memphis. Confederate troops that had moved north from Vicksburg to stop Grant reversed course and returned to their fortified positions. Grant's diversion had failed. Vicksburg was as strong as ever. And by then Sherman had already embarked from Memphis for his surprise attack. Sherman did not know he would be attacking an entrenched Confederate garrison. And Grant was helpless to warn him away.

Sherman's army was thirty thousand strong, traveling downriver on transport boats. His army, however, traveled without Major Ernest Butler, a.k.a. Gaylord Pritchard, the new Adjutant Provost for occupied Memphis. Pritchard had petitioned his commanding officer to join the Vicksburg offensive, feeling the opportunity to reacquaint himself with the Carthage family had finally presented itself. But his commanding officer had declined his request, saying a full Provost complement wouldn't be needed until Vicksburg had been captured.

Pritchard had briefly considered volunteering for a combat assignment, but decided he could wait for his chance to see Jeremy Carthage, wait until Vicksburg had fallen.

DECEMBER 29, 1862

General Sherman commenced his attack on Vicksburg under the false assumption that Vicksburg's garrison had been deployed to halt Grant in central Mississippi.

At noon, two full Union brigades assaulted the Rebels' northernmost positions. Five times they tested the Rebel lines, and five times they were thoroughly repulsed.

Sherman finally called off his disastrous attack, but not before he'd lost nearly two thousand men. Rebel casualties were one hundred and eighty-seven dead. Sherman had suffered his worst defeat. Four days later, he disgustedly withdrew from Vicksburg, wondering what in hell had happened to Grant.

December 31, 1862

Winston quietly tugged the cork free with a *pop!* Vicksburg was safe again, having survived a second Yankee attack. But the Yankees would return, he was sure of it.

The night was dark, but not terribly cold. He filled two glasses as his mind churned with memories. Four years, he thought. Four years ago this night, he had stood here on the veranda, and she had left him . . .

He was a man without purpose since Elizabeth's death. In every facet of his life, the word "lost" seemed to apply. He'd lost his wife to illness, lost his brother to greed, lost interest in his plantation, and now his son was exposing himself to death for a lost cause. Winston had no patience for everyday responsibilities. He didn't care if the house needed repairs or that cotton yields were dismal. He didn't worry with his appearance or feel social obligation or civic pride. He couldn't remember his last enjoyable meal, though his appetite was gluttonous. His spirituality had vanished. He scoffed at a god who would allow suffering on such an immense scale. He had few friends and no family. Morris was a good companion, but Morris had his own life to lead. And Curtis could never be a friend in the conventional sense. Not as long as Winston *owned* Curtis.

Winston strolled to the veranda garden and tried to picture Elizabeth, there on a sterling April day, cajoling life from the soil. He raised the champagne glasses and clinked them together. His lower lip quivered. He fought the tears and lost yet again.

"To you, my love." He drank from a single glass. Sparkling wine slid down his throat. He silently placed the second glass on the garden birdbath. Then he went inside to bed, his New Year's Eve celebration complete.

40

February 1, 1863
Dear Father,

Forgive the long delay since my last letter. We've been very active, though I can't say productive, for that would imply accomplishment. Instead, we are up to our old tricks, fighting and retreating, dodging Yankees like obnoxious guests at a social function.

Our latest misadventure was in central Tennessee at a hamlet called Murfreesboro. We fought hard, thousands of men died, and nothing was gained by either side. We retreated, and the Yankees let us leave—it is a familiar routine. The 9th Mississippi has seen hundreds fall and the Hill City Cadets are many fewer than when we left.

We learned Vicksburg was attacked in December by Sherman, and he was rejected. I am content that you came to no harm. I wanted to write, but we are an army in the fight (as well as in flight), and our time is precious.

My attitude has turned sour. I hate this war and all who are a part of it. Such words might be treasonous, but to imply otherwise would be a fabrication. Death is tragically common. Good men die, and the war doesn't care. It consumes life and starves for more. The best that can be said is that I have so far survived it.

Please write me back, Father. As you might have guessed, my application for Christmas furlough was denied. I have applied again for this Spring, but am not hopeful it will be granted.

Over a year has passed since I gazed on Magnolia's splendor. Home is a fetching dream I enjoy nightly. Reality is the nightmare of my waking hours. I miss you more than a grown man should miss his father, but feel only pride in that admission.

Love,

Andrew

Andrew wanted to write *What about the bonds?* but dared not. Too much was at stake for such a risky question. Vicksburg might be captured by the time his letter arrived home. Then what? Some Yankee soldier would read it.

With each passing day, Andrew knew the bonds would be his family's salvation. He hoped again that his father had prepared for the worst.

"Shhh!"

For a moment, all was quiet. Then the group of chattering slaves resumed their excited buzz.

"Hush, dammit!" They quieted again as the insistent white man climbed onto the wagon's buckboard.

"We have four wagons, and I counted sixty-seven of you altogether. You will be very crowded."

Giggles and buoyant talk.

"We'll take Cain Ridge Road down past Warrenton. If we see anyone along the way, keep quiet. Y'all belong to me and we're on our way to work on the Port Hudson breastworks. Right? Past Warrenton, there'll be a boat waiting on the river. Get on board as fast as you can. Does everyone understand?"

The chatter was more nervous this time. The group had collectively declined to accept that this moment would ever come. But here it was.

A hesitant old voice called out. "Whass we gonna do when we get there?"

The white man chuckled. "That's not my problem. Just make sure you get there."

Rumblings of muted agreement faded away.

"Form a line over here." He pointed to a pile of sacks. "Come by one at a time and pick up your food."

The slaves didn't move.

"We don't have all night!"

The diffident slaves formed a line. Each was given a sack containing a loaf of bread and salted pork, rations for several days. The white man then slipped them each a twenty-five dollar gold piece. Arguments commenced almost immediately over the money. The white man silenced them.

"Listen! Everybody got one coin, that is all. Everybody should have one coin when y'all get to New Orleans. You're gonna be free. Act like you know how!" Morris rubbed two damp palms on his trousers. Aiding runaway slaves was technically illegal.

Impending freedom once again seized their mass psyche, and they climbed aboard the wagons in good cheer.

As the slaves rolled quietly into the night, Winston Carthage watched from a hidden vantage. At least there were some things that still made him feel good. By law, he had to petition the state legislature to grant slaves their freedom. This was far simpler, no complications, nothing to explain. If he didn't report them missing, they would make it all the way to New Orleans.

41

March 25, 1863

Jeremy ached for a shot of whiskey or, short of that, a pinch of opium. But he had neither, so he could only wait. The damp night was shrouded in fog brewed from unseasonably cold air whipping across New York Harbor. He peered at the intrusive sign above the warehouse: ANACOSTE INDUSTRIES, it pronounced brazenly. Why did Benjamin insist they meet here?

A carriage rattled onto the narrow road before the warehouse. Benjamin Anacoste and two anonymous men rode abreast. They climbed down, Benjamin dressed in a clean blue suit, his companions in long black coats and low hats.

Benjamin jerked his head at the warehouse. "Inside." His ugly stare discouraged further discussion.

Jeremy followed him into the dark warehouse through a side door. One nameless man lit a lamp, the other silently watched Jeremy. The lamp's circle of light extended outward along a ten-foot radius and was swallowed by the hugeness of the warehouse. Iron rails could be seen stacked along the nearest wall.

"So?" Jeremy knew he should be nervous. Benjamin's intimidation game was well planned. "What is all this?"

Benjamin puffed a cloud of breath into the frigid air. His scarred cheeks were hollow in the shadows.

"These two gentlemen are employees of Anacoste Industries. They are personnel specialists." Benjamin wheezed and a veil of vapor momentarily obscured his face. He carelessly tossed a dossier at Jeremy's feet.

Jeremy collected the package and pulled it open. He couldn't see what was written on the half-dozen pages. "What is it?"

"Your biography, Mr. *Carthage*."

Jeremy froze.

Benjamin's grim mouth turned down even further. He spoke softly. "Your reaction confirmed its contents."

Jeremy's chest tightened. Of all the reasons to be here, this was least expected. Gambling debts, infidelities, drunkenness—Jeremy had provided many opportunities for Benjamin's attention. But *this*? It had been four years since he'd discarded the Carthage name.

"So you know my secret." Jeremy's play at off-handedness was natural. Minimize the importance of the revelations, he reasoned, and the damage will be less.

Benjamin's face betrayed nothing. "Well?"

"Old news."

Benjamin spoke. "It is grounds for an annulment."

Jeremy waved the dossier. "This is interesting, but I'm still your son-in-law, your daughter's husband. The Catholic church says so."

"You're not Catholic." Benjamin pointed at the dossier. "Jeremy Carthage is a Presbyterian."

Jeremy folded his hands across his chest. "And Jeremy *Harper* was confirmed in the Catholic Church a few weeks ago. I attended counseling sessions with a priest for months. So you see, Sophia and I are both Catholic, we are married, and nobody short of the Pope can change that." Jeremy smiled. "I am a bona fide fish-eater."

Benjamin's substantial self-control was tested. "Congratulations on your conversion." His eyes shone like candles. "As a longstanding *fish-eater*, let me offer you a helpful suggestion on the road to a more pious existence. Catholics do not commit adultery."

"You brought me here for a religious lesson?" Having outmaneuvered Benjamin preemptively, Jeremy's confidence soared. The men with Benjamin were intimidators, nothing more.

Benjamin stared at Jeremy, weighing, deciding. "How much are you in debt at your club?"

Jeremy's perplexed look was like dousing a fire with dry hay.

"*How much*?" Benjamin roared.

"About . . . eleven thousand, give or take—"

Benjamin's response was instant. "I will write a bank draft tonight for twelve thousand dollars. You will pay your debts and use the balance to leave New York."

"Where am I to go?" This time Jeremy was genuinely puzzled.

"I don't care. You'll leave and not return here. And if I have to, I will make you wish you had never met my daughter."

Jeremy let the obvious remain unspoken. "You're exiling me?" He snorted. "You can't do that."

Benjamin shook his head. "How could such a slow man ever deceive my daughter? You came from a wealthy family. You ought to know money's power."

"You can't force me away from the woman I love." Jeremy managed a straight face.

"Don't be a fool."

"What about our marriage? Catholics can't divorce."

"Nothing is impossible."

Jeremy smirked. "Religious convenience can be bought? That sounds so . . . Protestant."

"I will worry about that."

"I'm not leaving."

Benjamin's eyes probed Jeremy. "You're a scrupulous man." He took a small step backward and turned his head slightly. "Don't kill him."

The dossier suddenly felt heavy in Jeremy's hand. "Benjamin." His voice faltered. "You can't do this! I'll have you arrested!" The man on the left inched closer while the other reached into his jacket.

"Arrested?" Benjamin laughed. "In case you hadn't noticed, I am the largest producer of war materials in New York state. And you think I shall be arrested on *your* allegation?"

"Wait!" Jeremy's voice pitched higher, but they did not wait.

❧

"I regret to inform you that your position has become redundant." R. T. Stanton's heavy thighs spilled off both sides of the small visitor's chair. He could not meet Jeremy's eye.

Jeremy rose from his desk chair with a scrape. "I'm fired?"

"We're not having a good year, not good at all," Stanton squirmed.

"The year is only three months old!"

"I know but projections . . ." Stanton's sentence tapered. He was far too weak for terminations.

"Mr. Stanton, look at me."

Stanton slowly lifted his beaten-puppy eyes.

"Have I done something wrong? My performance has been adequate." And it had been exactly that, which in Jeremy's mind meant a lot.

"No. It's a business decision." Stanton was evasive, but there was something else, a frank curiosity.

"You think I've done something wrong."

"What? No, no. Business."

"Who— Why, that son-of-a-bitch . . . ."

Stanton gawked. "I hardly think that is necessary—"

"The old bastard got to you, didn't he?" Jeremy's voice increased an octave.

Stanton rose quickly from his chair ,which was an accomplishment for a man his size. "I think it's best we part company, Mr. Harper." He edged for the door.

"Was it a big deposit?"

"I don't know what you mean."

"Yes, you do." Jeremy slid around the desk. "My father-in-law!"

"Mr. Anacoste? Why would he—"

"Do you really think you'll keep his business after I'm gone? This bank has the worst reputation in New York, you idiot!"

Stanton stepped aside as Jeremy stormed from the office.

❧

"Why do you want to ruin my life?" Jeremy spat the words.

Benjamin Anacoste calmly regarded his son-in-law. "Why do you want to be a part of mine?"

"I never asked to be part of your life. You are my wife's father. Our relationship is rather unavoidable."

"And?"

Jeremy heaved a beaten sigh.

"I wasn't thinking clearly when we last met." Jeremy touched the lingering bruises on his forehead. "I'll take the offer you mentioned. My debts plus two thousand dollars."

"It was one thousand, but if you leave immediately, I'll consider two."

"On one condition: you must get me home."

"To Mississippi? Impossible!"

"Then to New Orleans. It is occupied by Union troops. You can arrange it."

Benjamin was silent for a moment. "New Orleans. Perhaps. I'll see."

42

Ulysses Grant's plan to sweep through central Mississippi had been an unmitigated disaster. Now he was trying a new strategy. In January, he linked with Sherman, and their combined armies floated from Memphis down the Mississippi to a point just north of Vicksburg. He was close, the closest he'd ever been to the elusive Vicksburg, the Confederate prize he had promised Lincoln.

To attack Vicksburg directly from the north invited disaster. Sherman's failure in December had proven as much. Thus, Grant considered many options, including an inland expeditionary force. Few of these ideas progressed beyond their initial stages, with one notable exception: an attempt to construct a canal that would cause the Mississippi River to bypass Vicksburg and leave the city dry and useless to the Confederacy. In the end, however, Grant's Canal was a dismal failure at the cost of many lives.

This brought Grant to the frustrating realization that he would have to go south of the city and attack from that direction. The flat landscape below Vicksburg was more amenable to a driving army. But he faced a daunting problem—how to bring his army south of Vicksburg past the vaunted river batteries on the bluffs.

Grant fumed over his lack of progress for several weeks. Finally he marched his army south through the Louisiana swamps. The plain and plodding solution was most effective. By May 1, Grant's entire force was reassembled thirty-five miles to the south on Mississippi soil. The Confederates at Vicksburg, under the command of General John Pemberton, were left guessing at Grant's true intentions.

❧

MAY 2, 1863

Winston coughed. "I'm catching cold."

Morris squinted in the morning sun. "How are you catching cold in May?"

"I don't know."

"Will you continue to stay here at *Magnolia*?"

"What would be my alternative?" Winston smiled sadly.

"Come stay in the city. You would be safer."

"And leave this place to the Yankees?" Winston coughed again. *Magnolia* was not within Vicksburg's perimeter defenses. It stood alone, southeast of the nearest Rebel lines, as visible as a lighthouse on a black night, proudly and completely exposed.

"Grant has taken Port Gibson. That's thirty miles from here. It won't be more than a few days . . ."

"If I come to the city, I'll never see my home again."

"Don't be so dramatic! You will come back when this is over."

"Sam, the Yankee army destroys plantation homes. Grant makes a point of it, Sherman too. This home is quite noticeable."

"Grant might never make it this far."

"That's reassuring."

"I've heard from reliable sources that Pemberton is dispatching a large force down to Grand Gulf to stop Grant even as we speak."

"Do I look sick *and* stupid?"

Morris chuckled. "You can stay with me. I have room."

"You're very generous, but you would evict me inside of a week."

"That's not true. You'd be much more comfortable there." Morris stared at the opulence surrounding him. "Maybe not more comfortable, but you'd have someone to talk to."

Winston's face colored a bit. "I talk to myself now, Sam. It's a sure bet that someone is listening."

"Stay with me for a night and see how you like it. Bring Curtis and Lou if you'd like. I just don't think you'll be happy here if the Yankees *do* come."

"You're probably right. I will think about it."

The commander of the Vicksburg garrison, General John Pemberton, had long been waiting for Grant's move, but was now at a loss to understand its significance. On May 2, Pemberton made a tactical decision, hoping to intercept Grant. He shifted several thousand troops to the fortified town of Grand Gulf, directly in Grant's path. Grant, rather than initiate a protracted engagement so far from Vicksburg, altered his plans accordingly. Instead of marching north, he turned northeast toward the state capitol at Jackson. Another small Confederate army lurked there which Grant hoped to eliminate from his flank. Accordingly, on May 13, he captured Jackson, then reversed direction and began his march back to Vicksburg.

Pemberton was frantic. He had watched Grant's campaign in confusion and dismay for months. Grant to the north, Grant to the west, Grant to the south, and now Grant to the east. Grant could move in any direction he wanted while Pemberton was tied to Vicksburg. But this time, Pemberton knew Grant was coming directly at him and would not veer away again.

May 16, 1863

Winston coughed once, twice, and was punished by a long fit. His eyes watered and his stomach muscles screamed for mercy. The fits came every hour and lasted a bit longer each time. He took a sip of water, but his inflamed throat objected and another fit ensued.

Finally it stopped. His breathing returned to normal. As it did, he heard a dull thump. And again. Cannons. The Yankees were close, fifeteen or twenty miles. Grant would be here in a day or two.

Without realizing it, Winston twisted his linen kerchief into a knot. How in God's name had it come to this? The United States was waging war on Vicksburg.

The day Winston had dreaded for nearly three years had arrived. Today or never. He wondered if he was up to what he must do.

Brown's Lake glistened brilliantly in the morning sun. Gnats and horseflies hovered near the surface as bream cleared the water for breakfast. Winston climbed from his carriage seat to the dewy grass, shovel in hand.

The blade struck ground with a lethargic thud. He carefully removed a square of sod. Slowly, he dug a hole two feet on its sides. With each thrust into the tough dirt, his arms screamed. His bad leg prevented him from driving the blade deep with his foot. Twice he was interrupted by coughing fits.

The soldier watched in silent fascination as the crippled man grappled with a shovel. He briefly considered an offer to help; instead, he waited in the tall reeds just a stone's throw away.

Winston was finally content with the hole. He limped to his carriage for a hand cloth and wiped perspiration from his face. Beneath the seat, he grabbed a mason jar, 10 inches tall, as wide as his fist. It was tightly sealed with a screw-on cap and hardened resin around the lid. Cane in one hand, jar in the other, he struggled to the lake's edge and submerged the jar for a full minute. He held it up in the sunlight and carefully studied its contents. Satisfied, he limped back to the hole and placed the jar nearly an arm's length into the earth.

"Whatcha got there, Mister?"

Winston wheeled around. "Who are you?" he asked, vaguely recalling the last time he'd been surprised by a stranger at Brown's Lake. Then it had been Pritchard. Today it was a Confederate soldier, a private.

"Easterling, Third Louisiana Infantry. You?" The soldier stepped from the reeds and approached. He was smallish, five-foot five, but stout with wiry brown hair jutting wildly below his cap.

"You are on my property. I'll thank you to leave immediately."

"Can't," he said simply.

"You can and you will." Winston's tone was more cautious than assertive.

"Nope. Lieutenant says this is my sector."

"Sector of what?"

The slow-witted soldier frowned, not entirely secure with his grasp of the word. "Don't know. But I'm supposed to be watchin' fer suspicious activity in this area." He pointed at the ground where Winston stood for emphasis.

Winston studied the soldier. "You are a sentry?"

"I reckon."

"And who sent you here?"

"Like I said, the Lieutenant."

"Where is your horse?"

The soldier laughed. "We ain't got enough of them to go around. I'm walkin'."

"What would you do in an emergency?"

The soldier shrugged. "Run."

"Are you alone?"

"Naw. My buddy is that way a piece." He pointed over his shoulder. Winston followed his finger, but could see no other soldiers. "Our company is back at the line, at the Baldwin's Ferry fort."

"Private Easterling, report to your lieutenant that there are no Yankees here."

"Not yet, there ain't. They'll be here by nightfall."

"What makes you sure?"

The private cocked his ear. "Them cannon ain't more than fifteen miles away."

"But a line to town would take the Yankees north of here."

"You think they'll line up and march straight in? Grant ain't that dumb. Naw, he'll surround the city, try to take it quick before we's ready. And this here property seems like a mighty easy way at our works. All these hills and hollows—good for sneakin' around."

"You're here to prevent that?"

Easterling didn't respond. He was inching closer, trying to peer into the hole.

Winston stepped forward, blocking his way.

"Private Easterling, I will watch this sector. As you can see, I have a carriage and can reach the lines very quickly."

Easterling frowned, not listening. "Whatcha buryin'?"

"Nothing important. Family heirlooms, personal items, that's all." Winston's voice betrayed a slight change. Easterling noticed.

"Did you want I should help? I mean, you got that bad leg and all."

"That won't be necessary."

The ragged soldier considered Winston's clothes and fine carriage. "That your house I passed coming out? The big one on the hill?"

Winston nodded.

"Ain't never seen such a place. Beautiful. This your land, too?" He didn't wait for an answer. "You must have a little money, huh? Some real money, I mean, not that Confederate shit." He looked at Winston again, his eyes thinning to slits.

"I have no money, Confederate or otherwise."

"Really? Ain't no money in that jar?"

"It is not money."

"'Cause if you got money, I can get us outta here quick. I know where there's a boat stashed at the river. That carriage of yours could get us there. Be across to Louisiana in no time. Ain't nobody gonna find us in Louisiana." Easterling's face brightened.

Winston pulled a money pouch from his trousers. "I have a few Union notes. Not much, about thirty dollars. You can take—"

Easterling unholstered his sidearm pointing the barrel at Winston's chest. The Rebel soldier's entire body seemed to twitch and his voice dropped to a whisper.

"Mister, I been fightin' in this war two years. Pittsburg Landin',

Corinth, Memphis, I been shot at by more goddamn Yankees than I could count. I got two dead cousins, friends, neighbors, all dead 'cause of people like you. Rich bastards with cotton fields and slaves and big houses. Folks who's too good to fight themselves. Folks who use the Twenty Nigger Law."

The "twenty Nigger" privilege held that any young man from a family with twenty or more slaves was exempted from military service.

Winston didn't flinch. "That law is a travesty, I agree. But before the war, I had close to a hundred slaves and right this minute, my son is in Tennessee, fighting just like you. When the war is over, I will have lost my house, probably this land. I beg the Lord every night not to take my son, too. Your sacrifice is admirable, Private, but hardly unique."

Easterling continued as if Winston hadn't spoken, his slow mind overflowing with resentment. "Every dime I ever saw went back to my wife in Chalmette," he hissed. "And you know what? That bitch left me cold. Ran off to Texas. Took my baby boy, my mules, everything. All 'cause Admiral Fairy-gut came upriver last year with a few boats. She got scared and skee-daddled. I got no money, no family, nothin'."

"What would you have me do?"

"Step away from that hole for starters. If you're carrying cash, I expect what's down there is a sight more valuable."

"Don't be stupid, son."

Easterling snorted. "I ain't gonna say it again, old man. *Move*!"

Winston didn't budge.

"All right, I'll see fer myself." Easterling stepped closer. As he did, Winston clutched his cane with both fists and swung. Easterling easily dodged the blow. Winston's cane whooshed through the air and he lost his balance. Easterling dropped his shoulder and sent Winston sprawling to the ground.

Easterling panted with excitement. "Old fool. I didn't want all of it, just enough to set me on my way." He reached into the hole and withdrew the mason jar, holding it up curiously.

"You was buryin' paper?" His mouth was contemptuous. "Dumb sumbitch." Something in Winston's expression made him reconsider.

“This here’s special paper, huh?” Easterling gripped the lid of the jar and tried to turn.

With the soldier’s attention diverted, Winston reached inside his waistcoat. He fired his Colt pistol once. Once was enough.

The dead weight was almost more than he could manage. Winston dragged the corpse to the reeds, then hurried to pull his carriage over the hole. If Easterling’s companion appeared, the gunshot could be explained away as a water moccasin, and no, he hadn’t seen another soldier. After ten anxious minutes, he concluded that either the other man—if there was one—hadn’t heard the gunshot or was unconcerned by it.

Winston returned to the reeds with his shovel and dug a shallow grave just as the rain began, first a few scattered drops, then a deluge. Water dripped miserably in his eyes and he fell twice in the mud. The entire process took an exhaustive hour after which he resumed his original task—burying the mason jar. On careful inspection, it seemed the soldier had not broken the seal, which was a good favor on a day of very bad favor. He planted the jar and covered it with mud. The job was done. And God help him, he had killed a man to accomplish it.

He struggled into his carriage seat. His expectant horse shuffled its hooves, waiting command, but Winston didn’t move. He sat, shivering, slumped forward, his head hung low. After a few lost moments, he mindlessly clicked his tongue and the horse tugged at its harness. The carriage inched forward. Fortunately, the horse knew its way home.

MAY 17, 1863

General Pemberton’s disparate Rebel army was in full retreat with Grant rapidly closing. Vicksburg was being overrun with Confederate troops who dragged into town and were immediately ordered into defensive positions. Pemberton needed a delay, if only twenty-four hours, to prepare for Grant’s attack. As a last resort, he ordered his army to hold the Big Black River bridge ten miles east of Vicksburg. But as dawn broke,

Yankees were already on the move. They fired on the exhausted Rebels, most of whom were more concerned about reaching Vicksburg's safety than defending a bridge.

The battle at Big Black River was over in less than an hour. The Rebels offered only a token fight, and their retreat became a mad dash for freedom. Almost as an afterthought, enterprising Confederate soldiers set fire to the bridge, by far their most effective defensive maneuver of the day. However, it came at the cost of nearly two thousand unlucky Confederate troops caught on the wrong side.

The fire delayed Grant by only a day. He had won another battle on his swath through central Mississippi. Port Gibson, Raymond, Jackson, Champion's Hill, and the Big Black River. The list required only one more name.

Winston read the critical words out loud: "To unearth the truth, one must know where to dig." He folded the letter into thirds and pushed it inside an envelope, praying Andrew would understand.

Vicksburg's regular mail service had been postponed; the war was too close. Curtis was being sent to Warrenton where the letter would be posted, hopefully before Union soldiers arrived and seized control of the entire area. Winston couldn't imagine how the letter would find its way to Andrew in eastern Tennessee—there were too many Yankee lines to cross along the way. But it was the best he could presently do.

He coughed thickly. Lou could be heard bustling downstairs, cleaning something. He wished he had the strength to tell her to stop. But she was bursting with energy after being granted her freedom; she cleaned to occupy herself while her mind struggled with the possibilities. Good for her. Winston could do more for her, and he would. Curtis too. But for now, his highest priority was that Andrew somehow get the damned letter.

He'd killed a man, a Confederate soldier no less, now buried on *Magnolia* soil. Winston wondered obliquely if Andrew had killed in the war. Almost certainly. But that was different; that was kill or be killed. Winston had killed over money. Could Andrew forgive him? Would he? *That* was most important.

43

May 19, 1863

The Union army had arrived outside Vicksburg. General Grant, hoping to capitalize on momentum, ordered an immediate, full-scale attack. Sherman's veteran division was the first to mount the Rebel works, uneasy but willing after its December fiasco.

For the Rebel defenders, Vicksburg was new. Most were from Louisiana, Texas, and other parts of Mississippi, but they liked the benefit of position and fought with renewed vigor. In three short hours of combat, the Yankees were completely repelled. Grant ceased the attack, realizing his quick strike was too poorly organized to break the Confederate lines.

May 22, 1863

Three days allowed the Yankees to regroup, but so too had the Rebels behind a serpentine collection of breastworks. Grant surmised that a single breach, one area of penetration where his army could pour through, would be enough to collapse the interconnected entrenchments.

At 5:00 AM, the Union army's full weight landed on Vicksburg. Five hours of artillery bombardment fell from every direction, including the river. At 10:00 AM, Grant ordered an infantry assault. The Yankees were surprised to learn the Rebels had been scarcely affected by the artillery barrage. In fact, the Rebels weren't whipped, they were angry. Many Yankees reached the Rebel lines only to be cut down by withering crossfire. At times, combat was hand-to-hand. All day the Yankees attacked and all day they were rejected. Grant called his attack to a halt. His losses were abhorrent, almost thirty-two hundred casualties, and not a single foot of territory gained. Only five hundred Rebels had fallen.

Grant learned a lesson Sherman might have taught him: Vicksburg, with its commanding geographical advantages, was impregnable to direct attack and would only be starved into submission. Grant's troops prepared for siege.

But some in Grant's staff were thinking ahead to when Vicksburg surrendered, as it inevitably would. A telegraph was sent to Memphis requesting immediate transfer of qualified officers to coordinate an occupational Provost's office. Within twenty-four hours, Major Ernest Butler a.k.a. Gaylord Pritchard, was en route to Vicksburg.

MAY 23, 1863

Sam Morris spent the first day of siege in his home. Grant was apparently bent on retaliation for the previous day's failed attack. Shells began falling at dawn and never stopped. Morris sat huddled beneath his kitchen table counting explosions to pass the time. He was scared beyond comprehension, but had only the walls to share his fear.

The shelling slackened late in the day, and he decided to venture to his office and prepare a short two-page edition of the *Reader*. Anything was an improvement on waiting for anonymous death. He approached his building and saw a pile of rubble near his office. He drew nearer and realized the pile of rubble *was* his office. A random Yankee mortar had silenced the *Vicksburg Reader* forever.

As the Union army settled into the monotony of siege, its attention gradually turned outward to the surrounding countryside. Like a typical conquering army, the Yankees were plunderers, thieves, looters, rapists, opportunists, and avengers. Local plantations were like plump cherries, providing food, building materials, farm animals, and in some cases, money. The giant farms where slaves had toiled provided ideological justification for their crimes. Cotton plantations symbolized the South, false idols to be banished from landscape and memory.

Part of the Yankee routine was to "inspect" plantation homes for signs of Rebel collaboration. Owners were pushed aside while soldiers appropriated the spoils of war. The Yankees needed only a day to find *Magnolia*.

Winston watched solemnly from the front porch. A column of soldiers emerged from the canopied driveway and gazed on *Magnolia*, the turrets and moat, the incredible front lawn. They stared, open-mouthed, torn between hate and admiration. The company captain noticed Winston and remembered his mission.

"Who might you be?" he called across the lawn.

Winston didn't respond, not from impudence, but to preserve his aching lungs.

The captain came closer, followed haltingly by his company.

"Are you deaf, mister?"

"Not at all," croaked Winston. New liver spots dotted his pasty skin. His breathing was forced.

"Oh." The captain looked self-consciously at his men. "What is this place?"

"*Magnolia*, my home."

"We have to look around."

"Be my guest. What are you looking for?"

"Confederate activities," the captain answered automatically.

"I'd be wasting my time telling you there are none."

"You would. Is there anybody inside, sir?"

"Not to my knowledge."

"No slaves?" the captain asked with disdain.

"I freed the last of my slaves six days ago."

"Just in time, huh? That won't win you any favor. I saw a Negro man on the side of your house. Who is he?"

"That would be Curtis, a free man."

"Why is he still here?"

"He's lived here most of his life." Winston's mouth and jaws sagged. "He has nowhere else to go. There is also a woman, Lou. She is free and also chose to stay. I'm paying them both wages."

"Where are the rest of them?"

"Most were freed earlier this year. The others left last week, to where I can't imagine."

"So you have papers from your state legislature indicating the slaves were officially freed?"

"No, I didn't do it legally. I sent them to New Orleans on a boat." Winston leaned forward and coughed wetly.

"A true humanitarian." The captain paused. "You say you're paying these Negroes? With Rebel money?"

Winston didn't waver. "I'm paying them in Union currency if it is any of your business."

A few soldiers chuckled. "Everything you Rebel trash do is my business." The captain leaned forward so only he and Winston could hear. "Where's your real money, mister? Your jewelry and your gold?"

"My money was invested in this property."

"Nothing buried in your gardens or your cisterns?" The captain smiled.

"Nothing that *I* put there. I'm very tired, captain. Please go about your business."

❧

Andrew had traveled for four days since receiving a furlough from the Confederate army. The company commander had allowed him to leave when word arrived that Grant was attacking Vicksburg. Many Hill City Cadets had sought leave, but since Andrew had been the company's only soldier yet to receive furlough, he alone was allowed to go. He'd been given nothing more than a clap on the back and well-wishes for his long journey. He had walked to Chattanooga and from there caught a train to Atlanta, continuing to Mobile, and then north to Meridian. From Meridian, he would have to make his own way across central Mississippi to Vicksburg. But Andrew suddenly realized he wasn't that far from Iuka, and was torn between diverting his journey north to find Emily or continuing home to Vicksburg. It was a horrible decision: the woman he loved whom he hadn't seen in a year or his father whom he hadn't seen in almost two years. Iuka and the entirety of northeast Mississippi was under Yankee occupation; Vicksburg was under attack by Grant. If he went north to Iuka, he risked almost certain capture. If he went west to Vicksburg, the same fate might wait him.

It was a fool's choice, and his heart was telling him to do both. In the end, he flipped a coin. He would go first to Vicksburg.

44

Sam Morris regarded the blank paper. As a journalist with no means of publication, he had decided to keep a journal. He would chronicle events and perhaps in the future, compile his thoughts into something more substantial.

May 25, 1863

Vicksburg has withstood two direct Yankee assaults, the most recent being last Friday. Grant's troops suffered badly, several thousand men dead by all accounts. A cease-fire was called yesterday so both sides could collect dead and wounded from the battlefield. The smell of putrefaction had become quite horrific. During the cease fire, opposing soldiers mingled together between the battle lines. They shared tobacco and spirits, chatted about the war, politics, and subjects varied. Some are relatives, cousins from Missouri and the like. By dawn, these men will again try to kill each other.

Vicksburg should fare well for a while. Food and water are plentiful. But Yankee forces surround the city on all sides, including the river. Shelling is incessant. Vicksburg's denizens, soldiers and civilians alike, dart from place to place in frantic detachment. Grant's bombardment pattern seems to be no pattern at all. Day or night, from all directions, the shells fall. It is his calculated method, one that allows the besieged no rest.

❧

The Yankee command staff had decided they liked *Magnolia*'s accomodations. Competition among officers to appropriate the best local living quarters was fierce. So a pushy Yankee general had moved in, undoubtedly at the behest of the captain who'd first inspected *Magnolia*. The general, a foul-mouthed Wisconsin native, claimed Winston's bedroom for himself. Winston was invited to either stay in the study downstairs or leave altogether. It was of no consequence to the general, as long as Winston didn't obstruct Army business.

Lou stayed to prepare meals, but only after Winston demonstrated he had U.S. currency with which to pay her wages, currency that Winston had secretly been hoarding for three years. The general established Lou's wages at one dollar per day. When Winston showed the surprised general a small clip of Union currency, he was immediately fined $10 for concealing contraband currency. The money went straight into the general's pocket.

With little to do, Winston was moved downstairs and instructed to stay clear of the important general. This he did gladly.

❧

May 27, 1863

Sky Parlor Hill, the prominent bluff on Washington Street, provides a commanding view of the river and outlying Rebel fortifications. People (mostly women) actually gather on the Hill for "combat watching" as it is called. For whatever reason, the Yankee batteries never fire on the Hill, or if they do, they always miss.

Today, as perhaps 50 people looked on from the Hill, a massive Yankee ironclad, the **Cincinnatti** came into view on the river. Its mission today was presumably to silence the northern defensive batteries in coordination with a land attack by the oft-rebuked General Sherman. Just after lunch, the Cincinnatti floated downriver along with a half-dozen smaller gunboats and proceeded to direct shells at Fort Hill. After a short battle, the **Cincinnatti**'s hull was pierced by a Rebel shell and she began to take on water. A gunboat came to her aid and her crew was evacuated. She finally sank, her smoke stacks still visible above the waterline.

Bolstered by the **Cincinnatti**'s sinking, Rebel defenders repulsed General Sherman's land attack.

May 28, 1863

I've begun working in my spare time as a volunteer at the Fisher House on Grove Street. It is one of the city's many infirmaries (sick houses as the soldiers call them). After only two days, I've witnessed the deaths of many men. Those who are shot are treated by the surgeons. One can barely imagine how ghastly the operating rooms become after a few hours of surgery. Blood flows in great volumes and amputated limbs stack like cordwood at the door. Screaming is constant. The surgeons are generous with ether and morphia, but drugs fail to alleviate the horror of losing an arm or leg to a dull blade.

45

May 30, 1863

Winston was fed three times daily and ignored by the Yankee interlopers. He was allowed to walk the grounds, but his strength had dwindled to almost nothing. His moods frequently swung between anger and depression. He clung to life only to see Andrew again but knew that opportunity was slipping away. He had no reason to believe his last letter had even reached Andrew. But he could hope, and in rare optimistic moments, he did.

The Yankee general who occupied *Magnolia* was a sloth. He had appropriated every convenience the house could offer, including Curtis and Lou. They were paid by Winston and subsequently served the general and his staff.

When the general pronounced suddenly and with great fanfare that he was leaving for twenty-four hours, Winston's guard was raised. His top staff, two colonels and a major, also made it plainly clear that they would be absent for some time.

Winston only had to wonder for an hour what was happening. He sat at his study window, staring at nothing in particular, when he saw movement. A head appeared in the bushes near the driveway. Moments later, a second and a third head appeared. More than two dozen men emerged from the woods, cautiously making their way toward the house. Winston shuddered. Their faces were obscured by black hoods. They wore Yankee uniforms, but their rank insignias were covered with cloth.

One soldier remained behind in the trees near the carriage path. He too wore a Yankee uniform. He was huge. Winston squinted hard at the hidden soldier, not sure of what he saw . . .

The house was empty, even the low-level staff finding other places to be. Winston reached for his pistol hidden in a desk drawer and holstered it at his left shoulder.

The Yankee soldiers moved closer, more confident. They reached the front door. Winston threw it open.

"What the hell do you want?"

The startled soldiers didn't answer.

"I said—" Winston was struck hard by a coughing fit. He doubled over and clutched his knees.

The Yankees relaxed and laughed as one. Then they ransacked *Magnolia*.

❧

Winston watched and listened from the great room while *Magnolia* was eviscerated. Paintings, crystal, draperies—nothing was spared. Loose floorboards were ripped up, then carelessly replaced. Suspicious walls were banged and prodded. Even the kitchen was scoured, where the wine cellar's discovery instigated a spontaneous party. Winston sadly watched as some of the world's finest wines were slurped and splashed away by the ignorant soldiers. But he held his tongue, particularly after the Yankees became drunk and obnoxious.

Some soldiers turned their attention outside where they dug in the gardens. It took them only an hour to find a cache of silverware Winston had buried beneath the rose bushes weeks earlier. Other soldiers remained inside and eventually discovered the wall safe in Winston's study. Winston, to prevent the use of explosives, opened the safe. The excited Yankees found nothing of value.

Their search and destruction continued. Every so often, a sergeant would slip away and report to the man who waited outside. At one point, a wine bottle was taken to him to ease his wait. The soldiers, Winston learned, were under strict orders to leave the house in good condition for the returning general. The man who waited outside was obviously their leader and wished to remain anonymous. In that, he failed . . .

At dusk, every inch of the house had been examined. The Yankees hauled away six burlap sacks of merchandise. The valuables would be missed, but nothing they took was worth Winston drawing his pistol. He was simply glad to see them leave. He made no effort to clean the mess, nor would he have been able. He was content, for this one night at least, to have what was left of *Magnolia* to himself.

He walked through the house, stopping every few feet to collect his breath. So frequent were his coughing attacks that he carried a spittoon in his free hand. His journey was endless and bittersweet. He drifted from room to room, sometimes pausing to sit in a favorite chair or recall a special moment. Memories swarmed him, pecking away at his resistance like hungry sparrows. Elizabeth, his parents, even Jeremy. He heard their voices, saw their profiles, wallowed in their fleeting presence.

Elizabeth's sewing room finally proved too much. It smelled of her, even after so many years. The Yankees had defiled it, had destroyed many of her handcrafts and sewing heirlooms. Her favorite armoire lay on its side, shattered. Winston drooped into a chair and wept uncontrollably.

46

Sam Morris's "Siege Journal," May-July 1863

May 31, 1863

Vicksburg now has a new architectural trend — cave homes. These dugouts dot the hillsides like giant gopher holes. Many existed before the siege (built during Farragut's bombardment last summer), but over the last few weeks, dozens, maybe hundreds, have been built. Enterprising Negroes are the primary source of labor. They charge $50, $100, even $200 to dig a cave depending on its size and complexity. Some caves are quite elaborate with foyers and separate bedrooms. But dressing up a cave does nothing to remedy the fact that one still resides in a cave.

Ona personal note, I choose to stay in my vulnerable little timber-and-nail home. Such obstinance may come at the expense of my life. But having recently visited a family's cave, I found it to be quite disgusting. The air was thick, the people too close, the mosquitoes maddeningly persistent.

Merchants are now taking advantage of the siege. Food prices have reached stupefying levels. This could quickly become a serious problem.

June 7, 1863

Grant's bombardment is ceaseless, even on the Sabbath.Service was held this morning at the Vicksburg Baptist Church. About ten people braved the entire ceremony. It was the most rapid service of God imaginable. The preacher's words were delivered with motivational alacrity, seventeen minutes from sinner to saved.

A story is circulating about mass this morning at St. Paul's Cathedral. During the service, a Parrott shell came hurtling through a side window while Father John Bannon presented his sermon. Whether Father Bannon recognized what had happened is not immediately clear. But according to witnesses, his ministration continued without pause even as his parishioners fled.

June 16, 1863

Winston had begun a new painting this morning. At least the Yankees were allowing him that one small pleasure. But his latest work, while expressive, was austere and unhappy, his bitterness reflected in every stroke. His color selections had become noticeably darker, his images stark and surreal. He couldn't bring himself to finish a canvas or display the work as he progressed.

One Yankee officer on the general's staff was an art aficionado and had tried to strike up conversations, but Winston had been unresponsive, disclaiming any knowledge of classical art. He didn't want to befriend a Union officer, or anyone else for that matter. He secretly suspected the young lieutenant came into the study when Winston was away to observe his work. He couldn't stop the intrusion, so he'd begun inserting minor flaws that were displeasing to the eye. His quiet rebellion made him feel a little better.

Winston was completely removed from Vicksburg's plight. Horrible rumors were emerging from the beleaguered city—people eating vermin and mule meat, living in caves, dying from diseases more steadily than battle wounds. The dissipation of foodstuffs would eventually end the campaign. How did one defend against hunger?

June 19, 1863

Food now determines one's wealth. Flour and meal prices seem to increase by the hour. Apparently, profit and patriotism are mutually exclusive. Many merchants now only accept gold currency or Union notes. The buying power of Confederate notes has become negligible. Prices are so high, many search for alternatives to their normal staples. Some have been eating mule meat for two weeks or more. Root tea, derived from vegetable roots, has become common. Soldiers drink beer fermented from corn.

It is hard to appreciate what starvation will do to the human body. The once-fat are now slender, and the slender have become apparitions. Some families who haven't the money to buy mule meat are chasing rats - and catching them. Stray dogs and cats, once the bane of this city, seem to have all but vanished.

❧

Four days after that entry, Morris trudged down Washington Street, as he often did, looking for an odd chore here or there that might earn him a piece of bread or fruit. As he neared a hardware store, the heavy thump of Yankee cannons and mortars commenced. Morris ducked under the store's awning and found himself crouched beside an emaciated Confederate colonel.

The bombardment lasted only a few minutes, but several shells fell directly on Washington Street.Morris surveyed the damage and decided it wasn't too bad. He then looked across the street and was dismayed to see a severely wounded horse writhing on the ground next to the post to which it had been tied.

"Poor creature," Morris muttered.

The colonel rose to his feet.

"She's mine." He ducked inside the hardware store and emerged with a sledge hammer. He crossed the street and bludgeoned the horse to death, then walked back to the store, cleaning blood from the hammer with a kerchief. He returned the hammer, nodded to Morris, and walked away.

"You're just going to leave her in the street?" Morris asked.

"Watch if you have the stomach," the colonel said over his shoulder.

Confused, Morris waited a few minutes. A Confederate soldier appeared, then another, and another. Soon a small fire had been built in the street and a dozen or more soldiers feasted on the fresh kill. Within an hour, little remained of the horse but a skeleton.

❧

July 1, 1863

Rumors fly as thickly as Yankee shells: General Johnston is coming to rescue Vicksburg. Pemberton will surrender. Robert E. Lee is on the verge of capturing Washington. The military heirarchy does little to dissuade such speculation.What is worse,the local press is all but non-existent. The city's only functioning newspaper, *The Daily Citizen,* is now being printed on the back of old wallpaper due to paper shortages.

Most people, myself included, only concern themselves with their next meal. My clothes hang on me like I am barely solid mass. The thought of rat meat seems less disgusting. Of course, thinking about something requires less effort and fortitude than actually doing it.

July 3, 1863

As I write these words by my last good candle, Vicksburg appears to be on the verge of surrender. Generals Pemberton and Grant met today behind the Yankee lines. They sat beneath an oak tree and talked for a piece. What words passed between them? History will know, but I do not. What is certain is that tonight, for the first time in weeks, Yankee shells are not falling. Silence cloaks us like a sheer garment. And we wait.

July 4, 1863

Independence Day brings no joy to Vicksburg. General Pemberton has surrendered. At 10:00 A.M., the Yankees arrived umolested at the Confederate lines. The Rebel defenders laid down their weapons and quit the fight. A scant few hours later the city was pervaded with bluecoats.

The siege has concluded, but peace does not sit easily. On a positive note, the Yankees brought plenty of provisions with them. I ate my first full meal in a month. If gluttony is a sin, write me in Hell.

The work of rebuilding Vicksburg must now begin. I will try to find useful work. I feel fortunate that I only lost my place of business. My home is remarkably intact. Others lost everything.

47

July 4, 1863

Yankee soldiers swaggered into Vicksburg like a true conquering army. They peered curiously at the city to which they'd lain siege for 47 days. It was different than they'd imagined, many buildings intact, the streets passable, the civilians gaunt but proud.

Along the road, disarmed Confederates watched through hollow eyes, quietly grateful their ordeal was over. They would eat and bathe and talk like human beings again. Vicksburg was lost. That wasn't their fault.

Among the Yankees was a robust Major, stormy-eyed and clean-shaven, with cropped hair. His stride was long and casual. He assessed the city with detached interest. He'd been here before. He'd killed here before, and never been paid for the job. He was glad to be back.

As Pritchard marched through the city, a timid figure in civilian clothes darted from house to house, carefully following his progress. The uniform didn't change anything. It was him. She knew it was him.

July 6, 1863

Winston hobbled to the carriage on Lou's steady arm. Curtis waited on the buckboard, the once ancient slave, now a free man, youthful compared to his sickly former master.

Winston was making his final trip into Vicksburg—that he knew. He would stay with Sam Morris. His health demanded he be near a doctor. The Yankee general and his staff had departed after the siege's conclusion. In their haste to appropriate new quarters in Vicksburg, they'd left the house a shambles. Winston had asked Curtis and Lou to clean up, to take care of *Magnolia* until Andrew returned. Winston had provided for them, making sure their lives would have meaning beyond their servitude. Lou had been deeded 50 acres of farmland on *Magnolia*'s western expanse. Curtis had received $1,000 in Union currency. Both had been so overwhelmed by Winston's beneficence that neither could form words to thank him. Lou tried.

"Massa Winston, we's real glad. . ." She toyed with the hem of her dress. "Me and Curtis just wants to say . . ." She couldn't bring her face up to his.

"What she means . . ." Curtis cleared his throat. "You didn' have to give us nothin'. We reckon you done it from the heart."

"You've both served this family well. I hope your life hasn't been too terrible."

Lou and Curtis tried to talk at once.

"Massa Winston . . ."

Lou spoke first.

"If we didn't work here, Lord knows, woulda been lot worser some place else. Ain't that right, Curtis?"

Curtis nodded slowly. "I's glad we free. But I ain't had all bad." He mumbled. "I thank you for that. And I hope . . . I hope Massa Andrew be home soon."

Andrew's name seemed to jar Winston. He grimaced and slowly climbed onto the wagon.

Newly employed black roustabouts teemed on the bustling Vicksburg docks taking shouted orders from Yankee troops. Cargo was loaded and unloaded from river boats as the business of occupation progressed. A river steamer approached and docked. A single passenger, Jeremy Carthage, waded through the chattering deckhands and organized mayhem. Fifty dollars had bought him passage upriver from New Orleans.

After so many years, he was finally back in Vicksburg. With any luck, he could walk unhindered past the preoccupied Yankee sentries.

"What's your business here, Mr. Harper?" A Union sergeant dubiously inspected Jeremy's identification papers.

"I'm a New York journalist. You've probably read my by-line."

"Yeah, sure."

"The Vicksburg siege is big news back east."

"So?"

"I'm here to report on its conclusion."

"Not without authorization, you ain't. We already have reporters here." The sergeant frowned at Jeremy's credentials. "You can't enter the city without my commanding officer's permission."

"Splendid. Who is your commanding officer?"

"Major Butler. Come with me please."

The Provost Marshal's office was a plain, cheerless building on South Street, a former dry goods store. It was undamaged from the siege and only a short walk from the waterfront. Jeremy entered with his Yankee escort and was instructed to wait in a holding area where incoming prisoners mingled with honest citizens. Two sentries near the door guarded a bizarre array of people on rows of rickety chairs and hard benches. Three young ladies in tattered dresses sat indignantly on a bench. A handful of bedraggled Confederate soldiers stretched on the floor. Jeremy was steered to a bench next to an elderly pastor reading from the New Testament.

Jeremy's escort disappeared through a side door. A moment later the door reopened. An officer entered. Jeremy went parchment pale.

"Small world, eh, Mr. Harper?"

Random terror streaked through Jeremy's brain.

Pritchard approached. "Come with me." His significant left hand fell on Jeremy's shoulder with a controlled squeeze.

Jeremy shuddered, and lost control of his bladder.

"Mr. Harper, there's no need for that. Please come with me."

"How . . .?" The word strangled in Jeremy's throat.

The timbre of Pritchard's voice changed. "*Move!*"

Jeremy looked frantically around the waiting room. The pastor to his left stared at the mountainous Union officer with open fear. Others had discreetly moved away. A Yankee guard grinned stupidly at Jeremy's plight.

Pritchard leaned over and whispered, squeezing harder on Jeremy's shoulder. "Do you know how easily a collarbone can be snapped?"

Jeremy shook his head no. He came to his feet. A stream of urine trickled down his leg and collected at his ankles. He numbly followed Pritchard from the waiting room.

48

JULY 17, 1863

"You have a visitor, Winston." Morris came close to the bed, his eyes shadowed and wary.

Winston struggled to rise, alarmed by Morris's expression. "Who?" he asked weakly.

"Harper. *Jeremy* Harper."

The revelation was slow. Winston's color drained away. "Why is he here?"

"Apparently, to see you. He arrived by boat from New Orleans, but is being detained by the Yankees. Will you see him?"

"He is here? Now?"

The spark in Winston's eyes was a welcome sight to Morris, regardless of the circumstances. "At the Provost's office."

"What does he want?"

Morris shook his head slowly. "You don't have to see him."

"Do me a favor, Sam. Go and make sure it's him."

"It is him."

Winston took a deep breath. "All right then."

"You will see him?"

Winston nodded. "Why not?"

Morris left the room. Winston reached beneath the bed and retrieved his Colt. He placed it on his chest, under the bed covers.

When Jeremy stepped through the door, Winston's emotions were disturbingly powerful, anger and bitterness and lingering questions all compressed into one moment. Love was conspicuously absent.

Jeremy was fit, a few pounds too heavy, his full face surrounded by a trim brown beard, his hair sprinkled with gray tufts. He moved more deliberately, but his familiar smugness was not softened by age.

"Winston."

"Jeremy."

Morris silently watched their strange interaction. Jeremy turned to him.

"May Winston and I speak privately?"

"Of course." Morris closed the door behind him.

"It's been a long time." Jeremy did nothing to hide his shock. Winston looked near-dead, eerily similar to their father in his final days. His long sideburns were stark white. Only his eyes were alive, quick and appraising, hostile.

"Five years." The strength in Winston's voice belied his physical appearance.

"You are ill."

"What do you want?"

Jeremy deflected the terse question. "I was sorry to hear of Elizabeth."

"Thank you. Answer me."

"I was detained for a few days at the Provost's office. They told me you were here." Jeremy came nearer. "What has become of *Magnolia*?"

"It was occupied by a Yankee general during the siege. He moved out afterward. I came here a week ago. Sam is looking after me."

"Who is tending *Magnolia*?"

"Curtis."

Jeremy smiled. "Really? What did the Yankees do to the house?"

"Looted it."

"Did they take everything?"

"Everything worth taking."

Jeremy's eyes were drawn to a point above Winston's head. "You still have your favorite painting."

Winston was unresponsive.

"The one that covered Father's safe?"

"Yes."

"The Yankees discovered the safe?"

"I didn't try to conceal it."

Jeremy was quiet for a moment. "Then where did you hide your money?"

"I *have* no money." Winston had expected the question.

"You lost all of your money? That doesn't sound like you."

"You were a business man in New York. *That* doesn't sound like you."

"Point taken." Jeremy folded his arms. "By the way, how did you know I was in New York?"

"Your wife."

"Ahhh. Meddlesome woman." Jeremy's scowl was momentary. "She discovered my identity years ago. I assume she wrote you?"

"She did."

"Not a terribly trusting consort, my Sophia. I had to leave her."

Winston's lips pursed. "Why her?"

"Because it was so easy. Her family was rich and I apparently resembled her dead husband. For some silly reason, she thought our personalities would be the same."

Winston did not smile. "You should have stayed in New York."

"No, actually I had a few problems there. I had to leave." Jeremy shrugged. "You can't imagine the difficulty of traveling from New York to Vicksburg. This war is very inconvenient."

"You had better leave."

"You can buy me off cheaply, Winston. Otherwise, I will take it all. You know as well as I do that Father's will said the oldest surviving male Carthage inherits that land."

"I was the oldest surviving male Carthage. Now it belongs to me and I can do with it as I please."

"I will find a judge to hear my arguments. You see, I'm considered a Yankee. General Grant is appointing new judges, most of whom are

Yankee sympathizers. And we know about probate cases, don't we? They can last months, years. From appearances, you haven't that long."

"If I had a million dollars, you'd starve on the street like a dog."

"If you had a million dollars, you'd have bribed that Yankee general to stay out of *Magnolia*." Jeremy sat on the edge of the bed. "Which returns me to the question at hand: how much *do* you have Winston?"

"The house, the land, that's all."

"And what of young Andrew? Suppose he doesn't return from the war."

"He will return. Your nephew is a resourceful young man."

"That makes me proud. But he can't start over with no money. He's not like our father."

"You'd be surprised how much like our father he is."

"Touching." Jeremy smirked. "You're smarter than that, Winston. I would wager you saw all this coming." Jeremy reached into his jacket and withdrew a small flask.

"Saw what?"

"This." Jeremy rolled his eyes irritably. "The war."

"I'm not a prophet."

"Just a saint."

Winston disregarded the taunt. "Andrew knows how to run *Magnolia*. He took time to learn."

Jeremy nodded and placed a forefinger to his lips. "You withdrew all that money from the bank before the war. So my guess is, you prepared for the worst. What did you hide—gold? Cash?" Jeremy frowned. "Say it wasn't Confederate cash."

"How do you know of my bank account?"

"Peculiar Fate, she placed a powerful acquaintance of mine in the Provost's office. He's an officer and has amazing access to just about anything, including bank records. Martial law and all. Anyway, you withdrew everything three years ago."

Winston stared evenly at his brother. "I bought Confederate War bonds."

"Really? As I recall, you were once a Unionist."

"People change. Look at you."

"Expedience, Winston, everything I do is for expedience. So where are these war bonds you bought?"

"Ask Milton Green."

"Green died during the siege."

Winston registered this news in the overworked portion of his brain responsible for cataloguing death.

"Strangely, Green had no record of selling war bonds to you."

"Maybe the records were misplaced. I kept them in the bank vault."

"And the vault was looted by Yankee troops. Did *they* steal your bonds?"

Winston wheezed, but didn't answer. Both men were suddenly aware of his failing health.

"What if Andrew doesn't return before your . . . departure?"

"No matter." Winston's breath was shortening.

Jeremy walked to the window and made a small motion with his hand. "You really ought to take precautions, Winston."

"You will get nothing." Winston slipped into a coughing spell. Spasms racked his frail body beneath the covers.

"You haven't changed." Jeremy turned, the amusement on his face pushed away by sudden fury. "The perfect son!"

Winston spoke in a whisper. "And you are an accident of nature."

"I *hear* you, Winston, but barely. You're fading, like Father when Mother died."

Winston closed his eyes.

"How long since Elizabeth passed?"

Winston blinked. He hadn't the strength to resist the question. "Four and a half years."

"What exactly happened?" Jeremy was sadistically curious.

"Her head. Dizzy spells. Lasted for months."

"Her head?"

"She took a fall."

"Her head . . .?"

Jeremy's disbelief was plain. The day in Jackson rushed back to him, the hotel room, her head hitting the wall, the wonderfully prone Elizabeth.

"Why does the manner of her death surprise you?"

"It doesn't." His answer was slow. Winston was saying something. "What?"

"I said Andrew is protected."

"From me?" Jeremy was smug again. "If he is protected, that means you have something to protect. What if he doesn't come home right away? What if the property taxes aren't paid?"

"I paid them."

"Yes, but, the Yankee army will pass an additional property tax to defray occupation costs."

"There is no such tax."

"It will be assessed shortly, my well-placed friend told me. Any property seized for delinquent taxes will be sold at auction. I will be there bidding."

"Get out!" Sweat beads formed on Winston's upper lip.

Jeremy calmly nodded. "You want to die in peace? You don't deserve peace. Since you won't tell me what I want to know, I will tell you something you *don't* want to know." He came closer to the bed. "About Elizabeth."

Winston's features automatically softened.

"She was such an exquisite creature, Winston. And you took her from me. I never really overcame that hurt."

Winston was incredulous. "She made the choice, not me."

"You betrayed me with her just like with Father!"

"She saw through you. As did Father."

"You never spoke ill of me to Elizabeth?"

"I didn't have to."

Jeremy accepted this quietly. His lips spread into a profane half-smile. "I laid with her, Winston."

"Lying bastard!"

"No, it is true. In Jackson, days before the lawsuit was settled. She came there to ask that I drop the suit." His eyes screwed into little balls.

"She wouldn't."

"With me? Not normally. I mean, she hadn't before then. But you see . . ." Jeremy savored his words. ". . . she bumped her head against the wall that day. It put her out of sorts."

"Her head?" Winston's voice went dead.

"An accident, of course. She fell unconscious." Jeremy upturned his palms. "When she woke, the injury must have lowered her inhibitions."

"Oh, God."

"She was quite amorous, trying to persuade me with her affections. I was surprised, a little disappointed."

Winston's face flushed red.

"Put yourself in my place." Jeremy snickered. "I guess you've been in that place a few times, haven't you? You know what I liked? The birthmark on her left thigh—"

"*No!*" Winston roared with all of his ravaged lungs, and an explosion shook the room. Tufts of down feathers burst from Winston's covers and floated above the bed. A small fire spread on the sheets.

Jeremy recoiled. His eyes dropped in wonderment to his chest. The bullet had passed through his heart. He fell to the floor dead as a stone.

"Winston?" Morris crashed into the bedroom nearly tripping over Jeremy. "Christ Almighty, what happened?"

The fire on the bed was growing; Winston was content to let it burn. He drew the smoking pistol from under his blanket and dropped it to the floor. Morris scooped a sheet from the bedside hamper and extinguished the flames.

"What in hell . . .?"

Winston was rigid and inscrutable.

"Winston?"

"He threatened to steal Andrew's inheritance." His monotone was mid-range, not loud or stressed, but serene.

"So you *shot* him?"

"Yes."

"Winston, my God, you can't just—"

"Shoot people." A deep voice came from the doorway, where stood a Union officer. "That is called murder. You are under arrest, Mr. Carthage." He unholstered his pistol. "Mr. Morris, you are under arrest too."

"For what?"

"Conspiracy. You lured Mr. Harper to this house."

"I did no such thing! He asked to come here. And his name isn't Harper, it's . . . it's . . ." Morris stared at the officer. "Wait a minute." He turned to Winston whose expression showed no surprise. "Isn't he . . . ?"

Winston cleared his throat. "Pritchard." He squinted from the bed. "Now apparently someone else altogether."

"I am Major Butler, gentlemen, and you are both going to jail." A hint of a smile turned the corners of Pritchard's mouth. He scooped Winston's Colt from the floor. "Please help Mr. Carthage to his feet."

"I will see General Grant about this!" Morris hissed.

"You'll have to wait your turn. He's rather involved in the process of paroling Confederate troops. A journalist has been killed, and you two are responsible."

"You know damn well Jeremy Carthage was no journalist."

"I *do* know he is dead." Pritchard stepped forward. "Will you come along or must I use force?"

The Vicksburg city jail had been appropriated to house recalcitrant Confederate sympathizers. Moreover, any person not complying with martial law was arrested and hauled before a military tribunal. Legal due process was forsaken in lieu of expedience. General Grant's intention was to quell lingering feelings of rebellion, which meant he administered swift and sure justice to all. But the Provost Marshal's office was given leeway as to who among the arrested were dealt with first. As such, Major Butler was able to forestall arraignment of his two newest prisoners.

Winston sat quietly on his makeshift cot. A blanket was wrapped around him, flouting July's insufferable heat. Jeremy's death caused him no remorse. Killing Jeremy was something he had considered many years earlier. Now it seemed appropriate, like a long forgotten chore he'd finally tended. The things Jeremy had said echoed in his mind . . . Elizabeth had hit her head . . . she had willingly lain with him . . . Of course, Elizabeth would never have seduced Jeremy. And since Jeremy had known of her birthmark, he had violated her person. The last few months of her life became clearer. The sudden mood swings, the sense that she was hiding something, her apparent feelings of guilt. These could all be explained now. Jeremy had raped her and she had hidden it from Winston, knowing to tell him would've meant Jeremy's certain death. A sickness swept over him at her awful burden. Tears dotted his face.

"Weeping for your brother?" Pritchard stood in the cell doorway where he'd been silently watching.

Winston didn't answer. He struggled to sit straight on his cot.

Pritchard entered the cell. "Jeremy owed me from a long time ago. Imagine my surprise when he walked into this office last week. Like an unexpected present."

"Merry Christmas." The bags under Winston's eyes were bluish and puffy.

"We made an arrangement that he was unable to fulfill. He thought you might provide a means of repayment. Now he is dead and you are responsible for his debt." Pritchard sucked on a cigar. Smoke filled the tiny cell.

Winston coughed bitterly. "Any arrangement you had with my brother is based on deceit and extortion."

"That's a matter of interpretation. I performed a service for him and was never paid."

"Jeremy was responsible for my wife's death. He is rotting in Hell where he belongs."

Pritchard's eyebrows furrowed. "Your wife's death?"

"It is a long story." Winston wheezed. "I shan't repeat it."

Pritchard shrugged. "Your brother owed me money, you killed him, now *you* owe me money."

"I am penniless."

"Is that a fact? And what did you do with one hundred thousand dollars you withdrew from the bank three years ago?"

Winston raised two red, weary eyes. "How the hell did you become a Union officer?"

"That is *my* long story and I shan't repeat it." Pritchard smiled. "So you maintain that you have nothing. What about your house?"

"Your colleagues looted it."

"But they found nothing of real value. Just an empty safe and some jewelry, a little silver."

"That's all there was to find." Winston's entire upper body trembled. Sweat poured from his forehead. "Did you enjoy my wine, Major?"

Pritchard's mouth turned down. "You knew I was there that day. . . No matter. You are obviously feverish. Wouldn't it be easier to tell me where you've hidden your money? I can arrange for your brother's death to be decreed self-defense."

"I have no money."

"You could live out your final days at your plantation. Surely that is preferable to a rat-infested jail."

"I cannot give you what I don't have."

Pritchard nodded and turned for the cell door. "Prepare yourself for a trip to *Magnolia*."

Winston looked up. "Why?" But Pritchard was already gone.

"That *is* a fine house." Pritchard gestured with a giant hand toward *Magnolia*. At his signal, two Union soldiers jumped from the wagon and approached the mighty house, studying its foundation closely.

"You are being given another chance."

"At what? I have nothing—" Winston's response degenerated to a low, ugly cough.

"Not without proper motivation."

Winston's tired eyes opened a little wider.

Pritchard pointed. "Demolition experts. Those bundles in the wagon are powder kegs. About three hundred pounds worth. That should do the job, don't you think?"

Winston didn't stir, having already guessed their purpose for being here. He tried to stare at his feet, but was drawn to the soldiers inspecting a turret foundation. "I told you, there's nothing left," he whispered.

"And I don't believe you." Pritchard stepped into Winston's line of sight. "What price to keep your house?"

"You can't destroy private property without cause."

"I can act on little more than a hunch that you've committed crimes against the Union. If you gave money to the Confederacy, I consider that treason."

"Treason? You are a murderer."

Pritchard's brow knotted downward. "As are you."

"My actions were justified."

"Killing one's brother is justified?"

Winston raised his gaunt face and asked a long-held question. "Did Jeremy know you planned to kill that prostitute at the River Club?"

Pritchard paused. "Of course he knew."

"What did he promise you?"

"Five thousand dollars."

Winston's face didn't change.

The demolitionists returned, talking excitedly, clearly enjoying the job at hand.

Pritchard listened as they explained their intentions. "Fuse it."

A dozen small gunpowder kegs were stacked around the foundations of *Magnolia*'s two turrets. Fuses were strung together to achieve simultaneous detonation. The process took some time during which Pritchard closely watched Winston. Winston tried not to notice. The cloying heat made the wait seem interminable. Finally, the demolitionists returned. "Done, sir." The end of a single fuse was handed to Pritchard.

"Are we far enough away?"

The soldiers nodded affirmatively. "Good. Wait by that tree."

They did as instructed.

"Last chance, Carthage." Pritchard placed the fuse on the wagon seat and extracted a match and flint from his pocket. "You don't really want me to do this, do you?"

"I can't stop you."

Pritchard shook his head in mock disappointment. "Such a magnificent house."

"You won't get what you're after." Winston's face was cold and sick.

"We shall see." Pritchard lit the fuse. A sizzling fire snaked toward the house. Nearly a minute passed. Nothing happened.

Pritchard showed no surprise at the misfire.

"Poor bluff, *Major*."

Pritchard grinned. "How did you know?"

"I didn't."

"I don't believe you."

"That is your choice."

Pritchard stopped smiling and turned to the soldiers. "Prepare a real fuse. Mr. Carthage is wasting our time."

The demolitionists re-strung a new fuse, connecting it to each of the shorter keg fuses. They returned and again handed a single fuse to Pritchard.

Winston watched like he was watching his own execution. The long fuse was a hangman's noose—Pritchard the executioner. His stomach turned cartwheels. His eyes grew misty as images of his life washed over him. He remembered the day his father had proudly introduced *Magnolia* to the world. He remembered exchanging wedding vows with Elizabeth on the rear veranda. He remembered the unfettered joy of Andrew's birth and the hapless misery of his father, mother, and wife all taking their last breath within its walls. So much of his life, good and bad, was anchored to its foundation. *Magnolia* was the enduring pillar of the Carthage legacy. It was to be Andrew's home, his children's and grandchildren's. Before Winston could fully comprehend his loss, *Magnolia* ceased to exist.

49

Morris sat in frustration on his cot, trying to conjure legal arguments that might win his freedom. Pritchard had promised him a tribunal hearing within a day or two, but Morris doubted that would happen.

He heard a door open. Slow-moving feet shuffled nearer. A soft click of wood periodically struck the floor.

A faceless voice spoke. "Come on, old man, a few more feet." The adjacent cell door opened, then closed again.

"Winston?" Morris called through the observation port.

"Shut up in there." The guard slammed a rifle butt into Morris's door.

"Is that Mr. Carthage?"

"Yeh, it's him." The irritated guard left the cell block, muttering a string of vulgarities.

"Winston?"

"Hello, Sam."

"Are you hurt?"

"I'm fine."

"Where did he take you?"

"*Magnolia*."

Morris winced. "And?"

"You probably heard the explosion." Winston's voice was calm.

"Actually—"

"Gunpowder kegs. Nothing left."

"God, I'm so sorry, Winston."

Both men were quiet for several minutes. Morris could think of nothing that might cheer his friend. He settled back on his bed, assuming Winston had drifted to sleep, which was for the best.

"I wish I could've seen Andrew once more."

Morris sat up, his emotions betrayed by his stammering voice. "You'll see him. It is only a matter of time."

"Tell him how much I missed him."

"Winston, he certainly knows that." Morris's voice dropped. "But I will tell him."

"Be sure he receives my favorite painting."

"I will but . . . which painting?"

"The magnolia tree. It is in your house."

"I'll be sure."

Winston slumped onto the flat cot. "Thank you, Sam."

Morris woke to jingling keys.

"Come on, Solly. This one's stiff as a Saturday night pecker."

Morris peered helplessly through the observation port as Winston's corpse was hauled from the cell block.

Morris's cell door swung open. Pritchard filled the doorway, an unlit cigar between his fingertips. "Mr. Morris, I am pleased to inform you the charge of accessory to murder will be dropped pending your cooperation."

"What do you want?" Morris was utterly subdued.

"Did Mr. Carthage share anything with you in his final hours?"

"No."

"Nothing at all?"

Morris felt bile in his throat. "Haven't you done enough to the man? He's dead! You can't kill him again."

"Mr. Carthage died from pneumonia and a guilty conscience."

Morris barked, "Guilty conscience? How dare you speak those words, you son of a bitch!" He stepped closer, indifferent to the fact he was berating a dangerous, and very large, man.

"Why glorify Winston Carthage? He was only a man."

Morris was near enough to see Pritchard's soulless eyes. "What have you against his family?"

Pritchard vaguely admired Morris's courage. "Nothing personal. They owe me money."

"For that prostitute at the River Club?"

Pritchard hesitated. "Precisely."

"That is your motivation for two mens' deaths?"

"I killed neither of the Carthages."

"You may as well have. You sent Jeremy to provoke Winston. You exploded his home before his dying eyes!"

Pritchard waved this away with a frown. "Did Mr. Carthage mention where he hid one hundred thousand dollars?"

Morris slowly repeated the number. "A hundred thousand . . ."

"He withdrew it from his bank just before the war. Where did it go, Mr. Morris?"

"I don't—"

"Come now. Who else would he trust with that information?"

Morris was disbelieving. "I know nothing."

Pritchard's voice became agreeable. "Your help might not be necessary. There is another Carthage."

"Andrew," Morris whispered.

"The Confederate hero."

"He can't know. He's been gone for a year and a half!"

"Then he will be returning soon." Pritchard struck a match to his cigar. "I am in no hurry."

50

July 23, 1863

The summer heat tricked Andrew's eyes as he plodded along the railroad tracks outside of Vicksburg. *Magnolia* should've been plainly visible by now, but it wasn't. Vegetation could have grown up since he'd left, or he might be looking in the wrong place. It just didn't figure. An uneasiness crept over him and his pace quickened. His long overdue reunion with his father was close, but where was the house?

As he drew nearer to Vicksburg, he was careful, having just been released from a week-long stay in jail. Patrolling Yankees had confronted him outside of Jackson, which was under siege, and arrested him as a Confederate spy. Ludicrous as the charge was, Andrew had been most aggravated by the fact that he'd made it nearly all the way home, just forty-five miles away, only to be captured by a random Yankee patrol. In jail he had learned of Vicksburg's awful siege and subsequent collapse, heightening his anxiety over his father. Eventually his Yankee captors released him, no longer caring if he went to Vicksburg. Grant was paroling most of the Rebel soldiers there anyway.

Andrew slowed to a halt near a railroad overpass. Several men in blue uniforms stepped onto the track. Sentries. They waved to him and called out, but he would not test Yankee justice again. He sprinted left into the woods. He heard a rifle report and ran faster, south, his line guided by instinct in the clawing vegetation. He was close to home, too close to be sidetracked again by Yankees. Fear of the unknown pushed him, and with each pounding step, his fear veered closer to panic. The Yankees would never catch him in these woods, but every few moments, he stopped and looked at the *Magnolia* hilltop to see only lazy blue sky, a mirage of summer engulfing the house. What in God's name had happened? He visualized his father and ran faster, crashing through vines and underbrush, up hills and down hollows, through small creeks without pause. When he burst from the heavy forest, he was near *Magnolia*'s property line. He closed the remaining distance across an open field and suddenly found himself facing a pair of Yankee soldiers.

"Whoa, boy, where you goin'?"

Andrew instinctively ducked into a crouch. Both soldiers drew their weapons on him.

"I am . . ." Andrew panted and indicated the *Magnolia* carriage path. "I am going up to my house."

"Ain't no house up there."

Andrew's breathing slowed. "What happened?"

"Casualty of war."

"And my father?"

Both soldiers looked perplexed. "Ain't sure. Think he moved into town."

"Then I will be on my way."

"Maybe. Just who are you anyway?"

"Andrew Carthage. I live here. This is my father's land."

"Where you comin' from?"

"East Tennessee"

"You a Rebel soldier?"

"I was."

"Were you fightin' here durin' the siege?"

"No, I was with the Ninth Mississippi under General Bragg." Andrew fidgeted.

"Got any papers?"

"I don't."

"Gotta have papers, especially if you're a soldier."

"*Ex*-soldier. I am unarmed and no threat to anyone. I just want to see what is left of my home."

The soldiers shrugged at each other. "Go ahead. If you ain't back in half an hour, we're comin' after you."

"Half an hour." Andrew trotted up the path.

❧

"My God."

Magnolia was an indistinguishable pile of debris. The once-mighty house was less than a skeleton, a spot on the ground. Timbers, rafters, bricks, any valuable building materials had long since been pilfered, even the turret stones. The basement remained, like a big box, filled with a giant craftsman's discards. Seared pieces of plaster and campfire trash littered the lawn. Andrew had seen battlegrounds with less destruction.

He was jarred from his shock by a voice behind him.

"I's real sorry, Massa Andrew."

"Curtis!" Andrew gasped. "I can't believe it's you." He clutched the old man around his neck. "What happened?"

"Yankees done it." Curtis stepped back, embarrassed by the overt affection. "Jes' last week."

"Where is Father?"

Curtis hesitated. "You ain't been to town?" His words were thick and slow.

"Where is he, Curtis?"

"Massa Winston took sick and stayed with Mr. Morris after the siege."

"Sick?"

"He come back out here las' week."

"What do you mean sick?"

"Powerful sick. Pneumonia."

"Where is he now?"

"Well . . ."

"Talk to me, Curtis!"

Curtis sadly knotted his hands. "He dead, Massa Andrew."

"*Nooo!*" Andrew's anguish rolled through *Magnolia*'s hills. He collapsed to the ground like he'd been shot. Black spots clouded his vision and hot tears rolled down his face.

For a year and a half, through the hell of war and death, the thing he'd wanted more than any other was to see his father again. They had so much to say to each other, so much time lost. His father was dead, and the woman he loved was hundreds of miles away. He felt crushed and hollow, cheated.

"You needs to go to Mr. Morris. That's what your pa tol' me 'fore he left."

Andrew was slow to respond. He struggled to lift his head. "Why Mr. Morris?"

"Don' know."

Andrew made a pathetic noise.

"Massa Andrew, you needs some water."

"Were you with him when he died?"

"Uhhh . . . no, sir."

"Where?"

"He's in town when he passed."

"With Morris?"

"I reckon you could say that."

Andrew's face contorted. "Why are you talking in riddles?"

"Massa Winston died in jail."

"He *what*?"

"Yassa."

"That's an important detail, wouldn't you say, Curtis?" Andrew was shouting.

Curtis nodded. "He was under arrest."

"Why?"

"Cause he . . ." Curtis stared down, ". . . kilt a man."

"Who?"

"Massa Andrew, I don' rightly know—"

"*Who*?"

Curtis looked at the young man he remembered more fondly as a boy. "He shot Massa Jeremy."

Andrew's rising anger softened. He spoke deliberately. "Tell me again why Father was arrested?"

Curtis was resolute. "He shot Massa Jeremy. Leastways that's what Lou told me."

"Lou told you."

"Yassa, she did."

"And how did she know?"

"She say Massa Jeremy was in town. He went to Mr. Morris' house to see your pa. That's when he got shot."

"Where is Father now?"

Curtis pointed toward the family cemetery.

Andrew's eyes clouded again and his lower lip quivered. "Who buried him?"

"I did."

"Oh, Christ." Andrew looked away. Gradually, the barren hilltop came into focus. He sniffed and croaked, "What happened to the house?"

"Yankees blowed it up," Curtis mumbled. "Your pa was with 'em."

"That doesn't make sense, Curtis."

"I seen the whole thing from over in them woods. Your pa didn' have no mind to be here."

"They made him watch?"

"Yassa."

"Why?"

Curtis shrugged.

Andrew rose to a knee. "I want to see his grave." He hesitantly stood, but the tears fell again, as did he. Curtis dropped an arm around Andrew's shoulders and tried not to cry with him.

AMNESTY OATH

STATE of MISSISSIPPI,

Warren County.

I, _______ , do solemnly swear, in the presence of the Almighty God, that I will hereafter faithfully defend the Constitution of the United States thereunder, and that I will in like manner abide by and support all laws and proclamations which have been made during the existing rebellion, with reference to the emancipation of Slaves. So help me God.

_________________________ (Affiant signature)

Sworn and subscribed before me, this____ day of______, A.D. 1863.

_________________________ *(Justice of the Peace)*

Andrew barely read the oath that had been thrust before him. He signed without a second thought. His war was over.

"The Major will see you now."

"Major who?"

"Major Butler, the deputy Provost Marshal."

"Why must I see him?"

The clerk indifferently lifted his shoulders. "He's in charge."

Andrew was led to a well-furnished office where a Major, a huge man, sat behind a desk. He looked up.

"Lieutenant Carthage?" His bottomless voice was unsettling.

"Not anymore. Just Carthage, Andrew."

"Sit."

Andrew slid into the seat, transfixed. The Major had an evil aura, a crude and convincing ruthlessness. Andrew knew many pure killers from the war. This man rivaled any of them.

"I am Major Butler, Deputy Provost." Pritchard tapped a pencil on the desktop. "Why did you run from my sentries at the Railroad Redoubt?"

Andrew wondered how the Major knew it had been him. "I haven't been home in almost two years."

"Home would be the *Magnolia* plantation?" It was more statement than question.

"Yes. What is left of it."

"You mean the house. Very unfortunate."

Andrew sat straighter. "Do you know why it was destroyed?"

"More or less." Pritchard's obtuse answer was measured. "The land will be placed at auction next month."

"What land?"

"Your father's land."

"What are you talking about?"

"Your father owed back taxes on his property and was fined for war crimes."

Andrew scowled. "My father never committed war crimes."

Pritchard acted as if he hadn't heard. "Crimes against the Union."

"What specifically?"

Pritchard stared hard, but Andrew wouldn't look away. "Your father's fines amount to three thousand four hundred dollars. If you want that land, you must pay the fine."

"I don't have such money."

"Pity." Pritchard showed not a hint of pity.

Andrew tried to push the Major from his mind. "Surely Father left me something." He was confused, thinking out loud.

"He left the property and house to you, no money to speak of, about eighteen dollars in his bank account. His final grasp at human decency was to free his slaves. It cost him." Pritchard sniffed. "A nice gesture, but no help to you."

"How do you know all that?"

"It is my job. Your father died six days ago. His will was on file in the chancery clerk's office, written by an attorney named Dobbins some years ago."

Andrew was beginning to understand. He observed Pritchard's casual menace and felt a coldness pass over him. "You blew up my house."

Pritchard was altogether benign. "Your father was harboring Confederate fugitives."

"That's ridiculous. My father hated this war."

"Be that as it may . . ."

Andrew rose halfway from his chair. "What did he ever do to you?"

"Nothing, really. Mr. Carthage, shall we end this interview?"

"Bastard."

Pritchard stood to his full height. "Be very careful."

Andrew gulped. The Major was simply enormous. "I just signed an oath that says I'm a citizen. You can't hurt me."

Pritchard's mouth thinned in faint disapproval. "Rather a pathetic position for a Confederate soldier to assume."

Andrew hesitated. "Am I free to leave?"

"Certainly." Pritchard allowed himself a smile. The boy was much easier than his father. "I must know where you're staying."

For the first time, Andrew sensed his own plight—homeless and destitute. Where would he go?

"I will be staying with Sam Morris."

"Excellent. Mr. Morris currently occupies a jail cell just down the hall."

51

The tiny visitor's room door swung inward.

"Andrew!" Morris nearly tripped over his shackles hurrying across the dirt floor. He was trailed by a bored-looking Union corporal.

"Mr. Morris." Andrew waited quietly at a small table, unbelieving that the waif in chains was really Sam Morris. He was thirty pounds lighter than Andrew remembered.

Morris slid gracelessly into a chair across from Andrew. "How are you?"

"I am fine, Mr. Morris, and you?"

"I've had better days. You look well."

"As do you."

Morris laughed "You're kind, but that is not true."

"How did . . . ?"

"I become skinny? Food was scarce during the siege." Morris coughed and nervously rubbed his hands together. "When did you return?"

"This afternoon."

"Then you know?"

"Curtis told me about Father."

Morris shifted in his chair and glanced at the sentry. "Did Curtis tell you everything?"

Andrew shook his head. "Curtis was confused. He's very old."

"Outlandish tales are sometimes true."

"I don't think so, Mr. Morris."

"Call me Sam." Morris dropped his voice. "By the way, that guard has probably been told to report everything we say."

"Hey!" The sentry stomped over from the door and poked Morris hard in the ribs with his rifle butt. "No whisperin'!"

Andrew rose from his chair, but the sentry was braced for a challenge. Andrew returned to his seat.

Morris struggled for breath. "Sorry. Won't happen again."

"See that it don't!" The sentry skulked back to the wall, sneering openly at Andrew. "And remember where you're at, boy. We don't take guff from Rebels in here."

Morris turned to Andrew, holding his palms up, urging him not to speak. "Let it be." Morris breathed hard. "Your father died under very unfortunate circumstances. I was party to the incident that prompted his arrest."

"What incident?"

"Winston became very ill during the siege. Afterward, he stayed with me. One day, he had a visitor named Jeremy Harper." Morris fumbled for words. "He was . . . they argued and . . . and your father shot him." Morris shifted in discomfort. "Harper was your Uncle Jeremy."

Andrew stared at Morris. "Why was . . . where did he come from?"

"New York, I think."

"And why did Father kill him?" Andrew's voice had lost its energy.

"Hard to say. Moments after, we were arrested. I am being held as an accomplice." Morris swayed in his chair. "Winston was too sick for jail. He passed away about a week ago, just after the house . . ."

Andrew incrementally assimilated each bit of news. "Why *was* our house destroyed?"

"That was a personal matter between your father and Major Butler."

"Who is this Major Butler?"

"I really can't say." Morris eyed the sentry.

An awkward silence developed. Andrew slumped in his seat, trying to imagine his father shooting his uncle. It was too incredible.

Morris changed the subject. "How did you come to be here?"

"I was given a furlough."

"You were in Tennessee?"

Andrew dully nodded. "Near Chattanooga."

"Must've been quite a journey home."

"Very long."

"Yes." Morris was at a rare loss for words.

Andrew spoke to the guard. "I will give you ten dollars if you leave us alone for one minute."

"Bribery is a crime, boy."

"I'd like to speak privately to Mr. Morris. Please."

"I got orders. No secrets. Can't let you Rebels be schemin'."

Andrew could think of nothing persuasive to change his mind. "Sam, when will you be released from here?"

"That depends on if they pursue charges against me."

Andrew furiously rubbed his forehead. He felt he was being checkmated on the third move of a match. "What will I do?"

"You can stay at my house. I'm certainly not using it. A few of your father's things are still there."

"Thank you."

Morris nodded and seemed to reach a decision. He suddenly began to talk. He spoke of the weather, his most fearful moments of the siege, the newspaper business. He talked for five minutes while a bewildered Andrew listened. The guard disinterestedly leaned against the wall and closed his eyes. Amidst all the blather, Morris fumbled with the semi-attached leather of his boot heel. He reached across the table and placed an object in Andrew's hand.

"Your father wanted the best for you."

The guard perked at these words, but his eyes remained closed.

"I know." Andrew recognized the gold coin at once.

Morris continued. "We spoke often before his death. He was lonely for you."

Andrew didn't know what to say. "Me, too."

"I'm very sorry, Andrew." Morris tried to hold Andrew's eye. "When he died, you were his sole benefactor."

"That will do me no good. Major Butler said *Magnolia* will be auctioned."

"Don't be surprised if he is the buyer."

"*What?*"

"Never mind." Morris had said too much. "We will talk again when I am released."

Andrew was drawn to the coin in his closed hand. He didn't care if the guard was listening. "He only gave you one of these?"

"Yes."

"There were two."

"Oh." Morris thought for a moment and smiled. "Oh."

At first, Andrew was too preoccupied to notice. Eventually, the same thought occurred to him. He was about to speak when Morris cut him off.

"You should go."

"I will." Andrew slid the gold piece into his pocket. "I'll come see you again if you'd like."

"Please do. And be very careful, especially of Major Butler."

Andrew shielded the afternoon sun with his hand and waited for inspiration. None came. He peered up and down the crowded street seeking a familiar face, but saw only Yankee soldiers and groups of newly freed slaves.

His father had forgotten to pay property taxes. That made no sense.

Andrew wandered from the jail, allowing his feet to carry him south, back toward home, or what once was home. He absently flicked drops of perspiration from his eyes. His mind drifted, wondering about his grandparents, his parents, his uncle, all dead in the last five years. Strangely, none had fallen to the war that had taken so many lives. Andrew was the only Carthage to have fought, and the only Carthage to have survived.

Familiar landmarks pried into his thoughts, houses of families he had known, obliterated for sport to satisfy a vindictive army. But what was Major Butler's motivation for destroying *Magnolia*? Greed? Revenge? Other questions puzzled him. What about the gold coin? The coins had been in the safe at *Magnolia*, but *Magnolia* was gone. Unless the Major knew about the bearer bonds. But how could he? Andrew himself didn't know where they were, or if they still existed. If they had remained in the safe until the end, they were surely gone. His father would've moved them before then, wouldn't he?

Andrew drew a breath as he neared *Magnolia*'s carriage path. He urged himself upward. The Yankees would've searched the house before destroying it. They would've found the safe, but he had to look.

He approached *Magnolia*'s rubble on unsteady feet, kicking disgustedly at a pile of soggy plaster. With little enthusiasm, he peeled off his shirt and began to search where he reckoned the safe-bearing wall to have stood. The sun worked hungrily on his exposed back. After a fruitless hour of burrowing, instead of the safe, he found Curtis standing silently nearby.

"Hello, Curtis."

"Massa Andrew."

"Call me Andrew."

"All right."

Andrew self-consciously toed a rubbish heap. "I'm sorry I doubted what you told me."

Curtis looked down. "Don't matter none."

"It does to me." Andrew squinted in the morning sun. "Curtis, there was a big man, a Yankee Major. Do you know what happened between him and Father?"

Curtis shook his head. "But that Major blowed up the house."

Andrew nodded. "My father used to have a safe, Curtis. It was—"

"In the study."

Andrew's face crinkled. "How did you know?"

"Ain't much I don' know 'bout this place."

A nagging thought entered Andrew's head which he summarily dismissed. "Did you see Father remove anything from it before he left?"

"Naw. He didn' never open it when I's around." Curtis rubbed the white whiskers on his chin. "Massa Andrew . . . Andrew, you ain't gonna find nothin' down in that mess."

"Probably not."

"Whatcha lookin' for anyways?"

"Hmmm? Paper, just paper I think."

Curtis frowned. "I reckon."

Andrew chuckled. "A special type of paper, a debt instrument."

Curtis's mind veered in the direction of musical instruments and he was more confused than ever. But he did know a few things.

"Your pa knowed the Yanks was comin'. He didn't leave nothin' he thought they wouldn't find."

Andrew nodded, not really listening. "What did you just say?"

"I think Massa Winston let 'em find some stuff so maybe they won't go lookin' for other stuff."

Andrew's rust-colored eyebrows squeezed together. "He deliberately let them find something?"

Curtis pointed to where a row of rose bushes should've stood. Instead, a dozen holes punctuated their absence.

"The rose garden? What did they find?"

"Silver, some jewelry."

"Where was it hidden?"

"Under a bush."

"Buried treasure." Andrew smiled. "So trite."

Curtis didn't know "trite" either, but gathered Andrew's meaning. "I seen where Massa Winston had been diggin' and he didn't hide it none."

"He was deceiving the Yankees. If that's true, then he had another hiding place."

"I s'pose."

"Where?"

"Maybe the bank."

"Too risky. It was a lot of money."

"I thought you said paper."

"Convertible bonds."

"Oh." Curtis stroked his white whiskers. "He was stayin' at Mr. Morris' house 'fore he passed."

Andrew slapped his forehead. "Damn! I meant to go there."

"Gettin' late. You can go tomorrow."

"I will, first thing."

Curtis frowned. "I forgot to give you somethin' earlier."

"What?"

"Letter from your pa."

"Why do *you* have it?"

"I s'pposed to go to Warrenton and mail it, but the Yankees got here 'fore I could." Curtis looked down. "You ain't mad, is you?"

"Of course not. Where is it now?" Andrew asked.

"'Neath my mattress. I didn't open it or nothin'."

"Show me."

"Yassa."

Andrew and Curtis made the short walk to Curtis's old slave shack. It was a simple sturdy building, a single large room with beds arranged haphazardly around the floor. It was the former home to all of *Magnolia*'s domestic slaves. Now, only Curtis remained. Lou had moved into town and taken a job as a seamstress for the Yankee army.

Curtis reached beneath his straw mattress and produced Winston's letter.

Andrew read it through quickly first, more slowly the second time. Each word tormented him. He pictured his father, lonely, sick, worried. Tears poured down his cheeks.

Curtis coughed. "I got some stew if you's hungry."

"I'm famished, thank you." Andrew accepted a bowl of vegetable stew. He hadn't realized Curtis had been cooking. He sniffed and tried to concentrate. An unclear question formed in his mind.

Andrew tried the door knob to Morris's house. Unlocked. He entered a small hallway. The house smelled musty and old, neglected. Andrew looked around and wondered how Morris had escaped any direct hits from Yankee shells during the siege. Every building in town seemed to have suffered some measure of damage, but not here.

To his right was a closed door. He walked straight ahead and found the kitchen. An old pot-bellied stove and a functional table were the only items in the room. Andrew passed through to a small sitting room, and beyond, a bedroom. He stopped. The bedroom, which he assumed was Sam's, had been ransacked.

Andrew cautiously retreated through the kitchen and placed his hand on the closed door. This room would have been his father's. He stepped inside and saw it too had been ransacked, only worse. He recognized the remnants of his father's suits. They were torn apart, cut open at the seams by a sharp object. The bed had been completely destroyed; somehow, even its oak posts had been split in two. A million down feathers were all that remained of a quilt. A painting had been ripped from the wall and cast aside.

Andrew's gaze drifted to the floor to a dark stain just beneath his feet. Blood? Uncle Jeremy's blood? He stepped away from it.

What did he hope to find? Surely the bonds weren't here. A clue? He scuffled across the floor. No papers, nothing as obvious as a diary. He dropped to his knees and searched below the mattress. He lifted the rugs and rifled a chest of drawers. Someone before him had searched the same places.

He sat on the bed's edge, not caring too much that he'd found nothing. The room was impossibly hot, even so early in the morning. He sweated freely. This was where his father had spent his final days, on this bed. What had he been feeling, what had driven him to kill his only brother? Uncle Jeremy had come home for a reason. Money seemed to have been the motivating factor in his life. Had Winston denied it to him? Probably. But then why kill him? Had it been self defense? No, Morris would have told him that.

Andrew closed his eyes and pictured Jeremy, standing there, smiling in his smart-aleck way. Winston would've shot him from the bed.

Money, they would've argued over money.

He stood and walked to the face-down painting on the floor. He lifted it. The magnolia tree, his father's favorite, the painting that . . . had once covered the safe.

Hairs on the back of his neck raised, but not from sudden realization. He heard breathing. He wheeled around and stared into the gray depths of Major Butler's eyes.

"What exactly are you doing?"

Andrew felt his stomach toss. "Looking through my father's effects." His voice halted.

"Actually, you are trespassing."

"Sam Morris gave me permission. Why are you following me?"

Pritchard ignored the question. "Did you make this mess?"

"I did not." Andrew studied Pritchard's harshly expressionless face. It was tranquil, without creases, but simultaneously violent. "Why are you following me?" he asked more insistently.

"Security reasons." Pritchard scanned the room.

Andrew knew who had ransacked the house. "Did you find anything here, Major?"

"Me? What would I be looking for?"

"I can't imagine."

Pritchard easily withdrew a pistol from his jacket. "Is that true?"

Andrew cursed his own carelessness. "What do you want?"

"Whatever brought you here."

As casually as he could, Andrew tossed the painting away. "There's nothing."

Pritchard removed his hat. "Such a smart man, your father. Did he protect his money from the ravages of war?" His smile was icy. "We both know he did. The only question is: how?"

"You told me yourself about the will."

"He wouldn't have been stupid enough to reveal anything in a will. Let us not deceive each other." Pritchard came nearer.

"You are wasting your time, Major."

"No, *you* are wasting *my* time." Pritchard struck Andrew hard across his right cheek sending him to the ground.

"If you want to try my patience, we can . . ." Pritchard was looking at Andrew's back pocket where an envelope protruded. He reached down and snatched it before Andrew could stop him.

Pritchard tore open the letter and read. Andrew sat glumly on the floor, a hand pressed against his swelling cheek.

"From your father. Not very interesting." Pritchard muttered. He read further. "He confesses to killing a man." Pritchard smiled at Andrew. "That would be your uncle."

Andrew looked away, trying not to reveal differently.

Pritchard finished the letter. "The last part where he writes '. . . one must know where to dig.'—what do you suppose he meant by that?"

Andrew was silent.

"Maybe he meant that he buried his money. What do you think?"

"I think you are a lunatic."

"Non-responsive, try again." Pritchard cocked the hammer on his pistol.

"He had no money, you said so yourself."

"He declared no money, but Winston Carthage took precautions." Pritchard nodded as if agreeing with himself. "He had to be practical."

"I can't tell you what I don't know."

Pritchard's face clouded. He held the letter up again. "If he was referring to your uncle, the date is wrong."

Andrew tried to disrupt Pritchard's thoughts. "He might've hidden—"

"Shut up!" Pritchard barked. "This letter was written before the siege even began. But he shot Jeremy after Vicksburg had fallen." Pritchard concentrated. "That means he killed someone else. Hmmm."

"What is the difference?"

"None, I suppose. Getting back to my original thought, what would he have buried? The obvious answer is Union currency. He was paying his slaves with Union notes, but I don't think that was it. Something negotiable."

"Why?" Andrew was curious to hear Pritchard's reasoning.

"Because I found a letter in his bank file. He went to New Orleans just before the war and transacted some business there."

"Perhaps what you seek is in New Orleans."

"New Orleans would have been no safer than here. He knew that. He would want it close, whatever *it* might be. Not stocks—too risky. Probably not gold—too difficult to hide." Pritchard snapped his fingers. "Negotiable bonds! He couldn't buy them in Vicksburg and went to New Orleans. The perfect solution!"

Andrew failed to hide his disappointment.

"So it *is* negotiable bonds, probably government bonds." Pritchard knelt down and softly spoke. "And you've seen them. Are they *bearer bonds* by any chance?"

Andrew mumbled, "I don't know what a bearer bond is."

"Where did he bury them, Andrew?"

"Like I said, you're a lunatic."

Pritchard kicked Andrew fiercely in the chest. His boot toe separated two ribs and ripped cartilage from bone. Andrew screeched.

Pritchard leaned so close, Andrew could see his razor stubble. "My patience is a precious commodity. Don't fritter it."

"I don't know anything." Andrew struggled to sit up.

"I think you do." Pritchard went to a chair near the door and sat, enjoying himself. "Logically, if your father brought his bonds to this house, they would still be here. But they aren't. On the other hand, if he buried them, then perhaps he left a clue here." Pritchard stroked his temple. "You came expecting to find something. What could it be?"

"I told you why I came here."

Pritchard waved this away. "Something we both missed, something subtle." He strolled across the small room and stopped next to the painting.

Andrew held his breath. He had to draw Pritchard away from the painting.

Pritchard was talking to himself. "He was too weak to do much."

Andrew jumped to his feet and ran for the door. Pritchard easily beat him there. He grasped Andrew around the neck.

"Very dumb."

He sent Andrew tumbling back into the room. Andrew landed with a *crack!* atop the painting. He sat, wondering how long it would take . . .

Pritchard frowned. "Stand up, please."

Andrew didn't move.

"*Stand up!*"

Andrew rose.

"Turn that painting over."

He did.

Pritchard came closer, his eyes thinning with interest. "Those signature initials—W.C." He laughed. "How did I miss that?"

Andrew seethed, but said nothing.

"That tree is familiar. And the lake." Pritchard nodded. "Winston made a point to bring that painting with him. You already knew, didn't you?"

"Bastard."

"An orphan to be precise, but let's not quibble." He wagged the pistol. "Shall we take a wagon ride?"

❧

Andrew's bound hands were secured behind his back. He was led to a wagon in front of Morris's house. Pritchard's pistol dug into the small of his back.

"Remember, don't yell for help, and I won't kill you."

"Why do you need me?"

"Silly boy. You will dig for me."

As the wagon pulled away, a lurker emerged from a bush row across the street. Momentarily indecisive, the hooded figure turned and walked briskly in the opposite direction.

❧

The desk lieutenant looked up from his newspaper in surprise. "Can I help you?"

"I'd like to see Sam Morris."

"Really. Why?"

"Do I need a reason?"

The lieutenant grinned, appraising his visitor. He slid around the front desk, thinking the good Lord's benevolence always arrived most unexpectedly.

"All visitors are authorized by—" His thought ended prematurely when he discovered a pistol pointed between his eyes.

❧

Morris nervously paced his cell. He had to speak with Andrew. He'd lain awake all night. It had come to him in the early morning. He knew where Winston had hidden the money.

The cell block door clanged open. Lunch time. It always came just after noon when the wise-assed lieutenant brought him a pail of table scraps.

Morris had to escape or convince the lieutenant to free him. He watched through the square port on his door. The lieutenant's face appeared.

Morris expected the usual command to step back. A set of keys jingled and the door came open. Instead of a food pail, the lieutenant slunk inside. His face was white. He moved to the bed and sat dutifully without speaking.

"What are you . . .?" Morris turned and saw a hooded figure in the doorway with a gun.

"Come along."

Morris was stunned. "Holy Christ. How did you—"

"We have no time. Come along!"

Morris needed no further persuasion. He glanced at the forlorn lieutenant and pulled the door shut behind him.

❧

Andrew's tightly bound wrists chafed with each bump in the road. He could've kicked himself for being Major Butler's easy prey.

Pritchard steered the wagon through a Union check point without a hitch. The deferential sentries worked for him and were uniformly afraid of their commanding officer. They didn't even offer a question about his prisoner. Andrew considered appealing for help, but decided the Major really *would* shoot him dead.

Midway through the long ride to *Magnolia*, Pritchard spoke. "Don't feel too bad. I've bested much better men than you."

Andrew wondered how the Major knew exactly what he was feeling, but didn't ask.

"You are still young," Pritchard mused. "You can recover from this."

"Recover from what?" Andrew was numb. With every passing moment, his heart closed more tightly around his emotions.

"Poverty." Pritchard smiled. "I was born into it, and I'm about to do well for myself."

"You had better kill me."

Pritchard chuckled. "Or else?" He laughed harder and seized Andrew by the hair, pulling him close. "Be nice and I *might* kill you." His eyes gleamed several dark colors at once. "There are worse things than death." He shoved Andrew back against the seat.

Andrew stared ahead, not as scared as he'd been earlier. The Major was right, there *were* worse things than death.

They reached the *Magnolia* carriage path after twenty long minutes and drove past.

"Where are you going?"

"To the lake."

"Use the carriage path and cut through the main property."

"Very well."

Pritchard reversed the wagon and guided them up the carriage path. When they reached the plateau, Andrew didn't look to where the house should have stood. He was searching . . .

Curtis walked toward them from the servant's quarters. He half-waved until he saw Pritchard. He stopped.

Pritchard turned and conversationally spoke. "You really thought an old man could help you?" He brought the wagon closer to Curtis. "Good afternoon!"

"Afternoon." Curtis hooded his eyes. "Massa Andrew, you all right?"

"Yes, I'm—"

"He is fine," Pritchard interjected. "Who might you be?"

"Curtis."

"Curtis, can you find a shovel?"

"I reckon. Why you gots Massa Andrew tied up?"

Pritchard aimed his pistol. "Fetch a shovel."

Curtis did as told. He was ordered into the wagon. They were all taking a trip to the lake.

❧

"What we lookin' for?" Curtis squinted up and down the shore.

"A gold coin." Andrew spoke softly and kicked through the grass beneath the giant magnolia tree. Pritchard conducted his own survey a few feet away.

Curtis watched Pritchard and talked low. "It ain't in the lake is it?"

"Under the tree, I think."

"Oh." Curtis nodded with realization. "Massa Winston's paintin'."

"Yes."

Pritchard came nearer. "Where shall we start, gentlemen?"

Curtis shrugged. Pritchard handed him the shovel. "Make holes."

Curtis began to dig. His strokes were slow and methodical. In moments, he was heavily sweating. Each time he bent, his bones seemed to creak and moan, reminding him his days of hard labor were better gone.

"Let me dig," Andrew said.

"In time."

"Why are you doing this?"

Pritchard's laugh was dry and humorless. "Settling a long overdue debt."

"What debt?"

"Nothing you would know about. It involved your uncle."

"You knew my father *and* my uncle?"

"Yes. We had a business arrangement some years ago. I was never compensated."

"That is a shame." Andrew's stare was level.

"You don't posture as well as your father." Pritchard drew closer. "Winston and I met once at this very lake. I remember being impressed by the beautiful magnolia tree."

"Shall we chop it down? Death seems to be your expertise."

"I've waited a long time," Pritchard said. "You would do well not to antagonize me."

Andrew bristled. "You are a Yankee. How did you ever know my Father?"

"Before the war. My business was more precisely with your uncle. He could not pay for services rendered and the responsibility became your father's."

"And the type of business?"

"Is irrelevant."

"How much are you owed?"

Pritchard frowned in thought. "I'm taking all of it."

Andrew snorted. "Go to hell."

"Undoubtedly. Your turn to dig."

Andrew was calculating the distance between Pritchard and himself.

Pritchard cocked the pistol. "That would be very unwise."

"Major, I won't help you. Are you prepared to kill two people to settle your debt?"

Pritchard showed a row of even white teeth. The pistol roared. A bullet sent Curtis careening into the lake. He sank in the waist-high water then floated to the surface. His chest wound busily exchanged blood for water as he bobbed.

Andrew couldn't find breath. He fell to his knees. "Curtis . . ."

Pritchard was nonchalant, a heinous smile on his face. "Slaves are expendable in your world, are they not?"

Andrew had seen sudden death a hundred times on the battlefield, good men who didn't deserve to die. But nothing had hurt him like this. Curtis, the sweet old man he'd taught to read, the man with whom he'd caught his first fish, the friend who'd once explained the mysteries of the female body . . . Andrew's rage caused him to instinctively coil.

Pritchard re-cocked the hammer, daring him to charge. "*Pick up the shovel!*"

Andrew looked at Pritchard for an eternity. He had never wanted to kill so badly, not in his worst moment. He raised himself from the ground. "Where?"

"Anywhere will do." Pritchard's voice was remarkably unchanged. "And that shovel is a poor match for a bullet. Believe it."

Andrew's lips were parted in dismay. He lifted the shovel and plunged it downward. Feverish tears rolled from his cheeks and were swallowed in the dark earth where he dug.

Pritchard walked in small circles. "None of this ground has been recently disturbed."

Andrew mindlessly continued to dig in the same spot.

"That's deep enough. Try somewhere else."

Andrew moved a few feet away and began another hole. He forced himself to talk, but his voice was trembling and arrested. "You never told me your business with my uncle."

"Why speak ill of the dead? Your uncle was not a good person."

Andrew stopped digging. "How dare you judge another man?"

"He hired me to frame your father for murder."

"That is ridiculous."

Pritchard waved the pistol. "Start a new hole. Your uncle was trying to affect the outcome of his lawsuit against your father."

"Lawsuit?" Andrew remembered. "My father was never involved in a murder, and he won that lawsuit."

"Jeremy's scheme failed."

"He failed or you failed?"

"I fulfilled my obligation."

"And you were promised money?"

"Five thousand dollars to be exact. There are some details I omitted."

Andrew swung a shovelful of dirt at Pritchard's face and missed. The gun discharged and a bullet lodged in Andrew's right shoulder sending him to the ground. He tried to gain his feet, but Pritchard was over him instantly and kicked him in the stomach. Andrew's breath left him in a rush and he was still.

A rope held Andrew fast to the giant magnolia tree trunk. The wound in his right shoulder seared with pain. Ironically, he'd fought a year and a half in the war and never received a scratch, only to be shot on his own property.

Pritchard removed his shirt in the afternoon sun. His physique, Andrew noted, was astonishing. His waist was narrow and his shoulders and chest were obscenely muscular.

Pritchard drove the blade downward and tossed the earth aside with casual flicks of his wrists. His holes were concise and sure. Soon more than a dozen dotted an area beneath the tree. He took a break and stood over Andrew.

"You know a way to shorten this search, don't you?"

Andrew didn't, but said nothing.

Pritchard struck him hard across his cheek, jarring him to the left. Andrew's head snapped back and lolled forward.

Pritchard strode to a different side of the tree and dug some more. Ten minutes later, sweat cascading from him, Pritchard again addressed Andrew. His question went unanswered and he pounded Andrew's face. This seemed to satisfy him and he made more holes.

The third time Pritchard approached, Andrew's silence was met by consecutive punches on his chin and nose. The final blow knocked him unconscious.

"What is this?"

Andrew woke from his stupor. His eyes had swollen shut and his lips were thick and shredded. Blood loss tolled him.

"This spot has been dug recently, within the last few months I'd say." Pritchard pierced the earth. Then again. Finally, he struck something. He carefully expanded the hole and bent over to see. Andrew couldn't tell what he saw.

Pritchard dug with his hands, rapidly at first, then slower. "What do you know about that?" he muttered. "A Confederate soldier. Been here a while." He stopped to ponder this development.

"Of course!" He turned to Andrew, who was drifting in and out. "Winston's letter said he killed someone else." Pritchard leaned on the shovel. "I wonder why a soldier?" He stared at the putrid corpse.

"This man is with the Third Louisiana Infantry according to his identification disk. His company fought here during the siege. He must've stumbled onto this place while your father was burying his money. Yes, Winston would've had to kill him. In cold blood." Pritchard nodded in approval.

Pritchard also realized the corpse was a confirmation that the money was close. Properly motivated, he started a new hole only a few feet from the grave. The shovel blade struck a solid object.

"Here is something!" Pritchard dug faster.

Andrew vainly tried to focus, but drifted away to the inexplicable sound of breaking glass.

Andrew's mind swirled with visions of blood and gore. In his vile dream, bad men took advantage of the unsuspecting. Everyone died, everyone except him. And no matter how hard he fought, no matter how many times he exposed himself to the enemy, he lived. He didn't want to be alone, he wanted to go where the others had gone, to their peace.

He was jolted awake by a sharp noise. His eyes fluttered open. He couldn't tell how long he'd been delirious. Pritchard was to his right, near the lake. He stood very still, the shovel in his right hand, the pistol tucked in the small of his back. He bore an odd, shaken expression.

What was it? Andrew strained to see. He looked left and . . . there were two people. They stared at him. One was Sam Morris, and the other was . . . Andrew tried to open his puffy eyes wider. It couldn't be. The dream was intruding on his conscious thoughts. He wanted to call out, to warn them, but he hadn't the strength. Morris spoke.

"You can't get away with this, not now." Morris inched forward, holding a pistol, but not with confidence. He stole a glance at Andrew. "Hello, there."

Andrew slurred, "Gunnnn," and his head fell forward.

Pritchard's face contorted. He had to pull his eyes away from the person who stood beside Morris. "Mr. Morris, you escaped from my jail. This . . . this *lady* must've helped you."

"On your knees."

Pritchard didn't move. "You are not sure with that pistol."

Morris drew back the hammer. Only fifeteen feet separated them. "I would enjoy killing you, Pritchard."

Andrew wished his dream would hurry and end.

"I can see that you're serious." Pritchard made a submissive gesture. "Of course, you're an escaped convict. What had you planned to do beyond this point?"

"On your knees."

"As you wish." Pritchard made as if to lower himself to the ground. At the last moment, he hurled the shovel high in the air toward Morris. A split second later, he charged.

Morris watched the shovel sailing at him. He ducked away and righted himself just as Pritchard's enormous weight crashed into him. His breath was knocked out and the gun flew from his hand. He tried to fight back, but was pinned to the ground like a small child by a bully. A punch shattered his nose. Bright lights exploded in his eyes and he gasped for air as blood filled his nasal cavities. Then he was pulled up by the throat.

"On *your* knees, Mr. Morris," Pritchard hissed.

Morris was limp as a rag doll.

Pritchard placed two hands around Morris's head, employing his favorite death grip. He tensed.

Click!

Pritchard looked up and saw the woman pointed a cocked gun at him. They stared at each other across a gulf of hate. She pulled the trigger and the gun roared. She missed.

Pritchard dropped Morris and leaped at her. She tried to re-cock the hammer, but was too slow. She was rooted to the spot, paralyzed in terror. Pritchard seized the gun and dragged her to a bare spot beneath the tree. She fell in a heap, her back to Andrew.

At first, Pritchard gaped at her. His expression was incredulous, angry, and finally, lustful. He dragged her to her feet by her hair. He tossed her pistol aside and in one savage motion ripped away her dress. Still holding her hair, his eyes roamed her body, "I remember this," he panted. "Rather enjoyable as I recall." He shoved her back to the gorund. He unbuckled his trousers and she whimpered, "I have work to do, so this won't take long." Then he was over her, his trousers to his knees. She frantically backed away, clawing at the ground. Her left hand fell deep into a hole. Pritchard came closer, muttering darkly as he pressed down on her.

Without warning, her left hand came out of the hole and ripped across his face. He howled and rolled away in agony. She scrambled to her feet.

Pritchard sat up, a thick shard of glass protruding from his right cheek. The glass had pierced his mouth wall so deeply, his tongue had been sliced. He carefully placed two fingers between his lips and, without even a grimace, pulled the glass through his cheek and out of his mouth. He examined the shard briefly and tossed it away. Blood flowed down his jaw and neckline. His eyes were smoldering and horrible. The woman was only a few feet away, the cocked revolver once again in her quivering hands.

Andrew had been shaken from his stupor by the gunshot. He fought with the rope at his wrists as he watched, enthralled by the unfolding scene, wondering how the woman had been able to divine glass from a hole in the ground. Pritchard was coiled on the ground, between Andrew and the woman. If her aim wasn't true . . .

"Well?" Pritchard's voice was hoarse and blood sprayed from his lips.

She squeezed the trigger. Pritchard took the bullet in his upper abdomen and fell backward. Amazingly, after only a moment, he came to his knees. "Nice shot."

Her lower lip trembled. She fired again and Pritchard was hit in the left arm. The shot passed through and kicked dirt into Andrew's eyes.

This time, Pritchard didn't recover. He lay flat on his back, and could only raise his head.

"Do you have a killer's instinct?" His defiance had lost its edge. He tried to pull himself up, but could not.

She came and stood above him, her face stretched in contempt.

Pritchard made no effort to defend himself.

She fired a third time, directly into his laughing mouth. A fair part of his brain was blown through the back of his skull.

The woman teetered, then collapsed, yet to have uttered a single word.

Andrew felt he might be dying of blood loss, but couldn't gather the sobbing woman's attention. She was slumped forward on her knees, silently weeping. Morris was unconscious, maybe dead. Finally, she looked up. Tears had washed a clear spot in the center of her face.

Andrew was too weak for niceties. "Untie me."

She hesitantly came to her feet.

Andrew saw her more clearly and realized his dream had not been a dream at all. "Don't I know you?"

She nodded.

"You are that prostitute from the Kangaroo."

"My *name* is Mary Tisbett." Her voice was raspy and tortured.

Andrew pulled his eyes away from her and stared at Pritchard's head. "How are you here? . . . and why?"

"I first saw him when the Yankees arrived in Vicksburg. Even in uniform, I knew it was him." She sniffled, then deeply exhaled trying to compose herself. "I saw you with him in the wagon today. I could tell you were in trouble, but I could do nothing to stop him. That is why I brought poor Mr. Morris. He was the only person in town who knew, really knew, about Pritchard."

Several questions came to Andrew at once. "You called him Pritchard. Why?"

"That is his real name." She struggled with the rope knots as she spoke.

"How did you free Morris from jail?"

"With that gun."

Andrew's estimation of her increased. "And how did you know Pritchard meant me harm?" He truly couldn't imagine.

Her hand clasped her throat. "He . . . hurt me once. And your father, your uncle. I couldn't let him hurt anyone else." Her words slowed. "In a way, I owed your father."

Andrew couldn't make all the connections. "You and Morris followed him here on foot?"

She nodded. "We assumed you would be coming to this place. Mr. Morris spoke of a painting."

The bindings fell away. Andrew stood unsteadily and went to Morris. He was still breathing.

Mary remained at the tree, staring immutably at Pritchard.

Andrew shook Morris without response. He staggered to the lake and collected a hatful of water, trying not to look at Curtis who still floated there, and returned to splash it on Morris's face. Morris murmured, but didn't fully regain consciousness. Andrew gently laid him back down, then succumbed to his own spinning head. He dropped to the ground. After a moment, he fashioned a tourniquet from his torn shirt sleeve. He tried to tie it around his upper arm with one hand. Mary was oblivious to his struggle. She hadn't moved an inch. Again Andrew came to his feet. He only made it halfway to where she sat before he swooned to his knees.

"Ma'am," he croaked. "I need some help."

She turned and nodded her head.

Exhausted, Andrew fell forward and caught himself with his one good hand. He looked down, his eyes only inches from the ground. He stared into a hole. Dazedly, he saw a glint of glass. His unanswered question from earlier returned. He looked more closely and saw the remnants of a mason jar. He reached down and brushed away the loose dirt. There in the hole, unmistakably, was a crisp sheaf of United States bearer bonds. He felt no elation or sense of relief. Another glint, a different type of reflection, caught his eye. He carefully slid his fingers around a circular object and pulled it from the earth: a gold coin.

Epilogue

January 3, 1864

Sam Morris wiped his nose with a handkerchief in the frigid winter air and watched from a respectful distance. He seemed to stay permanently congested these days. His nose was almost half-again larger than it used to be, gnarled and bulging like an unseemly tree root protruding from a pretty lawn. He no longer looked at mirrors.

Morris wished he could offer more than kind words and reassurance. Andrew suffered, coped, suffered some more. There were better moments when his face would brighten, always at mention of the woman Emily. Morris wasn't an expert on romance or the human condition, but the clarion change in Andrew at those times was an indication that his true salvation rested with her. But she was in Iuka, a world away from a man basically confined to his home by the suspicious Yankee army. Morris couldn't see how to facilitate their reunion, though he pondered the subject often. Maybe when the war finally ended . . .

❧

Andrew placed a bundle of freshly cut flowers on Winston's plain headstone. It rested immediately next to Elizabeth's and only a few feet from a third stone that simply read "Curtis." Andrew could've bought much finer markers, a whole wagon load of flowers. He was rich, but chose not to draw attention to his money, not as long as the Yankees occupied Vicksburg, and they seemed in no hurry to leave. He'd cashed a single bond, used part of the proceeds to pay his taxes, and lived off the remainder. The bonds were rightfully his, but the Yankees had questioned him at length about the mysterious disappearance of Major

Butler, whose body now shared an unmarked grave with a Confederate soldier next to Brown's Lake. With Pritchard gone, Andrew had paid a small bribe to the acting Provost Marshall to win Morris his rightful freedom. Morris still sought work. He refused to apply for a job at Vicksburg's only newspaper, which was run by Yankee occupational troops. For her part, Mary Tisbett had decided she would put Vicksburg out of her mind forever. Andrew had tried to repay the debt he felt he owed her. She had accepted a few hundred dollars as a down payment on the new life she hoped to make for herself in New Orleans. At first, she'd written letters of her progress. Eventually, the letters had stopped.

Andrew's shoulder wound had slowly healed. It had prevented him from doing much, as had the Yankees. They watched him closely and didn't allow him to leave the occupied area. In time, he would begin to build himself a new home. He would, of course, call it *Magnolia.*

Andrew came to the cemetery every week, sometimes bringing Morris for company. He would sit, often for hours, and quietly mourn. He allowed himself to cry—for his parents, for Curtis, for his home, for himself, for the woman he loved but could not see.

He frequently wondered if he deserved all his father had left him. He knew he had earned his father's pride. Was that enough? The answer was never obvious. And it urged him, compelled him to try and make the most of his life, to prosper and live decently, to prove that *Magnolia* was indeed his birthright. His first act was clear in his mind, a measure of himself, as a man of character and honor, a man in love. He'd planned for months. He was finally well enough to travel. Now was the time.

"Sam, I am leaving tomorrow."

Morris was jolted from his thoughts. He needed no further explanation. "Are you ready?"

"I can't wait any longer."

"How will you do it?"

"Best that you don't know."

Morris nodded in agreement. "Be careful."

❧

The sentry shuffled between his feet and carefully studied the very young major who stood before him. "Do you have orders, sir?"

"No, I'm on furlough. I grabbed the wrong haversack when I left my duty station." Andrew wore the uniform of a Yankee major, created secretly by his former slave and now seamstress, Lou. He carried identification papers taken months ago from the corpse of Major Ernest Butler.

"Your duty station is?"

"Vicksburg."

"Sir, you are a Provost officer. You know documentation is required to enter this area."

Andrew winked. "I'm here to see a lady friend."

The sentry didn't smile with him.

Andrew sucked in a quick breath. Posing as a Yankee officer was an offense punishable by death. He reached into his pocket and withdrew a sheaf of Union currency. "Sergeant, I haven't much time."

The sentry eyed Andrew's money. "You better put that away."

"I didn't mean to insult you, but it is imperative that I see her."

The sentry was skeptical. "If you're from Vicksburg, how did you come to know a lady in this area?"

"I was with Halleck's army when we took Corinth last year."

"She is in Corinth?"

"Iuka, actually."

"And what is the purpose of your visit?"

"I will take her to Vicksburg, then back to Pennsylvania when my duty is up."

"She is expecting you?"

"She is."

The sentry rubbed at his whiskered face and inspected the authentic identification papers Andrew had presented him. "Mighty young for a Major."

Andrew shrugged. "My father is an acquaintance of General Sherman. My commission was a political favor. I am not afraid to admit that."

Andrew's eyes narrowed. "And I still have those connections, Sergeant."

After a moment's consideration, the sentry decided he had no need to draw the ire of an influential officer. "How long will you be, sir?"

"No more than a few hours."

"Proceed."

"Thank you, Sergeant." Andrew pulled his wagon through the picket line.

❧

As Andrew neared the Gardner home, he urged his horse faster. His heartbeat intensified and his mouth was dry with nervous anticipation. She had never answered his letters. Would she still be here? Would she be glad to see him after twenty months? Angry?

The Gardner home came into view. At least the Yankees hadn't burned it. Andrew squirmed anxiously and peered ahead. When he drew closer, he saw someone sitting on the front porch. His breath nearly exploded from his chest. She watched him, probably wondering about the Yankee officer approaching her house.

He could stand it no longer. "Emily!" he called. She sat up straight in her chair, confusion painting her face. "It is Andrew!"

She rushed through the front gate just as he stopped. He leapt to the ground and they met in a frantic embrace. She kissed his cheeks, his eyes, his mouth, whimpering with delight.

"I missed you so much," she whispered.

Andrew felt hot tears against his face. "I came as soon as I could. Did you receive my letters?"

"Only one. I read it a hundred times."

"I wrote you at least once a month."

"The Yankees have occupied this area ever since you left. I was surprised even your first letter arrived."

Andrew hesitated, slightly unsure. "Did you try to write back?"

"I was going to, but then . . . I couldn't. My health was poor."

Andrew's face creased with concern. "But you are well now?"

"Oh yes." She reluctantly pulled away from him and indicated his uniform. "You had a change of allegiance?" Suddenly, she smiled and cried at once.

He lightly brushed away her tears. "This was the only way I could pass through the Yankee pickets."

"From where did you come?" She clutched him around the waist and lead him toward the house. Her smoky brown eyes fixed on him, as if she might look away and he'd be gone.

"Vicksburg."

"Oh." She stopped. "I heard what happened. Did your family . . .?"

Andrew's face darkened for a moment. "We have plenty of time for that. At least I hope we do." His mouth moved to speak again but no words came out. He looked at her in total supplication.

"We have a lifetime," she said, guiding him up the front porch steps. "A lifetime," she repeated.

Andrew spoke in a rush. "Will you come to Vicksburg with me?"

"Andrew, I must tell you—"

"Emily, dear, who is that?" came a call from the house.

"We have a visitor, Mother!" Emily turned to Andrew. "Let's go in."

"And your mother can come with us," he said. "If she can stand the sight of me."

Emily's face was a composite of emotions, happiness, excitement, optimism. "Things have changed."

Andrew nodded, not understanding, not really caring why. "Good. Then we should leave right away. I have a tenuous ally at the Yankee picket line who will pass us through. We must go while he is still on duty."

Emily laughed. "We can leave soon, but I really must tell you—"

She was again interrupted, this time by a wailing sound.

"What the devil . . .?"

"Come inside, Andrew."

They stepped through the door. Emily's mother was sitting on the sofa. In her arms, she cradled an infant child. Mrs. Gardner looked up. At first, she studied his uniform. Then she looked more closely at his face. "Hello, Andrew." She smiled.

"Mrs. Gardner." His voice was hushed. He took a hesitant step toward the sofa.

Emily pulled him closer. "This is what I was trying to tell you." She took a deep breath. "Say hello to Drew."

"Drew?"

"Short for Andrew." She intently studied his reaction.

"This is why you didn't write back," Andrew said in a hoarse whisper.

"Yes." Her voice was halting. "I had a very difficult term." She looked affectionately at Mrs. Gardner. "Mother took care of me. There were many times I never thought Drew would safely arrive in this world. The delivery nearly killed me."

"Oh my God."

"There was more." She looked down, then up into his face again. "If you had known I was with child, you would've been distracted from your duties, maybe injured or killed. And I didn't want you coming back to me out of a sense of obligation. It had to be your choice."

"I had no choice, none whatsoever." He kissed her.

Her tears fell unchecked and they lost themselves in each other's eyes.

Finally Mrs. Gardner spoke. "Andrew?" She held the baby up to him.

He turned in quiet fascination, delightfully lightheaded. "This is the most glorious surprise of my life."

Emily guided him to the sofa. "He doesn't say much yet." She smiled. "He'll be a year old next week. He looks just like you."